This

Deep

Panic

By

Lisa Stowe

Dedicated to the memory of

Sam P. Grafton

Our river spirit, gone too soon

CONTENTS

~Prologue~

The Hole in the Wall wasn't really a hole but a dead-end shaft with a steel door that could be barricaded from within and locked from without. And the Wall wasn't really a wall, but a granite mountain deeply fissured and hung with a dark and shadowed forest curtain. One that went straight up, creating a sense of severe vertigo overwhelming anyone leaning back, and back, and back, to see the top. Here and there, stunted fir and cedar and hemlock twisted and bent waiting to fall.

Occasionally the Wall would free boulders to plummet down and leave deep impact craters in the forest floor.

Few rock climbers, hanging with harnesses and bandaged knuckles, knew the door was there, far below them where the forest washed up at the base of the Wall.

Curtis Jonason locked himself in the Hole five days a week. Some days he imagined himself a climber suspended in the heights, able to see for miles, see the rushing white water of the Skykomish River, speckled with daredevil kayakers. Or to gaze down on the tiny, tiny town of Index, Washington nestled in the Cascade Mountains. But he wasn't an adventurer. And he had long ago come to terms with the reality that his adventures were found only in imagination and books.

Instead, each day, in cold weather gear, he unlocked the Hole with his smooth scientist's hands, slipped into the dark, and bolted the door behind him. There, he would spend fourteen hours alone burrowed into the granite, a small stream rushing under his workstation, a flashlight his only illumination.

Alone with his machines.

~Day 1~

1

It was technically spring but the slanting rain and gusty wind from high snowfields felt like winter. The river ran fast and gray-green with snowmelt. Curtis sat in his aging Volkswagen Bug waiting for the general store to open, his wool coat buttoned to the chin. He was still in full winter mode, with cold weather gear in a pack beside him. The small stream that ran through the center of his workspace would be rushing with spring runoff and the Hole would be chilly and damp. Which was why he waited for the store to open. When it did, he would fill two thermoses, one with fresh hot coffee and the other with Betty's turkey tortellini soup.

With the town so small, Curtis had come to know, at least by sight, most of the people who lived there. Like Rob, one of local river rats, who tapped the hood of Curtis's car with a fist and then waved as he walked by, a red kayak slung over a shoulder.

But one local in particular made a point of giving Curtis advice. Frequently. He saw Henry now, crossing 5th Street with his signature hurried walk, on his tiptoes and leaning forward as if racing with his own body. Or like a human quail. Curtis enjoyed debates with him over religion and other myths, over history and its lessons, over whatever scientific tome each happened to be reading. But occasionally Henry didn't stop at intellectual debate. Sometimes, the old man veered off into unscientific rants and conspiracy theories.

Henry was veering off right now, headed for the general store. Curtis pulled on his stocking cap to cover his short blond hair and brown eyes, and sank in the driver's seat. Maybe he'd look like he was sleeping. He liked Henry, but he also had to get back to work. And he definitely did not want to get trapped into one of Henry's monologues.

There was a sharp tap on the window, then a longer series of knocks. Unable to ignore the sound, Curtis sighed heavily and straightened, pulling off the cap. He rolled the squeaky window down.

"Oh, did I wake you?" Henry asked. His long, fuzzy gray hair was like a cloud around his head with rain dripping through.

"That's okay." Curtis managed a smile. Really, what else could

1

he say? His mother had, unfortunately, raised him to be polite. He opened the door and got out with his thermoses.

"I have been studying the types of gravity experiments you are doing in the Hole," Henry said.

Of course he has, Curtis thought, sighing heavily again. Henry had degrees in geology and physics, and even though the last time he'd seen the inside of a classroom had been in the dark ages before computers, the man was still brilliant. It was just that he talked so much. It was great when Curtis had time. And not so great when he had places to be.

"I have proof here that you are going about it all wrong." Henry held up a well-thumbed textbook so old its binding flapped. With dirt-grimed fingers, he fanned through the book, oblivious to the rain splattering the paper.

Curtis caught a quick glimpse of stained pages heavily annotated with cramped blue ink. He also caught a quick whiff of Henry's unwashed body. He sneezed and moved toward the store hoping Betty would unlock it and save him.

"For one thing, that boring equipment is drilling too deep into the mountain."

Curtis pressed his lips tight. There was no drilling equipment. He'd told Henry that several times. Three years previously a company had tested a boring drill for deep underground drilling. It was long gone, off to drill some tunnel under Tacoma or Seattle or Japan. Curtis didn't care.

"The tremors we have experienced the last two and a half weeks are a direct result of your work. I have complained to the University of Washington."

Curtis kept walking, his face pulling into a tight grimace with the effort to stay silent. He would *not* get sucked into another argument with Henry.

Betty flipped the neon 'open' sign and unlocked the front door. As Curtis walked inside and handed over his thermoses, the older lady in her long wool dress gave him a sympathetic smile. As always, her dyed black hair was in perfect waves and her tarnished gold crucifix hung in its place of honor against her throat.

"And if the drilling is not bad enough, this research you are doing on the Fifth Force is just making things worse." Henry gripped his book to his chest. "I have also refreshed my memory on the search for your parallel universes. Do you realize the damage you will cause?"

Curtis clenched his teeth as he took one thermos, now full of hot coffee, from Betty.

"I do not think anyone has given thought to the serious

consequences of messing with parallel universes. We must understand the ramifications, especially around all your drilling-"

"There is no drilling equipment!" Curtis grabbed his second thermos and headed out the door, trying not to run. "There are no studies on parallel universes! We're furthering our understanding of Newtonian physics!"

"Yes, yes," said Henry, trotting behind Curtis. "The known forces of the universe. Gravity, electromagnetism, and the two nuclear forces. You seem to think you are going to find the weaker force on the molecular level. Anti-gravity. Parallel universes."

Curtis jerked open his car door then turned, gripping his thermoses. "No, no, and no! We are not looking for parallel universes! It's a study on gravity at the molecular level, possibly anti-gravity; you have that right. And that's *all* you have right!"

Guilt immediately swamped Curtis. He flashed on his mother, teaching him to be respectful to his elders. He knew what her face would look like if she'd just heard him shouting at one of those elders. The disappointment would make all her soft wrinkles sag and her eyes go watery with unshed tears. He opened his mouth to apologize, but Henry caught his arm.

"I understand the need for secrecy. It is not like you can let just anyone in on what is really happening. Which is all the more reason why you should allow me to advise you. Have you not noticed the tremors growing more frequent? Have you not read the newspapers? Even reporters, dim as they are, have noticed the increase."

Curtis pulled his arm free and tossed the thermoses on the passenger seat. "For god's sake, Henry, of course there are tremors. This is the Pacific Northwest. That doesn't mean they have anything to do with my experiments."

Henry shook his head emphatically. "You're wrong. And you're making them worse. I am hiking to the top of the Wall today. I am going to follow my fault line and take readings. It might take me a few hours. When I have gathered data I will then join you at the Hole and we will compare results."

"Fine," Curtis said, getting in the car and starting it. "How many hours?"

"Approximately three."

Curtis backed up slowly but Henry paced beside the car, holding the edge of the open window frame.

"I will need to show you how to calibrate your equipment to handle my findings."

In three hours Curtis would make sure he was in the Hole with the heavy door shut and locked. No way was he letting Henry inside. For one thing it would screw up his research. For another he might just lose his mind.

"Let go of the car Henry. I'm leaving." He heard the curtness in his voice and flashed on his mother again.

"Track the tremors and record hourly notes on your impressions."

"Yes, yes. Bye now." Curtis forced a rictus of a smile and pressed down on the gas pedal a little firmer.

A horn honked, and Curtis whipped around to look over his shoulder. He'd almost backed into a school bus coming down the street. He waved apologetically. Then saw Henry opening his mouth again. Gripping the steering wheel, he backed quickly into the street and drove around the bus as it pulled over for group of high school students with backpacks. He couldn't resist a quick look in the rearview mirror.

Henry was still talking.

Henry McCaffrey was still in shape, even at seventy-two, and he moved quickly along the trail. His odd quail-like gait lent itself well to steep hills. He tugged up the collar of his old jacket but the rain still trickled down his neck and soaked into the back of his once-white tee shirt. He was used to the weather, but the tickling annoyed him.

There had been a minor tremor earlier but he felt confident Curtis would do as told and record the information. The young man was doing an acceptable job with his research into anti-gravity but Henry was disappointed Curtis would not trust him with the parallel universe work.

When he reached the tree line at the top of the Wall, Henry paused, as always, to enjoy the sweeping views. Oceans of fir, hemlock, and cedar washed up the sides of the mountains that today, unfortunately, hid their crowns in low-sagging clouds. The town of Index was nothing more than a tiny clear spot alongside the rushing Skykomish River, a small silver ribbon far below.

Henry loved the trees and knew their scientific names, their habitats, and where the old growth stands still hid. It was one of his self-appointed jobs to guard them from human interference. He was a well known, and he was sure, feared, presence at city council meetings and logging protests.

Today, his job was to look at the fault line that created a small crack running from the river basin to the top of the Wall. He fully expected to find that the fault had changed since his last visit. That would prove the tremors were having more impact than the scientists who ignored him believed.

He followed the ridgeline for a couple hundred feet and then dropped back down into the tree line where there was no path. Drizzle collected on fir needles and plopped on his head as he ducked under branches. He searched through wet fern and bracken looking for the crack in the earth that an uneducated person would never recognize as anything significant. But he had been here before and was definitely educated.

Henry stumbled as the ground suddenly crumbled away under his boots. Startled, he caught at a tree branch for balance and then stepped back to more solid earth. Where a small crack used to be, a larger, two-foot wide trench gaped. As he stood at the edge, flabbergasted, dirt and small rocks tumbled into the slit. The soil was still dry where the rain had yet to touch it. Henry smiled in vindication.

The trench was clearly new, as proven by the dry soil. And new enough to be the result of the earlier tremor. The fault line had shifted, just like he expected. Curtis would now be forced to admit that his experiments impacted the Wall. As always, Henry was right.

The underbrush rustled but he barely glanced in that direction. He was used to interacting with wild animals. Even bears didn't bother him. It was one reason he refused to bathe. His natural scent allowed animals to detect his presence, and removing the element of surprise from encounters with them drastically improved outcomes. Once animals detected him, they typically left.

Henry inched closer to the edge of the fissure and squatted, trying to see how deep it was.

The rustle, however, grew louder. Moved closer.

Henry glanced to the side. A dog also stood at the edge of the fissure. A huge dog. Possibly an Irish Wolfhound. Henry had never seen a wolfhound but had once researched breeds for a genome project, and knew they were taller than Great Danes. And this dog was definitely taller, with scruffy black fur littered with fir needles and dirt. Obviously dumped by someone.

He waved a hand in the air, dismissing the animal. "Go on, get out of here. Go fend for yourself." He didn't like dogs. They didn't have the intelligence of cats.

The huge dog turned its head and looked at him.

Its eyes were filled with blood. Horrified, Henry stumbled back and lost his balance, coming down hard on his butt. Pain shot up his tailbone but he was barely aware of it.

The dog stared at him through what had to be sightless eyes and growled, deep and low. Henry pushed upward, trying to stand on legs shaking so badly he only made it to one knee. The dog lowered its head and moved forward, teeth bared. Henry scrabbled in the dirt and came up with a chunk of granite.

He threw it hard. Saw it hit the side of the dog. Heard the hollow-sounding thump as the rock connected. Saw the dog flinch.

"I said get out of here." His voice trembled.

The dog didn't listen.

Ethan Reynolds sat behind Val, the middle-aged driver, ignoring the chatter of his high school students on the bus and watching the colors of the forest slide past outside the window. All the shades of green filled his soul like a deep drink of cool water. He flashed back on searing winds, colors of ochre and burnt orange, flaming sunsets, desert heat. Compared to his past this place was lush, exploding with life, a temperate rain forest slashed with granite. Something inside him that had been boxed away opened to these woods as if they were a sanctuary.

He'd felt like that since he'd been lucky enough to stumble into the job of teaching environmental science at the alternative high school. He was twenty-six, and eighteen of those years had been spent being dragged through third-world countries as his parents strove to save humanity. He'd felt like luggage.

He'd learned survival early and the lessons never left him, shadowing his dark eyes. On bad days his too-long black hair hung to mask those shadows. His father had been shot to death in front of him when their car hit a roadblock in Iraq. Ethan, shot three times, had been left for dead.

He limped out of the hospital and out of the country. He pushed himself through months of physical therapy, his eyes almost black with pain. He'd started university classes as he healed, and eventually found the teaching job. Found the Pacific Northwest. Found rain to soak into your soul and fill your heart. A place of deep loamy soil where equally deep roots could be put down.

"Mr. Reynolds? I don't have cell service."

Ethan twisted in his seat to look back at Payton Lang, one of his students. She stared fixedly at a smart phone in her hand and then brushed long brown hair out of her eyes in a practiced and provocative gesture.

"Why would you think there's cell service in the middle of a national forest?" he asked, honestly curious.

"I have a top-of-the-line plan. I'm supposed to have coverage anywhere."

John Delaney, in the seat behind Payton, leaned forward. "Want me to try?"

"Would you?" Payton asked, brushing her hair back again. "I'm so hopeless with technology."

Ethan turned away, hiding his exasperation. Payton, in her tight, low cut tee shirt was presenting John with a view he'd probably dream about for years. Ethan had seen Payton operating that phone with an expert's touch. *Hopeless, my ass.*

Payton was the student guaranteed to not be prepared on these field trips, to wear makeup as they worked to restore wetlands, to squeal when she walked through a spider web. But she'd been the first one on the bus this morning. Maybe, he thought, she was finally starting to enjoy the field trips.

The bus bounced over one more pothole on the rutted forest service road and juddered to a stop in the wide spot that signaled the trailhead. Val turned off the engine and opened the accordion door.

"Everyone out." She picked up a coat in an ugly shade of pumpkin orange and stumped down the few steps.

Ethan stood and moved into the aisle, zipping up his North Face jacket and shrugging on his backpack. "Get your gear."

He ducked his head to keep from hitting the doorframe as he followed the driver out of the bus. Val stood, arms folded, by the front tire. He knew from experience that she was a grumpy old bat who got grumpier if you talked to her. Instead he walked to the trailhead signboard, boots squelching in mud. The soft drizzle settled over his hair like fine cobwebs and he pulled his hood up.

Rowan O'Reilly was the first one out behind him. She was tall, with long auburn hair in a functional braid and hazel eyes that never seemed to see those around her. She moved through the world awkwardly, as if she hadn't grown into her height, hadn't learned to be comfortable in her body yet. A quiet young woman, she spent most of her time deep in notebooks, sketching the world around her and rarely interacting with others.

"Want to do the honors on the safety board?" Ethan asked her.

She always looked startled when someone spoke to her. As if she had no idea anyone was there until they said something.

At the trailhead there was a large board where forest rangers posted tips and warnings, and hikers posted trail notes. Ethan skimmed notes on how many spring-hungry bears were awake and the state of the log bridges. Seeing nothing they needed to be worried about, he gestured to the safety notepad where hikers signed in and out on a worn sheaf of papers.

Rowan picked up the string tied around a stub of dull pencil, and flipped the plastic cover back from the well-thumbed pages.

"Environmental Science senior class, eleven students, one

teacher." Rowan looked over her shoulder. "Should I say something about Val at the bus?"

"No. She's leaving, won't be back until tomorrow to pick us up. If you list her and something happens to us, search and rescue will waste resources looking for someone who isn't there."

The other kids gathered around in a semi-circle, standing in the misty rain in their wet-weather gear and backpacks. Except, of course, for Payton. She'd pulled a pink short-waist jacket on and stood shivering in tight yoga pants and shoes that looked more like ballet slippers. Even her backpack was small and pink. Ethan's jaw muscles tightened. He'd spent hours lecturing on how to survive in the woods, how to prepare. He'd told them right from the beginning that they had to come ready for anything on these field trips, that there would be no going back for someone who didn't. Now he knew why she'd been the first one on the bus. If he'd seen what she was wearing he'd have sent her home.

For now, Payton was going to be cold and miserable. He'd have to find the balance between letting her suffer to learn a lesson, and keeping her from becoming hypothermic. And keeping the guys in the class from rushing to her rescue. She'd never learn anything that way.

"Okay, all of you know the lichen we've been studying," Ethan said. "This is your chance to see it in the world where it belongs instead of books. Remember, it's critically imperiled so follow the conservation assessments. But you're also going to see more than just the lichen. We're headed into the old Silver Creek mining district. It's one of the oldest in these mountains and dates to 1871. There are a still a few old-timers running placer claims for silver, copper, and garnets. And if you pay attention, you might find signs of the old mines. But you are not to go into any of them. They're not safe. Am I clear on that?"

There were a few groans of disappointment.

"This trail has been washed out in the past," he continued. "And it's rough. But it's easy to follow as long as you pay attention and remember what we've talked about. Go at your own speed. Don't get too far ahead of others, or too spread out on the trail. I'll expect sketches and journal entries on anything that catches your eye, whether it's *Niebla cephalota* or something else."

Ethan waited as the students started up the trail with their packs. He knew from past hikes that they would sort themselves out depending on their hiking pace. Rowan, physically fit, would lead the pack, probably followed by Zack Swenson, who was the only one besides Ethan who had any chance of keeping up with her. Ethan worked off memories and nightmares by lifting weights. Zack on the other hand, had the lean, ropy muscles from being a serious rock climber and jogger.

9

Payton, of course, would tie for last in line along with an overweight kid named Michael. They'd be followed only by Ethan.

He always took rear guard.

He stepped onto the trail, under the dripping forest canopy, dark eyes scanning the twilight shadows among the trees. The intoxicating, fresh scents of earth filled the air and he breathed in deeply, cleansed.

Just before the woods closed around him, he took one last look back at the bus in its little clearing. Val, in her orange coat, was inside and starting the engine. As he watched, he saw the pale color of her face as she raised her head in his direction. And he saw an equally pale hand come up.

"Did you see that shit?" Sergio Costa, waiting for Ethan, shrugged a black-clad shoulder in the direction of the bus. "She just flipped you the bird, man."

"Or she flipped you the bird," Ethan said.

Sergio, also known as Spike, had long unruly black hair and pale blue eyes. An Infinity Ouroboros tattoo on a hard bicep. A pierced eyebrow. Eye-candy for teenagers. "No man, it was you she flipped off."

Ethan laughed and waited as Spike headed up the trail. A lot of teachers felt the kid was a lost cause. He definitely was someone familiar with being expelled and with juvenile detention centers. But Ethan reserved judgment.

Payton stumbled over a tree root, catching hold of John for balance. She pulled off a shoe and shook out a small pebble.

Ethan shook his head. It was going to be a long two miles.

Payton laughed at something John said, and slipped her shoe on. They headed up the trail, but as Ethan started to follow, movement caught his eye.

Above them a large raven circled, slowly riding currents of wind. As he watched, it dipped below the treetops, coming so close he saw the sheen of rain on its black feathers.

It cocked its head to one side almost as if studying him while it circled. He realized the bird was probably used to hikers and looking for a handout. He pulled a fruit and nut bar out of his pack and broke it into pieces, scattering it behind him on the trail.

But the raven was gone.

4

Ramon Saura sat in his car in the drive-through for McDonald's and watched a sheriff's truck fly by with lights strobing, headed east toward Sultan. He automatically calculated. Both nieces were in school here in Monroe. His sister-in-law, Therese, was at work at the hair salon in Snohomish. His brother, Tómas, was also at work. Hopefully.

So his family was safe. Well, only if his brother was actually at the lawyer's office where he was a partner. Ramon resisted the urge to call and check up. He didn't want Tómas to get suspicious.

Old habits died hard, Ramon thought, as he put his shiny blue Camaro in gear and moved a car's length closer to his junk food. Too many years of looking over his shoulder, too many friends and family gone. Whenever he heard sirens he'd flash back to what those sirens meant. Someone dying. A shootout. A car bomb. A drug deal gone bad.

Moving to the States had been the right thing for Tómas to do. Ramon was thrilled his nieces were brought here while they were still young, before they saw too much evil. He wanted them to hang on to their innocence as long as possible, to live a life free of fear. Tómas had made good money in Mexico, but had chosen to raise his family in the poorest neighborhoods he could find. There had been too many nights when Ramon had been called because their apartment had been broken into, or because Tómas had been in a fight. It had seemed like a good thing when Tómas suddenly decided to accept a job offer in the States.

When Therese asked Ramon to join them a few months after they moved, he'd hesitated only long enough to realize that without his family he had nothing. And when Therese told him she thought her husband was having an affair, he knew he needed to move. And so a couple months ago he'd joined them. It hadn't been too bad. He liked the area and had a good job machining for a cabinet manufacturer.

It made sense financially to live with his family, to pitch in. It also made sense because he was able to watch his brother. Not just because of the affairs he was clearly having, but also because he was spending a lot of money. More money than it seemed he could be making, even at a law firm. Ramon's priority was keeping the family together, which meant it was getting time to confront his brother.

He pulled up to the window, took his bag of grease, and smiled easily at the young woman with brown hair and glasses who handed him the soda. She met his eyes and blushed, then ducked her head and managed to return the smile.

Grinning broader, Ramon pulled out. His youngest niece, Alegria, called his car a chick magnet. He patted the dashboard. Maybe it was. The powerful engine accelerated as he headed back to work. He turned the radio on and bit into a fry.

"The most recent tremor registered 2.4 on the Richter scale, and appears to have been centered in the vicinity of Index, in east Snohomish County. Such tremors are not uncommon in this area, and to talk more about that, we have here in the studio with us Professor Dannie Megard from the University of Washington."

Ramon pulled back the wrapper on his quarter pounder. He hadn't felt any earthquake. But then 2.4 didn't sound like much of one either. He wondered briefly if he should check on his nieces, maybe call their cells. He didn't like the thought that they might be at school and unsettled or even scared, with no family around.

But then, if he hadn't felt the tremor, they probably hadn't either. The urge to pull family in close and keep them safe was a hard habit to break.

Movement caught Ramon's eye as he turned toward the industrial park at the west end of Monroe. Looking over his shoulder, he saw black birds, more than he had ever seen, lifting up from pastures that bordered Fryelands Boulevard. Ravens? Crows? He didn't know much about birds. But the black shapes on a gray, shadowy day were oddly unsettling. Maybe because he'd never seen so many in one place. He leaned forward to watch as the birds flew over his car and away into the drizzle.

The birds were probably nervous from the tremor. Animals felt things like that more than people did. Maybe birds did, too.

He crumpled the burger wrapper and dropped it in the paper bag. His thoughts wandered back to the blushing girl. He had a place to live, a job, a car. Maybe it was time to build friendships, to truly settle in to his new life.

Tomorrow was a half-day at school for his nieces. He'd surprise them and take them out for burgers. It would give him an excuse to drive the chick magnet back through the drive-up again, see if the car could work some more magic.

Grinning at the possibilities, the dreams, the shimmery hopes he'd had to stifle for years, Ramon and his chick magnet headed for work. But moments later, when he pulled into the parking lot, the birds were there. Black shapes perched on cars, on light poles, filling empty parking spots. He stopped the car. Honked the horn. But the birds didn't move. He inched forward carefully and tapped the horn again.

He was about to honk a third time when the birds rose into the air in one large mass and flew out over the industrial complex.

Ramon parked, got out, and stood a moment, watching the birds fly into the dark skies. Rain pattered on asphalt around him, dripped through his hair, and soaked into the shoulders of his jacket. Wind shook the leaves of trees. Out on Fryelands, cars flew by, spraying water into the air. He shivered, chilled more by the disquieting sight of all the birds than by the rain.

He waited a moment longer but the birds didn't circle back. Thinking again that they were just unsettled by the tremor, he shrugged off the odd sight. Locking the car, he headed for work, his thoughts already moving on to the tasks for the day, to what Therese might make for dinner, to his plans for impressing a girl the next day.

Life was good. That would change when he finally confronted his brother.

But for now, life was good.

5

Sharon Driscoll came out of Monroe Valley General Hospital with a polite smile pasted in place and something like panic simmering deep inside. She unlocked her blue BMW and tossed her cream-colored Bourne blazer onto the passenger seat, following it with her Hermes purse. But before she could get in, she saw one of the bitches stick her head out the hospital door. Checking up on her, Sharon knew. The woman had the gall to wave.

Wave.

What did they expect her to do? Pull out a gun and shoot herself in the parking lot?

That was a thought. Go out with a literal bang. Maybe she needed to buy a gun.

Sharon sank down into the low-slung car, started the engine and then pulled on the seatbelt, wincing as it slid across her breasts. She paused. Thought a moment, then let it retract back where it had been. She tugged down on her green silk blouse with a sense of purpose.

Maybe someone would hit her on the highway. Head on. With no seatbelt she'd be ejected. A fast death.

She pulled out of the parking lot, automatically flicking on headlights against the gray, drizzly afternoon. She headed east on Highway 2, toward Sultan and home. Once out of sight of the hospital she unclenched her jaw and drew in a deep breath. A brief dizziness washed through, leaving her fingers and toes tingling, as if she hadn't breathed for hours.

The oncologist had been so damn kind that it was condescending. Reading her the results as if she didn't already know them. Listing all her options, talking about statistics and how far treatment had come in the past twenty years. How he and his staff would partner with her for treatment like they were creating some business contract. With her life as the termination clause.

The light ahead turned red and Sharon hit the brake harder than she'd intended, jerking to a stop. A car behind her honked and she glanced in the rearview mirror. The small black Honda was right on her bumper. Had probably just missed rear-ending her.

Rage, white-hot, burned through her. Throwing the BMW in park, she shoved open the door and charged the smaller car, her heels making sharp slapping sounds on the pavement. The driver, a young man, dropped his mouth open as wide as his eyes.

Sharon slammed the palms of her hands against the mist-washed driver's side window.

"You fucking asshole!" she screamed, hitting the window again. "You almost hit me and then you fucking honk at me! Come out here!"

She heard the click as the driver locked the doors. She saw him grab a cell phone and dial. She fisted her hands and drove them down on the roof of the car.

"Come out here so I can rip your fucking head off!" Hot tears washed down her cheeks.

The kid held his phone up. "I called 911! I'm recording you!"

Sharon bent so her face was right next to the glass. She stared into the jerk's wide eyes but then he faded out of clarity until all she saw in the misty rain was her watery reflection staring back at her, imposed over the kid's pale face.

She saw a woman in her fifties who had never used profanity before this day. She saw formerly blonde hair now almost all gray, the styled curls going limp in the mist. She saw rage in the hazel eyes, and under that, terror.

She saw coming death.

Sharon slammed her hands into the car again, hearing sirens.

A man in a car behind the kid's stuck his head out his window. "Hey, knock it off!"

Sharon flipped the man her middle finger. She'd never done that before either. It felt good. She flipped the middle finger at the kid. She watched the sheriff deputy's truck, lights flashing, pull up at an angle in front of her car, and flipped him off, too.

"What's the problem here?" The deputy with dark red hair in a military cut spoke in a calm, level voice as he walked toward her.

The kid must have felt brave now that backup was there because he lowered his window. "This crazy woman just went nuts on me, officer. I was just sitting here waiting for the light to change, doin' nothin'."

The deputy held his hand up, silencing the kid, and turned to Sharon, waiting.

She drew in another deep breath, felt the tingle again. All those cells in her body, drawing life from the breath she pulled in.

All those cells drawing life so they could replicate and kill her.

"What's the problem?" she mimicked, looking at the deputy, with his military haircut and muscled arms and calm eyes. "The problem is I'm going to wrap my hands around this little turd's throat and strangle him because he almost rear-ended me. So you best just pull your gun out and shoot me now."

The kid raised his window until just a couple inches remained open.

"Sorry ma'am, but that isn't going to happen today. Why don't you tell me what the real problem is?"

"Will you at least arrest me?" She'd never been in jail before, but knew people died in jail. Suicide by crazy inmates.

"No ma'am. That's not going to happen, either. Maybe, after I talk to everyone and we stand around in the rain a while, you'll end up with a ticket."

"I'll press charges for assault!" the kid yelled.

"Sure, you can do that," the deputy said, his voice still calm. "And then you'll go up before the judge and say how you, a guy in his, what? Twenties? Got assaulted and scared by an older lady who never touched him." The deputy turned to Sharon. "You never touched him, right?"

"The little shit locked his door."

The deputy actually smiled.

Sharon, reluctantly, felt the rage cool. That made the tears start again. She put her fists on her hips, feeling the expensive tweed of her black slacks. Things that no longer mattered. "You can't do this to me. You can't just let me off. Let me go. Make me go home."

"Sure I can," the deputy said. "I expect you to get back in your car and leave. Whether you go home or not, that's up to you. But don't take whatever is making you so angry out on someone again. Because if I get another call about you, I *will* arrest you."

"Is that a promise?"

The humor left the deputy's blue eyes. "Ma'am, jail isn't going to allow you to escape whatever you're running from. I know that look. You go find someone to talk to. Get your head on straight. Quit punishing strangers for what's messed up in your life. I want no more calls about you. Is that clear?"

The deputy must have seen resignation in her eyes because he cupped her elbow with one hand and walked her to the car. He even opened the door and helped her in.

"What's your name?" she asked, wiping the back of a hand across her eyes.

"Max Douglass. You want my badge number, too?"

"I don't know. Can I complain that you didn't arrest me?" Sharon put her hands on the steering wheel and stared straight ahead, not looking at the deputy. She didn't want to see sympathy, kindness, compassion. She didn't want to see acknowledgement. Proof that she needed any of those caring emotions.

"You can complain, ma'am," the deputy said. He caught the seat belt and tugged it forward, holding it for her.

Sharon looked down at it, this synthetic material, this symbol of safety, of a future, and could only shake her head.

After a moment, the deputy let go and the belt once again retracted. He put a hand on her shoulder and she felt the warmth, the solidness, the reality of contact.

"There's always hope, ma'am." He took his hand away and pulled out a business card. "You can call me if you need to. And don't pull out on this highway without that seatbelt fastened."

Sharon watched the man go back to his truck, get in, and head west toward Monroe. She put the BMW in gear. When the light turned green she started forward, only to hear the long blare of horn again as the kid used the center turn lane to pass her. His tires sprayed her windshield with muddy water.

She could follow him. Pull him out of the car when he stopped. Beat him to a pulp. Make someone else suffer.

Instead she turned the windshield wipers on.

Get her affairs in order, the doctor had said. Make a will. Prepare for the worst, even though, with all the treatments they had planned, she had a fifty percent chance of survival.

Talk about what was making her angry, the deputy said. Sharon gasped on something that might have been a sob trying to escape.

Chemotherapy. Radiation. Baldness. For fifty percent. The doctors acted like that was a good thing. But really, fifty percent sucked.

The deep panic unfurled into something like rage. Sharon gripped the steering wheel so tight her knuckles deadened.

If she was going to suffer and die soon, she sure as hell wasn't going out leashed to oxygen and machines. Her body had betrayed her. Life had betrayed her.

So life had to pay.

She was going to die on her terms, not on the terms of microscopic fucking cells invading her breasts, spreading to her armpits.

Eating her.

6

Curtis emerged out of the Hole for a lunch break, peeking first to make sure Henry wasn't around. He was startled to see clouds had thickened and were now entwined in the branches of old evergreens, misting heavily on everything. He pulled his hat down over his ears and jogged to the car.

That morning he had driven the narrow track, bouncing over rough ground to the Hole, where he negotiated a several-point turn in order to back up as close to the door as possible. It was his daily routine. Just like in the afternoons when he sat in the locked car with the engine running so he could have heat and drink his still-warm soup.

And just like at the end of the workday when he came back out and it would be pitch black. Anyone who had ever been alone at night in the mountains knew that deep darkness. Knew that sense of being watched. Realized that humans might be welcome during the day, but that the night belonged to the wilderness. That was one of the fears he faced every evening. Which was why, by the light of his flashlight, he would scurry to the car, jump in, lock the door, and turn the headlights on as fast as his trembling hands allowed.

But for now it was afternoon and he was safe in his car. He felt the heater kick in and reached for his soup. He gave himself half an hour for lunch. It was plenty of time to warm up, work on his mystery novel, and get a mental break from the cold solitude of the granite hole.

Calibrations were going well. And there had been only one minor, very normal 2.4 tremor. Nothing out of the ordinary for mountains crosshatched with faults and pushed into existence by still-active plate tectonics. He looked forward to telling Henry that. He'd already formulated several responses, all of them clever. He knew the next time he got cornered by Henry he'd have forgotten those clever responses, but he enjoyed playing the scenes in his imagination.

No, his only concern for the day came from a fellow university professor who had sent him a text right before his break.

"Just confirmed. Hole has highest level of radon gas on whole planet. In granite though, not air you're breathing. That tests fine."

Curtis decided he better apply for cancer insurance. Even if the air tested fine. And maybe he should take more breaks outside the Hole.

Technically Curtis wasn't supposed to leave during his shift. The studies on the Fifth Force required more than just the mass of granite he worked within. They required him to start a pendulum in motion and record its crossings at two points every eight-and-a-half minutes, for one hour. Then he had to calculate the precise distance to the next test point, move the gold-plated pendulum manually, and start recording again. He did this, alone in the cold and damp under the mountain, for fourteen hours a day.

He figured science could sacrifice the time he took on breaks. Though he'd probably get fired if anyone ever found out.

His watch beeped at him. Sighing heavily, he finished the last of the soup, turned the engine off, and got out into the drizzle.

At the entrance to the Hole, there was a loud rustling in the ferns. He spun around, gripping his keys. With his heart racing and almost hyperventilating, he scanned the woods.

Nothing.

The safety of the car was too far away. The safety of the Hole was right behind his back. He fumbled the door open, jumped inside, and heaved the heavy door shut behind him. A small flush of shame filled him as he bolted the door with shaking hands. It was probably just a raccoon or something. Henry would know. But if Henry had been there, he would have laughed at him.

That was okay. Curtis was used to being laughed at. The only time he was without fear was when he was deep in science and studies and teaching. Then he was confident and sure.

But only then.

It was finally the end of the workday and Curtis turned on his flashlight, trying as always to ignore the flutter in his knees as he shut the Hole door behind him. Even though winter was over, the days were only negligibly longer, and by the time he was done with work it was pitch black outside. He locked the door, hitched up his pack, and turned, standing for a moment with his back to the granite.

There had been three more shivers of the earth, tremors in the two and three-point range on the Richter scale. Not that big of a deal typically, but Henry's concerns niggled at him.

Mist collected in the trees and dripped around him. Wind rustled leaves and tree branches. His Volkswagen sat alone, scattered with fir needles, the metal glinting in the shaking flashlight beam.

Curtis always needed a couple seconds to raise his courage as he went from the safety of the Hole to the safety of the car. He felt the solid mountain behind him, an ancient presence that gave the illusion of safety.

But then, so did the car. And it had very bright headlights. And locking doors.

And since he backed right up to the door, it was only a couple feet away. He gripped his keys and braved crossing those few feet.

The flashlight, only slightly wobbly, illuminated the keyhole. Curtis jammed in the key and twisted. Yanking open the door, he threw in his pack and quickly followed, not quite slamming the door behind him. He hit the lock and then finally drew in a deep breath.

The trusty engine started easily and Curtis flipped on the headlights and depressed the clutch. But something was there on the hood of the car, in the mix of fallen fir needles and collected drops of mist. He squinted. What was it? A small lump. A bird?

Well, it would fly off when he started down the logging road.

But what if it was dead, or worse, injured? And what was it doing out at night? His foot remained on the brake, clutch still depressed.

What was he going to do if it was injured? Put it in a pocket and take it home? And then what, into a shoebox where he could watch it die a slow death?

He lifted his foot off the brake, started to release the clutch, and the Bug lurched forward a little. His boot came back down on the brake.

The need to see for sure what was there, where nothing should be, overcame his fear of the dark. He pulled the emergency brake on, grabbed his trusty flashlight, and, feeling brave, got out on his rescue mission.

He left the car door open though. Just in case he had to make a run for it.

At the front of the car, he bent, peering at what was clearly not a poor, sweet, injured bird.

A bloody piece of raw meat.

His breath stuttered for a second as his heart fluttered. He stepped back, hand coming to his mouth to hold back the sudden queasiness.

It couldn't be meat. But that's what it looked like.

"Vultures," he whispered, nodding to himself.

There were turkey vultures in the area. One probably caught a mole or something and then dropped it as it flew overhead.

That's what had happened.

Drawing in breath and taking a firmer grip on his flashlight, Curtis leaned forward to get a closer look at what animal the vulture had caught.

Several tufts of long gray hairs were attached to the piece of meat.

Curtis stumbled sideways, falling against the door of his car. He lost his grip on the flashlight and it hit the ground with a crack. With fumbling hands, he scrabbled his way into the car, slammed the door and locked it. Then had to shove it back open to throw up. Wiping his sleeve across his mouth, he enclosed himself again and sat, gripping the steering wheel to control the shaking of his hands, the racing of his heart, the shortness of his breath.

Police. The police would want to see that. Test it or something. Those gray hairs. Henry. What else could it be?

There was no way he was getting out of the car again to retrieve the gruesome hunk. Instead he put the car in gear and drove into the dark mountain night, easing very slowly down the logging road in order to keep from jarring off those gray hairs. He gagged again, but pressed the back of one hand against his mouth and managed to swallow down the horror.

Once he hit pavement and got to where cell service worked, he would call 911.

Though they'd probably think he was insane when he told the dispatcher there was a piece of an old man on the hood of his car.

Curtis stood bathed in the red light of the neon 'closed' sign hanging in the window of the Index General Store. He'd called 911 as soon as he had cell service. Snohomish County Sheriff's Deputy Max Douglass had, luckily, been responding to a call about a bear in town. The two of them now stood under the store's wide eaves as rain splattered on the asphalt of the parking area.

The deputy wasn't as convinced as Curtis that the only thing remaining of Henry was a small chunk stuck and congealing on the hood of the Volkswagen Bug. Curtis had pulled in under the eaves so Henry wouldn't get washed off. Sure, the deputy said Henry wasn't home, but it didn't help that Henry was known for going bushwhacking into the mountains for days at a time and never telling anyone.

Until now Curtis had never realized how easy it was for someone who lived a solitary life to not be missed. It made him wonder how long it would take someone to notice if he disappeared. It saddened him to think there was only one person who might notice.

"I need to call my mother," Curtis said.

Deputy Douglass raised an eyebrow as he carefully packaged Henry.

"She's in Anacortes. Likes the ocean better than the mountains. I should call her more often."

The deputy didn't ask what caused the sudden spate of information he didn't need. Maybe he recognized that Curtis was simply thinking out loud.

Curtis was actually thinking that he needed to start calling his mother every evening. Not only so she'd miss him if something happened, but also, he suddenly realized, so he'd know if something happened to her.

Curtis blew out a breath, returning his focus to the here and now. "What will you do with Henry there?"

"Get it tested. See if it's human or not. First though, I'll take a quick run up to the Hole and poke around. Just in case. It might be days before we get any results and by then Henry might even be back. It hasn't been twenty-four hours since you saw him so legally he's not missing."

"I suppose it's possible the vulture grabbed some of his hair for a nest." Curtis's vivid imagination took over. "He might be camping out there right now with a headache and missing piece of scalp!"

The deputy shrugged. "Maybe. You *are* a scientist, right?"

"Sure. Why do you ask?"

"Just checking."

Curtis shuffled his feet as the deputy wrote down Curtis's contact information. "So there was a bear in town, huh?"

"The Smith family heard their garbage cans go over and said the bear actually tried to get in their house."

"What?"

Deputy Douglass shrugged. "That's what they said. They heard it breathing heavy, heard it outside the door. Probably was a bear. There were long scratches in the wood. And they'd been having breakfast for dinner. You know, lots of bacon. Though I only found big dog prints. But then I'm not a tracker."

"But still," Curtis said, peering into the darkness around them. "That seems weird behavior for a bear."

"I contacted Fish and Wildlife. Might be a tagged bear. Accustomed to people. They're coming next week to set up bear cages around town." Deputy Douglass closed his notebook. "Can you come by East County Precinct tomorrow to sign the statement?"

"Sure," Curtis said. "I'll stop in on my way up to work."

The deputy simply nodded and headed back to his truck.

Curtis drooped, exhaustion seeping through him. By now he was typically at home, writing up his notes from the day, checking email, finishing his solitary dinner.

Solitary, suddenly, didn't sound appealing. As he ducked against the rain and got back in his car he decided he'd stop at the Agate Cafe in Gold Bar. Comfort food and bright fluorescent lights.

As he drove over the bridge out of town he couldn't help glancing in his rear view mirror at the quiet street behind him. Index always had a few bears come through, especially this time of year when hibernation was done but berries weren't ripe yet. After all, Index nestled in bear country. But a bear trying to get into someone's house? That was just odd.

~Day 2~

1

Snohomish County Sheriff's Deputy Max Douglass pulled into the tiny parking lot of the Espresso Chalet and parked next to Deputy Casey Richards. He lowered the window of his whale. The black and white truck took ten points to turn and ten minutes to gain enough speed for a pursuit. He loathed it.

Casey's window was already down. She wiped raindrops off the edge before they dripped inside and shook her fingers. "Heard you had a road rage call in Sultan yesterday. What did the guy do?"

"Woman," Max said. "She lost it on this kid. Got out of her car at a stoplight and threatened to kick his ass."

"Really? Write a ticket?"

"No." Max thought a minute. "Something going on there. Looked like she'd just found out a loved one died. Know what I mean?"

"She was taking her grief out on the guy?" Casey asked.

"Maybe. Think we're going to see her again."

Casey smoothed her short black hair and put on a baseball cap with the Sheriff's logo. "As long as it's not suicide by cop. Ready for your coffee?"

"Always. You ready for your wimpy hot chocolate?" Max raised his window and got out of the truck. "I've never understood how anyone originally from Canada doesn't drink tea. You should drink tea. Isn't that a Canadian thing?"

"Tea, eh? Can't stand it. Plus, it's a British thing, not a Canadian thing." Casey looked up at him, who, at over six feet tall, rarely had anyone look down on him. "And, hey, isn't it your turn to buy the drinks?"

"Nope."

He followed Casey past a towering carved totem of Bigfoot. The legendary Sasquatch, as the creature was called locally in the Pacific Northwest, had a perpetually worried expression on its etched face. Today, in the drizzle, someone had placed a knitted orange and yellow cap with a big pompom on its head. The espresso stand was a quarter-mile east of Index, and the location where an old movie about Bigfoot had been filmed. It was also the location of the best espresso in the whole

Skykomish Valley.

"You heard from the ex?" Casey asked.

Max ran a hand over his head, slaking rainwater off his short hair and wishing he'd grabbed his hat. "Nope. Out east somewhere is all I know."

He used to rub the palm of his hand over the pain in his heart every time he thought of his ex-wife. But not anymore. She'd left him over two years ago, saying she couldn't be married to a cop anymore. He'd realized that she'd never been able to separate the man from the job. Thank god they hadn't had kids.

"That slacker you live with got a job yet?" Max actually liked Casey's boyfriend, Shep, who had recently been laid off from Boeing. Though Shep wasn't good enough for her. And lately he got a sense things weren't working out any better for her than it had for him. Romance and law enforcement were difficult bedmates.

"Who you calling a slacker?" Casey raised her fist and thumped his bicep. "Shep's in Snohomish today, applying at Soundair Aviation. It will be good again once he's back to work."

Max hoped the guy got the job. He didn't like hearing stress in Casey's voice.

Sandy was working the espresso machine and when they stepped up to the window of the tiny trailer, she was already pouring shots. Max nodded in greeting and then took his cardboard container of caffeine with a deep, contented sigh.

She called the drink a Lift Ticket. Four shots of espresso and four shots of heavy cream. He called it Priority Number One.

Casey paid for both their drinks, chatted briefly with Sandy, and then picked up her hot chocolate. Max shook his head as he always did, and they walked beside each other back to the trucks. But as he reached for the door handle, his cell phone rang.

"Deputy Douglass." He listened a moment then disconnected the call and looked over at Casey. "Want to go to Index? Maggie McMann is threatening to shoot some giant dog from hell."

Casey laughed. "Did you hear she wants to pass a law banning all dogs?"

"Yeah, good luck with that."

Max got into the truck and started it up. He toggled his shoulder unit to radio dispatch and then pulled onto the highway. Casey followed.

Max liked getting calls in Index. In such a tiny community, he knew most everyone and even liked some of them. Plus, the old mining community was in a beautiful setting, stuck between a big rushing whitewater river and a high, towering granite wall, with forests surrounding it like a giant blanket.

He drove over the bridge into town and took a deep drink of his Priority. He'd need it to deal with Maggie. While the older woman would be the first to jump in and help if needed, when she went off on a ranting tangent, she was like a hurricane. Casey had once said the best way to handle Maggie was to just wait until the winds died down and hope you were still standing afterwards.

But hey, it was a quiet day in the world of crime, and Index was a pretty good place to spend a rainy afternoon.

Even if it did involve a hurricane bottled in an old woman.

2

Curtis waited while Betty made him a turkey, cranberry, and cream cheese sandwich. He'd sneaked out of the Hole for his lunch break, thinking he'd go to the general store and ask about Henry. The rain was steady, too light to be a downpour but too heavy to be a drizzle.

He looked out the window of the store and watched the rain wash across his old Volkswagen, thinking that no one would ever know part of Henry had been on the hood the night before. He was relieved the rain had cleaned the car. And guilty for that sense of relief because maybe that had been the last remnant of the old man, now gone into the rain.

"Has anyone seen Henry?" he asked.

Betty wrapped the sandwich and handed it across the counter. "I haven't. Why?"

"Well…he was going to lecture me yesterday afternoon but never showed up."

"He does that all the time," Betty said, grabbing a stack of napkins and pushing them across to Curtis. "Says things and then gets distracted by something else. I remember one day he promised to come to church with me but chose instead to go hiking and got distracted by some type of beetle. So maybe he's out on a bug walk."

"Well, then, has Deputy Douglass been around?" Curtis asked. "He wanted to talk to Henry, too."

"Haven't seen him, but I know old Maggie was going to call him about some dog problem."

"Okay, thanks anyway." Curtis paid for his food. "Hey, if you do see Henry, ask him to come pound on the Hole door."

"Why would you want to encourage him?" Betty asked. "I've learned over the years if you give him a chance he'll talk for hours. And about things you don't even understand. I enjoy the times he's gone, God forgive me for saying so."

"I know. But I'm worried."

"Don't be," Betty said. "You're sweet to be concerned, but Henry does this all the time. And if he was here, he would be driving you to distraction. Enjoy the break while you can. Besides, the Lord protects, so he will be just fine. You wait and see."

Curtis wasn't too sure about that. Henry was annoying. Pompous most times. Unwilling to admit others might know more than he did. And yet, Curtis had to admit he enjoyed their debates. He liked having someone who understood that books and science were a world more real and tangible than the one he moved through. Someone who understood when the science became dizzying and thrilling with limitless possibilities. Someone who knew how study and research pulled a person into imagination, like being thrown out into the beauty and mystery of the universe.

There were even moments when Curtis imagined Henry as his father. He didn't remember his dad, who'd died when he was young. And Henry would have made a good dad because he listened and understood.

At least until he headed off into his conspiracy theories.

Curtis went out to the car and drove the three miles back to the Hole, then sat eating his sandwich and looking through the rain-washed windshield at the sheer granite and surrounding forest. He knew there was a steep and narrow trail nearby that Henry used to access the top of the Wall. Henry told him once that the trail was an ancient pathway probably originally used by animals. Curtis had been intrigued by his use of 'ancient' and immediately imagined a mystical path used by the indigenous Skykomish tribe for sacred quests.

But he'd never been on the trail himself. He wasn't a hiker. And who knew how many bears were out there. Or cougars. Or even raccoons. He'd heard raccoons got rabies.

He licked the last of the cranberry sauce off his fingers and then suddenly realized it looked kind of like that little scrap from the hood of his car. Minus the hair. He gagged and got quickly out of the car just in case he lost his lunch.

As he went through the rain to the Hole, he looked up at the low clouds hanging in tendrils through the cedar and fir trees. Henry could be up there in the woods. Maybe injured. Maybe more bits were missing than just from his scalp. And no one cared. No one would look for him because he took off all the time.

He thought about his job and his solitary life. If he died in the Hole would anyone notice? His mother would eventually, but other people were used to not seeing him. Just like they were used to not seeing Henry.

How could someone just walk away and not be seen, and no one worried? It wasn't right that it was so easy to disappear. He knew people cared, but they weren't so worried that they were out searching. Because he knew, without a doubt, that those tufts of gray hairs had come from Henry's head. Yes, the old man irritated him sometimes, but no one deserved to be forgotten. And if it was him, lost out there, he'd want someone to at least be concerned enough to look.

So it was up to Curtis to march into the rain-soaked forest, find the injured man, and carry him out to safety. He pictured himself staggering out of the trees with Henry, over his shoulders in a fireman's carry. He'd be a local hero.

He went into the Hole, but only long enough to slip on his raincoat and grab his backpack. It wouldn't hurt to go up the trail, at least a little way. Just in case.

Henry's 'ancient pathway' was steep. Rocks and tree roots were placed just right to trip Curtis. Tree branches hit him in the face and rain-soaked salal, ferns, and salmonberries brushed against him. His jeans were soaked to the knees in minutes. Oddly, the discomfort made him feel proud. He was taking on nature, persevering against all obstacles. His chin came up, and his shoulders, he was sure, squared with determination.

But it took him much longer than he'd expected to make it even a short way into the woods. Partly because he kept stopping to catch his breath and debate about giving up, and partly because he kept stopping to peer into the trees. The low clouds made the afternoon feel more like twilight and the woods also blocked light and created deep shadows that moved. A few times Curtis was convinced a shadow followed him, and that slowed him down, too.

The snap of a branch breaking made him spin around so fast he stumbled. Breathing fast and shallow, he struggled to hear over the thunder of his pounding heart.

Before he could think it through, he ran back down the trail, feet racing as fast as his heart. But after a couple yards he tripped over a large cedar root and came down hard on his hands and knees. His backpack rode up his back and banged the back of his head. He crouched there for a long moment, convinced he'd hear something chasing him. But all he heard were the birds singing cheerfully in the drizzle.

He pushed to his feet, tugged his pack into place, and wiped mud from his hands onto his jeans. His knees stung, but not bad. He glanced side to side, but there were no witnesses to his panic.

Now would be the time to give up and go back. He'd made the attempt. He could leave and have no guilt. He gritted his teeth. Would he want someone to give up on him so easily? And so he went up, wanting nothing more than to go down.

The woods opened up when he reached the area of Henry's fault and he relaxed a little out of the shadows. He listened to the peaceful sound of rain pattering on leaves and the forest floor and the hood of his raincoat. The Skykomish River was a gray ribbon far below, like a piece of old tarnished tinsel draped around the tiny town. The view alone was worth the hike.

A few feet away, clump of ferns shuddered and he jumped back, gasping. Before he could catch his breath, the ferns disappeared. Curtis stared, his mouth open in disbelief. Maybe the ferns were sucked off into one of Henry's parallel universes. Suddenly, that crazy theory didn't seem so crazy.

"Henry? That you?" His voice trembled.

He took a couple steps forward. "Henry? I found your scalp. Thought you might need some help."

No sound. But a salmonberry shrub tilted slowly and then fell. Disappeared.

Curtis took a few more steps forward, knees shaking. Still nothing. He pushed through some bracken and stumbled as the earth gave way under his boots.

He threw himself backward and hit the ground, rolling away from the deep crack in the ground. As he stood, heart racing, more dirt crumbled away and another clump of ferns fell out of sight. What was happening?

Clearly something had happened to the fault line. Henry had talked about it being a crack, not a deep trench. Had Henry fallen in?

He reached up to a nearby fir tree and grabbed a branch, then inched tentatively forward.

"Henry?" His voice was tremulous and nothing more than a whisper.

He wasn't sure he wanted an answer. He didn't want to go any closer and an answer meant he'd have to.

But he listened intently anyway, tilting his head to one side and squinting as if that would help. He heard the soft sounds of earth crumbling away. The sharper clacking of rocks tumbling downhill.

He called again, louder this time.

Nothing.

Curtis carefully backed up, not letting go of his branch until the ground felt firm and solid and no ferns shivered. He didn't know what to do next, which answered the question for him in a way. He had to go back. Tell someone what he'd just seen. Pressure someone, anyone, into taking it seriously that Henry was gone, that he might be lying, broken, at the bottom of the fault.

He was done pretending he was a hero.

It was time to get help.

3

Anya Lindgren sat on a granite boulder at the narrow footpath that led away from her cabin. Her German Shepherd, Bird, sat on his haunches next to her. Mist cobwebbed her coffee-colored hair, collected in her eyelashes, and dripped into her brown eyes. She swiped a hand across her face and shivered in the chilly spring day. Fine tremors moved upward from numb toes and fingers.

The woods were quiet around her, the forest sounds muffled under water dripping from leaves and fir needles. Clouds hung low, caught in treetops like a high fog. A breeze whispered through her damp clothes, raising goose bumps. She'd been here too long, waiting.

She knew better than this. She'd lived off grid in the national forest near Index for a year now. It was stupid to get wet and cold when it was going to take a couple hours to walk home. But she couldn't bring herself to leave yet. And so she sat in the muted late afternoon light, watching the empty trail.

Earlier, as the sun came up, Devon had brought her out a mug of coffee where she'd been planting rosemary, thyme, and rue around a young yew tree. Herbs for remembrance. She'd got up stiffly, the knees of her jeans damp from the rich humus of forest floor, and reached for the mug.

And then she'd seen his backpack.

"Going in to town?" she'd asked, wondering briefly what supplies they were short on.

Devon nodded and ran a hand through his shaggy blonde hair, not meeting her eyes.

"Can you pick up some evaporated milk?"

"The thing is, Anya, I'm not coming back."

She shook her head. His words made no sense. "What? Leaving? Leaving us?"

"Us?" Devon asked. "You want to talk about us? About this?" He threw out his hand, gesturing at the newly planted herbs.

"I understand you need a break," she said, her voice higher than normal, as if desperation lifted her words into the cold air. "I can handle things here for a few weeks."

Devon stepped away from her. "I'm not coming back. I never signed on for this...this Daniel Boone shit. I thought a summer would be, like, fun, living in the cabin, running the placer claim, maybe finding enough garnets or silver to pay for another college semester. I didn't plan on being here all, like, winter, chopping firewood, hunting-"

"Hunting?" Anger flushed heat through her veins and Anya let it fire her words. "You didn't do any hunting. You sat on your ass all winter while I kept us from starving. Me, in the condition-"

Devon held up a hand. "I didn't sign on for that either. And now…now you won't let it go. It's messing up my head."

"Go then." The welling emotion chilled. Died.

"You could, like, come with me," Devon said. "We had some good times together before. And the sex, man, that was mind blowing. If we got away from all this we might, like, get that back. We'd have to find another home for Bird though. The apartment my parents got me doesn't allow dogs."

"Apartment?" Anya felt the punch of his words deep in her heart. "How long have you been planning this?"

"Not long." He looked away from her, shifted his weight from boot to boot.

She saw the lie in his eyes, turned her back on him and knelt, sinking to the earth, to her plants. Last year's dead leaves rustled under his boots as he shuffled his feet and she heard him draw in breath as if to speak. She held hers, waiting for him to repeat his offer. Would she go? Could she go?

But he didn't speak, didn't give her another chance. He blew out breath and she listened to him leave.

Then waited for him to turn around. To wrap his arms around her and tell her he'd made a mistake. When a couple hours passed and he still hadn't returned, she took her pack with its emergency gear, her grandfather's Henry 45-70 rifle, gestured for Bird to come, and set off cross-country. She walked to the closest trailhead and waited there; waited to greet Devon when he showed up, convinced that by now he'd have changed his mind. Be on his way back.

But now the day was ending.

Movement to Anya's right caught her eye. She turned to see her shepherd patiently waiting, alert, ears forward, watching the trail. She saw how the mist collected in droplets on his fur. He shivered. She'd been away from home too long.

She stood and rubbed the ache in the small of her back. Bird looked up at her, head cocked to one side.

"You're right," she told the dog. "We've waited long enough." She looked back down the trail and swiped tears away. "He's not coming back."

Saying the words out loud, setting them free, made the whole thing too real. She was alone now.

Off-grid. On her grandfather's old placer claim in the national forest. Miles from the nearest road.

Anya ran a hand over her dog's wet fur. She had no idea what she was going to do. The only certainty was that she couldn't leave her home now.

She started across country, heading northeast through woods that rarely felt the presence of people. The trail she'd waited by was the result of her grandfather's repeated trips over many years toward civilization, when he took garnets in to sell, when he stocked supplies for winter, when he sent her rare letters talking simply of a simple life. Letters that had planted in his granddaughter the same yearning to test herself against an indifferent nature.

His trail led to a more popular one that took day-trippers to the old Silver Creek mining district where mining had gone on in the 1800s. Few of those hikers saw the small break in fern and salal, and even fewer recognized it as a path. To follow it, to find her cabin, someone also had to know landmarks and sense which way was north.

Anya touched Bird's head. Having a dog with a strong desire to be in his bed by his fire also helped point the way home.

Devon might never come back. She'd have to decide if she wanted this life, alone. If the reasons to stay outweighed the reasons to go. She recognized a tiny seed of relief, buried deep in the grief, that had been filling her for months. She and Devon had slipped effortlessly into a relationship born of great sex in a college dorm. When her grandfather died and left her the cabin and mining claim, she'd decided to walk away from forestry management courses and live it instead. And Devon, hearing about the mining claim, had been only too willing to drop out and follow her into the woods, dreaming his dreams of easy riches.

He'd had no clue how hard running a placer claim was, let alone how hard survival was. They'd fought a lot about everything. Anya, hiking steadily, let her subconscious point out what she should have seen.

That he'd been leaving a long time before he left.

Bird stopped suddenly and barked. The sound startled Anya out of her memories and she turned back to see the dog standing still, hackles up, teeth bared. She brought the rifle up and smoothly chambered a round, then turned, expecting to see a black bear. It was the time of year they came out of hibernation, hungry. And the time of year that berries weren't fully on yet to satisfy that hunger.

But she saw nothing. No movement in the trees, no shadows of something that shouldn't be there.

Bird, nose up, continued barking. Anya's heart rate shot up with the frantic noise. She spun in place, searching for the threat.

Several yards away she saw movement. Drawing in a deep breath to steady her hands, she raised the rifle and looked through the hunting scope. Surprised, she lowered the rifle to stare, then went back to the scope to bring the odd sight closer.

Douglas squirrels raced across the forest floor. Not just a few, but dozens. More than she'd ever seen together. They ran fast, in a mass, all of them headed east.

"What the hell?"

Anya glanced at Bird, still barking.

He wasn't even looking at the squirrels.

Confused, Anya lowered the rifle and stepped closer to her dog. She touched him, felt the rigid muscle. The slight jerk with each bark. "Bird! That's enough!"

The dog ignored her.

And then the forest floor breathed.

Anya stared, too confused to take in fully what she saw. The ground seemed to undulate, to rise up in waves as if the very trees exhaled. She lost her balance. The movement sharpened. The earth sagged down, out from underneath her. She followed, slamming into the ground only to be thrown back up. A deafening roar rose like an epic avalanche. Louder cracks came from above as trees snapped.

Anya fell again, grabbing the terrified dog as she went down.

Earthquake.

Breath coming in shallow, panicked sips, Anya managed to climb back to her feet. She grabbed Bird's collar, dragging him with her. She stumbled for one of the truck-sized granite boulders. She plastered herself against the cold flank of rock, sank to her knees and folded around Bird to keep him from bolting.

The quiet woods transformed to a maelstrom. Trees splintered, slammed into the earth with dynamite explosions that sent debris flying. The ground roiled beneath her. A tree hit the boulder above them. Heart pounding, Anya could only close her eyes and hang on as the primal instinct for survival shot adrenaline through her. She barely felt the pain of flying debris hitting her, barely registered her dog's cries, was barely aware of the screams that tore her throat.

And then the world stilled.

4

The key fob chirped as Ramon hit it with his thumb, locking the car. Traffic in Monroe sucked, and trying to find parking on Kelsey Street sucked even worse, even in the middle of the afternoon. He walked down the sidewalk toward his brother's small, two-story house to pick up his nieces for their lunch date. Yesterday had been soft and misty but today the rain was more defined, soaking into his short hair and the shoulders of his jeans jacket. Used to warm, dry weather, he shivered. This was spring?

A block from the house he shivered again, a quick dizziness. He stumbled. The vertigo deepened. He reached for the neighbor's ratty board fence to catch his balance. It didn't help. What was wrong with him?

But then the earth moved upward, a wave he couldn't surf. He fell against the fence, heard a loud crash, heard, dimly, screaming.

The sidewalk cracked under his feet. The fence collapsed, leaving him gripping a wooden slat. He struggled to stand as the noise around him became a cacophony of terror. A car and a pickup truck slammed into each other head on. A tree came down, hit the street like a bomb, disintegrating.

Ramon fell as the ground sank beneath him.

Earthquake.

He heard it, the roar of something that should be solid giving way. A telephone pole went, the lines ripping free, zinging through the air, tangling in another tree with sparks and smoke. And still the ground rolled.

Parked cars tumbled against each other. More trees splintered, snapped. Houses moved, seemed to waver.

Ramon tried to stand, heart pounding, and was thrown against a fire hydrant. Pain sliced through his right side. He fumbled, trying to grab the solid hydrant, an anchor in this sea of destruction. But even as he gripped the cap he saw a crack at the base open. He lunged backward as water shot out and up.

There was nowhere to go. No safe refuge in the chaos.

Nothing but pandemonium and horror and obliteration.

5

When the quake hit, it was a sign. Sharon knew she would die fast. While others in Sultan ran screaming, while buildings collapsed and streets convulsed, while the bronze Sultan John statue came down hard, she held arms out. Waiting.

Take me.

Trees fell around her.

I'm here.

The brick façade of the strip mall crumbled, exposing the inside of Vinaccio's Coffee, where rows and rows of flavored syrup bottles fell from shelves, shattering, shards flying.

I'm right here!

Thrown to her knees, Sharon came down hard on the sidewalk, grit cutting into her knees, the palms of her hands.

A man and woman stumbled past, the man stepping on Sharon's hand. She cried out with the pain but he didn't slow down. A hundred feet further down the sidewalk the Tobacco, Cigars, and Vape store blew. The door and windows convulsed outward, pushed by explosive flames that engulfed the man and woman.

And then they were vaporized and Sharon still waited on hands and knees for a quick death to find her. As she struggled to her feet, cradling her bruised fingers, a thought flashed through her brain. If that man had paused to help her he'd still be alive. Followed by the realization that if she'd kept running rather than standing so dramatically with arms outstretched, she'd be dead.

She laughed bitterly even as the heaving earth tossed her back to the ground and she came down on her tailbone. Sharp pain raced up her spine but all she could do was breathe through it as she was thrown around. There was nothing to hang on to even if she'd wanted to try and save herself.

The movement surrounding her slowed and the air filled with sound. Sirens, flames, screams, the crash of poles and buildings and glass hitting the ground, the crunch of cars trying to get somewhere, anywhere.

Sharon stumbled across the narrow parking lot to her BMW sitting unscathed on a patch of still-level pavement. She sat, cold and alone, in the car as darkness fell, convinced the quake was a sign. She exalted in the chaos, knowing her time had come. Something this major, there would be aftershocks.

Death would find her here.

6

Max stood in the tiny parking lot of the Index General Store. Casey, next to him, patiently listened to Maggie, who was describing, yet again, some big black dog that had growled at her and had blood-red eyes. Max had a hard time focusing on the story. Every dog in town growled at Maggie. Every dog she described was always the dog from hell. The short woman stood there with a half-finished wool afghan draped around her shoulders, crochet hook in her hand. The more upset she got, the faster she crocheted.

Max figured whatever she was making would be finished before her story about the crazed dog from hell.

"I understand your concerns," Casey said in a well-practiced tone. "Let me get your signed statement and-"

"Statement? I'm not signing any statement." Maggie's hook never paused. "All I need is for you to shoot that dog."

"And where is the dog?" Max asked, making a point of squinting down Avenue A.

"I'm not going to do your job for you," Maggie said. "This town pays the sheriff's department for your service. Get out there and earn it."

Max ducked his head to hide his grin.

"We can't take any action without a signed statement from you," Casey said. "But Deputy Douglass will certainly go look for this giant dog and wrestle it back here. Won't you, Deputy?"

Casey reached up and punched him lightly on his bicep.

Max staggered, reached out for Casey, and came down hard, hip and elbow slamming into asphalt. There was a brief second of disconnect, that Casey had actually knocked him over. But then she came down on top of him and he saw her fear-filled blue eyes, her hands splayed out to stop her fall.

Max caught her and held on from pure reflex as the pavement lifted them into the air then dropped away from them. He hit the ground again and sharp pain sliced up his back. Casey's mouth was moving like she was shouting at him but he heard nothing past the thundering impact of something hitting the ground. Off to the side, he was vaguely aware of Maggie falling forward.

He struggled to get up but the earth was having seizures. In the middle of a parking lot there was nothing to use for a handhold. For a brief moment Casey made it to her hands and knees before slamming back to the ground. Her chin split and blood bloomed, splatting on the ground.

A huge crack in the pavement opened just a few feet away and water shot into the sky as a water main broke.

Max slammed onto the rolling ground again, hitting chest first. The Kevlar vest took the brunt of the impact but the wind was still knocked out of him. He struggled to breathe even as he was tossed up again and again and again.

And then it was over. A deep, heavy silence fell and it took him a moment to realize it wasn't really silence. His sudden lack of movement just felt like silence. He could hear his own gasping for breath. He could hear shouting and screaming, glass shattering, loud crashes.

He groaned and managed to get up on one knee. Casey, a foot or two away, spit out blood. Grit bit into the palm of his hand as he pushed himself up.

"Okay?" he asked.

Casey shook her head, spit blood again, and then struggled to her feet. "Yeth."

"What?" Max said. "You hurt?"

"I'll live." Casey spit blood again. "Get on the radio. Aftershocks."

Max simply nodded and reached up for the radio on his shoulder unit. But then he saw Maggie on her side and not moving. Glass from the store's broken windows was scattered across her and her crochet hook was impaled in her eye. Dark blood washed over her cheek and down her neck. He staggered over and dropped to a knee, reaching for her neck, frantically trying to find a pulse. The hook angled upward from her cheek toward the top of her head. The majority of its length was out of sight.

One filmy, old lady eye stared at him, but there was no life behind it. And there was no beat of life under his fingers. He pushed back up to his feet, pain shooting through his hip, back, and chest. He looked at Maggie and forcibly shut down the sorrow. There was no time for that now.

Casey jiggled her radio then jogged the short distance to him. She glanced down at Maggie, recognized death, and her brain automatically clicked into their training. Triage and things they might be able to fix. "Radio's out. Bridge is down."

The flagpole behind them slammed to the ground with a loud crash.

"What?"

"I said, the Index bridge is out. Gone. So is the railroad trestle.

Unless the old back road is open, help isn't coming soon."

Max scanned the area. A familiar Volkswagen Beetle had been thrown into the telephone booth at the side of the general store. He saw the driver's head slumped forward. One wall of the store had completely collapsed. There were screams in the distance, the tang of propane and smoke in the air, and gushing water from the broken main.

"Get over to the fire department," he said, gesturing across the street.

Most of that building still stood, although half the roof of the bay had come down. It was going to take work to get a fire engine out. "See who's in district. Get a jump kit. We need to get everyone who's not injured searching for those who are."

She sprinted across the street. The lack of sirens or flashing lights from the tiny volunteer department didn't bode well for anyone being around. But then he saw someone in uniform come around the corner of the store from the direction of a small house where firefighters lived. He recognized an EMT, a young man he thought was named Samuel.

Max yelled for the guy to follow and ran for the car that had hit the telephone booth. He wrenched open the door and recognized the driver but before he could do more, Samuel was there, pressing his fingers against the man's neck.

"Curtis! Come on man, wake up now." Samuel glanced at Max. "I've got a strong pulse."

Max drew in a deep breath in relief as Curtis's eyes fluttered, opened, and stared uncomprehending.

"Can you tell me where you are?" Samuel asked.

Curtis looked around, struggling to focus, as if he'd been deeply asleep and was only just now waking. He stared at the sign for the general store.

"Index. I'm in Index. The sign fell."

"It sure as hell did."

Max saw no blood, no signs of broken bones, no sign that Curtis had impacted the windshield. When he saw Casey coming back across the street hauling a jump kit, he gestured her over. She gave the first aid supplies to Samuel and then got out of the way.

"Samuel, you good here?" Max asked. When Samuel nodded, he turned to Casey. "I'll clear the store next, you start triage out there."

Inside the general store, Betty, the owner, was on her knees surrounded by collapsed shelving and shattered goods. She was pale, her eyes dilated with shock, and her arm self-splinted with a belt. Max pushed aside a small table and broken coffee pot and lifted her to her feet, scanning the rest of the store. She spoke but her teeth were chattering too hard for him to make any sense of her words.

The lights flickered, catching glass shards everywhere, and then went out leaving the store in semi-darkness. A sharp vinegar smell filled the air from broken pickle jars. A freezer case was tipped, pinning a man who was still moving weakly, trying to pull himself free. A woman sat on the floor in the back corner where the tiny post office was. She stared wide-eyed at her hand, still clutching mail.

"The front door is clear," Max yelled to the woman, making his way to the trapped man. "If you can move, get out. Go now, before aftershocks bring down the rest of the building."

"The door," the woman repeated, like she didn't know what the words meant. But Betty went to her and, one-handed, helped the woman to her feet.

Max climbed over a shelving unit, kicked aside a chair, and made it to the freezer. But the man under it was no longer moving and the widening pool of blood under him no longer flowed. Max felt for a pulse anyway, even though he knew it was too late. Just like Maggie, this man was gone.

He quickly searched the rest of the store, flinching and ducking when a portion of the back wall came down with a crash that shattered the icemaker and sent ice cubes skittering into glass and debris. When he found no one else, he stumbled over canned goods and headed outside.

The tiny town was a scene of chaos. People sat in yards or in the street, staring in shock or crying, or with faces buried in hands. Some stood, clinging to each other. Some stood, alone, eyes glazed with shock. Some headed for the fire department as if that was the place they'd be safe in this newly destroyed world.

For a brief moment he was incapable of action. He stood, frozen, simply unable to take in the dramatically changed world. How was he to fix this? And then he saw Casey.

She stood in the middle of the street doing fast evaluations of people, talking and gesturing. She was organizing search parties, pulling the least-injured people into her hastily assembled work crews. He drew in a deep breath that made his ribs ache and kicked his brain into gear. What was the highest priority? The children.

He ran toward Fifth Street and the school. Thank god it was Friday afternoon. That meant a half-day, but there might still be kids inside, and definitely some staff.

The school looked relatively intact, in spite of, or maybe because of, its age. But inside was the same chaos he'd found in the store, with collapsed shelving, scattered books, and tables and desks broken and knocked over.

The school's secretary knelt next to a stylish dark-haired woman he didn't recognize. The woman's blouse was torn and a small shard of glass poked out of her side, but she still clutched a massive red leather purse as if that was more important. The secretary had one hand on the woman's waist, keeping her from moving. A small amount of blood seeped around the sharp edges of glass.

"I need an aid car," the woman said, gasping fast and shallow. "A paramedic."

Max dropped to one knee and met the secretary's eyes. He carefully lifted the torn edge of the blouse on the woman.

"I didn't know if I should pull it out," the secretary said, her hands shaking. "It looks pretty minor."

"Minor?" the woman asked, eyebrows going up. "I'm impaled. I need a paramedic. An ambulance."

"Leave it in place," Max said. He leaned toward the woman. "Look at me."

The woman met his eyes. He saw anger there, but knew that was often the form fear took. She clutched her purse closer.

"The two of you are going to get out of this building before there's an aftershock. The glass shard stays in place. This woman will take you to the fire department where the injured are gathering. You'll be seen as soon as possible. But there will be no paramedic and no aid car. The bridge is down. We are on our own for a while. Do you understand what I'm telling you?"

"I demand a paramedic."

Max's patience disappeared. "That's fine. Go to the fire department and demand all you want. But you're leaving this building now."

He stood and helped both women to their feet. "Take her to the fire department and then see if you can help Samuel there with the injured. Is there anyone else in the building?"

The secretary shook her head. "No. Everyone left early. Our half-day. I stayed because Ms. Martin came to meet about our curriculum."

"Okay. Get going." Max watched the secretary tug the woman toward the door and then followed them out into the light rain.

Outside on the street, Casey jogged over to him. Rain dripped down his neck and under the collar of his uniform jacket. He shivered. The town had always felt so small. A hundred and fifty people. But now, with no help coming and the responsibility for these people squarely on him, Casey, and the lone EMT, the population was suddenly overwhelming. *One step at a time*, he told himself. It wasn't enough to quiet the small voice of fear deep in his chest.

"The main part of the fire department is pretty solid," Casey said when she reached his side. "Samuel is doing a good job with triage. He's got people helping him with the injured we've found so far. Some are going to die. There's no way around that. We don't have any way to treat internal injuries. I can't make radio contact with dispatch and cell phones aren't working so I think the repeater towers are down, too. I've got some crews organized to search houses. I'm headed over to Index Avenue."

"I'll go with you," Max said, and then caught something, a shadow, in Casey's eyes. "What?"

She pulled off her baseball cap, ran a hand over her hair, and put the cap back on. Raindrops collected on the shoulders of her jacket and she felt the damp chill sink into her skin. She shook her head and looked past Max, up at the high wall of granite over them. She didn't want to answer, didn't want to say something that would make him think less of her. And didn't want to follow that thought any further down its road. But he stood there looking so…safe. She drew in a deep breath.

"I'm scared shitless." She caught his arm. "I don't know what the hell we're going to do, Max. I think this quake was the big one everyone's been predicting for years. And it's just us here. People are terrified, hurt, and isolated. It's going to be dark soon. And you know what comes out in the dark, how it changes people. Looting, vandalism."

Max looked at the ground. He knew how hard it was for Casey to admit to any weakness, let alone fear. But this…it was legitimate. She *should* be afraid. They all should be. He met her eyes.

"So am I. Scared shitless that is. And if you tell anyone, I'll never pay for your hot chocolate again."

That lame joke got a shaky smile from her.

"I think you're right about the quake," he said. "That means no help for a long time. No infrastructure. Tsunamis along the coast. You've seen the projections. Water all the way to Monroe. The freeway destroyed. Bridges down. Sultan's dam will breach if it hasn't already. It's going to be a long time before anyone can reach us, unless it's by air. And these little towns in the Sky valley aren't going to be a priority. The cities will be. Seattle. Everett, what's left of them."

"So what do we do?"

"No clue." Max ran a shaking hand over his face. "What we can, I guess. But we need to be thinking long term."

"So for right now, help out the crews we got going. Find the injured that we can. Figure out how to find shelter for everyone."

"Yes. And let's try to get everyone together before dark. Maybe we won't see the vandalism and destruction here that the larger cities will face tonight."

"Let's hope," Casey said.

They both knew what kind of people crawled out of the shadows in chaos like this.

Max looked at the deep worry still in her eyes. "Shep will be okay. Your guy is resourceful."

Casey, startled, looked up at him and then simply nodded. She couldn't think of anything to say so she headed toward Index Avenue knowing Max would follow. But her chest felt light and hollow, with something almost like shame settling in there.

She hadn't once thought of Shep.

What did that tell her? She wasn't sure, and wasn't sure she wanted to know.

7

"Curtis."

Curtis opened his eyes. He had a vague sense that someone had been calling him for a while.

"Can you tell me where you are?"

He looked around, struggling to focus, as if he'd been deeply asleep and was only just now waking. He saw the sign for the general store. There was something wrong with it.

"Index. I'm in Index." He thought for a moment. "The sign fell."

"It sure as hell did."

Curtis looked up at the young man speaking and slowly became aware of the fire department uniform. And then saw the deputy standing behind him. "What happened?"

"An earthquake. A big one. Maybe *the* big one. Can you tell me if you're hurt?"

Curtis thought for another slow moment. "No, I don't think so. Maybe...I think I hit my head."

The young man aimed a penlight in Curtis's eyes. He winced away from the bright light and raised a hand to wipe his cheeks as his eyes watered. He started to move but was restrained. He looked down and realized he was in his car and still buckled in. He reached for the release on the seat belt and let it go.

The deputy gripped Curtis under his arm and helped him out into light rain and then left them, heading toward the town hall. He stood carefully and leaned against his car, shivering. The old phone booth no one used except the few local drug users, rested in pieces of metal and shards of glass across the front of the car. The front fender and hood were crumpled.

"Oh wow, I hit the phone booth," Curtis said. "What happened?"

"Like I said, earthquake." The firefighter studied Curtis. "Look, it's crazy right now and we have lots of injured and missing people. I think you're okay, but if you start feeling worse, like dizzy, nauseated, blurred vision, come find me. Ask for Samuel. Okay?"

"Okay," Curtis said faintly, his head throbbing.

Samuel left him, jogging across the street toward the fire department.

Earthquake? Had Samuel said earthquake?

Curtis ran a shaky hand over his face and looked over his shoulder at the general store. One back corner of the building was collapsed in a mess of shattered timbers, hanging wires, strips of insulation, and broken glass.

He frowned, thinking hard.

He remembered coming down Fifth Street and pulling into the parking lot. A flash of movement, a second of realization that a utility pole was falling. He'd swerved to avoid it. That was how it happened, swerving. He must have driven, or been thrown, right into the telephone booth.

Sounds started to filter through the haze that was his brain. Distant thunder that rolled, silenced, rolled again. Voices, some panicked, some angry. Someone in the distance screamed but he wasn't sure where it came from. The rotten-egg scent of propane was sharp in the damp air.

Soft rain pattered around him and on him. He shivered and bent, head pounding, to pull out his raincoat from the back seat. He slipped it on and tugged up the hood.

The bridge that curved so gracefully over the North Fork of the Skykomish River was missing. Just gone. The old rusty train trestle downriver from the bridge was also gone. The far bank of the whitewater river had collapsed, sending dirt and boulders into the water. Cables and pieces of concrete hung where the bridge had been. Water gushed up in front of the general store, where a water main had obviously broken. The tiny town wasn't recognizable and Curtis could only stare.

The town hall still stood although it listed heavily and the front steps had pulled completely away. The flagpole rested against the roof of the Old Fire Hall, a small community center that was next to the town hall. Some houses were completely flattened like someone had stepped on them, some were in pieces, and all were impaired. One, a gray-blue historical home that had been expensively renovated, had only one historical wall still standing.

Curtis pushed away from his car and moved out into the street. His legs shook and he shivered uncontrollably. The extent of the damage terrified him but he had to see. Had to know the reality. What his eyes told him, his brain was simply unable to grasp. This wasn't something that was going to be fixed in a day, or a week, or even a month.

Another thunderclap echoed in the town and rumbled down the canyons. Curtis jumped. What he heard wasn't thunder. Couldn't be. The sounds were too close to the ground, too close to the town. It had to be boulders coming down from the granite Wall.

Curtis walked toward Index Avenue, making his way carefully over the torn up asphalt of the road. The Railroad Hotel, another historical building recently renovated, had massive damage. The top floors had collapsed like an accordion. A piece of one balcony hung from the corner, and as Curtis watched, it fell with a crash. Relief flooded him as he remembered the owners had never opened for business. He wondered, briefly, where the building's local ghost had gone.

He stumbled down Index Avenue and saw a body in the grass. With heart pounding, Curtis ran across the street. His mind was a sudden panicked blank, years of first aid trainings gone. But then he saw movement and recognized Bert.

The man rolled on his side and pillowed his head on his arm. "Brother, I'm show drunk."

Curtis knew that without being told. Even from a few feet away he smelled the fumes.

"I mean, brother, really drunk," Bert said. "You should have sheen the earth jusht rolling, brother. Rolling."

Locals had jokingly named Bert and his partner, Ernie, because no one knew their real names. The two homeless men, with scruffy long hair and longer beards, had worked their way into the psyche of the tiny mountain town.

Curtis stood there a moment longer, but when he realized Bert was snoring, he turned back toward the town center. Let Bert think the earthquake was the result of alcohol a little longer. And sleeping in the rain was the least of their worries.

Back on Avenue A, the double doors of the Old Fire Hall had been pulled open and leaned, crooked, against the outside walls. People milled in the street, some with rain gear, some with umbrellas, some just getting soaked. The mayor, Albert, was asking for tents, or anything that might work for temporary shelters, for generators, for search teams. His voice was a calm center in the crowd and people gravitated toward him.

Two sheriff deputies moved through the crowd, stopping to talk, to listen, to hand out first aid supplies. Curtis recognized the deputy that had helped him out of his car. And he realized now, it was the same deputy that had helped him with the piece of Henry's scalp.

He joined the people but stood at the fringe of the activity, not sure what to do. A slight, older man wearing a metal hardhat said something about getting on the radio with emergency management. No one seemed to be listening as they milled around the mayor and the deputies, their eyes dull with shock.

Betty, from the general store, stood by one of the doors, an arm in a sling made from a belt. She glanced at Curtis, but then waved at a young man standing a couple feet away. "Don't you have a huge canopy that you rent out for weddings?"

The young man nodded. "We can get that set up. Maybe some kerosene heaters."

"Um…excuse me?" Curtis said, raising a shaking hand as if in school. "You might want to save that kerosene until we really need it. Maybe assign some people to start gathering firewood instead. Build fires to gather around."

"Save it?" the young man asked. "Why? Snohomish County will get the bridge fixed. I'm a councilmember. If I ask our state representative, I can get this taken care of quickly."

Without even being aware of the transition, Curtis slipped into lecture mode. "No, we can't. For one thing, how are you going to contact them? Maybe fire department radios if we're lucky. Maybe a ham radio if anyone has one. Cell phones won't be working. And with all due respect, responders are not going to prioritize Index."

"Of course they will. I have contacts. I'll have help here quickly." The young man started to turn away.

Curtis grabbed his arm. "Look around you. This wasn't a local tremor. I bet this was the quake they've been predicting for years."

"Don't be ridiculous," the young man said. "You're just scaring people."

But the mayor, Albert, nodded toward Curtis. "Keep talking."

"Well…freeways beyond use for one thing. Tsunamis from the Sound coming all the way to Monroe." Curtis's voice shook. "No one will even be able to come up our two-lane highway, let alone help out a tiny town. All the bridges will be down. Resources will be tied up with big cities and infrastructure."

He stumbled to a stop, fear making him oddly breathless. His words, with their ring of truth, overwhelmed him.

"Who are you again?" the young man asked. "And what makes you the expert?"

"Well, I'm not an expert," Curtis said, his cheeks warming. "Just a University of Washington professor. But you don't have to be an expert to know this was major. People need to think long term."

The young man threw up a hand as he turned away, as if blowing off Curtis's words. "You don't know what you're talking about."

Curtis watched him leave, but then the old man with the hardhat spoke, making him jump, startled.

"You're right. Help won't be coming soon. We need to find a way to communicate with the outside world and figure out what resources we have here."

Albert shook his head. "Okay, but right now we have to find the injured. House to house searches."

"And don't forget Henry," Curtis said quickly.

"Henry? What's he got to do with anything?" Albert asked. He raised his hands, waving people toward him.

"Well, a piece of him was on my car," Curtis said. "I thought maybe someone should go look for the rest of him. I found a fault fracture on the Wall. He might be down in there."

"There are lots of people missing," Albert said. "I'll add him to the list and we'll do what we can."

A long, undulating scream from down the street made everyone turn. A man, walking with stiff dignity, came down the middle of torn up pavement. In his arms he carried the blood-covered body of a small girl, lifted as if in offering. Her head lolled to one side, her brown hair trailing over his arm. A woman behind him caught his shirt, her screams now sliding into keening. Samuel came out of the fire department and ran to them.

Betty touched Curtis's arm. "Samuel's the only medic here. No one can get to us. What are we supposed to do?" Rain soaked in to her hair and trickled down her face.

Samuel took the little girl and lowered her gently to the ground, his fingers going to her neck. There was a long pause, and then he slowly shook his head.

Curtis brushed warm tears away from his face with cold fingers. "We help," he said simply.

8

Ramon's fingers left bloody tracks on the cell phone. He flipped it shut, struggled to control his rage, and then blew, throwing it at the pile of rubble that had been his brother's house.

"Fucking hell!" He raked fingers into his dark hair, digging into his scalp as if he could forcibly pull a solution out of his brain.

Sirens wailed in the distance, drew near, then faded away. They'd been going like that for almost an hour now. But was anyone coming to help him, or any of the people around him? No. Could he get anyone to answer when he called 911? No. Because the stupid piece of shit cell phone wasn't working.

He coughed from the smoke that moved in tendrils through the rain. Several collapsed homes were on fire. He was surrounded by a nightmare scene of rubble. People staggered down the street, some sat in shock, some wept, some, like him, raged. Blood and bones and bodies. Isolated by their terror, frozen in their individual horrors, no one came to help.

He bent again to the debris and heaved bricks aside, cut his fingers again on broken glass, stumbled when his boots broke through wedges of sheetrock. This had been a beautiful small home, built in the 1960s, renovated last year when Tómas moved in with Therese and their daughters. Ramon's nieces, home from school on their half-day.

No way to get hold of his brother and sister-in-law, no way to get through to 911, and his nieces were trapped, injured, maybe dying, alone. He was supposed to keep the family safe. *He* was. Not Tómas, who had never been good at it.

He dug into the rubble with a vengeance. A shovel clattered down beside him.

"Use this, son."

Ramon, panting with exertion and a stomach-wrenching panic for his nieces, grabbed the shovel and glanced upward. Standing next to him was an old man with another shovel. The stranger didn't speak, simply went to work. He was stoop-shouldered under the weight of years, with the fuzzy remains of gray hair creating tufts over his ears. Ramon took in the blue bib overalls and the old fashioned black framed glasses and without a word started digging in earnest. With the old man helping, they cleared debris away, creating a sizable hole where the front door had been.

Ramon hoped he would find some sort of way in but as he worked that hope died. He saw only downed beams that had once supported the ceiling. He dropped to his hands and knees.

"Alegria! Marie!" Ramon shouted then held his breath, willing a response.

"Hear that?" the old man asked. "Someone's there."

Ramon lunged forward, slamming the shovel into the broken home. Pain arced through the muscles of his shoulders and arms. He barely registered a woman's voice behind him.

"Be careful now. You won't do those girls any good if you get hurt yourself."

Ramon shook sweat and rain out of his eyes. An extremely overweight elderly woman stood above him, holding out a bottle of water. He shook his head, no breath to answer, no time to spare. The woman, her white hair curling up from the rain, offered the bottle to the old man.

"Later, Mother. Got work to do."

She stepped backward, and Ramon was barely aware of a hurt expression in her eyes.

"I want to help," she said.

"Mayhap you can, Mother, when this man's family is out," the old man said. "Right now stay out of the way."

Ramon squatted down and crawled into the opening they'd created.

"Careful now," the old man said, coming in behind him. "Got to go slower, shore up these beams so we can get back out."

Ramon saw the wisdom in the words, but shoved through debris anyway, leaving the old man to brace and secure the small space. Ramon paused only call out, to listen, to follow the responses that became clearer as he forced his way forward.

He saw the small foot, the slender ankle, Alegria's bright hot pink tennis shoe half on, half off.

"Alegria, talk to me."

"Tío Ramon?" And then, sobbing.

"Hush, baby," Ramon said, carefully lifting a two-by-four from across her ankle. "We're here. Talk to me, tell me where you're hurt."

"My arm is broken, I think," came the thirteen-year-old's voice, choked with tears. "My head hurts." Her voice rose. "I did what teachers said at that stupid drill! I stood in the doorway!"

"She's panicking," the old man said.

"No shit." Ramon grabbed a chunk of sheetrock, handing it back to the stranger.

"Calm her down. Talk, touch her."

"Alegria, listen, baby." Ramon spared a brief second to put his hand over her ankle, the only thing he could reach. "You're not alone. You're going to be okay."

"I seriously doubt that," she said, sounding suddenly like her mother in spite of the catch in her voice. "And I'm never going back to school. They don't know shit."

"Alegria," Ramon said, ignoring the laugh from the old man. "Bad words. Remember what your mother says."

"I heard you say 'fuck'. When you couldn't hear me."

"Listen now," Ramon repeated, squeezing her ankle slightly. "Is Marie with you?"

"She ran for the bathtub. I told her that was for tornados. I called her an idiot!" Sobs broke out again.

"Alegria!" Ramon raised his voice. "Cry later. Right now I need you to calm down."

He heard muffled sniffles. And then her voice, quivery, but more controlled.

"Okay. But I hurt."

"I know, baby. We'll take care of that." He passed more of the wreckage back to the old man.

As he worked to shift broken boards and shattered glass, Ramon tried to picture the layout of the house. But now it was like he'd never been here. How far was the bathroom? And then he thought *which bathroom?* God, had Marie gone upstairs?

Alegria was slowly coming free of the debris.

"That there doorframe looks pretty solid," the old man said. "You get your shoulder under it, mayhap I can pull the young lady out."

"What's your name?" Ramon asked as he maneuvered under the frame.

"Benton Volker. Ben. That's June, outside. You?"

"Ramon Saura." He grunted with effort and as he pushed upward his back muscles screamed. His breath caught on the pain.

Ben didn't waste time, shoving under Ramon and grabbing for Alegria. "This is going to hurt."

Alegria screamed as she came free, and the instant she was clear, Ramon lunged back and let the shattered doorframe settle. He caught his niece up to him as close as he could in the confined quarters, trying to protect the arm she supported as she cried.

"I'm truly sorry young lady," Ben said.

Alegria sniffled loudly and buried her face against her uncle's shoulder, trembling against him. But then she took a deep breath.

"At least you didn't lie," she said. "I hate it when grownups lie." Tears rose to the surface again. "I ripped my school uniform."

"Don't matter none," Ben said. "You did say you weren't going back."

The matter of fact words seemed to help as Alegria once again sniffled down tears.

"I'm going after Marie," Ramon said. "Can you get Alegria out?"

"Yep."

Ramon shifted in the small space, handing Alegria carefully over. "Which bathroom?"

Alegria gasped in pain as her arm brushed against the remains of the wall. Ben pulled her to him, and started backing out of cleared space they'd come in through.

"I don't know," Alegria said. "I haven't heard her."

"Don't worry baby," Ramon repeated, turning back to the space Alegria had just been pulled from. "I'll find her. Everything's going to be okay."

Her voice grew fainter as Ben hauled her out. But he still made out the words.

"See? Grownups lie."

9

Marie was unconscious in the bathtub. Ramon lifted the slight fifteen year old out gently, searched bathroom debris for a hand towel, and then carefully pressed it against his niece's head wound. Her crazy hair, those long wild curls that drove her mother nuts, was matted with blood. More stained the white blouse of her school uniform, and the blue cardigan had a rent in the shoulder. Holding her against his chest to avoid jostling her as much as possible, he backed his way out of the ruins.

Ben waited at the opening, and helped Ramon to stand. In the front yard, June sat on the grass with Alegria, oblivious to the rain. The two men joined her, and Ramon, legs shaky with exhaustion, sank down with Marie braced against his chest.

"Duct tape," Ben said, gesturing with his chin toward his wife.

June was splinting Alegria's right arm with a *Sun* magazine and the duct tape. The elderly woman was sweating and wheezing, and Ramon wondered briefly how they'd get her back up on her feet.

"I don't think the arm is broken," June said. "I think it's just banged up pretty good. But the splint will help either way."

Ramon could only nod.

"Just keep that towel on her head." June gestured at Marie. "Use that umbrella of mine on the ground there, and I'll fix her up soon as I get done here. Now, child, this is only a temporary splint so keep your arm as still as you can. It will help with pain until we can find a doctor."

"It sure hurts," Alegria said in a shivery voice.

"I'm sure it does, honey," June said, putting the roll of tape on the ground.

"You got that taped on firm enough, Mother?" Ben asked.

"Of course I do."

Ramon rocked Marie gently as June scooted over to them and carefully lifted the towel.

"Oh, not so bad," she said. "Head wounds always bleed heavy."

"But she's unconscious," Ramon said. His back ached, his hands and forearms were scraped, cut, and raw. His side felt deeply bruised where he'd hit the fire hydrant. But he had his nieces. They were alive and out of the house. Gratitude filled his soul.

"Well, she got knocked on the head by something, that's for sure," June said. "They'll probably want to watch her for signs of a concussion if we can get to the hospital, and if it's functioning. But I don't think it's that bad."

"How long do you think she'll be out?"

"I'm awake," Marie said in a soft, drowsy voice.

Alegria immediately started sobbing and crawled awkwardly to Ramon, where she tried to climb into his lap with Marie. He gripped both girls and held them tight, head bowed over them.

"Where's mama?" Marie asked.

"No idea, honey," June said. "But you're safe here until your mother comes home."

"She's going to be mad," Marie said. "Her nice home all broken up." Her eyes fluttered, her breathing deepened, and she seemed to drift back to sleep.

"Are you sure it's not bad?" Ramon asked.

June nodded. "I've seen my share of injured children."

Ramon clutched the girls, his mind suddenly blank with the exhaustion that follows adrenaline-fueled fear. "So...you have children?"

"Ten," Ben answered. "Mayhap more. You kind of lose count, right, Mother?"

June pulled her huge purse over and rummaged inside, coming up with another small bottle of water that she handed to Alegria. "He's pulling your leg. We have two boys. Both grown now. Charles and his husband have twin girls and live in California. Frank is in Wyoming and him and his wife have three boys."

Ramon struggled to focus on her words, and when she reached again for her purse he feared she was going to pull photos of grandkids out. But she came out with a tissue that she wiped her nose with.

"The boy don't need our whole history," Ben said. "You sure it's not ten?"

Ramon managed the weak smile that the old man seemed to be hoping for with his lame humor. He gripped Marie and started to stand when Ben suddenly turned.

"Hey! Get out of there!"

The suddenness of the old man's bellow startled all of them, and Ramon jerked around to see Ben stomping toward the house.

"What?" he asked.

"I saw someone going in the door hole." Ben bent into what had been the entryway. "Hey!" he shouted again.

"Who was it?" Ramon asked, exhaustion sinking into his pores.

"No idea," Ben said, still staring into the house. "Just saw him out of the corner of my eye. Gray clothes. I think. Not even sure he went inside."

"If he did, he's on his own," Ramon said. "I've got to get these girls to the hospital, figure out where their parents are."

"Right," June said. "Father, stop that hovering. You probably were just seeing things. Come on over here and help me up."

Ben waited another moment, head cocked as if listening. But finally he straightened and came back to where his wife waited. He took hold of her arm, and stepped back, bracing himself. To Ramon, it looked like old habit, heaving his wife up.

"Shouldn't have had that last donut this morning," June said as she got up on her knees.

"Mayhap shouldn't have had donuts the past forty years." Ben grunted with effort as he hoisted her upwards.

Ramon ducked his head, swallowing an inappropriate laugh. Both girls snuggled closer to him, Alegria shivering and Marie seeming to surface and sink, wake and sleep. He wasn't sure how he was going to find his brother and sister-in-law, he was afraid for Marie, worried about Alegria. Yet all of that faded under profound relief. He'd found his girls before an aftershock took the house down all the way. What if he hadn't been on his way here? What if the old house hadn't held up so he could get inside? What if the place had caught on fire like some of the others? He tightened his grip on his nieces.

Thank god he wasn't a parent.

"Come on, son," Ben said. "Let's get your family loaded up."

"My car is just down the block," Ramon said. "A blue Camaro."

"Your car isn't going anywhere, honey," June said. "Just look at the streets."

Ramon twisted around to look fully at carnage he'd been oblivious to when focused on his nieces. Houses collapsed, utility poles down, wires across crumpled cars like odd fishing nets. But worse were the streets. The noise had been nothing but background for him moments before. But now he saw people staggering, bleeding, many simply sitting on curbs in profound shock. Horns honked and engines revved as those with working cars tried to get down the road. Where they thought they were going, he had no idea, but the neighborhood streets were clogged. One Suburban tried to simply push its way through two cars honking at each other, and only succeeded in jamming all three up against a fourth.

Ramon had no words to give voice to what he saw. It was a world gone insane. Three hours ago he'd been driving past Lake Tye Park, thinking about the level of his savings account. Taking his nieces out for burgers. It had been a normal rainy afternoon. And now, all was strange and terrifying. The shock of the destruction left a hollow chasm inside.

"We'll take my truck," Ben said. "She's old but she's built for rough going. Plus she's got a winch out front and reinforced bumpers. She'll get us to the hospital."

Ramon helped Alegria up and then managed to somehow stand with Marie in his arms. The truck was older than dirt, a rusty dark green Ford with a camper obviously homemade, its thick plywood siding painted barn red. And the reinforced bumpers were simply huge slabs of wood bolted on to the frame.

"Does she have a name?" Alegria, her voice rough from strain, pointed at the truck with one hand and clutched a wad of Ramon's shirt with the other.

"Old Crusher," June said.

The name fit, Ramon thought. It probably would get them through to the hospital better than his car. He scanned the street as they walked over to the truck. The area was so changed it was hard to pick out where he had parked.

And then he could only stare, no words left for the catastrophe.

"What's wrong?" June asked.

"He just saw his car," Alegria answered. "Not a chick magnet anymore, huh?"

"I liked you better when you were clingy and teary," Ramon said, turning away from the shiny bright yellow Hummer half on top of his Camaro, like an odd, car - mating ritual. "Should have left you inside and saved the car."

Alegria tugged on his shirt. "Tío Ramon. You're so full of shit."

No, he thought as he carried Marie to the truck. He was empty. His normal world was now insane. His nieces had no one but him in all this chaos.

And he had no idea what to do.

10

The Index museum blazed, fully engulfed, and the fire lit the surrounding area brightly. With the broken water main, the firefighter and two deputies hadn't been able to get enough pressure for hoses. And with the partial damage to the fire department bay, they hadn't been able to get the tanker out. Instead they'd run a hose to the nearby river and put in a pump. Between that and the rain the fire would soon be out, but the building was obviously a complete loss, all the history now gone forever.

Curtis stood on the far side of the street from the fire, helpless to do anything but watch. Throughout the town, other small fires burned, with shadows of people gathered around the points of light. It amazed Curtis how dark the world was when electricity ceased to exist and the only light came from flames. At least the rain had eased from drenching to something softer.

Leaving the remains of the museum, he walked down the street, searching faces of those he passed, pausing outside remains of houses, looking for some way that he might help.

Someone had put up a canopy behind the Town Hall and bodies were being placed underneath. Or at least all that they'd been able to find so far. Curtis knew the number would grow as the searches continued.

He wandered from fire to fire but there was still no Henry. Some people had left town before dark, walking along the back way that led to Reiter Road and eventually the city of Gold Bar. It was highly doubtful the narrow, twisting road was even passable. But it was the only way out on this side of the river, and people wanted to get away, like they still believed the quake had just devastated Index and not the whole area.

Curtis had thought briefly about going with them, but more people than just Henry were still missing. How did someone walk away from that?

Curtis passed into the deeper darkness beyond the clustered circles of firelight. Exhaustion made his eyes gritty and watery. Fatigue was as deep an ache as the one in his head, but he didn't know where to go to find rest.

The mountains were a solid mass surrounding him, invisible in the dark, but felt. The Hole, under those mountains, was probably gone, all his equipment with it. Even if the Hole itself hadn't caved in, it was doubtful the access road was still intact. All that work, all those experiments searching for the Fifth Force, gone. He remembered Henry harassing him all the time about parallel universes, and wished he could argue with the old man again. Sadness seeped through him and he wiped tears away.

He thought about how afraid he got at night, sprinting from the Hole to his car, knowing something scary was out there in the mountain night. Now here he was with a world gone insane, walking through the darkness by himself. If only his mother saw him now. He knew he wasn't fully alone, that there were people nearby, but the world, oddly, had become much less terrifying in the dark, when you couldn't see the truly horrifying devastation and death.

He passed the remains of the little community church on Index Avenue and rounded the corner. As he did, something like a small flash of light caught his eye. Behind him, across from the church, a narrow dirt driveway climbed up steeply to what used to be known as Schoolhouse Hill. Now it was a private residence up there, in a prime location with a view of the town and nothing but wild forest and high mountains behind it.

At the base of the driveway Curtis saw the movement again. Like the flash of a tiny red LED light.

Or maybe ambient light from fires making something glow red.

"Hello?" Curtis said. His heart thudded heavily in his chest.

The light moved, and then there were two. Something had just turned to face him.

"You okay?" Curtis stepped back, not sure he wanted an answer. So much for the dark not being scary anymore.

The low growl sounded loud against the softly pattering rain on pavement and the distant snapping and popping of the museum fire. Curtis stepped back again. Wild animals had to be just as scared as people were. Why else would they come so close to town?

"It's okay," he said, his voice shaky. "I'm not going to hurt you."

The shadows around the glowing eyes moved and Curtis realized the size of the animal. Maybe it was that bear someone had called the deputy about.

Curtis froze, his breath coming fast and shallow. *Bear. Oh, god. A bear.* "I know kung-fu. And karate. And Ju-jitsu. You know, in case you're thinking of eating me or something."

"Curtis? Is that you?"

Curtis jumped, his feet actually leaving the ground as he let out a high-pitched squeak.

"Sorry, didn't mean to scare you."

A headlamp beam kicked on, aimed at the ground, and in the reflected glow Curtis saw the older man still wearing his metal hardhat. The guy who'd wanted to contact emergency management.

Louis. That was his name.

"Are you okay?"

"Shine your light over there," Curtis said, voice shaking. "Right over there by the driveway. Some animal. Big animal. Really big."

The beam swept across the road and in the low light a dark shadow moved and took shape.

"A dog," Louis said.

"That's an awfully big dog." Curtis kept his voice low. "And why are its eyes red?"

"Just light reflection. I'm going back to the fires. If it's a stray who knows what it will do."

"I'll walk with you, if that's okay." Curtis had a shaky fear that the huge black dog, now fading back into the woods, was no stray. He didn't know what it was, but he was pretty sure it wasn't just some poor dog dumped in the woods.

"Come on." Louis sounded impatient.

"You'll keep the light on?" Curtis fell in step next to Louis, keeping close.

"Sure." Louis turned back toward Avenue A and the fire.

"I'm scared of the dark," Curtis said with no shame. "Always have been. Kind of a nameless fear of everything. A few minutes ago I was thinking maybe I wasn't anymore. But then that animal growled and now I think it's worse because it's no longer nameless. You know what I mean?"

"Everyone's going to be afraid for a long time," Louis said. "You're not alone."

"That's good. Not being alone." Curtis thought about the glowing red eyes. "Maybe *no one* should be out alone."

Louis said nothing as they walked down the street, the mountains around them quiet, ancient, and hiding their secrets.

"Did you get hold of anyone?" Curtis asked. "You know, out there? When you were trying the radios earlier? Maybe help is on the way."

Louis pulled off his hardhat, ran a hand through his short, curly gray hair, and put it back on. "You're the one working on the UW experiments, right? On gravity?"

"Yes."

Louis stepped over a crack in the road and stopped. "Do you have any radios or equipment in the Hole?"

"No," Curtis said. "We never got radios to work underground. Besides, I doubt the Hole exists anymore."

"I was hoping you might have a CB or ham radio in there. Because I think that's what we need to make contact with the outside world. Something old school."

"But the fire department has that new radio system. It cost taxpayers millions of dollars."

Louis smiled sadly. "Yes. That system. But the repeaters are down. The towers are up on the top of the Wall. If any survived."

"In other words, no contact with anyone."

Curtis felt his stomach bottom out as if he'd been punched. This quake, if it was the big one predicted for years, would have devastated the whole region, including Anacortes, on the coast, where his mother lived. There would be tsunamis. Was she still alive? Henry, and now his mother. He pressed his hands to his temples, and then dropped them, turning to Louis.

"Hey. I've just had an idea."

Louis looked unimpressed as he started toward the nearest fire. "That's nice. I see the mayor over there."

"No, really." Curtis caught his arm. "I think Henry is up the Wall somewhere. And I wanted to search for him anyway. Once it's daylight maybe we could get a group together and try to climb up to the top. We could look for Henry and also maybe figure out a way to get one of the repeaters working. I mean, you know, if there's anything left to work with. I know some about electronics."

"Maybe." Louis drew the word out as if hesitant. Or just being polite.

"Okay, I get it," Curtis said, his face flushing. "You think it's a stupid idea. But I'm going to look for Henry anyway. I'm going to find a way to call out. Get us help before there's an aftershock."

Louis said nothing as Curtis turned his back on the man and walked into the darkness between fires. Let them all gather in their little groups, backs to the mountains and the unknown. Let them all huddle around their fires like flame made them safe. He'd go out anyway, even if he had to go alone. One more time trying to find Henry. And maybe a solution to the repeater would be easy. Maybe it was just wires that had come unplugged or something. He could fix it. Maybe save the day.

But not until daylight.

11

Ben shut the front passenger door behind his wife, and put a hand on Ramon's arm as they stood together next to the truck. "Mayhap this might be impossible even for the Crusher."

Ramon glanced in the truck where his nieces waited on the cracked vinyl of the old truck's back bench seat. Even though they couldn't hear him with the windows up, he lowered his voice.

"The hospital, all emergency services are going to be overwhelmed."

"I agree," Ben said. "Roads are going to be clogged with terrified people with their own injured loved ones."

"You got a suggestion?" Ramon asked.

"You got a gun?"

"Maybe." Ramon hesitated, then lowered his voice further. "How's a gun going to help?"

"Think broader." Ben hooked his thumbs in the straps of his overalls. "This for sure isn't going to get fixed in an hour or so. You may not find your brother. You got yourself two little girls, injured. We got to feed ourselves, keep our girls safe. Laws are gone now, son."

Ramon felt an inordinate relief when he heard 'we' in the old man's words. "I got a gun in the car, if it's not destroyed. A Glock I picked up when I was working nights on the waterfront."

"Get it," Ben said. "And anything else in there you need. Then we got to find us a place to stock up. Mother and me, we got the Crusher pretty well able to be self-sufficient, traveling like we do, but we need more food, water, first aid stuff, anything we can think of. And we need it fast. Maybe faster than getting to the hospital. Your girls are stable for now."

"Vandals," Ramon said, his mind racing now that Ben had shown it the road.

"Yup. It's going to be a hell of a free-for-all. The police are going to be overwhelmed and it's going to be a while before the military gets here. This here earthquake is going to have devastated way more than we can imagine."

"Be right back," Ramon said, and placed the palm of his hand against the back window to reassure the girls.

He ran down the street toward his car, dodging people like him, trying to figure out what the hell had just happened, trying to find

something normal to ground themselves back in reality. He stumbled to a
stop when he reached the car. The yellow Hummer that had climbed up
the back of the Camaro tilted at a dangerous angle. Any aftershock
would topple it. He saw the driver, motionless behind the wheel, staring
straight ahead.

Ramon went to the driver's side of his car, staying well back in
case the Hummer slid. "Hey! You okay in there?"

There was no answer.

He couldn't see the driver from where he stood. Carefully, he
climbed up on the hood of his car, standing cautiously. His breath caught
on pain under his ribcage and he pressed a hand against his waist where
he'd hit the fire hydrant earlier. When the pain eased, he stepped
forward. Neither vehicle moved.

"Hey!"

Still no response. No movement either. The guy was either
unconscious or dead.

"You coming?" Ben shouted from his truck.

Ramon stared at the driver a moment longer, willing the guy to
move, then shook his head and chose his nieces. The guy was on his own
to make it or not. Ramon had no way to help him.

Back on the ground, he wormed his way inside the gaping hole
where the front windshield of his car had been and fought to free the
small black box from under the front seat. It was jammed in tightly, but
the side had broken out and he was able to work the handgun free.

Bullets. Add that to the list of things they'd need. By god, if
anyone went after his girls he wanted to be able to shoot.

He backed out of the window and jumped to the ground, moving
away from the two vehicles. Was there anything else in the car he
needed? His wallet was in his jeans pocket. The Camaro didn't have
anything, he realized. He drove it back and forth to work, he drove it on
dates, on errands, always on the assumption that he had ready access to
anything he needed. His life had been complacent.

He jogged back, thoughts ricocheting. Blankets. Flashlights.
Camping stuff. Would debit cards still work? He didn't have any cash.
How was he going to find his brother in all this chaos? How would his
brother find him? If he could get to the hospital, west of Monroe, then he
could get to Snohomish, another ten minutes west. At least on a normal
day. Maybe find his sister-in-law.

At the Crusher, Ramon went around to the driver's side. "You
got something to write on?"

June opened the glove box and pulled out a pad and pen that she
handed across Ben. Ramon took them and went back to the house.

"Girls with me," he wrote. "Trying for the hospital. Call the cell when service is back." He signed his name, tore off the sheet and impaled it on a nail near the entrance hole.

He turned to go but then paused. There had been a brief second of movement inside. He wasn't sure he'd actually seen something. He dropped down to one knee and leaned into the hole they'd made, staring into the shadows. Had one of them moved? Was someone in there? Ramon's stomach bottomed instantly. Had his brother or sister-in-law been home after all?

No. No, there was no way. Tómas and Therese were both at work.

Ben thought someone had gone inside the house.

Ramon straightened up as anger coursed through him. Vandalism already. He wanted to crawl inside and grab the son of a bitch and beat the crap out him.

Ben honked the horn and the sound startled Ramon. He turned back to the truck. Priorities. Right now, he had to think about the girls, not about how good it would feel to whack the bastard crawling around inside their home. But, as he reached the Crusher, he saw movement again out of the corner of his eye and had a sense of someone tall, gray, slipping inside the place next door. He shook his head as he got in the back seat next to Marie and checked seatbelts on both girls. People breaking and entering already. He was glad Ben had thought about protection.

June had provided Alegria with a pillow and it was in her lap to help support the weight of her taped up arm. Marie was sleeping again, her head against Alegria's shoulder. It had to have been painful but Alegria was silent, dark eyebrows drawn down. Ramon reached under Marie's shoulders and gently transferred her to his shoulder. She settled against him and snuggled close without waking.

"Gracias, Tío," Alegria whispered. She blinked furiously and Ramon realized she was trying not to cry. "Where's mama? I'm afraid." Her voice was a bare whisper.

Ramon understood that she did not want Ben or June to hear so he spoke softly. "I don't know, baby. But we're all afraid."

June obviously heard anyway. She twisted around from the front seat as Ben pumped the gas pedal and started the truck. "And there's nothing to be ashamed of. People are going to be afraid for a long time. But you know what helps me?"

"Having Ben to take care of you?" Alegria asked. "Like I have Tío Ramon?"

"Well, sure, that helps." June said, and patted Ben on the

shoulder. "But what also helps is when I can close my eyes and think about the worst case scenario, the most awful thing that could happen. And then I try to figure out what I would do."

"Really?" Alegria asked.

"Of course," June said, nodding her head as if agreeing with herself. "It makes me feel like I'm prepared. And being prepared is the best, isn't that right, Father?"

Ben inched the truck out onto the street. "Yep. But right now we need to make a decision here. Hospital's going to be overwhelmed. There's that clinic in Sultan but that's east."

Ramon looked at his nieces, at Alegria's face pinched with fear, at Marie, asleep. "I say get out to the highway and see which way looks more open."

Ben drove the truck up over a curb and through the small parking lot of a chiropractor whose business was now in need of serious adjustments. He bounced back down over another curb and out onto Kelsey where he paused. "This might take some doing."

Ramon looked at the street. Debris, people in shock and injured, cars piled against each other, trees down. "No shit."

"We need a spotter," Ben said.

June and Ramon both opened their doors and got out. June dug around in the back of the camper and handed him a rain poncho, then got in the back seat to support the girls. Ben moved the truck forward slowly and Ramon walked beside it, guiding, moving obstacles where he could, pulling cable from the winch when they needed more than muscle. Ben maneuvered up curbs, over chunks of pavement, and in some places, over formerly manicured lawns.

It took three hours just to get down Kelsey Street and on to the highway, which surprisingly wasn't much worse than rush hour. By then full dark had fallen but the rain had at least eased to something softer. Ben pulled the truck over and got out.

They stood shoulder to shoulder, silent. With power out there were no streetlights to illuminate the highway, but headlights from cars pierced the chaos in slanted beams. Light shown in all directions, including canted upward. People roamed the highway, climbing over and around piled cars. Sounds of breaking glass came from the few businesses still standing and voices shouted.

A man with congealing blood covering half his face staggered into the side of the truck, mumbled something and headed down the street before Ramon could offer to help him. A family, mom and dad, infant, three young children went past, the man saying something about the hospital. Ramon saw the family reach the man who had staggered by.

The father took hold of the man's arm, supporting him as they kept going.

As Ramon and Ben stood there, frozen in shock, a loud concussive boom rocked the truck, followed by a giant rolling ball of flame a few blocks away that went skyward so fast, and so high, that it seemed to ignite the very clouds. Ben grabbed the door handle but Ramon was thrown into the side of the truck and then hit the ground.

Alegria and Marie were screaming. Gritting his teeth, he pulled himself upright, feeling the scorching heat as he struggled to draw in a breath. It was like the air had been sucked into flame.

"The overpass just collapsed." Ben clung to the door handle with both hands like it was the only thing keeping him on his feet.

Ramon stared in horror. The concrete 522 highway overpass was gone. And in the rubble was the outline of some sort of tanker truck in the heart of the inferno.

"No way we're getting through that." Ben pulled open the driver's door. "Calm down girls. That fire's not going to reach us."

Ramon grimaced. And there was no way they were going to reach the hospital, or his sister-in-law, both on the other side of the overpass. "Guess we're headed east to the clinic then."

"We got a stop to make first." Ben started the truck. "Get in, son."

Ramon got in the front seat, leaving June in the back with the girls. Alegria reached forward with her good hand to grip his shoulder and he covered her cold fingers with his own. Ben pulled out onto the highway, simply pushing two small cars aside with his massive slab of wood bumper. He worked his way across the intersection.

Ramon didn't want the girls to see the human suffering surrounding them. He didn't want his nieces vulnerable to the people coming out in the dark. He wasn't sure the locked truck doors would be enough. About half way into the intersection he pulled his gun out and kept it in his hand, resting across his thigh.

The night was full of screams, shouting, distant pops and nearer explosions. The tanker fire was the main source of light. Smoke filled the air and the stench blended with smells of propane and gas. Ramon tried to breathe shallowly and crossed himself, something he hadn't done in years. They needed to get out of there before residential gas lines completely ruptured and blew everything to hell.

They passed people wandering as if lost and sitting right in the highway as if oblivious to the madness around them. They inched by a fistfight between six or seven young men and Ramon tensed, gripping his gun. But it wasn't until Ben pulled into the parking lot of Fred Meyers that a young man ran to the truck, grabbing the driver's door handle.

Ramon shoved the door open, making the boy stagger back. He followed, grabbed the boy, and then twisted to shove him against a wrecked car.

"Get the fuck away from us."

"Please," the young man said, holding up his hands. "Please help me."

In the weird flickering light of the night, Ramon saw the beginnings of a black eye, the dried blood across the front of the kid's shirt and in his short brown hair.

"Please," he repeated. "I have to get out of the city. I need to get home, to get to my brother."

"Where's home?" Ramon asked, adrenaline ratcheting down as recognized the panic in the boy's eyes.

"Index."

"Long ways from here," Ben said through the open window. "But we got room for another if you're willing to help us. Mayhap we can get you partway at least."

"Thanks. I mean…thanks." The kid backhanded tears from his eyes. "I'll do anything."

"Come on then," June called from the back seat. "You can sit up front with the men."

The kid ran around the canted door, climbed in, and scooted across the bench seat to make room for Ramon.

Ramon got in and slammed the door. "We going to save the whole city?" he asked Ben, over the kid's head.

"Nope," Ben said, stopping the truck. "Just the ones that ask."

Ramon glanced toward the department store. "What are we doing here?"

"Shopping," Ben said. "Then we're going to try and get to the clinic. If we're lucky we'll make it there by the time they open in the morning."

12

There were a few people going in and out of the Fred Meyers store, but nothing like the chaos on the highway behind them. Ramon realized, as Ben parked in a handicap spot right by the front doors, that the customers were predominantly young men carrying electronics. He snorted. Idiots. When did they think electricity was going to come back on?

Ben reached across the kid and dug around in the glove box. He produced a handicap placard and carefully hung it from the rear view mirror. It was an odd juxtaposition between how insane the world now was, and how normal his motion was. Ramon stared at the placard a moment, then shook his head and got out. The boy followed, and then Ramon pulled the seat forward and June began the laborious process of levering herself out of the back seat.

"No one's thinking long term yet," she said, wheezing.

"Works for us," Ben answered. "Gives us time to get what we need. We got to be fast though."

When they were out of the truck, except for Marie, who still slept, Ben faced them.

"What's your name, young man?"

"Artair Beaumont."

"Think you can keep this young lady here safe?" He gestured back to Marie.

Ramon opened his mouth but Ben held his hand up. "We need to get as much as we can, as fast as we can. Alegria, even with her injured arm, can get clothes for her and her sister." Ben pointed a finger at Alegria. "Warm clothes, not fancy."

Ramon shook his head. "No way. Sorry kid, but I don't know you."

"He's our only choice," Ben continued. "She can't go with us and she can't be alone."

"I can do this," Artair said.

"There's a billy-club under the front passenger side," June said. "Lead lined."

"There's no time for arguing, son." Ben gripped Ramon's arm. "If we're going to make it we need supplies. Now, before more people get here. And if it turns ugly in the store, you look to me like you can handle yourself. We need you in there with us."

Ramon's thoughts raced. And then he got in Artair's face. "You let anyone, *anyone*, get to my niece and you won't see your brother ever again. Got it?"

"Got it," Artair said, and to his credit the only expression on his face was grimness.

Ramon waited until Artair was in the truck and the doors locked before following Ben, June, and Alegria as they maneuvered through the obstacle course of the sidewalk.

At the doors, Ben corralled them again. "Each of you take a cart. Alegria, stay with June. She knows what to look for. Ignore the freezer section. Get canned goods, boxed goods. Camping gear. First aid stuff. Flashlights and batteries. Headlamps. Glow sticks. Anything non-perishable we can use. Fill your cart, get it to the truck and throw it in the camper, then come back for more."

"What about paying?" Ramon asked.

"Son, that's the least of our worries. I'll take care of it. Just get going."

And they were off, as if in some weird reality television show that featured racing consumers. Ramon quickly lost sight of the others. The aisles were a mess, shelves tilted, scattered with debris, and difficult to maneuver through. Fred Meyers obviously had an emergency backup system though, as harsh light flickered, creating weird shadows that moved around him. He encountered a few people, but most of them didn't seem to know how they even got there. Some realized what he was doing, though, and it seemed to wake them up. He saw a few going for carts and knew the trickle would soon be a flood.

The pharmacy was open but no one was manning the counter. Half of the ceiling had collapsed and rain splattered onto linoleum. Ramon vaulted the counter, almost landing on a woman. He twisted at the last moment, grabbing the counter to keep from stepping on her.

"Sorry…" His apology faded.

She was maybe in her forties, tall and slim, with cropped dark hair and wearing a pharmacist's coat. Shelving that held prescription bottles had collapsed across her. Both her legs canted at unnatural angles, broken in multiple places. Bone shards slit through skin and her slacks were soaked in blood that no longer flowed. She stared off into a distance she no longer saw. A pill bottle rested, empty, next to her open and slack hand, on the floor.

Ramon backed away. There was nothing he could do for her now.

He rubbed the bruised ache in his side and then grabbed a handful of plastic shopping bags and started filling them. Any medication that sounded even vaguely familiar, he took. Back out in the main part of the pharmacy, he threw the bags in his cart, then added vitamins, bottles of electrolyte water, bandages, and cold medicine. He barely registered what he was doing, simply going row by row and taking anything he'd ever needed in the past. He almost passed one aisle and then remembered his nieces. He doubled back and took boxes of tampons and pads. Multiple sizes. He had no idea what teenage girls used.

When the cart was full he simply jogged outside, past a young woman standing at a cash register. Ben was talking to her.

"You got to take this cash young lady, because we don't want to steal. But you also need to get out of here. Fill your car with supplies. Don't worry about this here job. It's going to be dangerous for you to be here much longer. Do you hear me?"

When Ramon came back, she was gone.

In the camping aisle he filled the cart with sterno cans, propane bottles, a camp stove, waterproof matches, a whistle, a compass, space blankets, sleeping pads, tarps, rope, dehydrated food.

And so it went. Fill the cart, run outside, throw everything in the camper, run back in. He lost track of how many times he passed Ben and June with full carts. How many times he pushed aside people standing with glazed expressions. How many times he pushed aside someone reaching to take what he picked up.

Alegria had one of the smaller carts and pushed it one-handed. It wove back and forth but her eyebrows were drawn down in deep determination. Ramon chose to smile at her instead of telling her to take it easy, knowing she wouldn't listen.

He couldn't remember what he'd already grabbed and what he still needed. He tried to be methodical, but the store was slowly filling up with people doing the same thing. And as more people came in, his level of panic grew. He didn't want to miss anything. He didn't want strangers to get something his girls might need. What if he forgot something vital?

It was a surreal nightmare of need and greed, of fear and something almost like a feeding frenzy. One of those dreams where you just keep running, and wake up exhausted. Protein bars. Granola. Bags of chocolate because Alegria loved Reeses Peanut Butter Cups. Peanut M&M's for Marie. Plastic wrapped bundles of kindling. A heavy winter coat for him. Boots. At one point, back at the truck, he asked Artair what size clothes and shoes he wore, and then grabbed what he could find.

Finally, Ben caught up with him in the sporting goods aisle where they were both started on fishing supplies, ammunition, and guns.

"Make this our last load, son," Ben said. "The camper's getting full and there's too many people in here now. Won't be long and it's going to turn ugly."

"June and Alegria?"

"Already told them. They headed out a few minutes ago."

Ramon nodded, taking a rifle and a shotgun and working them into the pile in the cart.

"We're as stocked as an army," he said, pulling knives out of the shattered display case. "What do we need with all these weapons?"

"What we don't need we can barter," Ben said. "If things get back to normal fast, then we can return it."

"But you don't think it will," Ramon said, pushing his cart toward the doors.

"No, I don't," Ben said. "I've been in quakes before, but never one like this. Even the bad one up in Alaska back in the '60s wasn't this bad. Mayhap the devastation reaches farther than we think. Months before things get back to normal."

The weight in Ramon's chest agreed with the prediction. This was not just a trembler that shook people up and reminded them they lived in a fault zone. This felt like all those apocalyptic movies come to life.

"I can't thank you enough," he said. "For helping me, taking us along."

Ben waved a hand in the air as they came out into the parking lot. "Gives me someone to help haul June around. Getting hard for me to lift her."

At the truck, Artair stood by the open door of the camper, shoving in the last of the things June and Alegria had brought out. If they had taken the time to carefully pack things they might have fit in more. But there was no way that could happen now, so things were tossed in, shoved in, wedged in.

The parking lot didn't seem any more chaotic then when they started their mad shopping spree. People came out carrying plastic bags, some wandering away on foot, a very few filling cars and trucks like they were doing. A very few.

"No one wants to admit it's this bad," Ramon said.

"No one ever wants to admit things are out of their control." Ben slammed the door of the camper and reached into a pocket. "No one ever does."

He pulled out a package and a pocketknife, cutting open plastic around a large padlock. He put it in place on the camper door, and then handed Ramon one key, keeping the other for himself.

"What next?" Artair asked.

"Now we go east," Ben said. "Get to the clinic. Get Alegria's arm looked at and make sure Marie is okay. And then keep going east. Out of the city, the crowds. Away from Monroe. All this flat farmland."

"What?" Ramon asked.

"Puget Sound," Artair said. "You think the earthquake will send a tsunami?"

"A bad one like this?" Ben asked. "Sure as shootin'."

Ramon shook his head. "Can't worry about that right now. Let's get out of here."

But at the door to the truck, all three of them just stood and stared.

June, Marie, and Alegria were eating ice cream. Small pints of Tom and Jerry's. With plastic spoons. June waved hers.

"I thought I said stay away from the freezer aisles," Ben said. "Nothing perishable."

"We did." Alegria balanced her pint on the pillow supporting her arm. "Until the last trip. And then I said I was hungry and June said it was all going to melt anyway so we might as well have a treat and I saw Moose Tracks and that's Marie's favorite and I thought it might make her feel better." She stopped talking to take a bite. "We got you some, too."

"How'd you know what flavors we like?" Artair asked, one eyebrow up in bemusement.

"Oh, we got a variety," Alegria said. "This is so cool. Mama never lets us eat this much ice cream."

"There's a reason for that," Ramon said as he climbed in the back seat next to the girls. He shook his head as his niece offered him a pint of dark chocolate with cherries.

"It's going to melt," Alegria said, waving it under his nose.

He gave in and pulled the top off, suddenly too exhausted to argue. June, grunting with effort, pushed herself across the front seat to sit next to Ben and Artair climbed in next to her, slamming the truck door. June handed Artair a pint of ice cream and the young man stared at it as if it was alien.

Ben turned around in the front seat, holding a spoonful of what looked like strawberry ice cream. He gestured at Marie with it. "How you feeling there?"

"I have a headache," she said.

"Sleepy? Nauseated? Dizzy?"

"No, nothing like that." Marie spoke carefully, as if thinking through each word, or as if guarding her thoughts. "But everyone is kind of glowing. Like they have halos. It's beautiful."

Ramon's stomach did a slow roll of anxiety. How bad was a head injury when you started seeing auras? He pushed her hair back from her face, clueless what to do.

"You tell us if you start feeling worse," Ben said. He looked around the parking lot and then met Ramon's eyes in the rear view mirror. "We need to move on out of here before this parking lot is jammed and we're stuck good. Buckle up and hang on."

Ramon saw the tension in Artair's shoulders. The kid had to be worried sick about his brother. Ramon didn't know what Artair would do once they reached Sultan. Index was further east. Ramon wanted to come back this way after getting medical treatment for the girls. Try to find his brother and sister-in-law. Yet Artair had helped with Marie. He deserved hope.

"I agree with Ben," Ramon said. "Get to the clinic. And get out of the cities. Maybe there will be fewer people, a little safer. Maybe find a place to camp, hang tight until things clear up. Until the National Guard or something gets things back in order. Maybe someone can get Artair out towards Index."

"There's our plan," Ben said, starting the truck. "Clinic, then out of the city."

A loud explosion shocked them all, rocked the truck. Ramon twisted to look out the side window and saw a ball of flame roll up from a car at the edge of the parking lot. A group of people, generic in the shadows, danced, fists to the air.

"Time to move," Ben said.

Ramon saw the glint of tears in Marie's lashes. He put a hand on Ben's shoulder. "Wait. I want the girls safer. Not by a window."

When they pulled out, Alegria was up front between June and Ben, and Marie was in back between Artair and Ramon. It wasn't much, but it made him feel like they were a little more secure.

The black night was turning charcoal with dawn as they inched out onto the street. Ramon tossed the barely touched ice cream out the window.

Maybe they were overreacting. Maybe by tomorrow night the police would have everything under control. He and Ben would sheepishly return all the stuff to the store and apologize. He'd go back to machining, to trying to forgive his brother. Back to the things that had seemed important hours earlier.

Ramon briefly closed his eyes that burned with fatigue. But then he heard the muffled sound of another explosion.

Maybe they were over reacting.

But maybe they weren't.

13

Ethan smelled something metallic. A scent so strong, so wrong, he could taste it on the back of his tongue, in his throat. A scent he was familiar with. But remembering why was too hard.

There were other smells in the darkness. Things that reminded him of terror, of a past that lived in nightmares. Urine. Sweat. Vomit.

In a different lifetime, he would be up and in action. But now the memories and the smells were just another weight on him. It was simpler to remain still, to slide once more into sleep.

He didn't have to close his eyes. He'd never opened them.

When he did open his eyes later, there was no change in the total darkness. No light to orient to. He vaguely remembered an awareness of smells, and those were still in the air around him. Along with higher, cleaner scents. He drew in a deep breath. Christmas.

Why would he think about Christmas? He waited a long moment before realizing it was the strong resin scent of tree sap.

And now there were sounds coming into his slowly reawakening brain. Soft shufflings, faint moans. Someone cried, the sobs muffled. And someone was having problems breathing. He heard the labored, wet panting several feet away.

What the hell was going on?

Ethan tried to move and pain was the bright light he needed to bring him into full awareness. His breath caught on it, and he stilled, evaluating. Something he was good at.

He thought he was lying down but the angle seemed wrong. One leg was twisted underneath him, but as he tentatively tried to straighten it, he could tell it wasn't broken. He felt deep bruises, wetness on his side, his cheek, his hand. But knew nothing was fatal.

He knew fatal. He'd seen fatal.

He shifted again and dislodged something that rattled against metal.

A school bus. That's where he was.

The environmental science class. The overnight fieldtrip to Silver Creek. They'd made it to the old town site in time for lunch. No one complained about the drizzly rain. Everything had gone well. Ethan shifted again, slower this time, allowing the pain to tell him where his injuries were, to aid him in regaining a sense of what had happened.

He remembered hanging around the next day, kids wandering

around, taking time to pack up their tents and gear, heading back down the trail in the afternoon. Rowan lingering, sketching Jumpoff Ridge above them.

He remembered the hike back out. Payton injuring her ankle. So she said anyway. It allowed her to lean on Zack, the rock climber, who had pulled out a cold pack and massaged her ankle. Jennifer, a bookworm always in Zack's shadow, had helped and been oblivious to Payton's manipulations.

Ethan flashed on lecturing Payton. Something about hiking boots instead of ballet slippers. Payton had been offended. Spike told Payton she was stupid. Payton cried. Ethan reprimanded Spike. Again.

So the hike back out took longer than it should have. It was late afternoon, almost early evening, by the time they came out at the trailhead to where the school bus waited. Val had been sleeping. She'd had her ugly pumpkin orange wool coat pulled up over her face and the kids laughed.

Ethan remembered being nervous about Val. About the road that switched back and forth and was rough in spots. He wasn't sure Val could manage it in the dark. He'd offered to drive. She'd been pissed.

Had she driven them off the road?

Sounds were coming back now. Screaming, tearing metal. Had they rolled?

Of course they had. That explained why he was all twisted up and stuck. Adrenaline kicked his body in gear.

The kids.

He shifted, pushed, shoved, pulled, until his arms were free. He raked a hand over his face, feeling the stickiness of clotting blood. Where was his pack? It had been at his feet, but had it stayed there? He maneuvered until he felt the rough material, and the relief was so strong it nauseated him.

Tugging on the pack frame, he inched it forward until he was able to reach the pocket where his headlamp was. As he stretched for the pack, sharp hot pain sliced into the calf of his leg as the muscles gripped in cramps. Ethan sucked in air, his jaw clenching. He managed to shift until he could reach his leg, massaging the charley horse until the pain ebbed to a dull throb.

When he could breathe again, he pulled a headlamp out of his pack. And with a click there was light. He slipped the headlamp on and fingered his scalp, finding a shallow cut that still oozed a little blood. He aimed the light over his body and saw a cut on his bicep that had bled down his arm and hand. The blood was dry though, and the cut shallow.

With the bright beam of the headlamp came a sense that he was back in control. Even though he saw only chaos, at least he could see. He coughed to clear his throat.

"Rowan O'Reilly." Ethan's heart thudded with a sudden fear that none of his kids would answer, that he'd lost them all, the lives he held in his hands.

No response. He spoke again, louder, forcing his voice into 'teacher' mode.

"Rowan O'Reilly."

"Here," came a faint response. Automatic, the habit of roll call kicking in.

"Zack Swenson."

"Here." His response was closer, clearer.

"Payton Lang."

"Here." Her voice shook distinctly.

"Michael Bangor."

"Bitchin'."

Ethan scowled, but now wasn't the time to take issue with Michael. The overweight young man tried too hard to be cool and only succeeded in irritating Ethan and alienating the other students. Ethan continued, going down the list from memory, calling out the kids he'd come to know. And some to even like. There were a few gaps. No answer from Jennifer or Amy. A few kids barely able to respond. His gut clenched. He had to get out of this bus, assess the injured, figure out how bad things were, figure out a plan.

That stupid bus driver. He knew he should have insisted on driving.

Ethan paused. Something that felt large edged into his memory. Trees falling. Earth shifting. Val hadn't been at fault. An earthquake. The terror at not being able to do anything, at not being in control as the whole mountain seemed to slide away.

He forcibly shut down the panic.

"Mr. Reynolds?"

"Yeah?" Ethan tried to identify the male voice as he shifted the beam of the headlamp around.

"Amy's dead."

The light found Spike, face pale.

"Make sure. See if you can find a pulse." Ethan forced calmness into his voice.

"There's a huge piece of metal sticking out of her chest," Spike said, swinging his flashlight around. "Don't think there's going to be a pulse." His voice broke on the last word, emotion taking over his attempt at sounding in control.

Someone broke into wild sobs. Someone else screamed. There was a frantic upheaval of suddenly panicked students and the bus rocked.

"Freeze!" Ethan shouted.

The struggle to get out of the bus slowed but the light from Ethan's headlamp illuminated faces white with shock, wet with tears, streaked with blood.

"Listen carefully. I need all of you to calm down so we can get out of here. Find your gear. Find your headlamps or flashlights. Let's get some light going so we can see where we're at."

Rowan spoke up from somewhere near the back of the bus. "But Amy-"

"There's nothing we can do for Amy," Ethan said, struggling to shut down emotion. "Right now we focus on the injured. Check the person next to you. See if you sense an opening or way out. I know you're all scared, but focus on the immediate. Focus, evaluate, act."

"Yeah, yeah, we know," Spike said. "You've drummed that into our heads."

Ethan met Spike's eyes in the yellow light and nodded his head slightly. He'd heard the tremor in the guy's voice. Spike might be an asshole most of the time, but right now he was taking the right note, attempting to sound normal, to control his fear. Ethan had to honor that even if it surprised him.

The bus was on its side and cocked at an angle. As kids started moving around, Ethan felt it shift slightly again. He turned his light upward at the emergency exit. It was going to be damn hard to get up there and open it, let alone get people out. But then he heard the sound of boots on broken glass.

"Front windshield is gone," Zack said. "I think we can get out that way."

Ethan shifted in that direction, even as he saw Zack's headlamp exposing the jagged edges of the window.

"Val's gone, too," Zack continued, and even in the low light, fear filled his hazel eyes. "Maybe we should stay in here until daylight."

"We can't evaluate the injured here," Ethan said. "And we need more secure shelter. We don't know how the bus is situated and we don't know if there will be aftershocks."

He worked his way forward as more beams of light came on, illuminating the remains of the bus. Kids started talking, some crying, someone gagging.

"I still don't have cell service," Payton said, with distinct rising panic in her voice. "I can't even call 911!"

Ethan spoke over his shoulder. "Payton, don't worry about the phone. Find Jennifer. She didn't answer role call."

Payton's eyes were wide as she looked back at him. There was blood at her temple, and her dark hair was matted with it on one side. "I don't have a flashlight."

"Why are we not surprised?" Spike said.

Ethan pulled himself up and over the twisted remains of a seat. "Use the light from your cell."

At the edge of the window, Ethan put a hand on Spike's arm. The young man had been about to climb through. Ethan understood the overwhelming desire to get out, but he shook his head as Spike's pale blue eyes locked on him.

"Evaluate, Spike. Evaluate." Ethan aimed the headlamp outside. "Won't do you any good to step off a cliff right now."

Their lights exposed the immediate surroundings. A forest turned into a slash pile. Trees down, crisscrossing each other like a giant's game of pickup sticks. Boulders caught in huge root balls, tossed as if pebbles. The earth torn, ravaged. Mist thickening into rain. But they weren't on a cliff. The road had slid away and taken the bus with it. They were about a hundred feet down from where the road had been. And luckily for them, the landslide had piled up against leaning trees, slowing the downhill movement of the bus.

"Aftershocks?" Zack asked from behind them.

"Most definitely," Ethan answered. He wasn't paying close attention though. His light reflected off something.

"I still say we'd be safer staying here in the bus until help arrives," Zack continued. "Aftershocks will bring down more trees and there's no place out there to get away from them."

"I wouldn't count on help," Ethan said. "We don't know how bad the quake was. Or how long it's going to take people to remember a school bus that went out on a field trip. And the bus isn't stable. Like I said, we can't assess injuries or even find space to get kids comfortable for the night in here."

"Our parents will remember," Zack said, almost defiantly. "They'll know where we went. They'll be looking for us."

"I'm sure they will." Ethan hoped he sounded reassuring but his attention was caught by something in the trees a few yards away. A reflection from his light. Like eyes. Not moving though. He reached for his pack. "But if this quake wasn't localized here, and was this bad down below, it's going to take a while for help to get here, if they even can."

"What are you talking about?" Zack asked.

"Think of the bridges between here and Monroe, just to start with." Ethan opened a zipper. "Whitewater river you can't just wade across. Then there's Highway 2. Two-lane route that's going to be clogged with panicked drivers and wrecked cars. It might take days for anyone to get out here. You want to sit in this bus until then?"

Zack was silent a moment, his face white and eyes wide with shock. "But...our parents..."

Ethan put a hand on his shoulder. "One step at a time, Zack. Focus on what's in front of us, what we need right now." He moved to the shattered window.

"What are you doing?" Zack's voice was shaky.

"I see something," Ethan said, working his way out of the window opening. "Might be Val."

"Should I go with you?"

Zack sounded like he hoped the answer was no, but Ethan realized he needed a job that made him feel in control before he slipped further into shock.

"No. I need you and Spike to help everyone out of the bus and calm them down. Find a place to gather. Alongside the bus if it seems stable enough. Set up a camp for the night. See who has space blankets and first aid equipment."

"Got it," Zack said, and now relief crept into his voice.

There was something about giving a traumatized person a task to concentrate on, to feel responsible for, that was vital in emergencies. Ethan had learned that a long time ago. He just never thought he'd need to worry about it again, and especially not with his students.

He stumbled on the rough ground and grimaced as his bruised body complained. He leaned his pack against the side of the bus and slipped his hand into the small pocket on the side. The cold feel of metal was reassuring and his hand slipped along the too-familiar shape of the gun butt. Pulling the Walther out, he held it tight against his thigh, barrel down, finger automatically slipping to the edge of the trigger guard even as his thumb flipped the safety.

There was something about those eyes. The light from his headlamp made them almost glint red.

Could be blood, Ethan thought as he inched over the rough ground. If Val had been ejected out that front window she'd be pretty smashed up. Matter of fact, the way those eyes didn't move, she was probably dead.

He didn't want the kids seeing that.

But when he got to the spot where he'd seen the reflection there was nothing there. He moved the light around. If Val had been ejected she wouldn't have been thrown too far. Maybe she was in shock. Had wandered off.

"Val!" he called out, and then held his breath, listening for the faintest of sounds. Heard nothing but the rain.

The kids were his priority right now. He had to get them set up and warm before they started going even deeper into shock. He had to assess injuries and figure out a way to get them all down the mountain in the morning.

He walked a short perimeter though, stumbling over the rough ground as he shown the light in a wide circle. No sign of the bus driver. Not even blood. No sign of whatever it was that had seemed like eyes glowing in the dark.

Back at the bus, Spike and Zack had managed to get most of the kids out. Rowan tied the corner of a tarp around the bus axle by the light of her headlamp as Payton held a corner of the tarp. When Ethan got closer, Spike came through the gap where the windshield had been.

"Found Jennifer," he said. "She was out cold but seems okay. We can't move her though. She's wedged under one of the seats."

"Alright," Ethan said, putting a hand on Spike's shoulder. "You and Zack get started on freeing her. I'm going to do a quick triage on injuries then come help. You're doing great."

He opened the main pocket in his pack and pulled out heavy work gloves, slipping the gun back inside at the same time.

"Man, is there anything you don't have?"

Ethan thought for a second that Spike had seen the gun, but the seventeen year old nudged the gloves. "I think we'll find out in the next few days," he said. And then instantly regretted his honesty. "We'll be okay though."

Spike stopped. "Look man, we're not a bunch of idiots. Don't lie to us. That'll be worse."

"You're right," Ethan said. "Sorry."

"It's cool," Spike said.

But before Ethan could warm to the kid, or start thinking maybe he'd misjudged him in school, Spike continued.

"Don't treat us like kids and we'll try not to treat you like an asshole teacher."

Ethan shouldered past him, resisting the urge to explain, explicitly, just what kind of asshole he could be. He also swallowed down the impulse to shove the kid up against something and get in his face. He recognized reaction settling in, and knew the signs. Some people collapsed in the face of fear. He responded the opposite, as if punching something straightened out the bigger picture. The past two years he'd channeled that into pushing himself physically, to abate tension, ease rage. His parents would have been disappointed in his methods.

At the uphill side of the bus, he reached for the cord Rowan was trying to grab and tugged it down to her.

"I thought the slide might be too steep to set up tents," she said. "Or should we try to get up to the top?"

"For right now, let's use the bus and the tarps. The ground looks pretty stable and most of the trees around us are down. If an aftershock hits, we're in an open space. If the bus slides it will take the tarps but not us. Plus I don't want to try to get injured kids up that slope in the dark." Ethan tested the rope. "Tie it so the tarp makes something like a lean-to," he told her. "Something we can get behind. Use rocks for weights. Then get some kids to help you collect branches. Stack them over the tarp, along the sides, and layer them on the ground underneath. Cedar will work best."

"I can help Rowan." Nathaniel Salvatore, an angular, bony seventeen year-old who was proudly and openly gay, came forward. "What are the branches for?"

"Insulation and padding," Rowan said.

"People in shock need warmth. So work as fast as you can." Ethan raised his voice so everyone could hear him. "I want all of you to get a granola bar or protein bar out of your packs and eat it. Something with sugar. Trail mix if you have it. Drink some water. Share with those who didn't listen in class. Don't eat more than one though. We're going to have to hike out in the morning and once we hit the highway we don't know what shape we're going to find things in. So as of now we're on rations. Got it?"

The kids looked back at him, pale and scared, in the wavering light of flashlight and headlamp beams filtered by the light rain.

"Take responsibility for each other. Once the shelter is ready get inside and wrap up warm. Use your space blankets, any cold weather gear you packed. Take inventory of injuries and then report to me. Use the buddy system. A couple of you come help me. And shut off any headlamps you don't need. Conserve batteries."

"Can we start a fire?" Lucy Hsu was a tiny Asian girl of fifteen, the youngest in the class. She'd been bumped ahead in grades and was overwhelmingly shy.

"Good idea," Ethan answered. "Just not under the tarp."

"What are you going to do about Amy?" Michael asked. "Leave her in there to rot? You're responsible for her death, forcing us all out here."

Ethan pushed up against the kid who glanced side to side as if looking for an escape route. But there was obviously nowhere to run except dark woods.

"You go ahead with the asshole theme." Ethan let the icy control he'd once been known for frost over his words. "And we'll see where it gets you. We need to be safe and warm and treat those who are alive. We don't have time for your shit."

There was fear in the young man's eyes, but he tried to swagger, running a hand over the dark stubble on his head. And then he scowled and pushed away from Ethan. "Back off and don't touch me."

Ethan let him leave but knew he was going to have to deal with Michael soon. The kid's insecurity and belligerence was a bad combination, especially now, and he couldn't let that endanger everyone. "Someone come help me with Jennifer."

Nathaniel and Paul Larsen, an acne-scarred seventeen year old, joined him and they went back into the bus where Zack and Spike worked on the mangled seat pinning Jennifer. Ethan let the headlamp play over the blond-haired girl. He saw tracks of tears in the dirt on her face, saw the fear in her eyes. A small amount of blood was on the seat behind her but it was drying, not fresh.

"Whacked your head pretty good, huh?" he said, squatting down and ignoring the pain in his leg.

"Am I going to burn?" she asked, tears starting a fresh journey down her cheeks.

"Burn?" Ethan asked, confused. "Where'd that come from?"

"You know, when they have the wrecked vehicles," she said. "There's always someone who gets trapped and the others can't get them free before the leaking gas explodes."

Ethan laughed. He didn't mean to, but the sound escaped anyway. Thankfully it seemed to lessen her anxiety. "You're not going to burn. Take a deep breath. Do you smell any gas?"

Jennifer breathed in. "No."

"Besides, idiot," Spike said. "The bus is diesel. It's not as flammable as gasoline. Takes longer to ignite."

Ethan started to castigate Spike for calling the girl an idiot, but then realized what was going on when he saw Jennifer manage a trembling smile. Spike was talking like he always did to the others in class. Slightly condescending, slightly aggressive. Now Ethan saw that the normal tone was doing more than any of his reassurances.

"Okay, let's get you out of here," he said. And then couldn't help it. "Before the bus explodes."

They all laughed, more than the lame joke warranted. But their tension eased and the tears dried up in Jennifer's green eyes.

With the muscles of teenage boys to help, Ethan was able to peel back the wreckage. It took a good twenty sweaty minutes to free Jennifer.

Once she was loose though, a quick assessment showed that her worst injury was the small cut and bump on the side of her head. Ethan told Zack to take her on as his buddy. He explained what symptoms to look for in case her head injury was worse than it appeared to be.

And was thankful when Zack simply met his eyes, agreed, and didn't ask what they'd do if the injury was bad.

Since the reality was there was nothing they could do.

14

Anya sank onto a large downed tree, breathing heavily. The rain-saturated moss leached dampness into her jeans, but it made little difference to her soaked clothes. Bird sat next to her, close enough she felt the fine trembling in his body. She placed a hand lightly on his head, grateful for his warmth.

She had to get to her cabin soon. Get dry. Get a fire going. Take stock of what she had left. If there was a cabin left. But she had to stop to catch her breath and ease the burning in her side from running. She was wasting energy and it wasn't like she could escape the ruined world around her. She propped the Henry rifle against the log, within reach, then dropped the backpack and groaned in relief. She rolled her head and rotated her shoulders, trying to ease the ache of sore muscles, of her bruised body.

The woods were silent, in a way that spoke of trauma. No birds sang. No wind whispered through ferns, salal, tree branches. Just her breathing, the sound of life. She swiped chilly sweat off her forehead and then wiped her shaking hand down the front of her plaid shirt. Not that it did any good. The shirt was too damp.

There were so many trees down. So many old friends who would never again provide her with shelter, back rests, shade in the summer. Fir, cedar, alder, yew. There was too much light in the woods. Before today the forest would have been shadowed, dark shades of greens only occasionally lit by stray light that fell through branches. This temperate rainforest was heavy with thick underbrush, moss that grew like carpets and hung like curtains, and trees that held hands, leaned together, supported each other in an intricately entwined knot-work of bark, needles, leaves, and lichen.

But now the woods had been weakened as if some giant's hand had shaken them. When one tree had gone, it had taken its friends, like a person who trips, grabs someone to regain balance, and ends up taking them down, too. So many trees had lost the battle that there were huge holes to the sky. Anya felt exposed, raw, and vulnerable under the unfamiliar openness.

The rain thickened, fell heavier, felt like it might hang around. She badly needed shelter, especially since it was already late afternoon. She stood, rubbed the small of her back, and then reached up to re-braid her wet hair. She shouldered on the backpack, picked up the rifle, and scrambled over the downed tree. Bird immediately followed, glued to her side and for once not roaming the woods in wide circles.

Her goal was the rough-built cabin she hoped still stood. She needed the security of something familiar when more trees came down.

Because there would be aftershocks.

Anya bent to duck-walk under an alder propped against a fir and too high to climb over. The backpack caught on a branch and she tugged on it. The suddenness of its release caused her to lose her balance and she tumbled forward onto her hands and knees. The jolt sent hot pain up through her joints, but after kneeling there for a moment, the pain subsided and nothing seemed broken.

She reached out to the rough bark of the tree for balance to stand and heard an odd cough and a low growl from Bird. With stomach sinking, she turned very slowly.

A bear. Please, a black bear. They did not want to be around her any more than she wanted to spend time with them.

Grizzlies, though, were a different matter. Rare and elusive, no one really believed they had started migrating back into the high alpine areas.

And yet, there he was.

Her breath flinched away. Her mind raced and her heart screamed for flight.

The grizzly had seen her, and the massive brown head lowered, exposing the huge distinctive hump on the back. Its head slowly moved from side to side, as if there was nothing more important than looking for grubs. That swinging, swaying head meant the bear was nosing scents, determining what she was, deciding how hungry it was. She grabbed Bird's thick ruff of fur, hanging on tight. Her heart froze in terror for herself and her dog. He would try to defend her and end up dying.

With her back to the alder and the distorted, earthquake landscape around her, there was no way Anya could run. She slowly, slowly, slid her hand toward the rifle. She wouldn't be able to kill or even seriously wound the bear with it. But maybe the loud noise would make it reconsider eating her.

There was nothing else to do.

She brought the rifle up and sighted down the barrel, her hands shaking too hard to aim.

The grizzly reared up to stomp down on the ground, slamming its colossal weight in a display of strength. Paws larger than dinner plates caved in the soft loamy earth.

It had decided.

Tears filled her eyes.

Not like this.

Her breath came short and shallow.

She couldn't die here, away from the young yew tree. Life that was.

Movement flashed to her left. Bird whimpered. Anya risked glancing away from the bear. Walking through the dense forest underbrush was a boy, maybe eight or nine years old. Long brown hair, brown clothes that made him blend with the trees. He caught her eye and smiled, and the smile was so joyous that Anya's heart broke.

The boy walked toward the bear, trailing dirt-engrained fingers gently through fronds of fern.

"No. God, no." Anya's voice broke on a sob. She jerkily raised the rifle. "Wait! Stop!"

The boy glanced over his shoulder and smiled again. And then walked past the bear and kept going.

The bear rose up and slammed his massive front paws into the ground again. Then it turned and followed the boy. After a few yards the boy looked back and beckoned to her, as if he expected her to follow. Then he continued moving through the forest until both he and the bear were lost to sight in the shadows.

Relief caught her breath but then without warning grief burned through her. Hot tears coursed over her cold cheeks. She sank to her knees, overcome with loss that broadsided her. This boy, too young, alone, with so much love in his smile, brought everything back in an overwhelming wave.

She pressed her hands to her mouth to hold in juddering breath that broke on choking sobs, her whole body shaking. Bird nudged her elbow, whining.

For several long moments she crouched there in the rain and the devastated mountains breathing deep and struggling to regain control. When the soul-deep pain eased somewhat, she pushed herself to her feet, memories flooding her. There was no sign of the giant grizzly or the small boy.

Two months had passed and she thought she was healing. That tiny baby, born too soon in a cabin too isolated, with a father too inexperienced to help.

Anya had held her son so close, cupped the cooling face with her palms trying to warm him, to will life back. She'd failed.

Hours later, alone, she'd wrapped the tiny, tiny body in the soft blankets she'd made for his life and, still alone, buried him under the yew tree. The grandfathers of the forest, the trees that lived for hundreds of years. Her son would be sheltered forever.

Devon had done nothing but sit by the fire and weep.

But she hadn't cried. Not then, and not until now.

Anya brushed tears away with her palms and saw blood across her lifelines. She stared, then touched fingertips to her face. It was only then that she felt pain and found the cut above her right eye. She probed the swelling and the warm stickiness of congealing blood. She had no memory of being struck during the quake.

Bird whimpered again and nudged his nose under her hand.

She slowly shouldered her backpack and then her rifle. She touched the wound on her forehead again, then ran her hand repeatedly over Bird's head and back feeling his soaked fur.

"Shock and a head injury," she whispered to her dog. "I'm hallucinating."

Bird barked once, sharply.

"Shock," she repeated. "Okay. Okay Bird. I hear you. You're right."

The backpack slid off again. With shaking hands and blue fingers, she fumbled open zippers. She stripped, tugging and fighting to get out of the rain soaked clothes. Her teeth chattered as she pulled on wool pants, a heavy flannel shirt, a wool hat, and topped that with rain gear. Her battered and bruised and aching body responded with deep shudders as it tried to warm itself. She opened another small pocket on the pack.

Two high protein survival bars. She used her teeth to open them, giving one to Bird and forcing herself to take a bite of the other. It tasted like cardboard but would do its job.

After a few moments her hands steadied enough to shove wet clothes into the pack and haul it back on.

The bear and the boy, her hallucinations borne of grief and trauma, were long gone. But they'd disappeared in the direction of home and so she followed them with Bird close beside her.

She'd felt tremblers before. After all, this area was full of faults, of mountains that were constantly shifting. But this quake had to have broken records. The outside world was probably devastated.

She wondered briefly if Devon was safe, and struggled to care, still drowning in the raw loss that had blindsided her. She'd held so tightly to her emotions over the past weeks, so afraid that if she let go she'd never come back from the deep heartbreak. Devon leaving her was the first crack in that anguish. The terror of the earthquake took care of the rest.

And there'd been something in that little boy's eyes. Something like love.

"I'm okay now," she told Bird, swiping at fresh tears. He merely twitched an ear toward her. "We're okay, buddy. I hallucinated and saw what I wanted to see. That's all."

It took longer than normal to navigate the changed landscape, the shifted earth, the boulders, the trees. But as darkness seeped down to fill ravines, she drew close to home. One small stream to cross, one more stair step of ridge to climb and then she'd find her home, butted up against a granite that she hoped had protected the place. She pictured the heavy quilts she had made, focused on how wonderful it would be to crawl underneath and find the illusion of safety.

A salmonberry branch swiped across her cheek, tiny stickers stinging. She stumbled over mounds of damp ferns, broke through the dense understory brush and exhaled as if she'd held her breath for hours. She'd made it back.

It was pretentious to call the structure she lived in a cabin. Far from rustic or quaint, it was simply weather tight. It was nothing more than a small, rather ugly box of rough-cut logs with a slab of wood for a door and one small window in each wall. The roof was steeply pitched to shed snow, and inside, that pitch created a loft for storage. There were two small, rough-built structures on either side of the cabin. One was the outhouse, half hidden in the trees. The other was her chicken coop.

With Devon it had been a home. Now it was hers alone. Maybe no longer a home, but a place she couldn't, wouldn't, leave. Just her and Bird, managing survival one day at a time.

Anya crossed the rough, tiny, clearing, and even though she still shivered, even though she was desperate to be inside, enclosed, secure, she paused by the young yew tree.

"It was only an earthquake," she whispered to the life that should have been, reassuring the son she'd held so briefly.

She touched the tree and then, as she pulled her fingers away, saw the blood.

Anya looked at her hands. But there were no cuts, nothing she'd missed. The rain had washed her fingers clean. Except for the fingertips. She stared at the tree, seeing where branches had been broken off during the quake. Thick, deeply red liquid slowly seeped down the fissures in the bark. She touched it again then rubbed her fingers together.

A yew tree's inner bark was red. Maybe its sap was, too. Maybe the sap looked like blood.

Or maybe she was hallucinating again.

Bird barked and Anya jumped at the sound. She turned to see he hadn't waited while she stared at the tree, having visions. The dog, smarter than her, was at the cabin door.

Anya rubbed her fingers down the front of her raincoat and struggled to focus on the cabin, the immediate need for shelter.

There were tree branches on the roof and one large fir had splintered a corner of the roof over the rough deck. The fir itself rested on the ground next to the cabin. The death throes as it came down had scattered debris liberally. But the tree missed the building itself and for that Anya was grateful. The door of the chicken coop hung askew and her motley flock clustered in the opening, obviously too rattled to come out. Luckily Bird was too rattled to chase them. The outhouse tilted slightly, but nothing she couldn't fix.

Bird barked again, and pawed the door. She took his hint and left the rain and yew tree.

Inside, she went straight to the wood stove, pulling it open with one hand while she grabbed kindling with the other. Bird made a beeline for his bed next to the stove. He curled up, nose tucked under his tail, eyes tracking her every movement. Anya saw the fine trembling in her dog and knew he needed the heat of a strong fire as much as she did.

The scratch of a match on the stove sounded overly loud, even with the rain pelting down on the roof. She touched match to dry moss and watched the infant flame catch and spread.

When the wood started to snap she jerked off her hiking boots and rain gear, then grabbed a quilt from the dilapidated couch. She gave in to the simmering fear, the deep exhaustion. She dropped down beside Bird, wrapped her arms around him, and pulled the quilt over both of them.

If there were aftershocks she wasn't any safer inside than out. But for the moment, the warmth of the wood stove and the close presence of her only companion gave her the illusion of safety and security. It might not last, but for now it was enough.

15

Ethan sat on the ground, wrapped in a rain poncho and propped against a log as he tended the fire. Under the lean-to, kids slept. He heard them shifting occasionally. The small sounds of a bad dream or someone hurting. He dozed off periodically, waking when the warmth of the fire on his face lessened. Or when some forest sound came to him. Some time during the night the rain had slackened and that allowed him to hear more.

Though the woods were quieter than they should be. No owls hunted, no coyotes sang. He had the impression that the wilderness was hunkered down in fear, just like his group was. He thought at one point a bear passed close by. He'd heard the distinctive cough they made when they wanted to warn you they were near. He'd kept his gun close and it had taken several minutes for his heart rate to slow.

It had to be well past midnight. The blackness was a solid wall around him, with only the tiny hole of light from the fire in front of him. But more than the darkness, the night had that heavy feeling, that sense of muted time that came in the small hours when even the earth seemed dormant.

And that's when the sound came.

Ethan held his breath, listening.

A wet panting.

He'd heard that before, in the bus, right after he came around. He'd thought then that one of the kids was having problems breathing. But he realized now that none of them had.

A wild animal then. Maybe a bear again. But the sounds were different. He had the gun on his lap and now he slid his finger over the safety, grateful for the familiarity.

He heard no snapping of branches or other sounds that would indicate something creeping closer. But the panting did seem nearer. He scanned the perimeter of firelight, trying to see into the darkness beyond. He pulled his legs up, shifting weight so he could rise fast.

No headlamp yet, he thought. He wasn't sure it would penetrate much farther than the firelight anyway.

And then he saw the same reflection of light on eyes that he'd seen from the bus. This time the firelight flickered in them.

Ethan stood slowly. There was no way he was going to be caught sitting on his butt. He realized the eyes were on a higher level than his. A

90

bear, reared up on its back legs? That wet slurping of air just didn't sound like it. What kind of wild animal was over six feet tall?

Bigfoot? He snorted. As if that old hairy legend actually existed. Besides, according to stories they were supposed to stink.

He sniffed.

No stink.

The eyes moved, dipping as if the animal lowered its head momentarily, and then shifted to the left. Ethan went right, keeping the fire between him and the animal. It shifted again and he did the same. There was a sense suddenly of being tested. Or pushed. Adrenaline flooded his system. His heart raced. His muscles twanged with the need for fight or flight.

The animal shifted. He shifted.

With adrenaline came training. Focus, evaluate, act.

And that brought clarity as he suddenly realized what was going on. With each slight movement, he was being manipulated. Moved just a little farther past the tarp where the kids were sleeping.

"I don't fucking think so," he whispered and stepped back the way he'd come, putting the lean-to, his kids, squarely behind him.

He heard rustling back there, as if someone might be waking up. But he didn't have time to spare for that. He was watching the eyes. As he moved back into position, they dipped again and Ethan had the distinct sense that evaluation was going on over there, too.

"What the hell is that?" came a whispered voice behind him.

"Some wild animal," Ethan responded, keeping his voice low and calm. He risked a quick glance over his shoulder and saw Zack. "Stay back there."

"Got it."

The animal tried moving to the side again, but Ethan wasn't falling for that game a second time. He stood his ground, holding a hand up to keep Zack from getting suckered in to the weird wilderness dance.

"Put some wood on the fire," Ethan said, keeping his voice low. "Let's get a better look at what the hell that is. I'll cover you but I don't think it's going to come closer to the fire."

Zack's eyes widened when he saw the gun, but he didn't say anything. He simply grabbed up branches the kids had gathered earlier and poked them into the fire. Sparks shot up into the night as cedar caught and sizzled.

As the fire grew and the circle of light expanded, the animal seemed to step back, keeping to that twilight perimeter.

Ethan had had enough. "If something happens to me, use the fire to defend yourself."

"What?"

Ethan didn't answer. Instead he strode around the edge of light, reaching up to flick on his headlamp.

The animal was gone. That fast. No sound of crashing through the trees. Just gone. Ethan scanned the area, but was reluctant to go too far from the kids in case it came back, or circled around behind them. He looked at the ground but with the soft mat of forest floor no clear tracks were discernable. He saw indentations though, as if what had stood there was heavy. And for some reason the shape of the indentations made him think of human feet. But those sounds hadn't seemed human.

And there was something else there, at the edge of one of the divots. Ethan bent and scooped it up, letting the scrap lie in the palm of his hand. Pumpkin orange fabric that could only be from the bus driver's coat. Had it been Val standing there? If so, why hadn't she shown herself or called out? If that had been her breathing she was injured. But if it wasn't her, what was it? Ethan closed his fingers over the orange scrap and shoved it into his pocket. He returned to the fire.

"See anything?" Zack's voice was shaky.

"Dog tracks. Too big for a coyote." He kept his voice calm and matter of fact.

"Then what?"

"Remember that report from the Department of Fish and Wildlife? That they thought wolves might be migrating back into the area?"

"Oh, yeah. We had that big debate on whether that was a good thing or not. How farmers were going to be pissed."

"Right," Ethan said. "That's probably what it was." Thankfully Zack wasn't thinking too clearly or he would have realized wolves were big, but not that big.

Zack relaxed. "That's kind of cool in a way. I mean, being that close to a real wolf. Wild. In its habitat."

Ethan just looked at him.

"I know," Zack said, and managed a shaky grin. "I'm just trying to, you know, make you think I'm not terrified."

"I don't know why. I am."

"Guess we're going to keep that fire built up the rest of the night then, huh?"

Ethan sat back down on the log he'd been leaning against and added a piece of wood to the fire. "You guessed right."

His affected nonchalance seemed to work as Zack relaxed a little more. The young man also added wood, and then sat near the fire, using a long stick to poke the flames. Ethan noticed Zack periodically glancing around and understood. His back felt too exposed, with nothing but the black night behind him. Nothing but mountains and wilderness and whatever walked among the trees.

It was going to be a hell of a long night.

16

Some time before dawn, when the mountains felt dense and ancient and the night at its darkest, the low growling of Bird roused Anya. They were both in bed and she had even allowed the dog under the blankets. She pushed the heavy quilts away from her face, feeling cold air seep in. The fire must have gone out because there was no glow and no warmth. She listened intently, wondering what Bird had heard.

He growled again but didn't charge the door like he normally did when wild animals came too close. Instead he pushed up against her and she once again felt him trembling. She rose up on her elbows, peering into the heavy blackness of a night with no ambient lights from electronics or streetlights. Nothing here gave out light once the sun went down.

After a few moments of quiet, she collapsed back onto the pillow, resting a hand reassuringly on her dog. And that was when she heard odd slobbery sounds outside.

Was it the bear? The boy? Injured? No. They were hallucinations born of shock and loss. Weren't they?

Anya threw back the covers and out of long habit her fingers found the headlamp beside the bed. She flipped it on then grabbed the heavy flannel robe Devon had left.

All that took only a few seconds but it was long enough for Bird to beat her to the door. He stood, blocking it, staring at her with eyes that glinted yellow in the headlamp beam.

"Out of the way, Bird."

He refused to move. He wasn't growling. His hackles stood straight up though, and if anything he shook harder.

"Bird! Move!" She used her obey-me-now voice.

The dog didn't budge.

That gave her pause. It wasn't like Bird to disobey.

Anya went to the small window hoping the headlamp beam would shine outside. Which it didn't. The glare off the pane almost blinded her. She switched it off and wiped her watering eyes. Then she cupped her hands around her face and peered out the window. That didn't help either.

The odd gasping breathing seemed closer now, almost at the window. Maybe the boy hadn't been a hallucination after all. Maybe he was out there, scared and alone. Somehow he'd managed to find his way to her cabin. Maybe he'd followed her trail. Anya opened her mouth to call out, to tell the boy to come around to the door.

Bird whimpered. Once, softly. And her blood chilled at the sound. Her dog was a fighter. Yes the earthquake had rattled him, but typically he'd be going mad trying to get out the door.

If he was afraid, she better be, too.

With knees knocking, she stepped away from the window. Backed slowly into the deeper darkness of the room. She made her way to Bird, still by the door, and squatted next to him. Where was her rifle? By the bed where she always left it. It would only take a few steps to cross the small room and get it. She wouldn't even need the headlamp.

But she couldn't move. Couldn't get her legs to support her. Couldn't find the courage to leave the side of her dog. As if that proximity protected her.

There was a shuffling outside, a scuffling along the outside wall. She'd had wild animals do this before. Raccoons on the roof, black bears at the windows, especially before winter when food was scarce and the scents of her cooking wafted out into the forest. But those sounds didn't freeze her in place, didn't terrify her. A scratching sound now followed the top of the doorframe. No raccoon reached that high. And a bear would be clawing, not...not almost fingering, seeking.

She was still shook up from the quake. That was it. Just jittery like Bird. She dug her fingers into the thick fur of the trembling dog. She tried for a deep breath to ease the rapid-fire panic of her tripping heart. She failed.

The sound of heavy breathing was on the other side of the door now. Right behind her. The heavy slab of wood moved, shifting inward slightly. Anya quickly put her hands against the door and pushed back. As if she could hold the door shut, hold whatever it was, out. The door moved again and the iron bolt squealed.

She needed her rifle. Badly.

Swallowing down the bitter copper taste of fear, she forced herself to her feet. She'd have to pass in front of the windows. But it was so dark, surely nothing would see her move across the room. Holding her breath she ran to the bed and felt around beside it until she found the cold barrel of the rifle. Sliding her hand down to the stock, she lifted it. Braced the butt against her shoulder. Tried to hold it steady.

And then waited.

The cold night air eddied around her bare feet, wrapped icy fingers around her ankles, climbed to her knees and made them shake harder. Moments passed. Bird left the door and came to her, pressing against her side. She ran a quick hand over his head and down his neck, feeling his hackles still up.

The shuffling, lapping sounds moved around to another wall. Anya heard a scraping noise, and something scratched at the window.

She couldn't breathe. It was going to crash through the glass. The rifle suddenly felt too heavy to hold, the muscles of her arms watery.

Nothing happened.

After several minutes, or maybe hours, Bird sighed heavily. Touching him, Anya realized his hackles were back to normal. She was so cold her joints ached and her nose ran. Sharp pain in her biceps warned her she couldn't hold the rifle up much longer. But still she stood, straining to hear.

The deep mountain night was quiet. Whatever walked out there in the woods had moved on.

Anya stepped stiffly back toward the bed, propped the rifle against the wall, put the headlamp on the table, and climbed under the quilts without taking off the robe. A pocket of warmth still held and she slid her ice cube feet into it. Bird, without waiting for permission, nosed under the bedding and plastered against her. She was grateful for his furry warmth and familiar doggy smells as they shook together.

But she felt very, very alone.

~Day 3~

1

The rain had stopped but heavy clouds hung low down the sides of mountains. Curtis bent, stretching to touch fingertips to the ground. His spine popped as he slowly straightened. He'd slept, fitfully and shivering, curled tightly on the backseat of his crumpled car with a musty smelling blanket tucked around him. He kept starting awake, convinced the ground was shifting under him, that the car was tilting into a fall that would never end. Every time he woke, he'd see faint light from scattered fires refracted across the shattered windshield.

He put his hands on his hips and twisted side to side, making his spine pop a few more times. The ache in his head had dulled to the point where Tylenol would probably help. He pulled his pack from where he'd stowed it on the front seat and dug around in a pocket for the bottle. He downed two capsules with the last of his coffee, now cold, then capped the thermos.

He had his cold weather gear in the pack. He'd need bottled water and some food, which he could get from Betty. The store, though damaged, still had some supplies. And she'd be willing to help since he was going on a quest to find Henry. And maybe fix the repeater tower.

But once inside the store, Betty crossed her good arm over her splinted one and shook her head.

"I don't have anything to spare."

Curtis looked around the store. Half-filled cardboard boxes blocked the small aisles where Betty had clearly been up all night, packing. Most of the supplies left on the shelves were broken, shattered, or spilled.

"But, your boxes…"

"I've been thinking about what you said yesterday." Betty wouldn't meet his eyes. "About no help coming for a long time."

"I said that?" Curtis thought back. "Oh, right. Well, it's a strong probability, for sure."

"Exactly. And the Lord helps those who help themselves. So I need to hang on to what I've got. Who knows how long it will take to get supplies. If I give away everything now, what will happen in the winter? I need to think ahead."

97

"Well, you don't need to give things away," Curtis said, thinking through worst-case scenarios. "You need to barter. You know, trading something someone else needs for something you need."

Betty stared at the floor as wind whistled in through broken windows and gaps in the collapsed back wall. She looked up to meet his eyes. "So what would you have that I need?"

Curtis thought about what might be in the car or in his pack. "You can read the novel I'm writing since there's no television or smart phones working. And if need be you can use the paper to start fires with."

"That doesn't sound real valuable to me," Betty said.

"Probably not," Curtis scanned the store around him. "But juices in that cooler aren't going to be real valuable to you before long, either. Or the lunchmeat in your deli cooler."

In the end, he traded Betty his manuscript, two pens, the blanket from his back seat, and an old collapsible snow shovel they'd found in his gaping trunk. In exchange he stowed in his backpack three bottles of cranberry juice, four slices of sourdough bread, and a small stack of turkey and Havarti slices. And the most valuable thing of all, a cheap plastic flashlight with fresh batteries. Betty traded the flashlight for his taking a few minutes to kneel and pray with her for their salvation. Curtis didn't share her beliefs, but he thought it wouldn't hurt anything to support her. Plus, he got a flashlight.

He felt a brief sadness leaving the novel behind to be fire starter. Even if it was bad, his mother had enjoyed it. Leaving it felt a little like admitting he might not see her again. He clamped down on that fear before it fully surfaced and headed for the door.

When he came out of the store, the Sheriff's deputy was headed across the street to the still-smoking ruins of the museum. Curtis was itching to start on his quest, but deciding someone should know where he was, he trotted over to Max.

"I'm headed out to look for Henry," he said.

"Alone?" One of Max's eyebrows went up. "You sure you want to do that?"

"Oh, I'm sure I don't. But people either don't want to go or have important things to do here. I'm also going to look at the repeater and cell towers to see if they can be repaired."

"Uh-huh." Max stared at the museum remains and poked a glowing coal with his boot.

"And I wanted to tell you there was a big wild dog over by the church last night. It might have been injured."

"Uh-huh." Max took a shovel and threw dirt over the hot coal. "We got lucky with the rain last night. This fire could have spread through the whole town. Did you say a dog?"

"Yes." Curtis nodded. "A big dog. A really big dog. I told it I wouldn't hurt it."

"You talked to it." Max turned toward him. "Wonder if it's the same one Maggie saw. Her dog from hell. Maybe the one that left tracks by your car the night you found that hunk of meat on the hood."

"Tracks?"

"Remember I said I'd go poke around up by the Hole the night you found that hunk? When I was up there I saw huge dog prints around where you'd parked."

"So some dog may have attacked Henry?" Curtis's heart rate bumped up. "He might be out there bleeding from a dog attack?"

Max shrugged. "No way to know, and now there's too much going on here for me or Casey to head out into the woods looking for Henry or a dog from hell."

"Well, I can't imagine any dog coming from hell. That is, if hell exists. There are some interesting theories...wait. I'm getting distracted. I need to go. If I don't go I'll never make it back."

"That's certainly true." Max smiled.

"No, I mean, I'd like to make it back before dark."

"Better get going then." Max caught his arm, smile fading. "Seriously Curtis, think this through. You shouldn't go alone."

"Oh, I know I shouldn't. I'll let you know when I'm back." He patted Max's hand and hoped it felt reassuring.

What he wanted to do was grip the man's sleeve and drag him along.

His car started in spite of the crushed front end, which he supposed was one of the advantages of having an engine in the back. He still had a quarter tank of gas. He'd drive as far as possible on the damaged road then walk from there.

Come night, whether he ended up on the back seat again, or out in the woods somewhere, he'd probably be sorry he traded the blanket. But Betty was a hard person to negotiate with.

As he drove past destroyed homes and shattered lives, he wondered what the coming days would hold for everyone in town. In an area where driving to a grocery store meant a couple hours on the highway, most people kept full cupboards. So that would help depending on how badly everything was damaged. And he knew there were people in town who hunted. So if it did take weeks, or months, for assistance to start making its way up the Sky valley, there might be those who would be able to feed the community.

As long as everyone didn't react like Betty and close themselves off.

Curtis understood, in a way. How did you balance keeping your own family alive against helping those around you? It was a moral dilemma societies had faced through the ages. When he found Henry, he'd bring it up and they could sit around a fire and have a long debate while they ate turkey sandwiches.

He was only able to drive a couple blocks. The road out of town was impassable, with so many trees down that he could barely see the big chunks of pavement that had heaved upwards as the ground shifted. He parked the Bug off to the side, got out, and shouldered his pack. For the briefest moment he considered locking the car, but then pictured Betty, arms crossed, unable to give.

He left the keys in the ignition. Maybe that quarter tank of gas would help someone out. It wasn't like the car would do much good anyway, with the bridges gone.

When he shut the door and turned, he saw the tall and lean form of Rob, a red kayak over his shoulder, and wearing a life vest and helmet. Curtis glanced at the river that raced beside Avenue A, broad and full of debris. The Skykomish was so powerful that even on a calm summer day the rapids were rated the most difficult Class V.

"What are you doing with the kayak?" Curtis asked. "Surely you're not going rafting?"

Rob smiled his typical amiable grin as if the river was an old familiar friend. And it reminded Curtis of the stories of Rob taking a kayak out in floodwaters. For fun.

"I'm hiking upriver to Skyko One," he said.

Curtis thought about the old houses gathered under tall evergreen trees. "Skyko One is on the other side of the river. And there may not be anything left."

"Exactly," Rob said. "I'm going to cross the river and check on them. Bring back anyone I can. That old river rat, Malcolm, has a raft we can use to evacuate people."

"Oh. Okay."

Something moved in the life vest and Curtis jumped back, letting out a small yelp of fear. Rob laughed and tugged the vest forward a little. Tucked inside his wetsuit was a tiny ragged and mangy dog with one eye filmed with cataracts.

"You're taking a dog?"

Rob shrugged. "I inherited my mom's dog when she died. He's older than dirt. Don't want to leave him behind. He can help me scout the river."

Rob left with a wave, walking up Avenue A as if he was headed for a normal river run. Curtis thought about what lay ahead of the man. Getting across the river. A two-mile slog through the destroyed landscape. He might get lucky and find some of the road remaining. Rafting people across to town. Repeating the whole thing.

Just to help in any way.

Something in Curtis's heart warmed the disappointment that Betty's behavior had left. Rob was helping people and Curtis would do the same. Encouraged and feeling a little braver, he turned to face the remains of the road out of town.

He wished though, that he'd been able to drive a little further. It was going to be a long walk.

And a hard one. Curtis had to climb over downed trees, their branches catching at the pack and his clothes as if wanting to hold him. The torn pavement made walking more like scrambling. Or stumbling. There wasn't a single tiny piece of the road that was easy passage.

He'd gone about a mile when he heard voices and saw movement up ahead. He paused, wiping his coat sleeve across his forehead. Coming toward him was a small group of men and women, one carrying a toddler in a sling contraption on her back.

"Everyone okay?" he asked when they got close enough. A few faces looked familiar. "Are you from Sky Country Club?"

The club was a sister community to Skyko One, but on the same side of the river as town. A few people lived there year round, but most cabins were owned by weekenders. As the people drew nearer, he saw the stress and fear in their wide eyes, their shaking hands, their thrown together clothes.

"There's no Sky Country Club left," one of the men said. "Most of the houses went into the river. The bank just gave way, man." He pressed fingers to his eyes as if to block the images.

"Then everything just sort of heaved up," the woman with the toddler said, tears starting to track down her cheeks. "And the ground just dropped. We're the only ones who managed to get out of our homes in time. Everyone else…" She drew in a hitching breath and didn't seem able to continue.

"Everyone else is gone," another man said, his voice blunt. "Gone into the river."

"How bad is town?" a woman asked. "We're going there for help."

Curtis saw hope light up in their eyes. He thought again of Betty and her crossed arms, the cardboard boxes.

"Town's been hit pretty hard, like everywhere, I imagine," he said. "But there are fires to warm up by. That should help."

"Where are you going?" the man with the blunt voice asked.

"To the top of the Wall. I'm looking for a friend. And I want to see how bad the repeater tower is damaged. If it can be fixed we might be able to call out. You haven't seen Henry have you?"

"The old guy who walks like a quail?" the mother asked. "He took me mushrooming one spring. Is he the one you're looking for?"

Curtis nodded hopefully, but her headshake killed that brief blossom.

"No, sorry. I haven't seen him for about a week."

"Okay then," he said. "Well, be careful. The road's a mess."

"No shit," said the blunt voiced man.

They worked their way around each other, heading in their opposite directions. The blunt-voiced man nodded tersely to Curtis, his eyes on Curtis's backpack with something like hunger in them. Not physical hunger, Curtis thought, but the hunger to possess. As if safety came from things.

And maybe, in this new world, that wasn't so far off the mark.

He'd only gone a few yards when the ground suddenly heaved up under his boots. Curtis was thrown to the ground, hitting hard. His breath was knocked out of him and what should have been a scream came out a breathless whimper. He rolled, tried to get to his knees, and was thrown down again. Someone screamed and more trees splintered like gunshots.

And then, almost before he had time to register the thought, the aftershock was over. Tentatively, he stood, wheezing for breath. His hands and knees were scraped, his hip ached where he'd hit the ground, and his elbow felt strangely warm. When he craned around to look at it, he saw a hole in his raincoat and shirt, and an abrasion on his elbow that was seeping slowly. He pressed his hand against his elbow and started back to the people from Sky Country Club.

"Everyone okay?" he managed to shout.

They stood frozen, staring in one direction. Curtis came up behind them.

The blunt-voiced man was dead. Impaled and pinned to the ground by a fir branch at least six inches in diameter and several feet long. It had come down with such speed and force that it had gone clean through the man's neck, almost severing his head.

Curtis staggered to the side and threw up in a fern. Someone was retching behind him, someone else crying. When his stomach settled a little, he wiped his mouth and went back to the others.

"Is anyone else injured? The baby?"

The woman shook her head, her face white as bone and her eyes so dilated they were black. He scanned the small group and saw scrapes and cuts, but nothing else looked major. Just the man, in the wrong place at the wrong second.

"It's not that far to town," he said. "You need to get there as fast as you can. You don't want to go into shock out here."

"What about Big Al?" a man asked. "We can't just leave him."

"Sure you can," Curtis said. "This lady needs to be taken to the fire department. Get that done then come back for...Big Al? That's his name? Come back for Big Al's remains. You can't do anything for him now, but you can for this mom here."

"Can't you help us?" the woman asked, shaking with deep tremors.

Yes, Curtis thought. He could. He could stay with them all the way back to town, then gather others to come back here. Help with body recovery. It would all take time and it would be a legitimate reason to put off his quest.

It would be so easy.

But it wouldn't help Henry.

He swallowed. "I can't. I have to find Henry."

Slowly, as if lost, the small group of people turned toward town. Curtis watched them for a moment and then resolutely turned his back to them. His elbow had stopped seeping and none of his injuries gave him an additional reason to give up.

So he kept going.

He clambered up over a fir, the sharp resin of crushed needles biting into his sinuses. The rain had moved down the sides of the Wall, hiding granite and trees in a soft gray curtain. The pattering of drops hitting pavement and rocks and earth was almost soothing. He pulled the hood of his raincoat up and concentrated on climbing over the next log. And the next.

It was early afternoon by the time Curtis reached where the Hole should have been. Huge boulders had calved off the Wall and hit so hard they'd cratered deeply into the ground. If the quake had hit when he was at work, he'd be dead and his car would be a thin smear of metal under one of those hunks of mountain. The door itself was only partially blocked, but he had no desire to work his way through the cracks and go inside.

The path leading up the Wall was still faintly visible and he was almost sorry because that meant he had no excuse to back out. Plus, parts of the trail had slid away. His knees fluttered in anxiousness. He'd thought the road with downed trees had been hard.

There was nothing for it but to take one step at a time. Henry was out there somewhere.

He deeply wished there was someone else to go. A hero. Someone strong. Someone capable. Someone who knew how to save lives and stitch the world back together.

Someone who wasn't afraid of everything.

He waited a moment longer, hoping. The rain plopped on the hood of his raincoat. Leaves rustled in the damp wind. Somewhere in the distant forest canopy, a raven or crow cawed and then was silent.

But no one came.

And so he pulled in a deep, shaky breath, and started uphill.

2

Technically the sun was up. Well, some place flat, like maybe Montana, it would be up. But here it was still behind the mountains. The light was visible though, giving the ridgeline a halo that, unfortunately, didn't promise a day of sunshine. The halo simply illuminated the undersides of charcoal clouds moving in on morning wind. The brief respite from rain appeared to be ending.

Ethan entered the bus, his boots crunching on broken glass. The kids still slept, including Zack, slumped by the fire. Ethan though, hadn't slept all night and his eyes felt like the sockets held gravel instead of eyeballs. It wasn't the first time he'd gone without sleep though, and he knew how to function and just how long he could function well. He still had a while to go before his body's demand for sleep knocked him on his ass.

He moved carefully toward the back of the bus, assessing in daylight. The damage was a lot worse than it had looked in headlamp beams. It amazed him more kids weren't injured.

Near where one of the backseats should have been, he saw only twisted metal. And in that debris was Amy. The poor girl hadn't had a chance. She'd been impaled as the bus rolled and had bled out so heavily that the flow was just now starting to congeal. Ethan hoped she hadn't known what happened. He rested a hand on her forehead, smoothed her cropped black hair.

She'd been an average student. Usually B's and C's. Occasionally an A that got her a fifty-dollar bill from her dad. She saved that money, telling Ethan she wanted a Smart car because they were so cute. Who were her friends? He couldn't remember who she hung out with and that lapse made him clench his fists. Her brief life should have been more than this ending with a teacher who didn't remember shit.

She'd had a big, obvious crush on Zack. He remembered suddenly watching her at the sidelines of a track meet when the guy had crossed the finish line first. Of course, most of the girls had crushes on Zack. Ethan rested a hand over hers, relieved he had remembered something.

All that blood. He'd have to keep the kids out of the bus. He didn't want them seeing her, let alone that dark pooling blood. He looked away for something to cover her with, but then his eyes returned to the blood. What was niggling at him? He studied the coagulating mess.

Most of it had puddled under and around her, flooding over her torso and running downhill. But on one side the blood was smeared outward, uphill. It took him a moment to realize what he was looking at.

Something had been licking up the blood.

And there were slight smudges, almost like tracks, along the edges of the blood, as if whatever drank had rested there. Except that the marks didn't look like prints from paws.

They looked like handprints.

Ethan swallowed against rising bile, swallowed against the jolt of fear.

Just what the hell was out there?

Reflexively, he grabbed for his gun, only to remember it was in his backpack out by Zack. Stupid, stupid, stupid.

He stood to get it and then paused. From this height the tracks didn't look so much like handprints. They looked more like long smears. He blew out a breath of relief. Exhaustion was making him see things. Just to be sure though, he squatted back down and studied the marks closely.

Definitely handprints. Up close he made out the details of palms, and inches away, what could only be fingerprints. Maybe even nails. There were tiny red drops an inch or so out from the fingertips.

Okay, so maybe one of the girls had come in here during the night to sit with her friend one last time. Or to mourn in private.

Except for those long swipes where something very like a tongue had licked around the edges of the blood pool.

Ethan stood again and took a step backward. He didn't know what was going on but the gun had to stay with him from now on even if the kids saw it. And they needed to get the hell out of here and back down below where there were more people and someplace safe for the kids.

But what about Amy? What could he do for the girl now? It was going to be difficult if not impossible to free her body. And then what? How would he bury her with nothing but a fold up shovel and a crowbar in an area of ancient glacial till? In land that was nothing but rocks and boulders from a shedding, eroding mountain?

After thinking about it for a few moments, he rummaged around until he found a discarded coat and gently laid it over Amy. He'd come back for her after he got the other kids safe and to their parents.

He had to prioritize the living.

Outside the bus, he walked a perimeter, looking for signs of the animal or for anything that might tell him what had happened to Val, the bus driver. When he heard voices, he returned to the fire and camp.

106

"Find anything from last night?" Zack asked as he stirred the fire back up.

"Maybe some drag marks," Ethan said, reluctantly. "It's hard to tell with the forest floor here. All the underbrush is so lush and resilient. But maybe something was dragged through the salal over there."

"You think Val?" Spike asked.

Ethan turned. He hadn't heard the kid come up behind him, and a little spurt of annoyance hit him. He couldn't allow those kinds of lapses. "Maybe," he answered. "Look, I don't want to scare you kids-"

Spike held a hand up. "We're not kids. Some of us are old enough to vote. Some of us even have jobs. We're going to graduate in a few months and be out on our own. Some of us already *are* out on our own. So far you're treating us like we have brains. Don't stop."

Ethan cocked his head to one side as he evaluated Spike, with his tattoos and piercings. And a rough home life from the rumors. "You saying you want me to be honest with you?"

Spike nodded, once.

Ethan looked at Zack and decided that some honesty might be okay but definitely not all. "You want to tell him or should I?"

Zack laughed. "Dude, we had some kind of animal here last night."

Spike snorted. "We're in the fucking woods."

"No, not just a wild animal," Zack said. "Something big."

"Like what? And where'd it go?" Spike asked.

"Those are the questions. No answers though," Ethan said. "Let's hope wherever it went, it was some place far away."

"And you let me sleep through it?" Spike said.

"You needed your beauty rest more than I did," Zack answered, his fear from the night before obviously eased slightly.

Ethan left them to their brief moment of normal humor and went to the tarp, where he bent down underneath its flapping edges. The wind was picking up.

"Come on," he said, shaking the tarp for emphasis. "Let's get a move on."

When it looked like most of them were awake, he squatted in the opening. "Listen up. Check out injuries now that we have daylight. I want to hear how everyone is, in detail. Pack your gear, have a granola bar and some water but remember to ration. Come out to the fire when you're ready and report in."

"Mr. Reynolds?" Rowan asked, from the other side of the tarp. "I can't get John to wake up."

John? Had he been injured? Ethan stood and walked around the tarp to Rowan's side. John Delaney. Who wanted to be a racecar driver. The kid so anxious to help Payton with her phone.

Rowan moved back out of the way so Ethan could duck under the edge of the tarp. As he bent down, she spoke with her voice lowered for only him to hear.

"I think he's dead." Tears started to track down her cheeks. "I can't find any pulse. I didn't hear him during the night but when he got out of the bus he said his stomach hurt." Her voice broke on the last word and she drew in a shaky breath. "I made him my buddy like you said. But I didn't hear him die."

Ethan lifted the edge of the tarp and saw John there, eyes open and staring, skin bluish gray and flaccid. Beyond help. He straightened and caught Rowan's shoulder. She shook uncontrollably, her breathing coming fast and shallow.

"Look at me," Ethan said, taking on the voice he'd used many times in similar situations, following his parents through violence. Calm and in control, even if that's not how he felt. "Rowan, look at me. You helped him, you stayed with him, and he didn't die alone. He knew you were there. Sometimes all we can do is just be there."

"But I was sleeping. I didn't know." She shoved tears away with the palms of her hands. "I fell asleep when I shouldn't have."

"Shock does that to you," Ethan said. "But you were with him and he knew it."

She didn't look convinced, but then he didn't expect her to. Those kinds of words were platitudes, not truths. They simply filled the space around your brain and cushioned it until your heart figured out how to deal with the grief.

Squatting slowly, his leg complaining, Ethan went in under the sloping tarp and knelt next to John's body. The boy was on his side, knees pulled up and hands tucked between them. Gently, he pulled up the gray tee shirt.

A massive dark bruise stretched hip to hip across the swollen abdomen. Clearly John hit something that had resulted in internal bleeding. From the looks of it Ethan wondered if the boy hadn't been thrown out of the seat and into the metal bar of the seat in front of him. Damn school buses with no seatbelts. Anger whipped through him again at this wasted life, this death that shouldn't have happened. This death on his watch.

He'd thought a safe teaching job would allow him peace, allow him to leave death behind. Instead he was losing kids too young to die. Kids who should still be immortal and full of dreams.

Ethan ran a hand over his face as if he could erase the anger and pain, and then reached out to close John's eyes. He looked up and saw Nathaniel, Lucy, and Jennifer staring at John, immobile.

"Nothing we can do," he said, trying to keep the coldness from his voice. It was a frost he'd used to survive emotional pain, to keep from going insane years ago, but it had no place with these kids. It belonged to his parents. "Gather up your stuff and go out to the fire."

He pulled John's coat up over his face, and stood slowly, walking out from under the tarp. As he did, dizziness swept through him and he grabbed the side of the bus for balance. He must be more exhausted than he realized.

But the kids were grabbing on to things, too, and Payton screamed.

The ground under his feet shifted, rolled, as if he stood on a boat. And then lifted upward, tossing them around like toddlers in a jumpy station. Trees crashed to the ground, boulders rolled like thunder.

Ethan fell to his knees, tried to get up, failed, and crawled toward the others. He managed to catch Payton before she stumbled into the fire.

"Spread out!" he shouted at them, but got only glazed terror in return.

There was no place safe to go. No doorway to stand in, no table to get under. They didn't know what to do.

"Drop and cover your heads!" he shouted, pulling Payton down and shielding her.

This, the students seemed to understand. They dropped, some huddling up against boulders. He saw Rowan scrabble down tight against a downed tree, wrapping her arms around her head. If another tree came down, she might be protected by the one she huddled against.

And then it was over. Rumbling, a few more cracks and sharp breaks of branches, but the sounds were like the end of a heavy downpour, when all that is left is dripping water.

Cautiously, Ethan stood, helping Payton to her feet. She clung to his arm, crying. Jennifer still huddled on the ground near the bus, hands over her head, and shoulders shaking with sobs. Rowan, pale and shaky, stumbled to Jennifer, pulling her to her feet. Zack stood dazed, and then turned in a slow circle as if trying to figure out what had just happened.

Spike bent and lifted Lucy into his arms from where she'd fallen against a tree. He carried her over to the fire, still burning merrily, and lowered her down, before going back for Nathaniel who was on his feet but gripping one of the ropes and shaking.

"What the hell was that?" Michael's voice was a high-pitched scream.

"Aftershock," Ethan said, trying to keep his voice calm and authoritative. He knew they needed to see someone in control. "Bound to happen."

"Bullshit!" Michael shouted. "I almost landed in the fire! I might have burned to death!"

"Not in that fire," Spike said, carefully loosening Nathaniel's fingers from the rope. "Not big enough."

"You don't know that!" Michael's voice came down a notch in tone as his shoulders bunched up.

Spike took a step forward.

Ethan recognized the signs of panic giving way to fury in both young men. He pulled free of Payton's grip and moved in.

"Just shut the fuck up," Spike said. "Your little pussy panic isn't helping anyone. Grow some balls."

Michael launched forward. Ethan saw his hand go to a jeans pocket and come out with a knife.

Spike's fists came up, but Ethan got there first. With a quick raise of the arm and twist at the waist, Michael hit the ground and Ethan held the knife.

"Enough!"

Silence fell heavily, as if they all held their breath.

Ethan turned in a slow circle. "Everyone's scared. Whether you think you're too tough to admit it or not. We don't need this kind of shit."

Michael got ponderously to his knees, and then slowly to his feet. "Right. Here comes the motivational speech. We all have to pull together. We stick together and we're going to be fine."

Ethan took one step forward, pushing right into Michael's space and grabbing the front of his shirt. "No we're not okay and no we're not going to be fine. Two kids are dead, you piece of shit."

He released his hold on the shirt, pushing back as he did, so that Michael stumbled.

"You're going to pay, asshole," Michael said, his brown eyes shifting from one kid to the next. "I got you now. Teachers can't touch kids, beat 'em up."

Ethan threw the knife as far as he could into the trees. "You want to be a tough guy, go ahead. Just not here or I'll build us a road out with your fat ass."

Michael simply stared at him.

"Mr. Reynolds?" Payton's voice was as timid and meek as a little girl, breaking through the testosterone drama. "Should we, kind of, leave?"

"How do you 'kind of' leave?" Jennifer asked, wiping tears away. "Either you leave or you don't. Besides, we can't do either until you have some better shoes."

"I didn't bring extra," Payton said, her eyes tearing up again.

"But I know where to get some," Jennifer said. She looked around the group with defiance in her green eyes. "And before any of you say anything, Amy would have been the first to offer to help someone. We need to start thinking of ourselves. Not the ones who have died."

With that, she headed for the bus.

"Wait!" Ethan broke eye contact with Michael and caught Jennifer's arm. "It needs to be done but I'll do it."

Jennifer hesitated. Pale, and with dark circles under her eyes, she looked too frail to even contemplate what she was doing, let alone accomplish it. But Ethan knew by the tight jaw that her teeth were clenched, that her mind was made up.

"I mean it," he said, and then raised his voice. "Finish gathering gear and checking out injuries. We're heading out."

He left Jennifer and reentered the bus, now shifted more to the side from the aftershock. It rocked as he stepped in, and he moved gingerly through the wreckage. When he reached Amy's body, he struggled to remove her hiking boots. Rigor had set in and her feet didn't want to bend.

Payton's words diffused his anger as quickly as water poured on a campfire. He still steamed, but the flames were out. He shouldn't have let Michael get to him. These kids needed him to be calm and in control. And it shouldn't have been a scared teenage girl who came up with the solution to Payton's need. It was his job to fix things, to keep them safe.

The boots wouldn't come free. Thinking of Payton and her silly ballet slippers, he gripped Amy's ankles and pulled hard turning his head as if that would deaden the sound of small bones breaking.

He hoped Jennifer was right. That wherever Amy was, she'd understand.

3

Sharon must have slept because when she stirred into awareness, it was light outside. Yet nothing had improved with that light. The world was still destroyed. She was still alive. The vape shop still smoked. A light drizzle still fell, misting across her windshield.

The highway was frantic with activity though, jammed with vehicles trying to get somewhere.

At least until the aftershock hit, and then all the frantic activity became chaos.

Cars were thrown against each other, the last remaining wall of the vape shop came down with a crash of shattering bricks, and Sharon was thrown around inside her car like dice in a cup.

She hit the steering wheel and pain was white-hot with the struggle to breathe. A second wave of the earth tossed her against the center console. She was weightless and meaningless and without control. But through the pain, exhilaration burned. This was it, finally. Her death. Now, in this moment.

Until it wasn't.

Until everything stilled and motion stopped and she was bruised and breathless but with a heart still beating.

Until she climbed out of the car, now dented from where it had been thrown against a concrete parking post.

What kind of sick universe kept tantalizing her with near-death moments? Rage unfurled. Probably the worst recorded earthquake in generations and it failed to kill her. An aftershock failed to kill her. She pulled in a ragged breath and screamed until her throat burned and she tasted blood.

And no one noticed.

She staggered against the front of the car, chest heaving. Fury so burned through her that her skin was hot with it.

She would gladly grab the ending that these people fled from and yet it escaped her. She swallowed and her throat ached with the pain of her screams and the pain of her soul.

Her chest hurt from hitting the steering wheel and she rubbed the bruised skin. And then realized she was rubbing her breast. The one killing her slowly. She dropped her hand and snorted. As if rubbing would make *that* pain go away.

With nothing else to do, she got back in her car. And of course the engine started right up. Another sign that Sultan wasn't the place for her. She stared out the cracked windshield at all the cars jammed together in the road, struggling to get away.

An odd calmness settled over her. She couldn't just sit and wait for death to find her. She had to seek it. And so she worked the car through debris and out to the highway.

The road was backed up, bumper-to-bumper, cars angled across lanes, some crumpled against each other. Power poles were down and lines crossed the road like tangled yarn after a cat had been at it. But there were no sparks, no flame, no electricity to arc, and people simply drove around shattered poles and over and through lifeless wires. Sharon chose east only because there was a small opening in the traffic.

While drivers around her blared horns, screamed at each other to get out of the way, tried to use their vehicles as battering rams, Sharon sat calmly. She plugged her iPod into the console and turned up the volume when *A Deep Slow Panic* by AFI came on. Enveloped by the music, she sat encapsulated in her metal cocoon. While others fought to go, she carefully and serenely inched her way forward when space opened up.

Yesterday morning, before the quake, she'd walked away from her home. Left the place wide open and unlocked. Full of things that a week ago had been valuable, both in money and in memories. Value that she couldn't take with her, that no longer meant anything. Not even the memories. She'd left her purse, her identification, everything that defined who she was. Everything, that was now nothing.

The lyrics of the song spoke for her, putting into words the deep awareness of being consumed from the inside, of the engulfing panic that had no words. If an earthquake couldn't take her away forever, what else could she do? Sit here in that panic?

She needed to find that end, where she no longer dreamed. No longer thought. No longer existed.

Sharon gripped the steering wheel and inched forward again. Taking, in increments, her road to nowhere. As she neared the edge of city limits, a siren blared, loud enough to be heard over the iPod. She paused the music and cranked down the window. The siren continued. And continued. She knew instantly what that meant. The Culmbak Dam above the city. The quake must have damaged it.

Another chance. Death by drowning.

Drivers around her became more frantic. More cars tried to escape by force. Sharon smiled. She started the music again and continued inching forward. It didn't matter now if she made it out of town or not. It didn't matter where on the road she was when the water hit. It only mattered that she placed herself in the direct path of the flood from the breaching dam.

Something in black caught her eye. An old woman stood still on the side of the road. Her very stillness, surrounded by panic, made her unusual. A long charcoal gray dress hung loose around her thin frame and she held a tall walking stick. Sharon stared. For some reason the woman reminded her of herself. And then she realized there was no panic on the old lady's face. She wasn't begging for a ride from people and there was no terror, no visible desire to get out of harm's way.

Fascinated, Sharon paused the music again and leaned out.

"We're going to die, you know," she called to the old woman. "The dam has been breached. When the siren blows it's a half-hour warning."

The old woman made her way to the side of Sharon's BMW and stood there with one liver-spotted hand on the window edge. She said nothing. Her eyes were so black the pupils were indistinguishable from the irises. Deep wrinkles made fissures of age down her face.

"Hop in if you want to wait with me," Sharon said. "Might as well be out of the rain."

"You're inviting me in?" The old woman's voice was deeper than Sharon expected, scratchy and abrasive.

If a raven had a voice, this would be it. "Sure, why not? But I'm in no hurry to get out of town. And it looks like none of us are going to make it anyway." She twirled her hand in a circle, showing the traffic jam surrounding them.

The old woman cocked her head to one side. The odd movement was like she listened to something else. After a brief moment she nodded. "I have work to do first. Then we'll see." She moved around the front of the car and to the side of the road.

"Take your time," Sharon called after her. "I'll be right here. At least until the water hits. Then I'll be dead."

What would drowning be like? She drew in a deep breath and held it until her lungs burned with a crushing weight, then exhaled explosively. Would she die from breathing water or from being knocked around in the car as the flood hit? She would be terrified, that was a given. Would she fight to survive? That was more doubtful. Moments of terror versus weeks of being killed slowly. She'd made a choice, but she imagined her body would instinctively fight that choice when the moment came.

Sharon looked out the window but there was no wall of water racing down the side streets. When she tuned back, the old woman was gone. Sharon scanned the chaos but couldn't pick out even the tall walking stick.

A loud crash made her jump. Up ahead a bright red Ford F350 must have decided to make its own path. It had just slammed into the back of a small car. As Sharon watched, the truck backed up and then hit the car again. With each impact the car was shoved more to the side, until it was pushed into a small Fiat. Both then were shoved off the pavement and into the grassy shoulder. The truck took advantage of the opening to move ahead. It jerked forward, she heard metal on metal, and saw the backup lights come on again.

Horns honked around her. People wanted to press forward, to move into the open slot the truck created. As if a few feet forward would make any difference. There was a small jerk and her car bumped forward. Automatically, Sharon's foot came down on the brake and she stared into the rear view mirror. Some sort of Volvo was pushing, urging, forcing her to take those few feet of forward momentum so precious to them.

If she'd been able to pull off to the side, she would have. Let them have the openings, let them strive and hope and think they were going to make it. She'd just wait. She saw now that it had been a mistake to get into traffic rather than staying in the parking lot. But there were cars on both sides of her and the Volvo once again nudged her forward.

Sharon stepped on the brake harder and put her hand out the window, flipping off the driver. She saw an older woman behind the wheel, mouth open in a circle as big as the huge earrings she wore.

Let them strive, Sharon thought, resting her elbow on the window's edge. In the midst of all the fighting for movement, she felt detached and oddly at peace. This was her time, her last few moments. She'd chosen this. While others around her fought to get free of what was coming, she embraced the end.

What would her last thoughts be? Would she flash back on her life, like she'd heard happened? Would she remember those who had left her in one way or another? Would she decide, too late, that she wanted to live a few more weeks?

A man ran by her car, obviously deciding he had a better chance on foot. Maybe he did, she thought. The bright red truck's backup lights came on again. Sharon sucked in a gasp. The driver hit the gas and the truck flew backward into the man.

The driver either didn't know or didn't care because the truck moved forward, dragging the man as it pushed another car aside and into a third. The man come free of the trailer hitch and fell boneless to the ground.

He was clearly dead. Blood spread slowly across pavement full of white shards of bone. One arm, palm up, was too far away to still be attached.

This was what death looked like. At least for that stranger. The method she'd chosen would, by drowning in the coming flood, be just as violent in its way.

Yet that poor man hadn't chosen this. Without understanding why, she got out of the car, ignoring the honking of the Volvo. Carefully, she picked her way around cars until she reached the man's body. She was barely aware of the truck, gunning its engine and continuing its attack. After all, what would it matter if the driver ran over her, too?

The man's brown eyes were open and the light rain washed across them. Not widened in terror, just open. She searched his eyes for knowledge, some moment of awareness that this was the end, forever imprinted on his face. But there was nothing.

He was maybe in his thirties. Brown hair, cut short and neat. Jeans. A black tee shirt that had 'Clanadonia' stenciled under the photo of a man in a kilt. If she'd passed him on the street a month ago, she never would have given him a second glance.

But now he'd gone into nothing, as if showing her what was to come. And she realized she loved him. Just a little. Just enough to fill her heart, to grieve. To wish she could trade places with him, to wish she could have saved him by offering herself in his place.

She went to step closer and her boot slipped slightly. Glancing down, she saw she stood in his blood, already thickening, even in the drizzle.

"He's dead, lady," some guy shouted from a car. "You can't do anything. Just get out of the way."

Sharon didn't even glance at the person. Instead she bent over and rested her hand on the man's chest, where his heart no longer beat but where warmth was still there, under her cupped palm. The stillness would be hers, soon, when her heart stopped.

If only she could stop it now, give her pulsing heart and pumping blood to this man. Hot tears for this stranger filled her eyes, burned down her cheeks.

As she moved to straighten, she saw the wedding ring. A plain silver band. Someone had loved him in life. She held his hand a moment, as his skin cooled beneath hers.

Until her end, she would mourn this one who wasn't ready, who would never have chosen to breathe his last.

Sharon headed toward her car, then realized it meant nothing, just like all her other possessions. She'd once been so proud of that BMW. Loved driving it, showing off its immaculate midnight blue waxed gleam. It was a status symbol in a town of farmers and trucks and old beaters.

She walked back toward the bridge over the Wallace River, weaving around all the blocked cars. More people were leaving vehicles now, running breathlessly for higher ground. Sharon made her way around the end of the bridge and half-slid, half-climbed down the short embankment to the area where fishermen would park their trucks and trailers. From there she walked calmly to the water's edge.

She wanted to see death coming. She wanted to be one of the first taken by the water.

Up above, the bridge and the highway was a mass of movement. Sharon wished all those panicked people luck. She sat down cross-legged on the wet ground and felt the butt of her slacks soak up the water. The drizzle was thickening again to rain and she listened to the quiet, peaceful sound of drops pattering around her, of the soft murmurs of the little river moving over rocks.

It was a good place to wait for the water to get loud and hungry and demanding.

4

Ramon watched the small clinic in Sultan. Most of the building had collapsed, but a corner had been shored up for patients. It was early morning, the rain had eased to a drizzle from heavy, sullen clouds, and exhaustion lined the faces of those surrounding him. He waited, part of the huge crowd that spilled and overflowed the torn up parking lot. Ben was next to him, standing protectively over Alegria who sat on a curb at his feet. Ramon had managed to scavenge a folding chair and Marie rested in that, watching him silently. She was pale, her dark eyes wide with fear. He squeezed a piece of paper tightly in his fingers, as if he could make things move faster. The small scrap had a number written on it and once that number was called, his nieces would get help.

They had spent the night working their way along devastated back roads, avoiding the highway, jammed with vehicles with nowhere to go and no way to get there. June and the girls had slept fitfully while Ben and Ramon took turns throughout the long night driving the truck. Artair helped with running the winch when they needed to clear a path.

Just as they'd crossed into Sultan, just as Ramon drew in a breath feeling like they were finally going to be okay, the aftershock had hit. But Ben had just kept his foot on the gas, had just kept going. Only once had the truck slid as the road bucked under them. And now they were finally at the partially standing clinic.

June and Artair crossed the parking lot to the local pharmacy, also only partially standing. Ramon hadn't asked what mission June was on since they'd already stocked up on supplies. He had too many other things on his mind, like his exhausted and injured nieces.

No one seemed to know how far the quake had reached, but he'd heard the talk around him. Everyone knew it was devastating. No cell service or electricity. Even Ben's radio in the truck simply blasted the emergency broadcast warning. And there were no military rigs, no signs of National Guard, and no local police.

People talked in low voices and huddled together. It was strange, how quiet they were. There was no sign of the violence that had been in the Fred Meyers parking lot the night before. At least not yet. Ramon had expected to find crowds pushing and shoving to get loved ones inside, but instead they settled, waiting. He saw pain and fear, blood and broken bones, and one person with, oddly, a screwdriver sticking out of his arm.

"You seen anything like this before?" Ben asked, gesturing at the crowd.

Ramon hesitated, very aware of the girls listening. "I saw shootings all the time. Back home. Before I moved here. But nothing like this."

"Me neither," Ben said. "And I've been around."

"People are so...well behaved," Ramon said. "Handling this good. You know, waiting, no panic."

"Look at their faces, son," Ben said, lowering his voice. "You aren't looking at people calm and waiting. You're looking at sheep."

"What?"

"Everyone's waitin' for someone in charge to tell them it's going to be okay. Mayhap tell them what to do next."

"A doctor can't do that," Ramon said.

"No, but we're all hoping the doctor will have more information than we do. Right now, these medical people are the closest thing to authority around."

Ramon watched the crowd. Deep shock also explained what looked like calmness.

"Look closer, son," Ben said, poking Ramon with his elbow. "People are scared, but they're getting angry. Look at how they're inching closer to the clinic, starting to push against each other. Crowd their way up front."

Ramon saw Ben was right. There was a subtle shifting going on. Someone paced, one man suddenly threw up his hands and then shoved past the person next to him, going to the clinic and peering in the window. In the background a hum was starting, as one or two voices were raised.

"Can you feel it?" Ben asked.

Ramon could only nod. There was tension in the air, a side effect of fear and confusion.

Over the next hour, that tension grew and sharpened. Ramon was only distracted from watching the crowd when June and Artair came back holding white paper bags.

"What have you got there, Mother?" Ben asked.

"That nice pharmacist renewed my blood pressure meds," June said. "And gave me extra because of the quake. He didn't even check to see if I had a prescription. I told him I couldn't find my pills at Fred Meyers and he just started filling bottles."

"Lot of people in the pharmacy," Artair said. "And they're kind of getting angry."

A woman in a blue flowered smock came to the opening that had once been the clinic's doors. "Number sixty."

"That's us," Ramon said, relieved. The urge to get in the truck and lock the doors ate at him. He helped the girls stand but Marie suddenly latched on to his arm and plastered herself against him.

"Come on Marie, you're too old for this. They're just going to look at your head. Let's get it done and get out of here." Ramon tried to keep the impatience out of his voice. But Marie didn't respond, staring off to the side, eyes wide. He turned. "What?"

"Is that real?" Marie pointed.

"Is what real, honey?" June asked.

They all looked in the direction Marie pointed, at the outskirts of the crowd, the edge of pavement where parking lot became highway.

"I don't see anything." Artair squinted.

"What do you see?" Ramon asked his niece.

"There," Marie whispered. "The raven. Watching us."

"I don't see any raven," Artair said.

Marie clutched Ramon's hand and tugged him down so she could whisper in his ear.

"I think I'm dead."

Chilled fear avalanched through Ramon's body. He scooped up Marie and gripped her tight, as if his hold could keep her in one piece.

"You're not dead, baby," he said, and knew she heard the quiver in his voice. "Let's get to the doctor before they give our number to someone else."

Inside, the lights were on. That simple thing made Ramon take a deep breath. It was as if, with light, all things were fixed. But the low rumble of a generator running somewhere explained the lights. Deep lines of fatigue carved crevices in the face of the doctor who came toward them. Etchings that looked like they were there to stay.

"What do we have here?" the man asked, his voice scratchy and gruff.

"One injured arm and a head wound," Ramon said, not wanting to waste the poor man's time with unnecessary words.

Alegria though, caught at the doctor's hand. "My sister thinks she's dead."

"Really?" The doctor knelt next to Marie and managed an authentic smile. "That happens sometimes with head injuries."

"Why?" Alegria asked.

"Good question." The doctor talked to the girls as if this was a normal appointment in an exam room, instead of an overflowing destroyed waiting room with injured people lined up needing his time. "Sometimes, what happens is a temporary disconnect between your thoughts and your perceptions. Do you know what that means?"

"No," Marie said softly. "Not exactly."

"Your brain is doing two jobs at once, all the time," the doctor continued, as he parted Marie's dark hair with one hand and pulled out gauze from a tray on the floor next to him.

"Like my Tío," Alegria said. "His job that gives him money and his job watching my dad."

Ramon started in surprise. How had Alegria known he kept an eye on his brother?

"Okay," the doctor said, now snipping hair away from the wound site. "Your brain has an internal job. Where it keeps your body working, monitors everything. Then it has an outside job where it takes in everything you see, hear, taste, and so forth, and processes it into information you understand."

Marie watched the doctor intently, a frown pulling her eyebrows down into a sharp angle.

"Sometimes, when you've been banged around, the brain can't handle both jobs so it only does one. Usually it quits the outside job so it can work at home."

This brought small smiles to both girls.

"When it quits the outside job, it can give you a feeling that things aren't real. Because your brain just isn't processing the outside information like normal."

"Does it make you see things that aren't there?" Alegria asked, reaching out to hold her sister's hand.

"No," the doctor said, drawing the word out as if he thought. "Is that what happened?"

Marie shook her head and then winced. "It was there. Just no one else saw it."

The doctor looked up to meet Ramon's eyes and then went back to his job. "Well, let's talk a little more. I bet you have a headache."

The questions and answers moved into more expected channels as the doctor went through the exam. When he was done Marie had a bald spot on the back of her head with five neat stitches covered with a bandage. She'd been given two pills, and the doctor handed several sample packets to Ramon.

"Pain pills if she needs them, and antibiotics. The wound wasn't bad but since it's been awhile we don't know if any infection made its way in. Better safe than sorry."

Ramon nodded, pocketing the samples.

The doctor gestured for an assistant. "Your daughter can wait in that chair over there while my nurse takes care of your other daughter's arm."

Ramon didn't correct the doctor's assumption that he was their father. He realized, with stomach sinking, that right now he was the closest to a parent the girls had. And there was no way he was qualified.

"How long will they be?" Ramon asked, nodding in the direction Alegria had gone. "We came out here for medical help because we couldn't get to the hospital. But we need to get back to Monroe. Find my brother."

"I understand," the doctor said. "Are you injured? You seem to be guarding your side."

"It's not bad. Hit a fire hydrant. Just bruised." Growing impatience made his words curt. "Sorry. It's just…we need to get out of here."

"Believe me, I get it." The doctor leaned down to Marie still sitting in a chair. "Those symptoms of yours, that sense of unreality, should go away on its own shortly."

"What about her seeing things not there?" Ramon asked when Marie didn't speak.

The doctor shook his head. "Hallucinations. Maybe from the bump she got. Maybe from stress, fear, lack of sleep, shock. Who knows? Doubt it will happen again once she gets rest."

The doctor's assistant returned with Alegria. She was pale but proudly showed him a sling made of hot pink material with virulent green dragonflies.

"It's not broken," the nurse said. "Your daughter's arm. She compressed all the bones in the forearm so the nerves were pinched, and banged her shoulder up. But it's just deeply bruised, not dislocated. We've manipulated the bones but her arm is going to be sore as if she had a greenstick fracture. So keep the sling on to help her remember not to use the arm." The nurse handed him a handful of sample packets. "Pain meds if she needs them."

Someone outside shouted. There was a crash of breaking glass.

Ramon grabbed the packets without looking at them. He pulled Marie to her feet and caught Alegria's hand, prodding them both toward the door. The urge to scoop them up and run was overwhelming.

The crowd in the parking lot had grown, and grown more restless. Ramon pulled the girls close until they reached the truck where Ben stood waiting.

"Mayhap we need to get out of here, son," Ben said, his grizzled eyebrows drawn down.

"I know."

Ramon boosted the girls up into the truck where June and Artair already waited. Before he got in though, a siren, loud and long, made him twist around to Ben.

"What the hell is that?"

Someone in the crowd screamed and voices rose. A man near them grabbed a woman and child and shoved them toward a car so fast the child fell. He scooped up the boy but as he went by Ramon grabbed his arm.

"What's going on?"

The man yanked his arm free. "Warning siren for the Culmbak Dam."

"A dam?" Ramon's stomach filled with tangible terror.

"On the Spada Lake Reservoir." The man's face was bone white. "Thirty minutes, maybe, to get the hell out of here."

Ben ran for the driver's door and Ramon climbed in next to his nieces.

"What do we do?" Artair asked, staring out the window.

Ramon froze. The highway in front of the clinic was blocked. Cars sped out of the parking lot only to slam into other cars. Trucks pushed their way through by force, only to jam up, bottle-necked, against the small, narrow bridge that crossed the Wallace River just east of the clinic.

"Half an hour to evacuate out of the city," Ramon said, hopeless. "Through that."

"How?" Artair asked, his eyes wide with fear as he stared at the highway.

"Not by road," Ben said, his voice tight and grim.

"Buckle up and hang on," June said calmly. "You're about to see why I've been married to Father so long."

"Are we going to die?" Alegria asked, grabbing on to Ramon.

"No, honey," June answered. "We're going to bounce around a bit and then be fine."

Ramon checked each girl's seatbelt with shaking hands and then yanked his across to buckle. Artair, up front between Ben and June, looked over his shoulder at Ramon, eyebrows almost to his hairline. Ramon could only shake his head. There was nothing to do but trust the old man.

Ben hit the gas and the truck shuddered. Ramon saw no way to get through the parking lot, let alone down the highway, but Ben didn't even try. Instead he headed toward the back of the clinic. Mowing down a chain link fence around a Laundromat like it wasn't even there. Cutting right across a lawn.

Ramon threw his arm out across his nieces to hold them in place as the truck bounced and jumped a curb. Without letting up on the gas, Ben headed straight down hill and into a small gravel parking area where boats and boat trailers sat, some crushed under fallen trees. He swerved around vehicles, heading straight for water.

"That's a river!" Artair shouted.

"That's just a baby river," June said. "With nice sloping banks. That's nothing. You should have seen this river in Idaho-"

"Not now, Mother," Ben said, leaning forward and gripping the steering wheel.

Ramon glanced at the girls. He'd put his nieces right into the hands of a crazy old fart. They were all going to drown. He grabbed the door handle. Maybe he could get the three of them out before they hit water.

But then what would they do?

The truck engine slowed with a deep whine as Ben shifted down. He caught hold of another gearshift and went into four-wheel drive. Ramon lurched against the seatbelt as the truck nosed down into the swiftly moving water. Both girls clutched each other's hands with tears washing down their cheeks.

"The old Crusher is made for this," Ben said. "Relax."

They were thrown side to side as the truck bounced over rocks. Ben shifted into four low.

"There's an exhaust pipe for the engine," June said, one hand on the dashboard for balance. "See?"

A pipe came out of the engine compartment alongside the front windshield. Ramon sagged back. As long as they didn't get bogged down in silt, maybe they would make it. And now that they were in the water, he realized it really was a baby river. Only a few truck lengths wide. They'd be across in moments.

"Oh shit." Artair pointed out the driver's side window. "Floor it!"

The riverbanks overflowed and disappeared under rolling water.

Ben glanced quickly upriver and then shook his head. "Calm down, son. That's just the leadin' wave, not the flood. The bad part won't be a wave, just a giant swell."

"It's a hell of a lot of water!" Ramon pressed one palm to the window as if to hold back the wave.

The water hit the side of the truck, rocking and surrounding it. The steering wheel jerked out of Ben's hands, but he grabbed it as the truck lurched to one side. For a moment Ramon was sure the weight of the camper and all their supplies would send them crashing over. But the tires gripped, the hood of the truck came up slightly, and Ben hit the gas.

They lurched up the opposite bank, bounced over some rocks and kept going across the grass of a small park.

Ben didn't slow down and his knuckles against the steering wheel whitened with tension. "Not out of the woods yet."

Ignoring the highway, Ben headed down side streets, using yards and parking lots where he could. Ramon glanced down at his nieces, grinning broadly.

"We made it," he said.

Alegria met his grin. "That should be a Disney ride!"

"Look," June said. "There on the sidewalk."

There were people all over, but the crowds were moving. Throwing things in cars, running, grabbing kids and pet carriers. But where June pointed, an old lady in a long black dress stood perfectly still, holding a walking stick. The contrast with panic and chaos surrounding her stillness was eerie.

"We need to help the poor thing," June said. "There's no one with her."

"We don't have room," Ben said, but his foot came off the gas anyway.

"No!" Marie shouted, reaching forward to grab June's shoulder. "Don't stop!"

"We can't leave the old dear like that, all alone," June said, raising a hand to pat Marie's fingers.

But Marie jerked her hand back, threw off her seatbelt, and climbed over Alegria. She leaned between Artair and Ben, grabbing for the steering wheel.

"Don't you see it?" she screamed. "Don't stop!"

Ramon caught Marie around the waist, pulling her back toward him. She fought, sobbing.

"She's not for us! You can't stop!"

The old woman turned toward the truck, calmly watching as they neared. She made no effort to stop them, no hand came up as if asking for help. She simply stood there.

Ben hesitated, the truck slowing even more. "What do we do here?" he asked.

"Marie's just imagining things," Alegria said, although her voice rose in fear.

The old woman looked directly at them, her eyes black and bottomless, and Ramon shivered. He grew still, almost holding his breath as he gripped Marie.

The woman smiled, fissured wrinkles deepening across her face. And one hand came up, gesturing them onward, giving them permission to go by.

"What the hell?" Ramon said, tightening his grip on Marie, who pushed her hands against the back of Ben's seat as if trying to shove the truck forward.

Ben shook his head and rolled down the window. "You need help?" he called out, not quite stopping the truck.

"Not today," the woman said. "Listen to your little girl."

"You sure?" Ben asked, doubt deepening his voice.

"Go on," the woman said, impatiently flapping her hand at them. "You're not the one I'm waiting for."

Ben rolled up the window slowly, as if he was still undecided. But June reached across Artair and put her hand on Ben's arm.

"I think we'd best do what she says." June's voice was almost a whisper.

The warning siren went off again and the loud, jarring noise settled their indecision. Ben nodded to the old woman and pulled away.

Artair turned to look over the back of the seat. He was pale, his hazel eyes wide as he stared at Marie.

"How'd the old lady know what Marie said?"

Ramon rubbed the goose bumps on his arms. Trying to sound calm and in control, he turned to Marie.

"What did you see?" The silence that followed his question was heavy, as if time paused.

After a moment Marie wiped her eyes with the sleeve of her school blouse. Tears left tracks down her cheeks and she still trembled against Ramon, but her eyes reflected only a deep weariness.

"The raven on her shoulder," she said.

The hair on the back of Ramon's neck stood straight up. He carefully buckled Marie back in. She leaned against the back of the seat and closed her eyes. Alegria reached out and took hold of her sister's hand.

Ben shook his head as he maneuvered the truck onto pavement. The side street was relatively clear and he increased speed. But the evacuation chaos continued out on the highway. Ramon didn't think a lot of the people would make it out in time. For that matter, he wasn't sure they were going to.

"Why is the thought of a pet raven so creepy?" Artair asked.

"Because none of us saw it," Ramon said.

5

Casey knelt next to an older couple sitting on the curb in front of the general store. They sat, eyes wide in shock, shivering and clutching each other.

"Okay," Casey said. "Did you sleep last night? Have you eaten anything since the quake?"

She saw their relief, their hope that someone in a uniform would make all this go away. Would fix everything. Would keep them safe. That hope bloomed in every pair of eyes she looked into. And she had to be the one to kill that hope. Each time it felt like one big aching hole where her heart should be.

"Not much sleep," the older woman said. "But we shared a granola bar from Louis."

Louis. Casey had to think for a second before she remembered that Louis was the guy in his seventies who kept insisting they find some way to contact the Department of Emergency Management. It hadn't sunk in yet that they were on their own. But then, maybe it had, if Louis was handing out granola bars.

"That's good," she said. "So why are you sitting out here?"

"We wanted coffee," the old man said. "Just some coffee. We thought Betty would have a pot on like she used to. She has a camp stove going. But she won't share."

Casey saw tears in the old man's eyes and patted his shoulder. "Everyone is panicked right now. We're still in the rescue stage. Once that's under control we'll figure out what resources we have that can be shared. But right now everyone is terrified and the only thing making them feel in control is hanging on to what they have. Do you understand?

"But we just wanted a cup of coffee," the woman said. "We'd have even shared one."

"I understand. Is your house still standing?" Casey asked. "You'd be better under shelter than out here in the cold."

"I'm not sure. We live on Alley Oop. But we stayed by the fires last night."

Normally, when Casey heard the name the town council had given an alley that ran between Index Avenue and Avenue A, she had to smile. She loved the idea of a place small enough that they allowed humor into their city business. But now, she thought of the huge old fir trees that lined the Oop. Many had crashed to the ground in the quake.

"We have crews checking places now. If your place is still standing, you need to shelter in place. Can you do that? Make it back home?"

"Think so," the elderly man said. "But can we just sit a spell longer?"

Casey stood, her back aching. "Of course. Just not too long. It's too cold."

At their nods, she left them, moving out into the middle of the street. Index was still a nightmare, just like the day before when the quake first hit. Last night had been almost as bad as people huddled around fires, afraid to go into buildings, even if those buildings had been their homes before the quake.

And then during the night the museum caught on fire. She and Max, and Samuel, the lone firefighter, had managed to get a pump into the river and a hose to the museum, but by then it had been fully engulfed. The air still smelled of smoke, and wisps still rose from charred wood. So much history lost. But at least no lives.

Today was shaping up to be almost as bad. More bodies. More trapped people she and Max had no way of reaching. But Albert, the mayor, knew how to run a backhoe and he and the town's maintenance guy were using the heavy equipment to try and gain access to those who were trapped. And Albert had started a running log of names. Those who survived. Those who died. Injuries. The list was at the fire department and the last time Casey had looked, those who had survived outnumbered those who hadn't. She'd take whatever good news she could.

Like the fact that the rain had eased up some. And at least her hands no longer shook and the adrenaline-fueled queasiness had eased. But fear and helplessness were still there, trapped like a fluttering bird under her heart.

Water sloshed around her boots and bubbled up from the buckled pavement. Someone had managed to shut off the water main, but not completely. Water still fountained up from underground. At least it wasn't a gusher. Albert had said something about the broken main draining the town's water tank, but she figured the lack of potable water was the least of their worries. There was always the rain and the river.

She'd add it to the growing list of jobs. They would need a crew to find buckets and start hauling water to a fire. Find pots to boil the water in. She pushed the heels of her hands into her eyes, trying to force exhaustion away.

Up and down Avenue A, small clusters of people worked, the

result of the work she, Max, Samuel, and Albert had done to organize work crews. Someone had put up a canopy behind the town hall and bodies were laid out there under tarps. The part of the fire department still standing was working as a makeshift clinic. People were going building to building checking for propane leaks, shutting off tanks as they found them. Homes were being assessed and those unsafe for shelter were marked with red paint. Red for 'stay out'. Houses painted with big black 'X' marks meant they had been searched and there were bodies to recover. Green paint meant a place was good for shelter. Very slowly, a system was shaping up. Control was being gained in tiny increments.

Casey heaved out a heavy sigh. As exhausted as she was, she felt a seed of pride in all they had accomplished.

Max came around the back of the town hall. He looked haggard, his pale blue eyes rimmed almost as red as the stubble on his cheeks. Casey walked down the broken pavement and when she reached him, he handed her a granola bar then opened another, taking a big bite.

"You ran into Louis, I see," she said, opening her bar. Her stomach growled.

"And Curtis."

"Who?"

"The scientist from the Hole. He was worked up about some wild animal with red eyes they saw last night."

"Maggie's dog?" Casey had a moment of unreality flush through her and she had to draw in a deep breath to center herself. Had it only been yesterday that they'd been laughing about Maggie and her dog issues?

"Most likely," Max said. "That Curtis, he's on a mission. He's hiking to the top of the Wall to see if he can fix the cell towers."

"A fool's errand."

Max shrugged.

"Isn't that the same guy who called in a friend missing a couple days ago?"

Max thought a moment. "Yeah. Curtis said something about that. Henry, that old guy who walks like he's climbing uphill."

Casey started to reply but a piercing shriek cut her off. She whipped around, her hand going to the butt of her gun from pure reflex. Up and down the street people screamed and ran but she didn't know why.

Max grabbed her around the waist and jerked her backwards, lifting her off her feet as he stumbled back.

Pavement heaved and buckled around the broken water main. This wasn't an aftershock. Something moved, a dark shape pushing up from under the asphalt.

"What the hell?" Max dropped her on her feet, staring toward the general store.

Chunks of concrete buckled in a line almost twenty feet long.

"The water main is going to blow!" Casey shouted.

A deep roar came from the crack, louder even than the screams around them. The ground vibrated under Casey's boots as Max tugged her further back. The shattering pavement seemed to follow them.

"Run." Casey's voice came out in a shaky whisper. And then, louder, hauling on Max's arm. "Run! If it blows that asphalt is going to rain like shrapnel!"

She sprinted across Avenue A and Max followed.

"We need to get farther away," she said breathlessly.

"No shit."

Samuel stood in the bay door of the fire department. Max and Casey joined him, swinging round to stare back at the buckling pavement.

"What is it? God, Max, what is it?" Samuel's eyes were wide, but he held his arm across the doorway as if to protect the injured inside.

"Building water pressure," he said, pushing on Samuel's chest. "Get back under cover. The main's going to blow."

Casey froze. The two old people still sat on the curb, eyes and mouths wide open in terror. She'd run for her own safety and left them behind. Just left them without a thought.

She grabbed Max's wrist, fingers so tight she felt bones grind. "Oh, god."

"What?" Max asked.

"That couple!" she screamed over the growing roar of water and buckling street.

She leaped forward but Max grabbed her and jerked her back. He stared over her head at the water main, his face drained of color.

Something was coming up through the crack. Lifting concrete and dirt and rocks that slid down its sides and slammed into the ground.

It wasn't water.

She went limp in his arms as she, too, stared in horror.

A giant humped shape shrugged off asphalt as it lifted. At one end a flattened head shoved its way upward. A massive forked tongue cut through pavement like paper. The head swung side-to-side, opening more ground, slicing through it, sending boulder-size pieces flying.

As the crack widened the hump took shape like a long spine, twisted and coiled on itself like a tall tree warped by fire. Twenty feet away another head broke through, also with a forked tongue whipping through rock and asphalt. At first Max thought there were two creatures but as the long body surfaced he realized it was one, with a head at each end.

One head dipped and twisted, shedding pavement, then swiveled in their direction. The eyes were large dead ovals and as Max looked into them, icy dread froze his blood.

He flipped the safety off on his gun with a hand that shook, and stepped toward the nightmare. Casey's gun was also out and aimed. It wavered, but then she braced her feet and her hands became rock-steady.

The thing was almost fully out of the ground now, and as the creature roared the air filled with a stench like rotting earth.

The thing, fully out now, swung toward the general store. Both heads curved round to face the elderly couple. Mouths agape in terror, they pounded frantically on the door. On the other side of the door's glass window, Betty stood, eyes squeezed shut as if that would make the thing not real.

She didn't open the door.

"Run!" Casey screamed.

The creature surged upward.

Max fired. Walked forward, finger on the trigger. Fired again. Casey was right at his side, shooting her Glock. Someone came up on her other side, and she glanced over to see Albert, the mayor, jack a shell into a shotgun and raise it.

The thing pulled the old woman away from the door and gripped her with tongues from both heads. With the slightest flick it tore her in half as if she were nothing but tissue. Blood and intestines flew, splattering the ground. The old man screamed when both heads turned to him. The mouths opened and the roar was the wildest of winds. The old man was lifted by the roaring wind, spinning and twisting. And then the jaws of one head closed over him, swallowing him. It's throat bulged as the thing gulped the man down.

Casey backhanded tears away, struggling to do her job, to function. "We're not going to be able to kill it." She ejected a clip and slammed another into place.

"We're not even hurting it." Max couldn't see their bullets making any holes. He saw impact, but nothing more than if he was shooting an old BB gun. The shotgun had no impact either.

"Time to retreat?" Casey asked.

Max grabbed Albert's arm. "Time to retreat."

They ran back toward the fire department. The thing was now at the side of the general store, headed for the park and the railroad tracks.

It moved in an odd 's' shape with first one head taking the lead and then the other.

"The trucks," Casey said breathlessly.

Max veered away toward their two whales, parked next to the fire department. He climbed in and started up the engine, and then after a second, flipped the lights and sirens. Maybe the thing would follow the sound. Maybe he could lead it away somehow. But then his stomach sank.

There was no place to lead it. The bridges were gone. The town was sandwiched between the river and the Wall. The back road out was full of downed trees.

Casey had also flipped lights and sirens. He heard her tires squeal as she hit the gas and headed for the railroad crossing, the rear end of the truck fishtailing. Max floored the gas pedal, cursing the truck's slowness. But within seconds he was on Casey's tail.

Utility poles partially blocked the crossing but the thing slid up and over them. Casey spun the steering wheel, jerking the truck to the left. Gas pedal to the floor, heart pounding, she sideswiped a utility pole and hit the tracks with a bone-shuddering impact that lifted her up off the seat and slammed her back down.

On the other side of the tracks she jerked the wheel left toward Crescent Street. But she was going too fast and the truck spun out of control, its too-light rear sliding like she was on ice. She spun the wheel but couldn't get control back. The truck slalomed into the remains of a small white house. Casey was thrown against the steering wheel and then back against the seat. Her Kevlar vest took the brunt of the impact but the air was still forced out of her lungs.

The thing was down the railroad berm now and going up and over huge fallen cedar trees like they were kindling. One head faced back and its eyes stared straight into hers. She felt the terror crawl into her stomach and lodge there, a solid weight that froze her and pinned her in place. And then in her mind she heard her auntie's voice. She shook her head, struggling to refocus.

She clutched the wheel and tried to drag in a breath as Max's truck flew by her. He pulled to the right of the thing and she saw his window down, gun out and aimed.

He shot at the rear head from only a few feet away. She saw bullets strike. She saw holes, tiny and ludicrous against the massive contorted hide. The bullets didn't penetrate even far enough to draw blood. If the thing had blood.

Max's door flew open.

"No Max, no," she gasped, fumbling with her door handle. But she still couldn't get a full breath and lights began to sparkle at the edge of her vision.

No way in hell was she going to faint when Max needed her. She slammed her fist against the door, got it open, and clambered out.

An old Ford Aerostar van was canted against a laurel hedge. The thing shoved past the van, pushing it down the riprap embankment where it hit the whitewater river and was gone, joining trees and other debris from the quake.

The thing seemed to pause and then a long ripple moved the length of its body almost like it shifted shape. As Max came up behind it, palming another clip into his gun and raising his hands to fire, the thing slid down into the river as if following the van.

Max ran to the top of the riprap, standing on boulders meant to hold floodwater at bay, and stared as the thing surfaced and then sank below the rapids.

Casey's heart leapt as she caught movement out of the corner of her eye. But even as she spun to her left she recognized Albert. He passed her, heading toward Max, and she jogged after him.

"Mass hallucination," Albert said, breathing fast and shallow.

"No." Casey briefly pressed the fingers of one hand against her eyes. "I know what that was." Her old aunties would nod wisely if they heard her. And it would have been the first time she acknowledged their wisdom.

"You've seen that before?" Disbelief filled Max's voice. He holstered his gun and then put fingers under her chin to lift her eyes to his. "Did you hit your head?"

Casey pulled away from the warmth of his hand. "Seen one? No. But I know it. That was a Sisiutl."

"What the hell is a Sisiutl?" Albert asked.

"Legend," she said. "You know where my family is from, Max?"

Max shrugged. "You have relatives in Canada, right?"

"Vancouver Island." Casey's voice shook. "There, if you know who to talk to, Sisiutl is an old, old legend. Something I thought they made up to scare kids, you know?"

"Like a Coastal Indian boogeyman?" Albert asked.

"Kind of." Casey's hands shook and she cupped her elbows tightly. "It's a soul-searcher. In the stories I was told, it seeks people who can't control fear. It moves in water, even rain. And you never, never, want both heads to look at you at the same time."

"Because then it eats you," Max said.

"You will spin for eternity, no longer rooted to the earth." Casey's voice grew quieter and took on the cadence of a storyteller. "You will only know terror and your voice will forever be the screaming of wind."

"Unless, you know, it eats you," Max said.

Casey shook her head and then swiped tears from her cheeks. "In the old legends, if you face your fear and acknowledge it, accept it, Sisiutl will see Truth and supposedly then bless you with magic and leave. Some versions of the legend tell of it having three heads and being a god of warrior invincibility. After seeing that thing? I believe the version my aunties told me."

They were silent a moment staring at each other. And then Max started back toward the trucks. Casey and Albert followed him.

"I don't believe in myths or legends," he said. "I didn't believe in Godzilla when I was a kid, and I don't believe in Sisiutls."

When Casey opened her mouth to speak, Max held a hand up.

"Or at least I didn't." He met Casey's eyes. "Now I do. What do we do about it?"

"I have no idea," Casey said. "But if it comes back, getting away from it is going to be a bitch. The town is too small, too confined."

Max glanced at the river. "So what you're saying is, we need bigger guns."

Casey shivered. "I doubt bigger guns will help."

"Maybe we can get help from FEMA." Albert managed a shaky laugh, the sound so unexpected that the other two stared at him.

He shoved his hands into the pockets of his old jeans and shook his head. "We had this flood. Took out a lot of riprap here. To get emergency funding from FEMA, we had to do reams of paperwork. One thing we had to prove was that there were no Orca whales in the river."

"What?" Max asked. "What crazy idiot thought there would be whales up here in mountains and fresh whitewater?"

"FEMA," Albert said shrugging.

"The next time it floods, you're screwed," Max said. "No funding from FEMA."

"Right?" Albert asked. "No Orcas. But, hey, we do have a Sisiutl."

Casey didn't see the humor. She left them, heart-heavy, and walked up and over the railroad berm. At the general store she stopped, staring at the pools of blood and bits of bone and meat. The remains of two old people she had failed.

Samuel came crossed the street, his face white with shock, his pupils so dilated his eyes looked black.

"What the hell was that?"

Casey turned from the proof of her failure. How did you explain monsters? She didn't know and she hurt too much to try, so she decided on truth. "A Sisiutl. But it's gone. Into the river."

"Oh...uh...okay. It's not going to come back, is it?" He suddenly looked much younger than his twenty-three years.

Casey didn't respond. All she saw in her mind was the old couple looking to her for help. Grimly, she marched to the door and hammered her fist against the frame. After a long moment Betty slowly undid the locks and came out, shame and fear in her eyes.

It flashed through Casey's mind how many times she'd seen people, faced with terror, shut down, able to think of only themselves. She understood. She truly did.

But still.

She gripped the doorjamb and leaned toward Betty. "All you had to do was open your door. But you didn't."

"That demon would have gotten in." Betty's voice was high and shaky.

"I'm talking about coffee," Casey said, leaning right into Betty's face. "If you had shared one fucking cup of coffee. They'd have been safe inside with you when that thing came out. They'd still be alive."

Betty drew herself up. "And if you hadn't run and left them, they'd still be alive."

The words cut deeply and Casey felt the agony, knowing she would carry that failure, that grief, forever.

But she'd be damned if she'd show one ounce of weakness to this old woman. "One cup of coffee," she repeated, then turned her back and walked away.

6

Sharon sat at the edge of the river under the few remaining trees, waiting for the flood from the breaching dam. But when she heard the sound of a truck engine, she stood in surprise. Who else would be seeking out the flood?

Down the access ramp came a big old truck with a homemade canopy. It passed her and she caught a brief glimmer of a face, maybe a child, pressed against the passenger window. The driver, invisible to her, didn't pause, and she doubted they'd even seen her in the shadows. Without letting up on the gas, the truck drove into the small river and kept going, slow and steady. Obviously someone figured this was quicker than the blocked highway.

She gave a slight nod, wishing them luck. Children shouldn't die.

But then, when they were well over halfway across, the truck faltered, as if caught on something, and Sharon saw the water coming. Her heart raced. This was it. She ran forward and jumped into the path of the wave. The force of the water knocked her to her knees and she went under. Rocks shifted as she tried to regain her footing and she went under again. And then, right as her chest grew tight with coming death, right when she opened her eyes wide in the deep mossy green of underwater light, wide enough to see her ending, the wave passed.

Sharon scrambled to her feet, lungs sucking in rain-laden air. The old truck was long gone. She stood, soaked to her neck, shivering with the shock of the bitterly cold river. The water level dropped quickly until it was only about shin deep. And still dropped.

What the hell kind of flood was that?

A loud rattling rumble came from behind her and she turned to see another old rig of some sort coming down the access road to the parking area by the river. It was wide and boxy and rusty. Sharon watched it, shaking with cold and wondering if everyone was going to try and cross the river.

When the rig got to the water's edge, it stopped and the driver's window rolled down slowly, creaking as it went.

"The Culmback's breached," a young man said. "You need to get out of here. Climb in. We'll help you."

"The flood passed," Sharon said in disgust, throwing out her arm. "Piss-ant river."

"No, no," the young man said. "That was just the leading wave.

We saw it from the highway. Probably from when the dam first cracked. The flood's coming any second. We need to go, now."

A young woman in the passenger seat leaned across the driver. "We've got plenty of room."

Sharon stepped closer, cupping her elbows to hold the cold tremors in. Peering in the window she saw the young woman, plump, with brown hair and glasses. The young man was maybe eighteen but looked thirteen with fine tufts of whiskers, wide, scared eyes, and pimples.

There were two more kids in the back. She caught a glimpse of their movements.

But there was something else, in those few seconds that she looked at them. Something like gray shadows among them.

Something that felt like death surrounding them. Something that pulled at her. Maybe a faster way to die than drowning.

"Okay, thanks," Sharon said, going around the back of the vehicle.

A young man pushed open the small door so Sharon could climb in. The open space had a bench seat along each side. A girl sat there, clutching the edge of the bench. The young man pulled the door shut and then sat next to the girl. Scattered around the floor were backpacks and grocery bags.

"Hang on to something," the driver yelled, and hit the gas.

Sharon stumbled and the boy caught her, helping her to find a perch.

"Wow, man, like you're really lucky," the boy said. "We don't have much time."

Sharon wondered for a brief second why she didn't just wait for the real flood. But those odd gray shadows were still there, amorphous between the kids, fading around and through them like mist. It was only when she didn't look at them directly that they took on vaguely humanoid shape. Whatever they were, if she was even seeing them, she was sure of one thing. Death would be wherever these kids were going.

The front end of the vehicle dropped forward as if going down a steep hill, powered through the water, and then climbed the other side.

"We're following a friend of Tessa's," the boy said, gesturing up front toward the plump girl. "He's with an old couple. She saw them cross here, and it's, like, the only way to get out of town now the highway's fucked. But it took us a while to find something that would go through the water."

"The fire department had this just sitting by the station," the girl said. "It's an old 1940s Willys Jeep. Connor borrowed it."

The driver, obviously Connor, took a hand off the steering wheel long enough to raise a fist in the air.

"Where are you going?" Sharon asked.

"No idea, man," Connor said. "Just following Tessa's boyfriend."

"He's not my boyfriend," Tessa said, and even from Sharon's back seat view she saw the fire of a blush race up Tessa's neck. "I don't even know his name. He's just a guy that comes through work. But they looked like they knew where they were going and how to get there."

The jeep lurched sideways and Sharon fell against the girl, who caught her and then clung, as if Sharon could keep them both stable. When the jeep bumped up over a curb and made it to pavement, Connor hit the gas and followed rutted tracks into someone's back yard.

Sharon drew in a deep breath, teeth chattering, and finally looked past the shadows to actually see the young people. Connor and Tessa, and the two in the back.

All in McDonald's uniforms.

The jeep rattled like it was going to fall apart, but Connor managed to keep hold of the big steering wheel. Sharon saw the tracks he followed, and wondered if the optimism of these young people would end up saving them, or if they'd find the old truck they followed stuck.

But she remembered one of her father's sayings about necessity being the mother of invention. More cars were taking to the side roads in panicked attempts to get free of the gridlock on the highway. The Willys jeep had an advantage with its broad wheelbase and big tires. Out the small back windows Sharon watched cars getting stuck in boggy back yards.

"Dude, we're running out of time," the boy said, one hand splayed against the back window to hold himself steady.

"We don't need to get out of town if we can just find some higher ground," Tessa said.

Sharon wanted to lean back against the wall of the jeep, but they were bouncing around too much. She hung onto the edge of the bench seat like the other kids were doing, trying to brace herself. But where they were panicked, she was curious.

What were those shadows floating around the young people in the back of the jeep? It was like watching wisps of fog that had intent, softly moving from one person to another, tendrils wrapping around their bodies, almost as if stroking them.

"Something's smoking back here, dude," the boy said.

"Nothing we can do about it." Connor waved a hand. "Drowning or burning, take your pick, man."

Not smoke, Sharon thought. Definitely not smoke. If she looked directly at the shadowy movements, she saw only misty fog. But if she used her peripheral vision, looked out of the corners of her eyes, they looked human. She knew, somehow, that these shadows meant death.

None of them were drifting near her, though.

"Isn't this a back road to Startup?" the girl next to Sharon asked.

"Yes," Sharon said, not really caring. "What's your name?"

It seemed somehow like she should know the names of the people who were about to die with her. Because whatever these shadow things were, they sure as hell weren't there to rescue people from a flood.

"Oh, uh, Bea. Bea Jenkins." The girl reached out as if to shake Sharon's hand, then stared at her trembling fingers as if wondering what she was doing. She dropped them to her lap. "And this is Randall."

The boy just nodded, struggling to stay on the bench seat.

The jarring gait of the jeep eased somewhat as they reached pavement again, and Connor hit the gas. Then they were suddenly banged upward and slammed down as Connor barreled through a huge pothole that had opened up in the road. No one told him to slow down. When another car got in their way, he simply went out around it, over fences, down into drainage ditches, and at one point, straight through an outhouse-shaped board structure that looked like a homemade shelter for kids at a bus stop.

One of the shadows draped itself over Randall, who was still bracing himself with a hand against the back window. Sharon stared, transfixed, as a piece of fog slipped in to his open mouth. It slid in and in and in, paused, and then slowly withdrew. It looked…fuller…when it softly floated free.

A deep tremor shook Randall, and he bent suddenly, gagging.

"You okay?" Bea asked. She made it to her feet and stumbled over to his bench, dropping down to sit next to him.

Randall nodded, breathed in deeply, and then tried to speak. He coughed. "Just car sick I think."

"All this bouncing around and no side windows," Bea said, rubbing her hand between his shoulder blades. "You're freezing, too. Doesn't help."

No, Sharon thought. *It's not car-sickness. It's fog that wants to eat you.* She moved a hand gently through one of the tendrils. *Come on. I'm right here.*

The tendril coiled, cool and damp around her arm, sliding toward her shoulder. The piece shifted, took the vague shape of a hand, almost as if she was being caressed. She drew in a deep breath as it slid across her breast and paused over her heart.

Yes. Take it.

The ghostly hand withdrew, leaving her with a deep ache, with a

139

sense of not-yet.

Sharon's nipples were erect, burning with pain, and ultra-sensitive to the cotton of her bra. She bunched her hands into fists, flooded with an almost over-powering urge to reach out and beg the shadow to come back, to enter her, to take her, to take her life.

"You okay?" Bea stared. "You're, like, almost hyperventilating."

Sharon hung her head, gasping for air as a sudden rage twisted through her. She wanted to scream for the shadows to kill her. She wanted to leap into the fog.

But it was too late.

The shadows were sifting through cracks around doors and windows. Leaving her.

7

Ethan stood in the chilly morning air and listened as the students reported in on injuries. Paul Larsen had a deep laceration above his right hip but Nathaniel Salvatore had done a good job bandaging and wrapping it. Lucy Hsu's ribs were bruised but Ethan didn't think they were broken. Over all, the remaining injuries were minor. And Payton, never prepared, cried as she worked on the boots of her dead friend.

Gear was gathered and packed and the fire extinguished. Ethan looked at the site. John's body had been moved inside the bus with Amy and both covered with the tarp the kids had slept under. Ethan worried that the wild animal from the night before would find the bodies before they made it back, but there was nothing else he could do. He turned his attention to the living.

"Okay, listen up. We're climbing up to the logging road. The bank isn't stable. So go slow, double up with the injured. Test your footing before you commit, don't use tree roots for support unless you know they can handle your weight. Once you get to the top, find a secure place and wait. Don't wander off on your own. Questions?"

There weren't any. Ethan stood at the bottom of the slide waiting for each person to start the climb. Michael was going to have the hardest time, being the least physically fit.

Once all the students were working their way upward, Ethan looked back at the bus one last time.

No signs of Val.

Just the damp woods, leaves falling slowly in a twisting breeze, and two young people with their futures stolen. Taken during his watch. Taken by an earthquake. Something he couldn't retaliate against.

Shouldering his backpack, he started the climb several feet below Michael, watching the young man carefully to make sure he got to the top.

The logging road looked more like a narrow footpath but at least some of it remained. The slide had started high above them and rivulets of water ran downward, taking soil and rocks with them. The ground was clearly unstable, ready to give way if there was another aftershock.

"Where to?" Jennifer asked. "Back the way we came? Do you think the old bridge over the North Fork will still be there?"

Ethan thought a moment. "No idea. But if it's gone, we can follow the river to Index. So get some distance between us and this slide."

Rowan led the way, picking her footing over the most secure spots, heading for the undamaged part of the logging road. Ethan brought up the rear wondering just how far they were going to get over all the downed trees.

Although they made it to more solid ground, the forest around them was full of debris so solid ground didn't equate with easy walking. Tree trunks had to be clambered over or quickly scooted underneath. Boulders had to be maneuvered around. And the logging road was difficult to find in the traumatized landscape. Ethan pulled out his compass and took readings to make sure they were headed in the right general direction.

Rowan stepped off to one side and let the others pass her and Zack took the lead.

"What's up?" Ethan asked when he drew even with her.

"I think a wild animal or something is following us."

"Wild animals are going to be traumatized, too," Ethan said.

"I know." Rowan shoved loose tendrils of hair back behind her ear. "But I've seen something out of the corner of my eye a couple times now."

Before Ethan could respond, Zack yelled for him. He saw the kids clustered around the young man. Jennifer sank down on a log and buried her face in her hands.

"Oh my god! What are we going to do?" Payton's voice carried back to Ethan and he heard the edge of hysteria.

"Let me through," Ethan said, working his way through the group to where Zack and Spike stood motionless.

The logging road was gone. Another slide had simply taken out the side of the mountain in a more massive movement of earth than the one their bus had been involved in. Rivulets of water ran down the sharp sides of the slide, taking soil and rocks. As he watched, a tree toppled and went over with a loud crack, slowly sliding downhill.

"Any great ideas?" Spike asked.

Ethan shoved damp hair out of his face and studied the terrain. Even someone fit like Rowan would have problems, let alone injured kids. "We're going to have a rough time crossing that."

"Can we go up and around it?" Rowan asked. "Bushwhack?"

"Maybe," Ethan said, thinking. "But we're going to have to go back to find more stable ground. And we have to make sure we climb high enough above it. If another aftershock hits, we don't want to be anywhere near the edge. That slide's alive. It's not done moving yet."

"We're going to get lost," Payton said, her eyes wide.

"No we're not." Ethan shrugged off his backpack and unzipped a pocket to pull out a Green Trails map sealed in a Ziploc bag. "We're going to take compass bearings before we move. We're going to plot the route out on this topo map."

"But the topography is all different now," Zack said. "The map won't be any good, will it?"

"Compass readings will still read true." Ethan said. "All of you should have compasses and topo maps if you packed from the list I gave you. This will be a good exercise in orienteering."

Ethan unfolded his map as kids dropped backpacks and rummaged. He met Spike's eyes and saw Spike shake his head slightly. Ethan knew Spike had realized just how hard this was going to be. Following a trail with injured people would have been bad enough. Bushwhacking was going to be worse. And it was going to take a lot longer. Meaning the few protein bars kids might have left weren't going to go far enough. Ethan wished it was later in the season, when he might have been able to wild-forage food for the group. But this early in the season there wasn't much that was edible yet.

Rowan touched his arm lightly and spoke low. "What about the animal tracking us?"

"We don't know anything is, for sure," Ethan said. "Might have just been a deer."

"Maybe," Rowan said. "I didn't get a good look but I do think I saw antlers."

"Okay, listen up," Ethan said, raising his voice. "Take a break. Drink some water. Look over your maps and see if you can plot a route."

He saw them settle, gathering in small groups, then turned back to the slide. It was more like a boulder field and even as he watched, rocks shifted, trickled, tumbled. It was going to be too hazardous to cross, no doubt about that. He looked up at the high overhang of dirt and roots above the slide area. It would be worse to try and climb that vertical route of crumbling forest floor. Down would be equally steep. He hated the idea of backtracking and bushwhacking, but there didn't seem to be any other safe option.

"I say we go back to the bus," Michael said, coming up behind Ethan. They stood there watching as a small boulder slipped downhill, causing a tiny slide in its wake.

"And then what?" Spike asked from where he sat on a log, map in hand, next to Nathaniel. "We stay there until we run out of granola bars and starve to death?"

"Until search and rescue or someone comes for us," Michael said, lifting his chin and pulling his shoulders back in defiance. "People know we're here."

"It doesn't matter if they know or not," Rowan said. "We talked about this last night, remember? Think about the bridges between here and Monroe."

"What about them?" Michael asked. "Maybe the quake was just here."

"And maybe it wasn't." Zack said. "Rowan's right. We need to get as close to rescue as we can before we run out of food."

Ethan only half-listened to their debate, knowing Rowan and Zack were right. He studied the slide area intently, watching the movement of land, scoping out what just might be a fairly stable route.

"Maybe we could, like, hunt," Payton said. "Stay at the bus and build traps or something for wild animals. You know, like frontiersmen used to do."

"You know how to gut and skin a deer so it's edible?" Zack asked. "Because I sure as hell don't."

"We could try," Payton said, putting a hand on his arm. "If we stay together I know we can make it."

A loud snap, like a thick tree branch breaking free, came from behind them. Startled, Ethan swung around. He heard Payton give a small scream of fear, saw Michael step behind Zack. Saw Spike move in front of Lucy.

"What the hell?" Spike said.

Nathaniel pointed back along their route. "There's something back there."

Ethan saw it, too. A deeper shadow in the trees. Something human in size, but somehow off, as if denser.

"Maybe it's a bear. Like the one from last night," Zack said. His hands were clenched tight into fists at his side.

"Bear?" Lucy, one arm held protectively against her bruised ribs, took a step backward.

"That's not a bear," Rowan said.

"Where did it go?" Payton's voice rose in fear.

Ethan's neck hairs stood at attention. Rowan was right. It was no bear. But he didn't know what it was, either. Too tall to be a deer. And moving oddly, almost furtively. He flashed on the bus where something had lapped at Amy's blood. Then thought of Paul with his laceration. Lucy and her ribs. Vulnerable because of their injuries. The air scented with fresh blood.

"We're crossing the slide. Now."

"We'll never make it," Nathaniel said.

"Don't have much choice." Spike squeezed Nathaniel's shoulder. "Can't wait for that thing to come out of the trees at us. And I'm sure as hell not going closer to it."

"Listen up." Ethan gestured the group closer while scanning the slide. "There's a somewhat stable route, right above where that downed tree quit sliding. We go slow. Test every foot and handhold before you put weight on a rock. Spread out so if someone starts a slide it doesn't take all of us. Take your time. Don't get freaked out by whatever wild animal is back there. Just concentrate on slow and steady."

"Easy to say." Zack hitched his backpack straps more securely.

The others laughed tentatively, as if his words gave them permission to admit they were also afraid.

"I mean it." Ethan pulled his gun out of the pack. "I'm staying here until you're all across. Nothing gets past me. So you have plenty of time."

Rowan, Ethan noticed, had already stepped forward. The others watched as she cautiously made her way out onto the boulder field. She studied the ground carefully before each movement, testing each rock before trusting it.

"Watch what she's doing," Ethan said. "Do the same thing. Let her get about ten yards out and then another one goes. Don't go higher up the slide than the people in front of you so you don't bring rocks down on them."

Ethan turned his back on the slide, on Rowan, trusting her instincts. If the hillside gave way there would be nothing he could do for her anyway. There was movement again in the trees and he squinted, trying to see clearer. Had that been a flash of orange? He glanced over his shoulder. Rowan was moving steadily and Jennifer was now a few feet out, following.

"I'm not going," Michael said. "I'm going back to the bus."

"What about that thing back there?" Zack asked.

"It's just a bear or something." Michael stared into the trees. "It will be freaked out from the quake. I can scare it off."

"It's not a bear, and you're not going," Ethan said. "We stick together. I know you're scared, but you're crossing those rocks."

"I'm not scared." Michael crossed his arms over his ample belly and chest, but his eyes shifted back to the slide. "I'm just not going. It's stupid to leave shelter for the unknown. That's what you're always telling us in class. If we get lost, stay put."

"You're right," Ethan said, staring into shadows along the road. Wind moved through the trees making it hard to tell what was natural movement and what wasn't. "Glad you paid attention. But this isn't a normal situation and no one's coming for us anytime soon. And that bus wasn't on a stable slope either."

Zack moved out onto the slide. A few heavy drops of rain splatted on rocks.

Nathaniel pulled on his backpack straps to tighten them. "If I can do it, Michael, you can. I'm not much for physical activity either."

"What are you saying?" Michael swung toward Nathaniel. "You saying we're alike? Cause we're not."

"Oh, I agree," Nathaniel said. "I just meant neither of us is in physical shape. So if I can do it, you can."

"I'm in shape, you lightweight." Michael thumped his broad stomach. "All muscle."

"Shut up," Ethan said, his nerves and patience shot. "No discussion. Everyone goes. You see that?"

Everyone shifted to look where he pointed at the trees off to the side of the logging road. They clearly saw movement, climbing rapidly upward. The human shape was evocative but each time Ethan tried to focus, to convince himself that he saw arms, or legs, or a head, the shape seemed to shift. And there was something seriously wrong with the head. He remembered the fire, the way a creature had tried to manipulate him to move. It had to be the same animal, whatever it was.

"What's it doing?" Paul asked, hands pressed to his side.

"It's going to flank us, I think," Ethan said, stomach sinking. "Maybe go up and over and get to the other side while we're strung out on the boulder field. Payton, your turn. Get going."

Rowan was just stepping out onto more solid ground on the far side. Ethan, watching her drop her backpack and bend over, realized how vulnerable she was there, alone. Had he just sent kids to their death? If he called her back, if the kids tried to turn around on the slope, they'd slide for sure. And whatever that thing was would just circle back.

"Shoot it," Paul said, his face pale beneath the acne scars.

"He's right," Lucy said. "Can't you just kill it?"

Ethan's instincts screamed that shooting the creature, and killing it, would be two very different things. Not that he had a chance of hitting it, the way it moved through the trees, and him with just a Walther. He shook his head.

"It's too far away. Handguns aren't accurate, especially at a distance."

Nathaniel raised a hand to Ethan in farewell, and moved onto the slide. Ethan saw his rapid breathing, his jerky, nervous movements.

"Hey Nathaniel!"

Nathaniel paused and looked back, sweat glistening on his forehead.

"Take a deep breath and slow down. Remember, you have to

show Michael how to climb."

Nathaniel managed a weak smile, gave Ethan a thumb's up, and when he turned back to the rocks, looked a little more in control.

Ethan wished now he'd gone first. If whatever wild animal was following them got across the top before he did, those already there didn't stand a chance. "What the hell is it?" he asked under his breath.

He heard a small scream and whipped around in time to see Lucy, out on the slide, slip. She fell a few feet but caught up against a boulder that luckily held. He breathed out heavily in relief when her fall only dislodged a small cascade.

"Don't try climbing up to the others," he yelled out to her. "Just keep going."

Lucy raised a hand in acknowledgement and moved forward. He saw blood on her hands and seeping through a tear in her jeans. But she climbed smoothly, one arm tight to her side supporting her ribs. She looked so tiny and vulnerable out there that Ethan had to turn away.

Rowan straightened and Ethan saw her scanning the top of the slide, frowning. Jennifer made it across and dropped to sit on the ground, head hanging. Zack joined them and went up to Rowan, pointing toward the bluff above them. Ethan didn't have to hear him to know what he was saying. After a brief moment, Rowan dropped her pack, unzipped a pocket, and pulled out her large, folding serrated knife that she used for cutting tree branches. Ethan supposed it was better than no weapon but she'd have to be in close proximity to use it. His heart thudded. He needed to be over there.

Paul was now on the boulder field following Spike, and the only ones left were Michael and Ethan.

"Go," Ethan said.

"Ain't happenin'." Michael gripped his elbows in tightly cupped hands but even so he was shaking.

"Look buddy, there's no time to mess around." Ethan shoved the gun into the pack. "You go now, or you stay back here by yourself. Whatever that wild animal is, you think it's going to keep going after a group when it sees one easy prey all by himself over here?"

Michael stared into the trees so long that Ethan started to move out without him, hoping to jolt him into awareness. But then Michael shook his head and headed for the rocks, stumbling past Ethan. Ethan gave him a small lead but impatience wouldn't let him allow the same gap between them as he'd told the others to keep.

Granite immediately became his world. That and the backside of Michael. Grit bit into his hands and he wished he'd taken a moment to pull gloves out. Too late now. The ground shifted under his boots with the small rat-like scrabbling of falling rocks and pebbles. The urge to drop to hands and knees, to hug the earth like a leech, was strong.

Michael felt it, too. He had his arms wrapped around a large rock, breathing heavily.

"Take your time," Ethan said behind him, wishing he could push the kid forward.

Michael nodded, hung his head a minute, then let go of his anchor and took a step.

And up ahead, Paul fell.

8

The ground just gave way under him. It wasn't a big slip, and Paul managed to catch himself by grabbing on to the ragged edge of a huge granite boulder. He dangled briefly, kicked with his boots, and gained purchase on somewhat solid ground. Ethan saw those on the far side reach out to grab each other as if by hanging on there, they could help Paul hang on here.

There was a second where Ethan remembered to breathe, seeing Paul steady himself.

Until the huge boulder slid. Before Ethan's heart could jump out of his chest, the boulder seemed to briefly catch and hold.

"Holy shit," Michael said.

"Paul!" Ethan yelled. "Go!"

Paul looked up at the boulder and frantically scrambled sideways. His struggle to find purchase sent rocks and debris cascading out from under the boulder and down the steep slope. Ethan moved forward, oblivious to the danger he put Michael in by pushing past him. In horror he watched the boulder shift downslope, catch briefly again, and then almost gracefully, tip.

Paul never stood a chance. Tons of weight rolled right on top of him, pinning his torso and lower body. The rock slid a couple feet downhill, dragging Paul under it, and then came to a stop.

"Fuck!" Ethan went uphill above the boulder.

"We're coming!" Spike shouted from the other side.

Ethan saw Nathaniel and Spike starting his way, their faces tight and grim.

"No!" he shouted. "Stay there!"

He drew up beside Paul, small rocks sliding out from under his boots. The rain was coming heavier now, making the boulder slick. He saw the open eyes, the blood pooling out of nose, mouth, ears.

"We can push it off him." Michael, gasping for air, was close enough to reach toward the boulder.

"No," Ethan said. "No, man. We push it off, it starts an avalanche, and we go down with it."

"Then what?" Michael asked.

"We get to safety," Ethan said.

"No way. No way. You're the teacher! Fix this!"

Ethan saw the rising panic in the boy. He needed Michael angry and moving, not terrified and frozen.

"Quit questioning every fucking thing I say!" he yelled into Michael's face. "Get your ass moving, now!"

Michael stared into Ethan's eyes and Ethan saw the panic fade, saw the belligerent attitude slide back into place. He was still going into shock, pale, starting to sweat, hands shaking. But he was also getting angry.

Good.

"Come on Michael. Follow me. Step where I step."

Carefully they made it to the other side where hands reached for them, caught at Ethan, held on. Lucy and Jennifer gripped each other, sobbing. Rowan was pale and frozen, staring out at the slide with eyes dilated with terror.

"What do you need?" Zack, the rock climber, asked. "Can we make some sort of sling and lift the boulder? What?"

Ethan shook his head. "Nothing we can do." He dropped his pack, sank to his knees. "He's dead."

Michael took a step sideways and collapsed on a large clump of salal. He pulled an arm up to his face to muffle the sobs that shook through him. Nathaniel went to him and put a hand on his shoulder, but Michael shoved it off.

"Are you sure?" Payton asked, tears coursing down her cheeks and mixing with rain. "I mean, like, maybe he's just pinned."

"I'm sure." Ethan covered his eyes with one hand, elbow on his knee. Paul. Amy. John. Just kids. His responsibility.

The others crowded around him. Jennifer and Lucy still gripped each other's hands and Jennifer was breathing rapid and shallow. There were tears in Rowan's eyes now, but she brushed at them and walked away from the group.

Jennifer sank to the ground, gasping. Lucy's shoulders heaved with broken sobs.

Ethan reached for Jennifer and put a hand on the back of her neck. "Listen to me. I want you to take a breath in through your nose. Hold it, let it out through your mouth."

Jennifer shook her head, a hand going to her chest. Her face drained of color.

"You're hyperventilating and you're going to pass out," Ethan said, keeping his voice low and steady. "So you're going to do what I tell you. Look at me."

Jennifer shook her head again but then raised her face and met his eyes.

"Good girl. Now. One breath for me. In through your nose.

Now hold it. And let it out slow."

Lucy was curled on the ground but Spike, face pale and set, went to her and lifted her up.

"Okay, another breath," Ethan said, nodding to Spike.

Jennifer took a deep breath and held it. When she breathed out, some color came back to her face.

"Rowan, come sit with Jennifer and keep her breathing slow." Ethan stood and went to Zack, who was on his knees, cheeks wet with tears. "Come on buddy, let's get you up."

Spike deposited Lucy on a downed tree, went to Nathaniel and scooped him up, and put him down next to Lucy. Then he knelt in front of them holding their hands and talking. Ethan couldn't hear the words, but Lucy drew in a shaky breath and nodded.

Zack stumbled to his feet, deep tremors rippling through him. "We're all going to die."

"Maybe," Ethan said. "I'm not going to lie to you. This is bad. But I'm going to fight for you. You hear me?"

Zack swiped tears away with the wet sleeve of his jacket, hands shaking. He managed a nod.

Ethan's hands tightened into fists. This was supposed to have been a simple fucking field trip. An easy hike. An easy assignment. There and back. His biggest worry had been that bus driver. And Payton's preparedness. Now his kids were dying. His chest ached like the boulder that killed Paul sat on his heart.

Nathaniel came to Ethan, his cheeks wet with tears. "Should we go back out there and bury him?"

"We can't," Spike said. "If we start moving shit around the whole mountain is going to come down on top of us."

"We can't leave him like that," Rowan said. "We just can't."

"I'll go," Ethan said, his voice husky with heartache. "Cover him as best I can and mark the spot with something. When this is over we'll come back for him. For all three of them."

He bent for his pack but as he lifted it, Lucy screamed. Nathaniel grabbed her as Ethan swung back to the slide, where she pointed.

A man, a not-man, something, moved fast and sure-footed down the boulder field to the rock and Paul. Ethan stared, frozen. It was man-shaped but taller than normal. Skins, or at least things with fur, were tied around its body and draped over its shoulders. Something like huge antlers came out of its head. The hand that reached toward Paul had extraordinarily long fingers that looked almost, from this distance, like narrow claws. And wrapped around its waist like a surreal kilt was a pumpkin orange coat.

Ethan heard a thud behind him and glanced over his shoulder to see Jennifer collapsed, knees up and arms tucked in. The sight kicked his brain back into gear. With shaking hands he fumbled in his pack for the Walther. Fear and rain made his hands slick as he chambered a round.

"What's it doing?" Nathaniel whispered. "Oh, god, what is it doing?"

The creature was now bent over Paul. It reached out and seemed to gently stroke the side of Paul's face with a finger, like a mother would stroke away a child's nightmare. But then the hand came up and a long, bloody strip hung from one claw. As they stared in horror, the thing swallowed the strip of Paul's skin.

Ethan fired. He saw the bullet ricochet off the boulder near what would have been the thing's waist if it were human. It barely reacted, reaching out to Paul again. Ethan fired a second time. They all saw the bullet hit the hand that pulled another strip from Paul. The creature recoiled backward, staring at its hand.

Ethan blew out a breath and held it, pulling up his training. His arms steadied, his mind cleared. Slowly he squeezed the trigger, aiming for the thing's head. But at the last second it lurched uphill behind the boulder and the shot again ricocheted off granite.

And then it was back, the long arm coming around rock, reaching for Paul. Ethan suddenly realized the thing was going to be preoccupied with its meal. It might mean time for those still alive. He looked over his shoulder. Payton was on the ground in an obvious faint. He saw terror in their eyes.

"Go!" he shouted.

They didn't seem to comprehend him. Nathaniel and Jennifer stumbled to their feet, but then turned in circles as if lost. And then Rowan raised her arms.

"This way! Come on!"

Spike bent over Payton, straightening with her in his arms. He ran toward Rowan and his movement broke through the wall of terror and shock. When Ethan saw they were headed down the remains of the logging road, he turned back to the creature and raised the gun again.

But it was gone.

And so was Paul's head. Only a bloody stump remained, along with a trail of blood going back up the slide and into the tree line.

Ethan grabbed his pack, and keeping the gun in hand, went after his kids.

9

The rain stopped some time during the night. When Anya came out of the cabin the next morning, she was dressed in jeans, thick socks in heavy boots, a silk undershirt, a long sleeved tee shirt, and a logger's wool plaid coat. And yet she shivered, as if she'd never thawed after the events of the day before, or from the night before when something had stalked the cabin in the dark.

The quiet of deep shock hung over the place and the forest was devastated.

Anya gripped the rifle and stepped slowly away from the security of the cabin. Bird ventured further, but she noticed he stayed within a smaller perimeter than normal. She studied the torn up ground in front of the door then walked around the cabin, peering at mud and forest debris. There should have been tracks. Even with the rain, there should have been at least indentations left. But she saw nothing. No proof that anything had been out there the night before.

It was hard now, in the light of day, with misty clouds hanging low and dampness still in the air, to remember the fear. Had she really heard something outside the cabin, or had she simply been in shock from all that had happened? A nightmare maybe?

Bird snuffled something on the ground, then gave a short bark and backed away from whatever it was. He growled low. She walked to where he crouched.

A piece of coarse material was half buried in mud. She bent and pulled it free. Pumpkin orange. So something had been out there. She didn't have any clothes that color. Anya fingered the piece and then slipped it into a pocket.

She turned back to the cabin and froze. While there were no tracks on the ground, she stared at proof that something, indeed, had been outside the cabin last night.

Along the top of the door and the log lintel, out of her reach, long gouges cut deeply into the wood. She moved closer. Something was caught in one of the gouges. She stepped through the doorway, shoulders hunched as if whatever hung up there was going to drop on her head. Inside, she took one of the sturdy wood chairs from by the table and hauled it back outside.

Standing on the chair helped and she was able to reach up and tug the piece free. With one hand against the doorjamb for balance, she stared.

It looked like a five-inch thin strip of chicken.

"Damn it!"

In her fear and exhaustion last night she hadn't secured the chicken coop. She climbed down from the chair, dropped the strip, and ran around the corner of the cabin. Bird followed closely.

The coop door still hung from one hinge. The chickens were busy scratching in the debris of fallen needles and tree branches as if nothing had happened the day before. Anya quickly counted, then counted again. All twelve were there.

"Well that's weird."

Bird gave in to his favorite temptation and lunged at the birds, sending them scattering.

"Knock it off," Anya said over the squawking, more out of distracted habit then because she thought he'd finally listen.

She watched the chickens a moment longer, then, frowning, returned to the cabin. Maybe the wild animal from the night before had found an owl or something. When she looked closer there were traces of dried blood on the strip. Whatever it had come from, she had too much to do to waste time over a piece of meat.

She briefly thought about what wild animal was tall enough to leave behind something so high on the wall, but her thoughts skittered away. It was easier to ignore it than to let the fear at the edges of her mind sneak in.

The coop had to be secured. The cabin had to be evaluated, especially the roof. Anya didn't want to spend another night huddled in the blackness wondering if something could get in. When it got dark, she wanted to be locked up tight and secure inside.

Just in case it came back. Whatever it was.

Anya worked steadily in the damp and chill air. But she wasn't able to lose herself in the tasks like she normally did. She was deeply unsettled as she pulled branches into a burn pile, screwed hinges on the coop door back into place, and climbed the ladder to her roof. She kept pausing to scan the clearing, the forest fringe, looking for movement, looking for something that shouldn't be there. She kept her rifle close. She kept Bird close.

But it wasn't until early afternoon that her dog growled, low and deep.

Anya's boot slipped and she stumbled off the second to last rung of the ladder, hitting the ground harder than expected. Her hand slid on the wooden upright and a splinter bit into her palm. She barely noticed it over the racing of her heart.

Anya lunged to the wall of the cabin and grabbed up the rifle. She spun around and stood, back to the false security of solid logs. She heard nothing but her blood pulsing. She pointed to the ground next to her and Bird took up his heel position. Slowly, trying to not make any noise, she moved along the wall, edging to the corner. From there she could make a run for the door and get inside.

Bird moved with her, teeth bared, ears back, and head lowered. He stared to the east across the clearing but Anya saw no movement. She flipped the rifle's safety off anyway and raised the gun to her shoulder.

At that moment, she hated Devon with a pure, white-hot rage. He'd left her. Left her alone. There was no help, no salvation, no rescue.

If he'd come out of the woods she probably would have shot him.

But nothing moved that shouldn't. Trees swayed in the cold wind. Alder and cottonwood leaves shivered and turned belly up, like they always did when rain came. But now their pale undersides seemed weirdly vulnerable. Dark clouds stretched across the sky, also moving to the pull of the rising wind.

Nothing unusual.

But Bird snarled.

Anya reached the corner of the cabin. Leading with the rifle, she quickly looked out and then pulled back. Nothing happened, so she went around the edge, slower this time. Carefully, she stepped up onto the deck, the old wood squeaking under her weight. Bird followed. Giving in to the fear, Anya sprinted for the door, ran inside with her dog, and slammed the door behind her.

In the semi-gloom of the cabin, she crossed to the window and stood at its edge, peering outside. Her hands and knees shook, her bladder felt loose and hot like she was about to pee herself, and her scalp was tight as if all her hair stood on end.

And there it was. Something coming out of the trees. A tall man with sticks stuck in his long, scraggly hair. Anya, breathing fast, squinted but couldn't make out any details. She propped the rifle at her feet and grabbed her binoculars that hung on a hook by the door.

A man. Taller than normal. Angular and bony as if skin stretched too tight. Some sort of weird orange cloth tied around its waist, the same color as the scrap she'd picked up. And those weren't sticks stuck in his hair. Anya adjusted the focus on the binoculars. It looked like he had shoved antlers in to the tangles.

He looked left and right, then straight ahead at the cabin and stepped more fully out of the tree line. He carried something under one arm but it was still in shadow. He reached across his waist with one hand and she saw abnormally long fingers, almost like claws. He plucked something off whatever he carried and lifted it to his mouth.

He chewed as he walked forward with an odd, lurching gait.

Anya panned down with the binoculars, thinking maybe he was injured. But then she focused on what he held under his arm.

A head.

Blood was coagulated around long thin wounds along the face. Tendons and nerve endings hung from the neck like the head had been twisted off rather than cut. Horrified, Anya was barely aware of dark hair, of one wide, unseeing eye, of a hole where the other eye should have been.

The man, the thing, reached across again and with one long claw, or fingernail, peeled off a strip of skin and put it in his mouth.

The binoculars hit the floor. Anya went to her knees, rising bile choking her. She gagged and then heaved, and heaved again. She swiped a cold hand across her mouth and tried to stand but her legs shook too hard. She reached for the rifle but couldn't grip it and it slid to the floor.

"Oh god, oh god," she whispered.

She crawled forward and managed to take hold of the rifle butt. The door. She had to brace the door. She had to block the windows. Somehow.

Pushing a hand against the log wall, she managed to haul herself upright, hugging the rifle to her chest. Bird stood in the middle of the room, head still lowered, front legs braced, staring at the door.

How close was the thing? She didn't want to see. But the fear of not knowing was greater. With chattering teeth she came up to the side of the window and looked out.

The man, the thing, was close. Maybe fifty yards from the cabin.

Anya pulled back and scanned the room. Seeing the creature so close to her home froze her terror. Her breathing deepened, her jaw clenched, her heart thudded slow and heavy. Her eyes skimmed the room. There was no time to figure out how to block windows or the door.

She had to kill it before it got in.

"Bird, here."

The dog came quickly to her side. She gripped the rifle, checked to make sure a round was chambered, lifted it to her shoulder, and with one shaking hand reached out to pull open the door. As soon as there was an opening wide enough, she stepped through, holding the rifle steady, finger on the trigger.

The thing was only a few yards away, coming forward slowly, snacking. It stopped when she came through the door, studying her with eyes too big, too dark, too bottomless to be human.

"Get out of here, you fucker."

It dropped the head, which hit the ground with a wet thud, flexed its clawed hands, and bent forward as if to catch her scent.

Anya breathed deep and held it, resting her cheek against the butt of the rifle, siting in. The thing was going to launch and she was going to blow it back wherever it came from.

She caught movement to her left, and so did the thing. It swung away from her, fingers opening and closing, the nails clicking. Anya risked a glance away.

A huge grizzly stood in the clearing, near the yew tree. Possibly the same one she'd seen the day before. It reared up and slammed both massive front paws into the earth, coughing out a deep warning. And then it rose up on its back legs again and roared.

Anya, still with the rifle in place, swung back toward the man creature then back at the grizzly. Which was the bigger threat? Her breath came fast again as she lost her focus, her aim. The rifle butt jittered against her cheek.

Bird moved beside her and she saw he was focused on the creature, as if the grizzly wasn't even there.

That answered the threat question. The rifle steadied. She squeezed the trigger. The rifle kicked against her shoulder but she was prepared for it. She smoothly ejected the shell and slid in another bullet. Squeezed again.

Her aim was true. Through the scope she saw the bullets hit. She saw black blood oozing out of wounds. But the creature didn't even flinch.

The grizzly roared again, the terrifying sound of an apex predator, of something that wasn't killed easily. Anya glanced at it in time to see it charge. Quickly, she chambered another round and smoothly brought the rifle into place, firing. She kept going in her rhythm now, focused on the creature.

The grizzly was a massive blur coming from her left, attacking the thing. Anya fired until the bear was too close and she feared hitting it. She lowered the rifle and gripped Bird's fur tight in one hand. The dog was rigid, muscles locked, straining forward. She dropped to one knee and grabbed Bird tight but he broke free and launched off the deck.

"Bird! No!"

Anya, gripping the rifle, started forward but stumbled to a stop. The little boy was there, coming around the yew tree.

"Stay back!" she yelled at him.

He glanced at her, but his focus was on the battle before them. The bear, roaring, slammed into the thing, its massive jaws clamping down on the creature's middle. Bird danced around them both, darting in to snap at the creature. Anya fumbled a shell out of her pocket, chambering another round.

The creature's hands stretched out, long nails digging in on both sides of the bear's neck. The bear threw up its head, dragging the thing upward, and then tossed it to the side as if it weighed no more than a broken branch. The creature hit the ground, rolled, came to its feet.

Without thinking it through, Anya seized the moment, the clear shot. Up came the rifle and she fired, ejected the shell, chambered a round, fired again. And again, stopping only when the bear rushed the creature and crossed her line of fire. The creature's antlered head swung toward Anya. The black gaze was like ice, freezing her heart.

And then it turned, running in its jerky gait for the tree line. The bear followed, with Bird racing at its side.

The boy moved a few steps forward as if to follow the bear, but then turned toward Anya.

"Stay here," she said. "It's not safe to go after them."

The boy studied her, head tilted slightly. And then he made an odd gesture, touching his fingertips to his heart and unfolding them, palm up, toward her. Before she could do more than just stare, he turned back in the direction he'd come from.

Anya felt the vibration of the earth through her boots as the bear loped back into the clearing. Blood dripped from wounds on its neck and she saw the blacker blood of the creature around the bear's jaws. Bird came behind the bear, but angled toward her when they came out of the trees.

Anya's breath caught. Would the bear now turn on her? But it passed without even swinging its head in her direction. She stood, unable to move, as it followed the boy. They passed the yew tree and were lost to sight, slipping into the shadowed forest understory.

Anya sank down on the deck, the rifle beside her. Her muscles were suddenly like water, worthless. Bird flopped at her feet, panting heavily. Wind moaned through the treetops and a few fat raindrops hit the ground. More followed, a curtain of rain moving down the mountain pushed by the wind.

Anya sat there, watching the rain, unable to move.

The boy was gone and her heart ached. Twice in as many days wasn't a hallucination.

The creature was gone and her stomach twisted in fear. Whatever it was, wherever it had come from, she hoped it was dead. But the chill in her blood said it wasn't.

The head of a stranger wasn't gone. It sat out there, rain pooling in the empty eye socket.

"That's it," she said to Bird. "We're leaving."

Anya went inside, pulled her pack out, and tossed it on the bed. The rifle rested on the quilts next to it. She grabbed warm clothing and shoved socks and sweaters into the pack, then went to the kitchen shelves and started pulling down dehydrated packets of food that she took with her when hunting. She'd need her headlamp. Fresh batteries. Her bedroll. Her hands shook as she tossed things on the bed.

Being alone out here on a normal day was scary and intimidating. There were so many things that could go wrong. If she didn't know how to fix something, if she was injured or sick, she could easily die. Death was close in the mountains, a shadow always in the back of her mind. Nature in all its glory didn't care anything about the little speck of humanity on its flank. She knew this. She'd lived with that underlying fear for a long time.

She'd seen it up close when her infant son died.

In some ways she welcomed the day-to-day fear. It made her pause and think before doing something. It made her remember to take the rifle with her when she went out the door. To make sure Bird was within calling range. To make sure firewood was cut and dry before winter, that the food cache was full.

But she'd also had Devon there, even if he wasn't especially useful. He was terrible at chopping firewood. He threw up every time she gutted a fish. Yet he had been a warm body next to her in the deep night that said she wasn't completely, totally, alone.

But then, she'd lost the baby, that tiny life, after only being in her arms a few hours. And she'd realized even with Devon there, she was alone. The fear had been stronger in those weeks right after she'd lost that part of her. The sense of isolation had been overwhelming.

But now, Devon was truly gone. There was no one to lean on. No one who would believe a grizzly bear had come to her rescue. No one to believe a head sat out there in the thickening rain. And she couldn't face all of it alone. The low-grade fear slowly rolled over into terror.

So she'd leave. Pack up and head out now, so that she would be well down the trail before dark. If there was still a trail to follow. If not, it wouldn't be the first time she'd bushwhacked through the forest. She could make it through the devastated mountains. She could make it to Jumpoff Ridge that led to Index.

Eventually she'd find people. She wouldn't be alone to face whatever this monster was, this thing disgorged by the earthquake.

She wouldn't be alone.

Anya took a box of shells out of a drawer and dropped them next to the rifle. Her breath caught. She sank onto the bed, making the old mattress sag and the box tip, spilling the shells.

She wouldn't be alone. But she'd be running away. Leaving behind the strange little boy.

She'd already lost the child of her blood and bone. Could she leave a boy alone out here? If it was too dangerous for her, what would it be like for a child?

Anya leaned her elbows on her knees, burying her fingers in her hair. Was the boy even real? Was she going insane? She probed her scalp, pressing so hard her head ached. Maybe during the earthquake she'd been hit with something.

She stood and crossed the room, throwing open the door. Cool, damp air eddied in around her. She looked across the clearing and into the shadows under the trees.

"Two choices," she said.

Bird came up beside her and leaned into her hip. She rested a hand on the warmth of his head.

"We go now. Get out of here. Find people."

She would be exposed out there in the woods. Alone and with no secure shelter.

"Or we stay in case that little boy comes back. In case he needs us."

She would have shelter but she would be alone to face whatever the hell was going on.

And didn't that little boy have a huge grizzly bear to take care of him?

Anya slowly walked back to her bed. She scooped up the fallen shells and put them back in the box. And then put the box back in its drawer.

She swiped tears from her cheeks and blew out a heavy breath of resignation. She couldn't leave her child, or the bear's child. She crossed the room once more, calling to Bird. She'd have to figure out a way to barricade the door and windows before nightfall.

Bird came in from the small deck and Anya reached for the handle to pull the door tight against the woods, the unknown, the cold. But then she held her palm to the door, stopping its momentum as she stared out into the rain.

The head was gone.

10

The Willys Jeep survived a teenager driving it over a ripped landscape. The engine idled roughly but still ran. The young people, along with Sharon, stood outside in the rain, lined up along the side of the jeep, watching the end of the city below them. Bea sobbed behind hands pressed over her mouth. Randall stood frozen, staring at the jeep, refusing to see. Connor was silent, tears washing into the rain coursing over his face. Tessa was strong and silent, a plump girl with her chin up, facing the death of strangers as if the only way to honor their passing was by holding her horror in. Her hands shook, even clenched in tight fists.

The gray shadows had left the jeep. Sharon watched them disintegrate in the wind and rain like the fog they resembled. Ghost fog that wafted on currents of air flowing downhill toward what had been Sultan.

Sharon had imagined the flood of the Wallace River. A big wave that would overflow the banks and maybe take out the bridge. Maybe businesses and homes near the river. Definitely a big chunk of highway.

She hadn't pictured Sultan gone.

She hadn't pictured floodwaters following the highway, swamping east toward Startup and west toward Monroe.

She and the kids stood on their hill and watched an up-swelling of water higher than single story houses take everything in its path. The big berm the railroad had built to protect their tracks from the river on the other side simply slowed the flow from the dam a little before it kept going, shoving the tracks to the Skykomish River. All those cars that had been fighting to get out of town were now underwater. And not just flooded. They'd been picked up and thrown, tossed into piles against the barriers of railroad berm, bridge abutments, debris from the quake.

Some people down there were alive. Hanging on to whatever they could find. But most simply floated. At least, those who had been able to get out of vehicles or buildings. Sharon knew many more were still held underwater, and would be for a long, long time.

Even worse were those who fought to climb debris and get higher than the water. Some people made it. Some didn't. Some helped each other. Some killed those in their way. She saw people kicked, shoved back into the floodwaters, ruthlessly pulled down to make room for someone else to climb. Human decency, compassion, and empathy were now the minority. Now it was survival of the fittest. Or the most ruthless.

And there was no rescue coming.

"We have to help."

Sharon looked over at Bea, standing next to her. "How, exactly?"

"I don't know. Maybe we could get down there by the water's edge and try to reach people."

Sharon touched her arm lightly but the girl only glanced at her before going back to staring fixedly at the carnage below.

"Okay Bea. Listen to me. There's no way to get back down there. Look at the road we came up. It's gone. Look at how deep the water is. How fast it's still flowing."

"She's right," Connor said, his voice flat and emotionless with shock. He gripped the edge of the jeep's wheel well as if needing something solid. "If we try to go back there we'll die."

"But...my mom and dad." Bea's knees gave out and she sank to the mud. "We live over on Gohr Road. They might have been home."

Sharon rested a hand on the girl's shoulder but she couldn't tear her eyes away from the hell below.

Those shadows were reforming everywhere. Going underwater where cars and bodies were. Entwining around the people who floated. Slipping inside those who struggled. And then easing back out, leaving the person no longer struggling.

It was a feeding frenzy.

"It's so foggy," Randall said. He was pale, and his voice was almost dreamy with shock.

She saw the gray shadows spreading out over the surface of the choppy water. Inching back toward the base of the hill they were on. Starting back toward them.

"You kids need to get out of here." Sharon took a step away from the jeep. "There will be back roads still open if you stay up high. But you need to go."

"Go?" Tessa asked. "Go where, exactly?"

"Wherever your boyfriend went," Sharon said, her voice tight. "Just get out of here now."

Connor stared at Sharon then grabbed Bea's arm, hauling her to her feet. He jerked open the passenger door and shoved Tessa toward it then grabbed Randall.

"What's going on?" Randall asked, shaking. "What's happening?"

"I don't know," Connor said. "But we're getting the hell out of here."

Sharon ignored them, stepping forward to the edge of the hill where she could see better. There was arguing behind her and the jeep's engine revved.

The shadows were in human shape again. And halfway up the hill. Only a few were coming though. The rest were still feeding. Sharon took another step forward, stumbling as her heels sank into the saturated ground.

"Come on," she whispered. "Come back to me."

An arm came around her waist, jerking her off her feet and knocking the air out of her. Connor pulled her back to the jeep.

"No." Sharon tugged against Connor's grip. "I'm not going."

"Neither am I!" Bea shouted, climbing over Tessa to get out of the Jeep. "I'm going to do something!"

Sharon twisted free of Connor and pushed Bea back. "No you're not, you idiot! You're going."

"If you're staying, I'm staying!"

Tessa jumped down from the jeep. "Me, too!"

"You damn idiots!" Sharon caught Tessa's arm. "Get back in the jeep. Don't you see what's coming for you?"

Tessa paused, looking where Sharon pointed. "I don't see anything but those people dying."

"Not down there," Sharon said. "Coming up the hill. Almost here."

Bea, a few feet away, turned back to them. "Aren't any of you going to help?" Tears coursed down her face. "Are you just going to let them all die?"

"I'm with you," Randall called.

Tessa struggled against Sharon's grip but couldn't pull loose.

"Bea, get back here," Sharon yelled.

But the girl was already at the edge of the hill, Randall right behind her.

Connor came up to Sharon as Bea slipped in the mud and half-ran, half-staggered down the hill. Randall, a little more sure-footed, followed her. About a quarter of the way down, the pair stumbled and both fell.

The shadows floated over the two almost gently. Moving slow as if fog on the merest breath of a breeze. Bea stiffened, coming up on her knees. Her head was thrown back, mouth open in a scream that had to have torn her vocal cords.

Randall was almost back to his feet but then was thrown face down into the ground. Sharon, unable to move, watched as tendrils moved around him, flipping him over, racing for his mouth and his ears, sinking inside him. He convulsed, back arching upward.

Even where Sharon stood at the top of the hill, she heard his spine break.

Tessa screamed.

"What's happening?" Connor shouted, grabbing on to Tessa's other arm. "What the hell is happening?"

Bea and Randall were jerked downhill a couple feet as if pulled. Blood ran from the boy's eyes like thick tears. His fingers dug into the ground as if trying to pull himself back up the hill. But the rest of his body could no longer move.

Bea screamed again, but the sound was muffled. Her mouth too full of shadow. Her throat bulged obscenely. And then the girl's stomach expanded, moved, like a parody of pregnancy.

Sharon had seen enough. She turned Tessa and shoved her at Connor. "Will you now get the hell out of here?"

Connor's eyes were wide and full of panic. His breathing came fast and shallow. But he dragged Tessa toward the jeep, both of them stumbling. Sharon didn't know which one held up the other. She ran after them and shoved them into the Jeep.

"Get out of here."

"What's wrong with them?" Connor asked, his fingers, blue with shock, fumbling as he tried to put the jeep in gear.

"Didn't you see the shadows?" Sharon asked.

"What shadows? I saw fog. Just fog." Tessa said. "What's happening?"

"There's no time. Just get the hell out of here and don't stop until you're far away." Sharon stepped back. "And stay away from that fog."

"Please," Tessa said, tears filling her eyes, sobs filling her throat. "Please don't leave us."

Sharon looked at the kids in their McDonald's uniforms. Not kids. Young adults. But terrified and traumatized and looking to her, as the representative of adulthood, to save them.

She wasn't their parent. She wasn't their savior. She was a dying middle-aged woman who wanted death to come fast, on her terms.

There was movement in the trees above them. She turned and saw a large raven soar out of the woods. It was so black its feathers looked coated in an oily sheen. It flew overhead silently, but the kids lifted their heads to watch the bird.

The raven circled overhead, came lower, and landed on the roof of the Willys. It cocked its head to one side, the black eye looking right at Sharon. It stretched its wings, flapped a little, and then settled back on the roof. The dark eyes reminded Sharon of the old woman who'd talked to her before the flood. The old woman with no fear.

She reached for the door of the jeep to shut it on the kids. But the raven lifted into the air, dropped fast toward her, and pecked her hand. She jerked back as a bead of blood welled up. The raven stroked air with its broad wings and came down to ground behind her. It cocked its head again, studying her, and hopped forward. She saw her blood on the tip of its beak.

She reached again for the door. The raven spread its wings and moved toward her again.

She didn't understand what was happening. All she wanted to do was walk down that hill and join Bea in death. But instead she sighed heavily, giving in to the raven, whose fixed gaze seemed to command her.

"Okay." She didn't know if she was capitulating to the raven or the kids. "I'll go with you. But not for long, got it? I can't save you."

Tessa swiped tears away with the back of her hand. "Thank you."

The raven silently lifted into the air, circling back to the forest. The kids watched it go without comment. And in the grand scheme of things, Sharon imagined that a raven landing on their jeep was probably almost normal in their day of horror. She heaved out a heavy sigh that made her nerves tingle in something almost like pain. All those killer cells in her body sucking in oxygen to continue their work.

And then she climbed back into the Jeep.

11

What little light had managed to come through the rain was leaching away. Long shadows reached out from the tree line as the day ended. Anya shivered, as much from the cool air on sweat-soaked clothes as from fear. She struggled to hold a board in place over a window and nail it one-handed. It didn't help that she kept feeling eyes on her. Kept staring out the window at the darkening forest, waiting for one of those shadows to move, to step into the clearing.

Bird lay in the open doorway, also staring intently out into the woods. That didn't help her deep unease either. But at least his hackles weren't up.

The board slipped and hit the floor, just missing her hiking boot. She threw the hammer after it.

"You fucker!" She wasn't sure if she cussed the board, or the non-existent Devon, who should have been there.

One more window and the cabin would be barricaded. She'd made a mistake at first, boarding a window from the outside. But then it had dawned on her that whatever this creature was, it might be able to rip a board off, nailed or not. And so she'd switched to inside. She wasn't sure it would make any difference, but it felt more secure.

Anya picked the board back up, held it in place with her elbow and forearm, and seated a nail.

She had a huge stack of firewood inside the house. Enough to last a long night. She had a kettle of elk stew simmering on the wood stove. Something hot and filling after a day of fear and tension and work. She had the rifle cleaned, loaded, and within reach. Fresh batteries in her headlamp. She wasn't sure what the night would bring, but either way it was going to be long, lonely, and scary.

The last nail sank into wood and Anya put the hammer on the table. She pulled on a rain poncho and followed that with her backpack. But then she just stood there, holding the straps.

She had to go into the woods. There was no way around it. That morning she'd made the decision to stay rather than leaving the boy out there alone. Which meant she now couldn't just barricade herself in for the night without making some attempt to find him. And yet the thought of going into the forest alone terrified her.

She lifted the rifle.

"We'll make one attempt," she told Bird. "We won't go far.

Then we'll lock ourselves in. Okay?"

Bird stood and woofed once. When she took a step toward the door, he went out on the deck as if to lead the way.

Anya tugged up the hood on the poncho and crossed the clearing, circling around the spot where the head had been, even though rain had washed away the blood. Her heart raced the closer to the trees she got. What if that thing was out there, waiting? She swallowed. The fear made her queasy, made her muscles liquid.

Bird looked back at her, head tilted to one side. Still no hackles.

Okay then. She pulled in a deep breath and followed her dog into the trees. As they passed the young yew, she reached out to touch the bark.

"We'll be right back," she said under her breath.

Rain pattered on leaves and dripped from moss that hung from tree branches. The thick forest floor was spongy with water. High overhead, the tops of Douglas fir and Alaska cedar bent in a wind that didn't reach her where she stood. The air was that unique scent of the forest, of wet decomposing plant material and tree resin.

Anya walked slowly, trying to resist the urge to plaster herself against a huge tree and not move. She scanned the woods around her, eyes shifting from forest to her dog, and back. She looked for movement, for raising hackles. She knew she should call for the boy because the likelihood of stumbling across him was miniscule. But she couldn't bring herself to make noise, to attract the attention of anything that might be out there.

They didn't follow a trail, just roughly traced a wide circle around the cabin. The safety of her home was a strong rubber-band pull tugging her back. She was stupid to think she had a chance of finding someone out here in the middle of a forest without end. Of mountains that hid secrets for generations. She knew she was talking herself into giving in to the fear and running for home.

And then Bird stopped. He stared off to their left but his hackles weren't up. Anya went to him and placed a hand on his head, slipping the rifle off her shoulder with the other hand. She stared into the trees, breath coming fast, searching for movement in the dripping shadows. And saw it, movement, as if several shadows shifted. She raised the rifle to her shoulder. Was there more than one creature?

Bird looked over his shoulder at her and barked once, his tail actually wagging. Confused, Anya glanced back the way they had come.

The grizzly and the boy were behind her, not more than a few feet away. They, too, watched the movement in the trees.

Oddly reassured, Anya chambered a round and aimed. The

shadows coalesced into a group of people. A man with a gun. Young people clustered around him. One girl with dark hair raised a hand as if she was in a classroom and even with the distance between them Anya saw her trembling.

"Are you, like, real?" the girl called out. "Because, like, we're pretty scared right now."

12

Ethan and the students ran as far as they could and then slowed to a stumbling walk. Payton came out of her faint and Spike lowered her to the ground, rubbing his biceps and breathing heavy. Ethan brought up the rear, scanning the trees on both sides, wondering what the hell they would do once it was dark.

As the daylight faded into a rainy late afternoon, Zack, up ahead, yelled for everyone to stop, and then sank down to sit on the wet ground, head hanging. Ethan heard a low rumbling sound, and saw the others gather around Zack, staring through the trees ahead of them.

Ethan moved through them to the front of the line. Another slide blocked their route. And there was no way they were crossing this one. Because somewhere up in the mountains, a stream had diverted to follow the washout. Water cascaded down the steep incline, moving boulders and trees and earth with its power. The whitewater cut a new streambed, straight across their path.

"What now, genius?" Michael asked. "Told you we should have gone back."

For a moment, Ethan didn't have a clue. It was like his brain just gave up and shut down. There was no way he was going to get these kids out of the mountains, away from devastation and monsters. They'd all die out here, eaten by some freak.

"We're going to die," Zack said, echoing Ethan's thoughts.

"Speak for yourself." Spike turned, looking back the way they'd come. "There's gotta be a way around this."

Ethan pulled off his pack and opened it, keeping his eyes down. Of all of the kids, Spike would be the one to spot weakness in him. If he let that fear show he'd lose Spike's confidence. And once he lost Spike's, he'd lose them all and panic would take over. His thoughts raced, weighing options, as he struggled to swallow down the fear that this was where everything ended. And then his fingers curled around his compass. He straightened.

"Now we bushwhack. Same scenario that we talked about at the last slide. We backtrack some until we find solid ground then go around. Maybe up above the stream will be small enough to cross."

Zack pushed himself to his feet. "It's going to be dark soon."

"Then we better get moving," Ethan said. "Get someplace we can build a shelter."

"Maybe we can find a cave," Lucy said, one arm snugged against her bruised ribs. "You said there used to be a lot of mining around here."

"Right," Nathaniel said. "Like we want to go into a dark cave." He gave her a teasing nudge that took the barb out of his words and she managed a shaky smile in return.

"Come on," Ethan said, starting back the way they'd come. "We're wasting daylight."

"Which way?" Zack asked. "There's nothing but woods out here."

Ethan studied the compass, thought about his map, and then looked up for a visual marker. "Up. We can get to Jumpoff Ridge and follow it all the way to Index. That also means we don't have to worry about getting to the river only to find the bridge gone. Get your compasses out and orient on mine. If we get separated you should still be able to find your way out."

"Today?" Jennifer asked hopefully.

"Not today," Ethan said. "No way we're bushwhacking out in the few hours of daylight that's left. And it will be too dangerous to hike in the dark, even with headlamps. So keep your eyes open for anything that might work for a shelter. Something we can put our backs to. Check your compasses and maps often. Make sure you're following a true line."

Payton stared at him, eyes wide. "Can't I just, like, stick with you?"

Ethan sighed. "You didn't pack a compass. Right?"

"Jesus." Spike shook his head. "What *did* you pack?"

Payton scowled at him and when Zack sighed heavily and gestured for her, she went to his side.

This time Ethan led the way, orienteering from the compass and his Green Trails map. He put Spike and Rowan at the rear and Zack behind him, thinking they were the least likely to panic if something came at them. Although he didn't know what they would do with no weapons.

They bushwhacked for almost three hours without seeing a place that offered shelter. Cutting across country, battling uphill through the ruined landscape, was exhausting enough without adding rain and cold and fear. Ethan worried about the dying light and knew they couldn't go much farther. Their pace was slowing, Lucy was pale with exhaustion, and even Rowan was starting to flag. He finally called a break, telling them to drink some water and rest for a moment. But before they slipped out of backpacks, he heard the sound of something big crunching through underbrush.

"There's something out there!" Michael's voice was high with terror.

Ethan's heart jolted into overdrive. The gun was in his hand with no memory of having pulled it out.

"Oh, fuck me," Spike said. "A grizzly."

Ethan stared, his mind struggling to make sense of what he saw.

A woman stood several yards away. Even through the slanting rain he saw her, still as a statue, rifle to her shoulder, pointed at them. A dog stood to one side, alert. It barked once, and the woman held her hand up to silence it.

And just behind her, a giant grizzly waited. And just behind the grizzly, a shape, a small movement, like a child. He saw the woman glance back at the bear, then face forward again. She was like some mythic forest spirit with woodland guardians.

Except for that rifle.

"Are you, like, real?" Payton called out. "Because, like, we're pretty scared right now."

Ethan, startled, glanced at Payton. The one least prepared was the first one to speak in spite of fear. When he turned back, the bear and whatever had been with it were gone.

"Shit," Spike said. "Where did it go?"

"What are you doing out here?" The woman's voice was gruff, like she didn't use it often. Or like someone who'd been doing a lot of yelling.

"Where's the bear?" Spike yelled. "The fucking grizzly!"

The woman's eyebrows went up in surprise and she turned in a slow circle then raised her hand in a shrug. "It comes and goes. It won't eat you. I don't think."

Ethan's grip on the butt of the gun didn't ease. "We were out here on a field trip to Silver Creek. The earthquake cut us off. We're trying to find our way out to Index to get help."

"You won't get there before dark." The woman's eyes scanned the woods around them. "And you don't want to be out here after dark."

"No shit," Zack said.

"Can you help us?" Jennifer asked, tears on her cheeks.

There was a long pause. Long enough that Ethan thought the woman wasn't going to answer them. And to reinforce that impression, she turned her back on them and walked away. The dog went with her. But after a few steps she looked over her shoulder.

"Are you coming?"

Ethan turned to the group and shrugged.

Nathaniel shook his head and started after the woman. "Something's better than nothing. And she has a grizzly."

Ethan laughed, startled that he could. "Right. Let's go then."

They followed the woman as she headed uphill through the woods. But she seemed to know where she was going. And as the shadows deepened under the trees, as the gray light slanted downward, promising coming night, Ethan agreed silently with the stranger. They really didn't want to be out here after dark.

"Is the grizzly tame?" Rowan asked the woman, catching up to her.

The woman's eyebrows went up as if startled. "A tame grizzly? No way." She paused. "So you saw it?"

"We all did," Lucy said.

"Did you see...anything else?" the woman asked.

"A boy," Rowan answered. "At least, I think it was a boy."

"I didn't see any boy," Spike said. "I just saw a fuckin' grizzly."

"I saw something," Ethan said. "Maybe a child. Is he your son?"

The woman stumbled. Rowan caught her arm but she stood bent as if she'd just been punched in the gut. Ethan frowned. Were they making a mistake going off with some stranger who just happened to appear out of nowhere and looked a little unstable?

"No...not my son." The woman swiped the back of her hand across her eyes. "I don't know who he is. He's always with the bear. They come and go." She met Ethan's eyes. "I thought I was crazy. Seeing things."

"Not if we all saw them," Ethan said. "So just out of curiosity, where exactly are we going? I mean, you're not going to take us to some gingerbread house with that bear at the door are you?"

The woman managed a small, choked laugh. "You saw the bear so I'm not crazy on that point. But I might be anyway. There are other...things out here. So I'm going home. To my cabin. Still want to come?"

"Oh yes, please," Payton said. "I'd give anything for a hot shower and walls and a roof and a door that locks."

"No shower," the woman said. She looked out into the trees where shadows lengthened. "We need to hurry."

In spite of their terror and shock and exhaustion, they managed to keep up with the woman as she moved through the forest as if it was familiar territory, even in its wreckage. Ethan noticed she used no compass, and rarely stopped to get her bearings. He stayed at the back, making sure no one fell behind, scanning the land around them for movement. Of all that had happened, it was odd to realize the thought of a grizzly was the least of his worries.

Their progress was slow though. So many trees had come down.

Shifted earth, exposed boulders, unstable hillsides...every step they took involved some obstacle to be climbed over, crawled under, or stumbled on.

Nathaniel dropped back to walk beside Ethan. "Grizzlies aren't native to this area, are they?"

"Not here, no," Ethan said. "But they have returned in small numbers to the higher alpine areas around here. Like the Enchantments, or up around Evergreen Lookout."

"Guess the earthquake changed everything." Nathaniel gripped the straps to his backpack. "What do you think that thing was?"

"Honestly, I have no idea." Ethan caught movement in the distance to their left. He put his arm out, stopping Nathaniel, and then blew out a breath of air when he realized it was a black bear. A small one, running from them. "The quake was devastating. Who knows what it shook up."

"Can this woman save us?" A slight tremor shifted under Nathaniel's words.

"She can give us shelter for the night. Beyond that, I have no idea. In the morning we're going to have to make a plan. For right now, I just want us behind walls."

"You have a gun. She has a rifle. And a German shepherd. We should be okay, right?"

Ethan thought about his bullets hitting that creature. "Sure."

Nathaniel said nothing and Ethan didn't know if that was because he was comforted or had heard the lie in his answer.

The woman and Rowan pulled ahead of the others. Ethan lifted his chin in a nod. "Come on. Let's catch up. We don't want to fall behind."

And then, for a brief second, he saw the grizzly there, between the woman and Rowan. Indistinct, massive, and pacing with the two of them, like a guide.

And then gone as if it had been a trick of the twilight shadows.

13

One of the young people, a tall girl with long auburn hair, pulled ahead of the others to walk next to Anya.

"What's your name?" Anya asked, then cleared her throat. She hadn't talked this much in months. "And where did you come from?"

"I'm Rowan," the girl said. "We were on a field trip. Mr. Reynolds, Ethan, he's our teacher. We're seniors at the Environmental Science High school in Monroe. We came up to look at lichen and the old mining ghost town."

"Silver Creek?"

"Yes. But then the quake hit. And…things happened." Rowan told her about the students who had died, including one killed by a rock fall on a slide. She hesitated there, as if she wanted to say more, but fell quiet.

Anya waited a moment to see if the girl would continue with her story, but Rowan remained silent as they clambered over a downed tree. The fir needles were soft against Anya's skin as she pushed through the branches still remaining. The crushed and damp greenery left the astringent scent of resin on her skin. Bird jumped easily on to the trunk, and just as easily jumped to the ground on the other side. Anya watched him for signs that the creature had returned, but he paced calmly ahead of her, leading the way home.

When they reached the edge of the small clearing, Anya paused, holding out her hand to stop Rowan. She studied the area, staring into the fringes of forest around the cabin. The clearing was empty. There was no movement in the trees, but it was getting darker and hard to see. Still, she hesitated, not wanting to step out, be exposed.

The others gathered around her but no one spoke. She felt their tension though. As if they, too, feared the open air.

Bird made the decision for them. He wandered out into the clearing, paused to sniff a fallen branch, and lifted his leg on it.

"Okay then," the smallest of the young men said. "Guess we're good."

Anya followed her dog into the open and felt the others close behind her. Her breathing quickened and it was all she could do to not leap ahead and run for the safety of the cabin, now covered in shadow. No one paused to enjoy the view of surrounding mountains, dark silhouettes against charcoal clouds.

She unlatched the door and pushed it open, entering the shadowy cabin. The others crowded in quickly behind her, almost pushing her in their effort to get inside. Something hit the floor as one of them knocked into it. The small space smelled of simmering elk stew, bay and thyme, carrots and rich broth.

"Wait until I can get a light," Anya said. She crossed the room with easy familiarity, dropped her pack, and lit an Aladdin lamp. When the meshed wick warmed, she turned it up, letting the circle of light spread. She reached for a kerosene lantern as the small and slender young man picked up a book from the floor.

"Sorry. I knocked it off the table." He put it back and then stood with the others, awkwardly, in the middle of the room.

Where was she going to put them all? Anya had no clue.

But night was falling and she wasn't alone. The knot of tension inside loosened slightly.

"Want me to start a fire?" Ethan asked, gesturing to the wood stove. "And you mind if we spread out our wet gear?"

"Go ahead," Anya said. "Just open the damper. I banked the fire low to keep the stew warm while I was gone. And hang your stuff wherever you can."

"It smells so good," a small girl said. "We've been sharing protein bars."

Anya slid the rifle off her shoulder, moved past the students, and hung it on its rack. "There should be enough for all of us. I can make some biscuits. Drop your stuff wherever you can find room. Can one of you put the bar in place on the door?"

"It's sure dark in here." Rowan stood in the middle of the room, her arms tightly wrapped around herself. She moved closer to the Aladdin lamp.

"I boarded the windows," Anya said. She paused a moment, letting her eyes scan the group before meeting those of the teacher. "To keep anything out."

They relaxed, shoulders slumping as they glanced at each other with tentative smiles.

"Good idea," Ethan said. He added wood to the stove, closed the door until it left just a crack to let air stir the fire up, and then straightened. "Thanks for helping us out. What's your name?"

"Anya. And that's Bird."

Bird sniffed the discarded backpacks, wet coats and wool hats, and then crossed the room to claim his space, curling up on the dog bed next to the wood stove.

"How are you going to make biscuits with no oven?" the girl

with the dark hair asked.

"And this is Payton," Ethan said.

The others followed his lead, telling her their names. Michael sank onto her armchair as if he owned it, looking almost belligerent as if expecting someone to make him get up. She noticed the girl called Lucy holding an arm close to her side.

"Broken ribs?"

"Just bruised, I think." Holding her side carefully, she lowered herself down onto the dog bed next to Bird, who promptly pushed his head under her good arm, demanding a scratch. She wrapped her arm around him tightly and lowered her head to his shoulder.

The others followed her cue, slowly settling down as if unsure they were truly safe. Ethan stood near the heat of the woodstove with his back to it and hands in his jeans pockets. She saw him studying her cabin, watching his students, as if evaluating everything in his vicinity.

Two of the students, Jennifer and Zack, talked quietly, their heads together. Anya saw tears in the girl's eyes, and Zack put his arm around her shoulders.

Nathaniel was looking over Anya's bookshelves, running his hand along bindings and occasionally pulling a book out. He held up *Coming Into the Country* by John McPhee and raised one eyebrow in question. When Anya nodded, he sat cross-legged on the floor by the bookshelf and opened the old cover. He looked relaxed, if she didn't look too closely at how the pages shook, or how white his knuckles were, gripping the book.

Rowan had a journal out and appeared to be sketching. Her pencil moved in sure strokes across the pages and she seemed at ease. Or maybe, Anya thought, just deep in her world of paper, shutting out the reality around her.

Michael, the boy hogging her armchair, was focused on food. He stared at the Dutch oven of stew with a deep intensity.

"We've seen some strange things since the quake," Ethan said as Anya lifted a tin canister of flour off a shelf. "Including that grizzly. It's made us all kind of nervous."

"Scared shitless, he means," Spike said.

"Yeah, like he said." Zack left Jennifer and sat on the floor, leaning against his backpack with his knees up and his arms resting on them. He looked pale and even in the low light there were traces of fear in his eyes.

"It's been a weird couple days." She thought about telling them what she'd seen, but figured they'd probably run screaming from the cabin thinking she was insane.

"Um, excuse me," Payton said, raising her hand again. "Could you tell me where the bathroom is, please?"

Anya gestured to the door. "An outhouse behind the cabin."

"Outside?" Payton's eyebrows climbed in high arches. She glanced at the door. "I think I'll wait."

Nathaniel stood. "I'll escort you," he said. "I could use an outhouse, too."

Ethan straightened. "I'll walk you out." He glanced at Anya. "Just in case. You know. The grizzly or something."

"Or something," Spike said. "Are we going to tell her about the thing that killed Paul or not?"

"Oh, no," Jennifer said, her voice high with fright. "She'll kick us out! She'll think we're crazy. We can't go back out there."

Anya picked up a tin of lard and scooped some into the flour. "Maybe something with antlers?"

They all swiveled to stare at her.

"You've seen it?" Ethan asked.

Anya met his dark eyes for a long moment. He held himself as if calm and in control, but with a hesitant caution there, as if wondering which one of them would be the first to admit to the impossible.

"I saw it," she said finally. "It was here, trying to get in one night. And then came back with..." She sucked in a deep breath as realization hit her.

It came back with a head.

Maybe their friend Paul. She glanced around the room. These kids didn't need any more horror.

"With what?" Michael asked from the armchair.

Anya met Ethan's eyes again. "With blood on it. It came back with blood on it." She began cutting biscuit dough.

Ethan frowned as if he knew she wasn't being truthful. But after a moment he nodded to her and headed for the door. "Let's do the outhouse run before it gets full dark. Then we can talk about what's going on."

"Take your gun," Anya said.

"Always," Ethan responded.

By the time he shepherded the crew back in and dropped the bar down over the door, Anya was showing Payton the small cast iron box in the stovepipe of the woodstove that acted as her oven. The girl seemed fascinated, as if she'd never heard of cooking on a woodstove.

Anya didn't have enough bowls for everyone but found mugs and filled them with stew, then handed it out along with biscuits, warm and dripping with honey. And with the food, all conversation ended.

Anya watched the meal being devoured, and after she finished her bowl, she started another batch of biscuits. There had only been enough stew for one serving each, but she had plenty of flour and lard. She kept her hands busy, more than willing to let talk of scary things be delayed.

Payton rubbed her stomach. "That was the best I've ever had."

"Fear does that to you. Plus having a couple days of nothing but protein bars." Ethan took his mug to the sink and worked the hand pump. "What did you make the stew out of?"

"Elk," Anya said.

"Elk?" Payton's eyes widened and her face paled.

Spike laughed. "Elk. You know, like a big Bambi."

"Oh." Payton stared into her mug. "Well…it was good anyway."

The laughter at her words had the feel of relief in it. As if none of them were sure they'd laugh again.

When the second round of biscuits had been handed out, Lucy plucked pieces off hers. "Do you know…do you think…maybe the earthquake wasn't as bad down below? In town? Like, maybe our families are okay?"

Anya met Ethan's eyes and saw the same dilemma there. Protect the girl or break her heart with honesty?

"I don't know," Ethan said. "When you look at the extent of the damage here, it had to have been far-reaching. I'm sorry Lucy. If I could reassure you I would, but I won't lie to you."

"I don't want you to lie," Lucy said, lifting her chin and taking a deep breath. "I just, you know, want them to be there if I make it home."

"*When* you make it home," Nathaniel said.

"*If* we have homes to go to," Michael said, mimicking Nathaniel's emphasis, then pointed at him. "Your place is probably flattened. Don't you live in that mobile home park in Gold Bar? Low-income housing? Those things aren't meant for strong wind let alone-"

"That's enough." Spike stood.

"What?" Michael asked. "They don't want to be lied to and it's just the truth."

"There's the truth, and then there's being a fucker about it." Spike's hands tightened into fists.

Michael struggled to his feet. "What do you know? You're just a thug."

"That's enough." Ethan stepped between them and put a hand on Michael's chest.

Anya saw the way the teacher and student stared at each other. There was obviously some history there.

"This is my home," she said loudly. "Under my roof you're going to respect each other. You're going to be kind to each other. Trauma's no excuse to take your fear out on someone else."

"And what are you going to do about it if we don't?" Michael pulled his shoulders back as if that would make him taller than Anya.

"You'll leave," she said, keeping her voice calm and steady. "I'll take the rifle and my dog, and kick you out into the night. Do you want that? You want to go out there?"

Michael didn't speak but his eyes canted toward the boarded up windows.

The answer was in his face. She decided he'd got the point, and turned to Jennifer, who still stood, pale and shaking, by the door.

"Come stand by the fire," Anya said. "It will warm you up."

Jennifer jumped as if startled, then followed Anya to the stove. She stood over Lucy and Bird, but didn't drop down to sit with them like Anya had expected. Though Bird didn't seem to need more adoration. He was practically drooling into Lucy's lap, getting hugged and petted and fed bits of biscuit like he was the most important thing there. Anya figured he was just as relieved as her to no longer be alone.

"We need to talk about that thing we saw," Zack said. "We need to have a plan for when it comes back."

Lucy promptly burst into tears and buried her face in Bird's fur.

Spike crossed the room and sank down next to her, putting his arm around the girl's shaking shoulders.

Anya pulled in a deep breath. "I shot it. When it came back here."

"Did you kill it?" Jennifer asked, hope in her eyes.

"No," Anya said. "The grizzly and Bird went after it, but I doubt they killed it either."

Lucy straightened, wiped at the tears on her cheeks, and then rested against Spike's shoulder.

Anya stepped back against the rough wood table as if she could distance herself from these kids, from getting involved, from their scared faces staring at her as if trusting her to fix everything. But then she looked at Lucy and saw the deep grief in her eyes. The loss. The knowledge that no matter how much she might wish for something different, her family was probably gone and she was here to face monsters. Some things couldn't be changed.

For a brief second she felt the small weight of a baby in her arms.

Spike rested a hand on Lucy's head, holding her. Giving her more comfort than Anya had ever received from Devon.

Anya blew out a heavy sigh. There was no way she was going to be able to walk away from these kids.

Zack spoke, his voice startling Anya and pulling her out of her thoughts. "Do you know what that thing is? I mean, since you live out here? Is it some kind of wild animal?"

There was hope in his questions and Anya understood. He wanted her to name it, to make it real, to lessen the horror. She looked up at Ethan, meeting understanding in his eyes.

"No, sorry," she said. "I've never seen anything like it. I'm not even sure it's real. I mean, it's all kind of crazy right now. I've never had a grizzly follow me around, either."

A couple of the students laughed; a few managed strained smiles.

Ethan looked at the kids. "Any ideas? Anyone? Now that we are safe enough to actually think?"

Rowan placed a pencil between the pages of the sketchbook she'd pulled out, and closed the book. She folded her hands on the cover.

Lucy wiped her eyes on the sleeve of her shirt and looked around at the others. "Was the grizzly bear real?"

Ethan sat on a wooden chair next to a small table. "It looked real."

"It sure as hell has been interacting like it was real," Anya said. "I saw its tracks. I saw its blood. I saw it attack that thing. I've just never seen a grizzly come around people like that before. It's a killer. Not some kind of bodyguard."

"But they are," Rowan said, raising her head and pushing her hair back behind her ears. "If you read Pacific Northwest folklore, grizzly bears are ancestors, way-showers, teachers, guardians."

"And you just happen to know this how?" Michael asked.

Rowan shrugged. "I did the homework. Ethan had us read about bears when we were going to hike to the Heybrook fire lookout. And...well, I liked the idea of a grizzly as a guardian. Don't we all need guardians?"

"That was black bears," Ethan said. "What we were studying."

"I got distracted by the Native American stories." Rowan flushed as if embarrassed.

"Which is why you never turned in the essay on black bears?" Ethan asked.

Rowan shrugged again. "Guess so."

"What's it matter?" Jennifer asked, still shivering. "I mean, who cares if bears have some mythical meaning? That other thing we saw was real. It killed Paul. That wasn't some folktale peeling his skin off! We need something to make it go away."

Tears pooled in Lucy's eyes again and Payton covered her mouth with her hand as if to hold in the fear.

"The grizzly, and that thing, were real enough," Anya said calmly. "But nothing is going to kill us tonight. We're locked up secure. We have guns. We have Bird. Nothing's getting in."

"So you say." Jennifer's teeth chattered as her shivering grew into deeper tremors. "But that wasn't some wild animal. Who knows what it can do?"

"And tomorrow, Jennifer," Ethan said, looking directly at her. "We're getting the hell out of here. As soon as it's daylight."

Anya looked around the room at the people who had so suddenly filled her life. They were kids. They needed to be safe, to be taken care of. "Tomorrow." She spoke without thinking things through. "I'll help Ethan get you all out of the woods."

Ethan, eyes smudged with weariness, nodded to her in thanks.

Anya worked the hand pump until water flowed into a pan that she then put on the wood stove to heat. These people needed warmth and food and rest. A sense of security, whether it was real or not. And a goal, like hiking out of the woods tomorrow, no matter what devastation waited down in the flatlands.

She didn't want to go out into the woods. She didn't want to leave her home. But it would only take a few days to lead them out, and then she'd be back here.

With her son.

14

Curtis huddled, knees to chest, back to a still-standing tree. It didn't feel as safe as standing with his back to the granite wall, but it was better than having nothing behind him. The night was pitch black and late. Or early, depending on how you looked at it. He gripped his pack with one hand and the flashlight with the other. His eyes were gritty with fatigue and fear and no matter how hard he tensed his muscles, his legs shook. He told himself it wasn't fear.

It was just the chilly night air.

It was just his overly active imagination.

But then out in the woods, screams started. Somewhere above him in the forest, someone was dying. His breath hitched in his chest and tears filled his eyes. He tried to stand, put his shaking hand to earth to push himself upward, but each time the shrieks cut through his heart, sliced his nerves, slashed at his tiny spark of courage. Instead he pulled his knees up, dropped his forehead to them, and covered his ears.

But he still heard the cries.

He wanted to go help. He really did. After all, that might be Henry screaming, and hadn't he come out here to save his friend? But he couldn't do it. He could only hide, shaking so hard his teeth bit into his cheeks.

When the screams stopped, when the woods had been silent for several minutes, the terror began to seep slowly out of his bones. He fumbled on the ground for the flashlight, frantic with the sudden need for light. His thumb was on the switch when he heard something coming through the underbrush.

Whatever it was, it moved steadily in spite of the darkness and quake-damaged forest. Branches snapped and dislodged rocks tumbled. And then, gripping his pack and his flashlight, he heard last year's dead leaves rustle under a step, and then another. Something upright on two legs. A shape, darker than the night, passed between trees. Taller than a man. With something like branches coming out of its head.

Curtis felt the warm rush as his bladder let go. The sharp scent of urine filled the air.

The steps paused. Something drew in a noisy breath, scenting him.

He no longer wanted light, didn't want to see, didn't want to be seen. Tremors shook his body. Breath came in shallow tiny gasps. He squeezed his eyes shut. Pushed back tight against the solid tree trunk, and pulled the pack into his lap as if it could shield him.

There was a loud slurping, smacking sound, like someone eating something juicy.

After several moments the woods grew quieter. No screams. No sounds of eating. No sense of something standing out there in the darkness. Just the soft pattering of rain. His shaking slowed to fine trembling. Under his rain gear, his jeans were wet and itchy against his thighs. He finally managed a deep breath and wiped tears from his cheeks.

Eventually the darkness began to lighten to a deep charcoal, and then to gray. Curtis stood slowly, pushing himself up the tree trunk, still clutching his pack to his chest. Pins and needles shot through his legs as circulation returned.

The growing dawn light brightened under the trees and glistened off something small a few feet away. He limped closer.

A marble. It had to be a marble. He struggled to convince himself of that, but there was no way to avoid the reality. It was an eyeball, not a marble. Tendrils of bloody nerves lay daintily on top of a few thick, orange threads from some sort of material. Raindrops on glossy dark green leaves of salal were pink-tinged where blood had washed through.

Curtis had a moment to realize the eye was hazel before he was on his knees, retching.

He flashed on the sounds from the night before. Something passing close enough to smell his urine, to know he was there.

But not hungry enough to come for him.

His stomach heaved again, and again, until his vision narrowed from lack of oxygen. But then the muscles eased and he was able to suck in a ragged breath. He gagged and then was able to pull in another breath without throwing up. And then another without gagging.

Curtis pushed away from his vomit and collapsed to the ground on his back. Rain pattered softly against his face, cool and gentle. Warm tears leaked out of his closed eyes and trickled back into his hairline. He concentrated on breathing, on his slowing heart rate. When his insides seemed somewhat in control, he pushed up to sit, head hanging in exhaustion.

He'd always known the mountains at night were wild and dangerous and no place for mere humans, but that was because of the wild animals. Now something else was there, hunting. He felt a tickle in the back of his mind, as if he knew what the creature was, but fear kept him from being able to focus. All he could think of was how exposed he was.

Even in the growing daylight.

He'd wanted to be back in Index, next to the safety of people and fires, when night came. But he'd stupidly convinced himself to keep going as twilight fell, until suddenly it was too dark to find his way back down the trail.

And so here he was.

He stood and his still-damp jeans chafed against his inner thighs and groin. He glanced around but saw only trees and rocks and earth. Self-consciously, he shed his clothes and quickly wiped himself down with wet maple leaves. The cold, damp air seemed to chill him all the way through his skin. Even his testicles shrank in protest. Shivering, he pulled his cold-weather fleece pants out of the pack and then put the rain pants back on.

Using the straps on his backpack, he tied the jeans on the outside of the pack. It wasn't like he had more clothes in the car. He'd come to work two days ago planning on being home that night. So he couldn't toss his jeans, because who knew when he'd make it home. Or if he even had a home to return to.

He stared longingly down hill. It would be so easy to go back right now. No one expected him to find Henry, anyway. At least he would have tried, which was more than anyone in Index could say, down there safe by their fires. The fear twisting in his gut worked hard to convince him to go downhill, to justify retreat.

Instead, he shouldered his pack, turned his back on the forlorn eyeball, and headed uphill.

After all, Henry had blue eyes. Not hazel.

15

They went to bed early, sleeping bags and pads spread out across the floor of the cabin. Anya offered to share her bed with Lucy, since the girl wouldn't have been comfortable on the floor with her bruised ribs. Plus, she seemed more vulnerable than the others, more lonely and afraid. Bird, the traitor, chose to snuggle with Lucy. In the single-room cabin there was no privacy, and she slept fitfully, overwhelmed by the presence of others.

She woke once during the night to hear the soft, muted sounds of people shifting, someone snoring, the low whimper of someone having a nightmare. And then she heard the creak of the bar on the door being moved. Someone lifted the kerosene lantern she'd left burning low and shadows shifted as someone moved toward the door. Two people whispered together.

An outhouse trip, most likely.

She waited several minutes until she heard the door open and shut again and the bar come safely back down. And then she finally drifted back into a dreamless sleep for the first time in two nights. Not that she felt those around her would save her from monsters, but there was something about no longer being alone to face those monsters that lessened fear.

In the morning, Zack was gone.

~Day 4~

1

The early dawn was cool but at least the rain had stopped and the clouds slowly disintegrated as if filtered by old trees and older crags. Some time in the wee hours of the night before, Ramon and Ben found a place to not only pull over. After leaving Sultan it had taken them hours to make their way east on Highway 2. They'd gone as far as an area known as the High Bridge, but there they'd been forced to stop because that high bridge spanning the Skykomish river was no more. And the Skykomish, a large whitewater river, wasn't one they could simply drive through. Ben had chosen to take a small two-track forest service road off into the woods, looking for someplace to camp where they wouldn't be visible. After seeing how people had acted in Monroe, Ramon didn't argue.

Even making their way up the old logging road had taken hours. Every few feet Ramon, Artair, and Ben had to hook up the winch and cables to move downed trees out of their path. Or they'd have to inch along using the huge slab of a bumper to push a boulder out of their way. At one point Ramon had walked backwards in front of the truck, using hand motions to direct Ben and keep all four tires on the track instead of sliding down a washout. The others had walked behind during that maneuver so if the truck had gone it would have meant only losing Ben.

Only.

When they finally stopped it wasn't because of finding a prime location as much as soul-deep shock, delayed reaction, and exhaustion. But at least they were far enough from the highway that they felt safe.

They'd worked until it was too dark to see, organizing the over-stuffed camper. Now, though there was no room to sleep in it, they were at least able to find what they needed. Both girls, shivering, had crawled into the camper and changed into warmer clothes than their stained and torn school uniforms. When they were done, everything was packed tightly in the camper except for Ramon's Glock. When no one was looking, he'd slipped the gun under the front seat of the truck, securing it with a strip of duct tape.

Once it was full dark, Ramon stretched a couple tarps between trees, hanging them with rope. Exhausted emotionally and physically, his nieces burrowed into sleeping bags under the tarps and were asleep almost instantly. He sat in the dark, listening to the patter of rain on the tarp, and wondered what they were to do, where they could go. At some point Ben took over the watch and Ramon, chilled and bone-deep weary, crawled into a sleeping bag and eventually fell asleep.

Now, with the twilight of dawn, Ramon had a small fire going and over it, a pot with oatmeal just coming to a simmer. Movement stirred one of the sleeping bags and Marie sat up and rubbed her eyes. When she saw him, she unzipped the bag and brought it with her to the fire, wrapping it around her shoulders.

There were smudged shadows under her eyes and she slowly looked from side to side, scanning the forest that surrounded them.

"We're safe here," he said. "We'll hear anyone who comes this way."

Marie didn't acknowledge his words.

"Oatmeal will be ready soon. There's brown sugar and cinnamon. How is your head?"

Marie twisted around to look behind her. Ramon saw how her fingers, gripping the sleeping bag, trembled. He had to fight the urge to also look behind him. He wanted to reassure his niece that it was daylight, that they were going to be okay, that they were better off than most, that life would eventually get back to normal.

But the words were as thick in his throat as the oatmeal in the pot.

Ramon moved closer to Marie and put his arm around her, drawing her near. Her head dropped onto his shoulder and he saw the redness around the stitches. From healing or infection, only time and antibiotics would tell. Her dark eyes continued searching.

And deep in his soul, Ramon heard his instinct whisper, as if some primordial genetic code just woke up.

"What do you see?" he asked quietly.

"Shadows."

That didn't sound so bad. Ramon patted Marie. "Well, remember what the doctor said about your head injury."

"There's at least six. I see them out of the corner of my eye." Marie acted as if Ramon had said nothing. "They fade away if you look at them directly. They're not people."

"Of course they're not." Ramon patted her again. "That bump on the head just scrambled your brains for a while."

"No. They're moving around us, they start to come in closer and then pull back. I don't know how they can tell where we are because they don't have eyes or noses or mouths. They're just shapes. Like smoke.

But…"

"But?"

"They want us."

"I doubt a shadow can do much damage," Ramon said. Especially, he thought, ones that are the result of a head injury.

And then he remembered. That brief glimpse of a shadow, maybe a person, going into the house after he pulled the girls out. He shook his head. He wasn't going to let Marie's hallucinations get into his brain, too.

"Look Marie, you have to trust the doctor. He knew what he was talking about. There's nothing here that shouldn't be. And on top of your injury, the earthquake changed everything. That kind of shock messes with you."

Marie glanced upward and met his eyes, but only briefly before going back to scanning the woods.

"They're not the only ones here," she said. "But you don't have to believe me. I'll see if I can keep us safe."

"No, baby. That's my job. I'll keep you safe. You just rest and get better."

Cool wind whispered around them, passed over, fluttered the fire and made goose bumps rise on Ramon's arms.

Marie pulled the sleeping bag up over her head. "I don't want to see anymore. It almost touched you."

Another sleeping bag moved and Artair emerged. He rolled the bag up carefully before joining them at the fire, rubbing a hand over his face. Marie pulled her bag down slowly, keeping her eyes focused on the fire. Artair touched her shoulder lightly as he sat down on the ground.

"How's the head?" he asked.

"She's still seeing things," Ramon said. "Wish I'd thought to ask the doctor how long that's supposed to last."

Artair drew in breath as if starting to speak, but then seemed to change his mind. He picked up a stick and poked at the fire.

Ramon stirred the bubbling oatmeal. "Hungry?" he asked the two teens.

At their nods he spooned oatmeal into plastic bowls. By the time they started to eat, the others were stirring. Ben heaved June up off the ground, and June in turn helped Alegria to her feet. As Ben packed and stowed sleeping bags, June pulled out a battered stainless steel coffee pot and started coffee over the fire. Then she filled a pot with bottled water and placed it on a rock near the fire.

"When this is hot we'll have hot chocolate for the girls and warm water for washing up. Just because the world has collapsed doesn't mean we shouldn't brush our teeth and wash our hands."

Artair, cupping his bowl in one hand, looked at Ben with hope in his eyes as the old man unfolded a camp chair for June.

"What's the plan?" the boy asked. "How do we get across the river?"

"Don't think we can," Ben said gently. "That river is too much even for the Crusher. Someone might be able to get across on foot using the debris from the High Bridge, but that's going to be dangerous. Plus, we can't leave all our supplies and we can't carry them."

"Think we could get back to Monroe?" Ramon asked, thinking about his brother and sister-in-law.

"Doubt it," Ben said. "Sultan's going to be flooded. Monroe might even be. Mayhap once those waters go down. But now? Nope."

Artair put the bowl down on the ground next to him. "I appreciate all your help. More than I can say. But maybe here's where we separate."

"What do you mean?" June asked.

"I have to get home. My brother...we got in a fight. I took off. I don't know if he's alive or not." Artair swiped at tears and turned his head as if they wouldn't see. "If he is, he's going to be worried sick about me. I can get across the river on foot. If not on the bridge, then I can hike upriver until I find a way to cross. Upriver gets me closer to Index anyway."

"You can't go alone," Marie said. "You can't see what's out there."

Artair's hands fisted on his knees. "It doesn't matter. I have to get home. I was so stupid. Taking off like I did. I hated it in that nowhere town with nothing to do, getting nagged by my brother all the time. Now I just want to get back there. How messed up is that?"

"Bad times make you realize the importance of family," June said. "There may be a way to get you home."

Everyone stared at the woman, her gray hair flyaway from a night sleeping on the ground, her swollen ankles overflowing the tops of her tennis shoes, her rear end overflowing the edges of the straining canvas chair.

"Check that water, Father, see if it's hot." June pointed.

Ben did as she asked. "Not yet. What are you thinking, Mother?"

"Our Forest Service maps. Logging roads." June folded her arms over her shelf of belly. "We have all those Green Trail maps in the glove box. There's got to be logging roads that will get us into backcountry. Think about it. This area used to be nothing but mining and logging. Both needed roads."

"But they're probably overgrown or washed away, or destroyed by the quake," Ramon said.

Ben, surprisingly, grinned. "But there will still be ones in use. By the forest service, hikers, hunters. Good idea, Mother."

Ramon watched the old man go to the truck then return with a roll of well-thumbed maps. He glanced at his nieces, who watched him. He knew it was time for a decision.

"Okay girls. Family time."

Alegria came over to sit on the ground in front of Ramon and Marie. "Spell it out, Tío."

Ramon thought a moment. "Three choices. One, we keep going east with these people. It means supplies and not being on our own, and maybe help. Maybe places not as hard hit. But it takes us farther from home."

"Two?" Alegria asked.

"We stay here. Make camp more permanent. Hang out until water's down in Sultan, until things are in more control. This place is somewhat concealed. We have access to water from the stream and the river. But we'll be here a while."

"And three?" Marie asked.

"We start working our way back to Monroe. I left a note for your parents that we were headed for the hospital. If they survived they'll look for us there. It will be dangerous. Not sure we can get through the floodwaters in Sultan. But if we can, we might be able to find Tómas and Therese."

The sisters looked at each other. Alegria looked down, fingering her sling. After a moment she drew in breath and raised her dark eyes to Ramon.

"Tío. I vote for going back. To find mom."

Ramon nodded. "Marie? You're not saying much."

Marie looked at her younger sister and without warning, tears overflowed. "I vote for staying with Ben and June and Artair. For logging roads. We can't stay here. It's not safe. And we can't go back. There are too many."

June gently wiped Marie's tears away with the sleeve of her sweater. "Too many what, honey?"

"Shadows," she whispered.

June looked confused and met Ramon's eyes. He shook his head and June said nothing more. He wondered how long the symptoms of the head injury would last. Fear and worry for Marie gnawed at him. What would he do if she didn't start getting better?

"We'd like you to stay with us," Ben said, with hands folded over the maps. "But we understand that you need to decide what's best for your girls."

Marie broke into sobs. "We can't go back."

Ramon put his arm around the crying girl and drew her in close. "Hush baby. These things you're seeing. They're simply not real. Nothing will stop us from going back."

Marie pushed Ramon's hand away. "No. You're wrong."

Alegria stared at her sister and then gasped on a sob. She came to them, huddled close, tears streaming. Ramon clutched both girls, swallowed past the hard lump in his throat, and started to speak, to tell them again about head injuries, about the real world.

But Artair spoke first. "I think you got to decide something else."

"What?" Ramon asked, irritated by the interruption.

"You need to decide if everything Marie's seeing is from her head injury, or if something else's going on the rest of us can't see. Me? I think the doctor was wrong. I don't think what's happening has anything to do with the head injury." Artair glanced at Marie before focusing back on Ramon. "I believe her. She saw the raven."

Ramon remembered the tendrils of chill air that passed him earlier. And Marie's words that something had just touched him. Early morning breeze and a head injury? Or some freak shadow coming too close?

The logical side of him knew it was the head injury. That his brother and sister-in-law might very well be alive, maybe injured, out there looking for them. That an old woman hadn't had a raven on her shoulder only Marie saw. That shadow people without eyes or noses or mouths didn't move among the trees.

But then he thought about that deep buried instinct inside that stirred and woke. About his neck hairs standing up as if his body knew something his brain didn't.

He drew in a deep breath, studied Marie's face, and then looked around the group. "Okay. Not sure I believe in any of this. But I trust her."

"Mom," Alegria managed to say before folding over, sobs shaking her body. "I want to go home."

Ben blew out a heavy sigh. "I believe Marie, too. Against all my common sense. Last night…well, mayhap there's things around here we don't want to get too close to."

Ramon pulled Alegria up to his lap and wrapped his arms tightly around her as she cried against him. "We still have a choice to make."

"We have to stay together," Marie said, sniffling.

June opened packets of hot chocolate mix and poured them into splatter ware camping mugs. She stirred and handed them to Marie and Alegria. "Drink this girls. Something warm and sweet won't make your sadness go away but it will help you feel better."

Marie held her tin mug close in both hands. "We can't stay here. They're coming."

"And we can't go back," Artair said.

"Then logging roads it is." Ben unfolded the maps. "Let's finish up this breakfast before it gets cold, and then plot out our routes."

"And Marie," Artair said, reaching over to touch her arm lightly. "You need to tell us when you see things. We need to know what's around us."

Marie didn't answer, but she slipped out from under Ramon's arm and rolled up her sleeping bag.

And while she worked, her eyes scanned the woods around them.

2

Marie wondered what made shadows a threat. The way they circled? The way they paused, as if watching? Evaluating? Or the way they breathed?

They seemed to deeply suck in air when they got close to her family and the others. She could see the air, or something, moving like wisps of breath on a cold morning. The shadows drew close with a sound like wind, and then the fine tendrils, those wisps, would float out from her. From her uncle. From Artair. From each of them. And be pulled to the shadows.

As if something was being sucked out of their souls.

And each time a wisp left her, she felt colder. The chill deeper.

And the shadows grew. Like they were some kind of spirit vampires.

Her uncle wanted to protect his family. She wanted to feel safe next to him. But how could he protect them from shadows?

3

Ramon shut the camper door and snicked the padlock closed. He pocketed his key, turning back to the campsite. Artair kicked dirt over the fire, smothering it. June stowed the maps back in the glove box. Ben opened the driver's door on the old truck and a moment later the engine turned over, caught, and rumbled. Marie stood at the truck, waiting and watching. And Alegria…

Ramon's heart stuttered. He couldn't see his niece. "Where's Alegria?"

Artair looked around the site. "She was here after breakfast. When we started packing up."

"Alegria!" Ramon shouted, his stomach knotting into a heavy weight that pulled his heart down.

There was no answer.

Marie turned in a circle slowly, then stopped, pointing. "What's that?"

A small river rock sat on the hood of the truck, vibrating gently with the running engine. Ramon took two quick steps to the truck. Under the rock was one of the empty hot chocolate packets. He dropped the rock with nerveless fingers. His niece's childish handwriting scrawled across the brand.

I want mom.

Ben took the paper from Ramon's nerveless fingers, glanced at it, then wadded into a tiny ball. "Get in the truck, Mother. We all need to get back down the road."

"She can't have gone too far." Artair put his hand on Ramon's arm as if to reassure him.

Ramon pushed his hand off and jerked open the door to the truck. The kid didn't know Alegria. How stubborn she was. When they found her, he was going to figure out some sort of leash. Keep her tied to him from here on out so he knew where she was every moment of the day. Matter of fact he was going to leash both girls.

"You're grinding your teeth, Tío," Marie said, climbing into the truck. "We'll find her. She'll be sitting on the side of the road crying and waiting for us. You know how she is. Gets an idea, gets pig-headed, and then gets in trouble."

"She's going to get in trouble all right," Ramon said.

Ben worked the truck around to face the direction they'd come.

Ramon bounced against the doorframe as the truck went over the rocks that had ringed their fire. He gripped the back of the seat as if squeezing it would make the truck go faster.

And then the rain came back.

4

Alegria jogged down the rough forest service road, gripping her arm to her chest with her good hand to support it. Her shoulder ached deeply. Almost as deeply as the ache in her chest and throat that felt like her heart was broke. She wanted nothing more than to run back to the camp, to her sister and her uncle. Her knees were shaky with fear. Fear that her uncle would come get her and make her go back. Fear that he wouldn't come get her and something would come out of the trees. Fear that she would never see her mom again.

Fear made her keep going and fear made her want to turn back.

At least going back down the narrow track was easier since debris had been pushed out of the way when they drove the truck through.

Her dark eyes scanned the fringe of forest as she ran. She believed her sister. She knew there were scary things out there. But there were always scary things in the world. And it wasn't like she could do anything about it.

Besides, she knew how afraid for them her mother must be, and that meant she needed to be brave.

When her uncle came to live with them she'd been happy. The family all together like they were supposed to be. She couldn't remember when she realized that Tío knew her father was doing something bad, too. She couldn't tell her father that Tío watched him, and couldn't tell her uncle that her father swapped spit with the neighbor's babysitter. Either confession betrayed someone she loved.

And in the middle was her mother with her gentle voice and loving hands. She'd come home from standing all day in the hair salon, smelling like perm solution, exhaustion making shadows under her eyes. Any confession would break her heart.

Two days before the earthquake, her mother told Alegria that she was going to have a baby brother or sister. No one else knew. It made Alegria proud that she was trusted. Made her feel grown up. Maybe even more loved than Marie. It was their secret, her and her beautiful mother.

She knew then she'd have to be strong. Keep the secrets about their family. She would talk Tío into not doing something stupid like beating up her dad. Or better yet, she'd find a way to make her father stop. If he knew she'd seen him, he'd change. For her. She knew it. She'd keep the family together. Her mother would be happy again.

But then the quake hit. And her mother was cut off from home somewhere, pregnant, and without Alegria to help her.

Sitting around the fire eating the breakfast of oatmeal, the obvious action settled on her shoulders. The others could go on. But she had to go back. If the flood in Sultan wasn't gone, she'd swim. She was a good swimmer. And when she got to the collapsed overpass in Monroe that blocked the way, she'd climb. She was a good climber, too.

She'd get to Snohomish and save her mother.

A few fat raindrops fell, pattering softly on leaves. A few more fell, soaking into Alegria's hair and running down her neck in cold little streams. Maybe she should have taken time to grab her rain gear. Or at least a hat.

A low rumble came through the trees and she recognized the Old Crusher's big engine. So they'd already found out she was gone.

She tried to run faster but a sudden side-ache bloomed and made her breath hitch. She stopped, pressing her hand against her waist as she gulped for air. She couldn't outrun the truck. And her Tío would make her go back with them. She hesitated, torn between wanting to be saved and safe and wanting to find her mother.

She drew in a ragged breath. Her mother needed her.

So she'd have to hide. There were lots of hiding places now that the woods were so destroyed.

She scrambled over a downed tree, hitting her arm against the trunk and gasping at the sharp pain. On the other side, she dropped down into the wet earth, pressing back against the big log hiding her from view. She held still, trying to be quiet as a mouse, but then laughed.

They'd never hear her over the noise of the truck.

The rumble grew closer and she shifted in her hiding spot to get away from a rock poking her hip. The woods, with trees standing and broken from the quake and others shattered on the ground around her, was full of deep green shadows.

The brief laughter died. Something moved out there. Something solid. Not one of the shadows her sister saw. Something massive. A bear. A not-bear. Her shattered thoughts tried to form meaning out of what moved toward her through the trees.

But it was too big. She saw the body covered in black bristles. Saw the monstrous teeth and bear-like claws.

Screams tore her throat, ripped up into the rain.

And were drowned by the sound of the truck's passing.

Alegria scrambled to her feet and clawed her way on to the downed tree. Bark bit into her hands. Her knee slipped on wet moss and she came down on her stomach hard. She struggled to breathe as she rolled over the tree and hit the ground on the other side. Her shoulder made a sick, wet, popping sound and her arm went numb.

She got to her knees and pushed up with her good hand. The forest floor under her trembled with the impact of the thing coming. Branches snapped. Heavy breathing, like low grunts, drew close.

Alegria tried to scream but she didn't have the breath. She pulled herself up and looked around, eyes wild. Where could she go? The forest stretched forever. Help was gone. There was no shelter, no door to lock behind her. She stumbled onto the logging road, fell again to her knee, pushed up, and ran in the direction the Old Crusher had gone. They'd come back. They had to.

She didn't need to look over her shoulder to know the thing was coming after her.

Up ahead something else moved in the trees. Alegria gasped out a small, breathless scream. Another monster. Maybe she could get past it before it reached the road.

Pain bit sharply into her side and her breath hitched. Holding her arm tight to her chest to cushion her shoulder, she ran like she'd never run. But whatever was ahead of her was fast, too. She saw it in flashes of brown through the trees still standing. She saw glimpses of a shape as it moved through the destruction from the quake. It was going to pass her, to come out on the road ahead of her.

She couldn't help it. She risked a glance over her shoulder. The thing behind her was coming in a long-legged loping run. It was only a few yards behind her. She cried out, heart racing in terror.

The thing ahead of her roared. She twisted round, stumbled over a rock, and came down hard. Agony from her shoulder was a bright, white heat and for a brief second she was gone, carried away by pain and horror.

Something touched her and she screamed, brought back to cold ground and gray skies and monsters.

But it was a boy leaning over her. He caught her arm, pulled her to her feet. She twisted fiercely against his hands.

"Run!" Her mind screamed the word but what came out was a whisper strangled by pounding heart and heaving lungs.

The boy pointed.

The shape in the trees ahead of her was another monster, but one her frozen mind could wrap around. With a massive roar the grizzly bear charged. The boy pulled Alegria off the road. Her knee banged into a downed log and she felt something wrench inside. But the boy wouldn't allow her to stop. He hauled her up and over the log and then half-dragged her a few feet to a still-standing tree.

Behind her, the battle roared. Tears coursed down her cheeks and deep tremors raced through her body.

The boy's hands cupped her cheeks, turning her to face him. His hands were warm like summer sun. She tried to turn back to the battle, but he shook his head and held her so that she only saw the deep walnut-brown of his eyes.

He leaned back against the red bark of the tree behind him. His eyes were gentle. So calm. Alegria couldn't look away. Her racing heart slowed. Her breathing deepened. She thought he was hugging her. She felt his arms come around her. And then warmth. A deep, almost steamy, warmth that wrapped slowly around her body. For the briefest moment there was no air, she couldn't breathe, she was going to die, and then life came back.

The boy was gone but still there, surrounding her in a deep red-gold light like a setting sun after a storm. The moist air smelled of cinnamon and wood. She felt enclosed, cocooned. Pain receded and was gone. She couldn't move, but there was no need to run anymore. Time slowed and slowed and slowed. Her eyes closed but she saw all. Her feet sank into the beautifully loamy forest floor. Her arms stretched up, her hair moving in high, gentle winds.

She breathed deep, so deep, pulling life into her being.

Grizzlies and monsters and lost mothers were the merest irritation, like the minute flutters of wings against bark, meaningless in the long slow cycles of earth.

And then all sense of Alegria was gone.

5

Sharon bit into her second cold McChicken sandwich. Tessa and Connor sat next to her, rustling in bags and also eating cold burgers. She shook her head in disgust. They looked like some kind of weird product-placement scene in an apocalyptic movie.

At least it had stopped raining for the moment. The only good thing so far. The late morning was still cold and her clothes still clammy. Maybe she'd die of hypothermia. They had no fire and nothing to build one with. They had no blankets or cold weather gear and Tessa huddled against Connor for warmth.

Sharon swallowed the last congealed bite. If hypothermia didn't get her, maybe she'd die of food poisoning.

She wadded up the wrapper and dropped it on the ground when she stood. Connor opened his mouth as if to say something, but when he met her eyes he kept quiet. Maybe he realized there was no one coming to enforce littering laws.

She walked away from the jeep and young people, stepping carefully over torn up asphalt, lifted and twisted like waves. They were at the end of usable highway. Ahead of her the Skykomish River roared, underscored by the low rumble of boulders dropping and tumbling. The High Bridge was gone, nothing now but debris piled up in a river that was slowly backing up behind the mess. Eventually all that was going to break free when the pressure of the river became too strong. Sharon pitied anyone downstream when that happened.

It had taken them a full day and most of the night to get out of Sultan, past the high water, past the terrified people. All those vehicles pushing, pushing, forcing their way out of the city, seemed to have given up when they reached Gold Bar. But that city was so devastated Sharon saw no reason to stay, to become part of a crowd destined to starve to death. She'd pointed that out and the kids hadn't had the energy to argue. So Connor kept driving.

Until, sometime in the middle of the night, they'd ended up at the High Bridge. The end of the road. Literally. Exhausted and traumatized, Tessa and Connor fell asleep sitting propped against each other on a bench seat. But Sharon hadn't slept. She felt no need for sleep. Instead, she'd sat in the driver's seat, shivering in the cold and watching the black night slowly lighten to gray.

She knew it wouldn't be long before others came up the

highway. Until this spot became a logjam of cars and people striving to get some place the quake hadn't touched.

But for them, here and now, it meant they were done heading east. If the shadows followed them, there wasn't any place left to go, to get away. It gave her a deep sense of relief. She was no longer responsible for getting the kids someplace safe. They could camp out here or go back on their own. The decision was out of her hands. She could leave any time she wanted. Walk back the way they'd come, if need be. Once out of their sight, she knew she'd find any number of ways to die. She shivered again. Even if it was just hypothermia.

The greasy food sat like a stone in her stomach. All those years of eating healthy so she'd live longer. That had done a lot of good. If she had access to the now-under- water Galaxy Chocolates in Sultan, she'd gorge herself on their signature salted caramels. Or maybe she'd walk into Panera Bread, order a whole loaf of garlic and olive oil bread and eat it by herself.

Or, god, even a mug of strong coffee. She crossed her arms over her chest for warmth then winced, catching her breath. The pain in her breast was like a sharp knife being inserted and twisted. The doctor had told her the pain would get worse, had told her she'd end up taking morphine. She'd thrown the prescription at him. Told him she wouldn't be around long enough for the pain to count.

And yet here she was, still breathing. She should have taken the prescription and filled it instead of throwing a dramatic martyr fit. She could have overdosed days ago and missed all the McChicken sandwiches with their soggy buns.

At the cliff edge where the bridge should have been, Sharon stopped and looked over the rim. It wouldn't be hard at all to just step out into air. Either the rocks or the river would take care of things nicely.

"Don't get too close," Connor said behind her. "You might fall."

Sharon pressed a palm against her pounding heart. "No shit. Especially when some idiot kid sneaks up behind you."

"Oh, sorry. I wasn't thinking."

"Did you want something?" Sharon wondered how rude she'd have to be to get him to leave so she could face that cliff edge again.

"Well, yeah. I mean, someone's coming." Connor gestured. "We can hear an engine. Up that track there. Tessa thought maybe you should come back. We should stick close in case they're, you know, bad guys."

"Bad guys?"

Connor shrugged. "With the world gone to hell, no police around, and no way to call for help, people aren't going to need to follow civilized rules any more, are they? I mean, society's probably dead. Or at least going to be comatose for a long time."

He had a point. Sharon shoved her hands into the pockets of her slacks. "Lead on then."

Connor headed back toward the jeep and she followed, hoping for bad guys. Maybe she could sacrifice herself saving the kids. Go out in glory.

The sound of the engine grew louder. Sharon joined the kids and it dawned on her they'd just lined up in a perfect row of targets along the side of the jeep. Connor looked tentative as if not sure whether to be scared or not. Tessa just looked terrified. Their every-day lives gone, the things they took for granted, taken. Last week on the cusp of adulthood, striving to be so mature with jobs and lives slowly separating from their parents. And today they were children again, staring petrified into devastation.

Sharon realized suddenly that she didn't want anything to happen to them. They didn't ask for this, didn't deserve it, shouldn't die. She stepped in front of the pair.

A big old truck with a homemade camper came jolting down the logging road, going too fast. She recognized it as the one she'd seen crossing the Wallace River back in Sultan. She couldn't see the driver yet, but whoever it was hit the brakes. Before the truck came to a complete stop, the back door was thrown open and a Hispanic man leaped out. He ran toward them and Sharon saw something like panic in his dark eyes.

"Have you seen a little girl?" He grabbed Connor's arm. "My niece. Have you seen her?"

"No, man," Connor said, shaking his arm free and rubbing his bicep.

The man ran to the back of the jeep and pulled open the doors. "Alegria!"

Sharon watched an old couple and a teenage boy and girl get out of the truck, leaving the engine idling. The girl trailed behind the others, her eyes scanning side to side, as if searching. Sharon shivered, the hairs on her arms suddenly erect. She didn't think the teenager was looking for the same thing the man was.

"Is she here?" the old man said.

"No." The guy turned to Sharon. "How long have you been here? Which direction did you come from? Did you pass anyone on the road?"

"Ramon," the old man said. "Slow down, son, and think. There's no way Alegria made it this far on foot, in the time she's been gone."

"Unless someone grabbed her. Another rig, maybe, coming up that road."

The man, Ramon, was in full-blown panic, pupils dilated, hands shaking.

"Dude," Connor said. "We've been here most of the night. No one's gone by."

Ramon caught at the teenage girl's arm and half-carried her back to their truck. "We go back. We must have missed her. Turn this thing around."

"Wait!" Tessa shouted, taking a step toward the strangers.

Sharon saw a blush wash across her cheeks.

The old woman was the only one to pause. "We have to find our girl."

"I get that," Tessa said, her eyes on Ramon as he lifted the girl into the back seat of the truck. "But please don't leave us."

Something in her voice must have penetrated Ramon's panic because he paused, stared at Tessa, and took a step back toward them. "Do I know you?"

Tessa's blush deepened until Sharon wondered if she was going to self-combust.

"Yes." Tessa stared at the ground, and then raised her chin. "No. You used to come by where I work. Where we worked. That's all. McDonalds. In Sultan."

Connor's eyes widened as he looked from Ramon to Tessa. Sharon understood. This Ramon was muscular, fit, and probably handsome when he wasn't so upset. Maybe in his mid-twenties. He looked like someone who saved people from an apocalypse. All the things Connor wasn't.

"We've been following you, man," Connor said finally. "Because Tessa-"

And now, Sharon realized, Tessa was about to be humiliated. "Tessa saw your truck cross the Wallace in Sultan," she said, cutting in abruptly. "She figured if you did it, we could. Connor hot-wired this jeep and we followed you."

Tessa looked at her with gratitude. Connor just looked confused.

"Okay, but…" Ramon studied Tessa for a moment longer, and then seemed to finally see their clothes. "I do know you."

"Get in the truck, Mother," the old man said, ignoring the conversation. "Mayhap you kids should follow us. Be safer than being out here alone. We're going back to look for our girl. And then we're hunting up old logging roads to get us to Index. To find Artair's brother." He gestured at the teenage boy who was already getting back in the truck.

"Good plan," Connor said. "I mean, since Sultan is gone. There's no going back that way."

"Follow if you want," Ramon said, heaving the old woman up into the truck. "But we can't wait. We need to find my niece."

Tessa hesitated, then grabbed up their remaining bags of burgers and threw them in the back of the jeep. Connor jogged around to the driver's side.

While the old man got the truck turned around, Connor started up the jeep. Sharon hesitated, watching them. If she slipped away, right now they'd probably never notice. But then Tessa caught her arm and pulled her to the jeep. Reluctantly, she got in the back and sat alone on the bench seat.

She'd just go along a little further, she decided. Just to make sure Tessa and Connor would be okay. And then she'd find her death.

Connor pulled out and the jeep rattled over the rough ground, following the truck.

Sharon looked out the front window at the devastated woods they were entering. What was waiting for them? That teenage girl in the truck with Ramon. She'd seen something, Sharon was sure. Maybe the shadows, that fog, had followed them.

Either way, an unfamiliar emotion tickled deep inside. It was like a spark of light where there had been only the blackness of her death. She saw it as a final responsibility before the end. To make sure the two kids who had been kind to her made it somewhere safe.

But there was something else there, too. A tugging, a pulling forward. A tiny spark of anticipation.

It was strange to feel anything other than rage and pain, and Sharon wasn't sure she wanted it. She let her thoughts probe at it, like a tongue poking a hole where a tooth had been. There was irritation at being pulled from her goal, but at the same time there was something that just might have been relief. If she was going to die anyway, maybe going out as a hero was better than dying alone. She'd stay with the kids a bit. Just to make sure they were okay with these strangers.

The darkness, her end, could wait a little longer.

6

Ben drove back up the logging road slower than he'd raced down. Ramon gripped the door handle so tight his hand throbbed. He stared out one window, then swung around to stare out another, terrified that he might be looking the wrong way for the few seconds when they might pass Alegria. His neck muscles ached with tension and his heart felt like a trapped bird, fluttering frantically in his chest. Marie sat next to him, one hand a barely felt warmth on his arm. She wasn't looking out the windows though. Instead she sat with her eyes downcast. Every few minutes Ramon felt a shiver move through her but he couldn't tear his eyes from the passing forest to help her.

He might miss Alegria.

He put his arm around her shoulders and pulled her tight to his side. He didn't know if she was cold or afraid, but holding her close was all the comfort he could spare. A tremor moved through her again.

"It's okay, baby," he said. "We'll find her. Don't worry." Even to his ears the words sounded distracted and false.

They were roughly half way back to their campsite, with the kids in the old Willys jeep following, when Marie suddenly gripped his hand so tight he caught his breath. When he looked to her, he saw she also had hold of Artair's arm.

"Ben, stop the truck," Artair said quickly.

"Here." Her voice was slow and soft as if she talked in her sleep.

"What?" Ramon asked. "What's here? Are you going to be sick?"

"No…Alegria."

Ramon pulled loose from Marie and jumped out of the truck. He stood a moment, hands fisted, nerves screaming for him to go. Somewhere. Anywhere. The woods were quiet. A few small birds flitted through the branches of downed trees. He pulled in a ragged breath and ran to the edge of the road, staring into the ruined forest. Nothing moved. No shape of a small girl in the shadows. He jogged back to the truck, his insides twisted into knots of despair.

"She's not here." He stood in the muddy road, gripping the edge of the truck door.

Marie raised her head, pupils dilated, skin pale. "She's here. She's not here."

Ben and June had turned to look over the front seat and June reached out to place the back of her hand against Marie's forehead. After a brief pause she shook her head.

Ramon didn't know what to do. He'd agreed earlier to trust Marie, but she wasn't saying anything to trust. It sounded like she was arguing with herself. He met Artair's eyes and the boy shrugged. But then Artair opened the door, got out, and walked to the edge of the dirt track where he stood, looking around.

The truck idled roughly, the noisy engine knocking like an old man coughing. Ramon caught Ben's eye and signaled to him to turn the truck off. Then he walked down the road in the direction they were headed. Behind him he heard the jeep engine shut off and doors open. He scanned the ground, not sure what he was looking for. He didn't know anything about tracking. But maybe the mud and rocks were enough to show an imprint of a shoe.

"Ramon!" Ben called out.

He turned to see Ben standing next to the truck, one hand on the hood. Marie was outside as well. She stood in front of the truck, head down and hands up slightly, palms upward as if testing to see if it was raining again. And then she lurched backward as if yanked over, and came down on her bottom.

"No!" she screamed.

Artair ran to her side and lifted her in his arms. Ramon saw her speak to him, and then he was turning, running for the truck.

"Come back!" he yelled to Ramon. "Everyone, back inside!"

There was no hesitation now, no questioning whether Marie was suffering hallucinations or truly seeing what they couldn't. Behind him, the kids jumped into the jeep. Ramon ran the few yards back and climbed in the truck next to his niece. Artair slammed the truck door and reached across Marie to hit the lock button.

"There!" June's voice was low, cracking on fear.

Something moved through the trees. Too big to be Alegria. A broad, hulking shape moving over downed logs like they were mere branches.

"What the fuck is that?" Artair asked.

Ramon's thoughts stuttered over what his eyes tried to tell him. The massive body, moving on all four limbs, was covered in bristles. Its teeth and claws were long and darkly yellow.

The thing stopped in the logging road right in front of the truck and rose upright. It was large enough that its arms spanned the width of the hood as it grabbed both front wheel wells. The truck rocked violently as the thing shook it.

"Time to go, Father," June said, her voice oddly calm and even.

"Why don't you start the old Crusher up?"

Ben stared at her, mouth agape. The truck rocked again and then the thing lifted the front end a few feet, letting it drop so violently that they were thrown up off the seats. Ramon tasted the hot copper of blood as he bit his tongue. June reached across the seat to turn the key in the ignition. As the engine cranked over, she pushed against the steering wheel. A loud horn blew out the notes to the old song *Tequila*. The thing took a step back, cocking its head to one side.

Ben seemed to come to his senses. He shoved the truck into gear, hit the gas, and the truck surged forward.

The old Crusher slammed all of its weight, engine, old wood bumper, camper, everything, into the creature. Ramon heard the jeep behind them also laying on the horn. The thing went down under the front end of the truck, and the truck rocked heavily to one side as they drove right over it. He twisted to look out the side window and caught a glimpse of the jeep was coming fast.

"That'll take care of it," Ben said. "Both of us hitting it."

"Don't think so," Artair said, his voice high with strain. "It's getting up."

Artair was right. Ramon could the thing in the truck's side mirror come up on one knee, and then stand to full height as if nothing had happened. He saw no blood, no bones sticking out, no sign a big truck had just driven right over it. Instead the thing took the full impact of the jeep hitting it without even staggering back.

Ramon heard the screaming in the jeep. Connor must have thrown it into reverse because it started to back up. The thing caught the fender.

"This is the old Crusher," June said, still calm. "Might as well crush that thing, don't you think?"

Ben put the truck in reverse but Marie put a hand on his shoulder.

"Wait," she said.

Ramon's brain kicked into gear. He fumbled under the front seat and pulled the Glock loose with the sound of ripping duct tape. If a truck couldn't kill the thing maybe bullets would. But Marie caught his wrist.

"Wait," she repeated softly. She turned slightly as if listening and then lifted her chin, tears pooling in her dark eyes. "Alegria comes."

Ramon looked out the passenger window in the direction Marie pointed.

"What the hell?" Ben whispered.

Something as silver as moonlight moved through the shadowed forest. As it came out of the trees, Ramon saw a wolf. He'd never seen one outside of photos or the zoo, but there was no doubt in his mind that this large, muscled animal was a wolf. It leaped easily over a downed tree and paused, looking behind it as if waiting for something.

A girl came through the trees and put a hand on the wolf's head. Alegria. But somehow taller, older, a slender young woman instead of a gawky thirteen-year old.

Her eyes, meeting Ramon's, were a strange gold, almost a deep amber, instead of dark brown. Leaves and twigs were twisted in her hair, not like she'd just run through a hedge, but as if she'd hung them like ribbons.

It was Alegria. It was his beloved niece.

But it wasn't.

The jeans and pink tee shirt she'd had on that morning were gone. Instead she wore a long brown skirt and short-sleeved tunic. Bark. She looked like she wore soft strips of bark.

Marie reached across Artair, opened the truck door, and clambered over him even as he caught at her. She pulled free and ran toward her sister. Ramon shoved his door open and leaped out. Behind them, the thing shook the jeep again and kids screamed. Metal screeched as the thing dug claws into the hood. But all he saw were his nieces.

Alegria cupped Marie's face with both hands. Neither spoke. They looked at each other for only a brief second but Ramon felt like time slowed and stretched. He stopped near them, heart pounding. He wanted to grab his girls, hold them tight and safe, get them away from the insanity. But he stood still until Alegria lowered her hands and looked over Marie's head to meet his eyes. He stepped forward but she shook her head, stopping him. He saw a tear track down her cheek.

Marie came back and took his hand. "We need to be in the truck now."

"Not without your sister."

"We need to go, now." Marie tugged at him.

"Come with us, Alegria." The weighted pain in his chest was his heart, breaking.

Alegria glanced at him but then looked back into the woods. He saw movement again in the trees. Something else was coming.

"Now," Marie said, her voice tight with urgency. "She wants us safe. Please, Tío. Now."

Ramon gave in to her tugging and ran with her to the truck where he boosted her inside and then followed. With the doors shut again, he could only watch.

"Is that…" Artair's voice broke and he sucked in a deep breath. "Is that a…a grizzly?"

A young boy came out of the woods to stand next to Alegria. And behind him was an immense grizzly that dwarfed even the silver wolf. The four paused like some sort of avenging forest spirits. And then, with a thunderous roar, the bear lunged forward, muscles rippling with power. The wolf leaped after him. Alegria and the boy followed at a run.

The old canopy blocked the back window but as the creatures raced past, Ramon and the others leaned to watch the rear view mirrors. The bear's jaws clamped around the waist of the thing and flung it to the side of the road. The wolf jumped on it, biting into the throat and ripping flesh. Deeply black blood jetted upward, spraying the fur of the wolf. The bear sank teeth into the thing's legs.

It roared. Its claws raked the wolf and bright red blood bloomed in long gashes. But the wolf hung on, shaking his head, slinging black blood. The bear pulled backward.

"My god," Ben breathed.

The bear tore the thing's legs off and flung them with a shake of its massive head. Arteries hung from stumps on the creature like bloody rubber bands. The wolf braced its front legs and bit deeper, jaws working. It was only when Ramon heard the loud growling of the wolf that he realized the kids in the jeep were no longer screaming.

The wolf severed the neck and the thing's head toppled.

Silence fell. The wolf and bear stood over the carcass. Blood gushed, then slowed to a thick river. But the thing no longer moved. After a long moment, Alegria and the boy held their hands out. The wolf and bear turned as if they'd been called. Blood caked the fur on both animals. When they reached the boy and Alegria, all four walked into the shadows of the trees as if there was no truck, no jeep, no monster.

No family.

"No!" Ramon shoved open the door again, jumped out, and ran.

But in those few short moments that it took him to reach the forest fringe, they were gone.

7

Sharon sat, watching a fire burn, brisk and hot, sap snapping and sending sparks into the air. Ben, Tessa, and June moved through the motions of setting up the camp, gathering more firewood, simmering canned Dinty Moore beef stew in a cast iron pot near the flames. June stirred water into some sort of boxed biscuit mix. Artair and Connor had taken it upon themselves to be guardians and they walked the perimeter of the same small clearing they'd camped in the night before.

Sharon wasn't sure what they'd do if something like that monster showed up. But here they were, back where the others had started from.

Marie helped June, but Sharon saw the girl watching the spur track that led to the logging road they'd been on. Half an hour earlier Ramon had thrown down the hatchet he'd been splitting wood with and gone back that way.

Sharon sat on a rock a short distance from the others. She was pale and her skin felt clammy. She shivered but it wasn't from the soft mist falling, or the coolness in the air. It wasn't even fear as the sun left them and shadows lengthened, deepening between the trees.

The agony was sharp and white hot, her breast burning a hole all the way into her soul. Her nerves screamed against the invasion, her stomach twisted in nausea. But all she could do was grit her teeth and hope it passed.

She'd waited too long. She should have found a way to die sooner, before the pain reached this point. She pressed chilled, bluish fingers against her breast as if touch might cool the fire, put out the inner destruction as cells slowly killed her.

The pain was unbearable. She couldn't draw in a deep enough breath. She saw a sparkling halo around everything and knew she was about to pass out. She managed a shallow gasp. Her body shook as if trying to wake her, but she could feel herself slipping. She put her hand out as if to stop the pain, stop the darkness coming, stop the fall, even while something inside rejoiced in finally reaching the end.

But then someone caught her hand in a strong grip. She was lifted back up, her fingers held tight. Air, cool and damp and clean flowed into her lungs. The agony eased, became an ache. The world came back, the crackling fire, the trees, the dripping soft mist.

"No," she whispered. "Let me die."

"When it's time, daughter."

The old woman from Sultan stood there. The layers of her black dress moved in a wind that didn't exist. Her long gray hair blew across her face, hiding her eyes and then revealing their darkness. A raven, so black its feathers were like midnight, perched on the old woman's shoulder. In one hand she held a tall staff while with the other she gripped Sharon's arm.

"It *is* time," Sharon managed to whisper. "It's past time."

The old woman tightened her grip until Sharon felt her bones shift. "It's time when I say it is."

And the old crone was gone.

Sharon straightened, her skin now flushed with heat. Her breast throbbed, but it was manageable. She shook her head, wondering if everyone saw hallucinations as they fainted.

But then she saw Marie staring at her, eyes wide, and knew if it had been a hallucination, Marie had shared it.

8

Ramon walked down the logging road, following the path the truck had cleared earlier. The soft mist and low clouds diffused any light, and the coming night stole even more. Long twilight shadows lengthened around him and he knew he should turn around. Knew he didn't want to be out here alone in the dark. His jaw, his fists, were clenched so tight both ached. It was hard to breathe past the even deeper ache in his chest.

Family was everything. The only thing. It was the whole reason he'd walked away from his life in Mexico. Uprooted, left it all behind, in order to come here and keep his family together. He'd thought his brother would see reason, stop his affairs. Keep the family intact. Then when the quake hit, everything tilted toward keeping his nieces safe.

And now Alegria was…what? Gone? This new, damaged, dangerous world shifted reality around him and his whole body ached with deep grief. He'd lost his niece but didn't even know if that meant she was dead and he was mourning her, or if she'd changed somehow and was simply lost. Was there any part of his little girl left in that young woman who moved through the trees as if part of them?

He had failed at keeping them safe. What kind of man was he, that he couldn't protect them, couldn't fix whatever the hell this was? He hadn't even been able to save Marie when that thing attacked them. That had all been on Alegria and the boy with her. And their pets.

Some pets.

If it hadn't been for those wild creatures, Marie, Ben, all of them, would be dead right now.

So what could he do? Stay here to find Alegria, get her back somehow? Or leave her to keep Marie safe?

Something moved through the trees off to his left. He froze, breath hitching in his chest.

The deep shadows in the damaged forest shifted and he saw the silver wolf, his fur so pale it was like moonlight. Ramon took a step back. That animal had killed a monster. No way was it a real wolf. His mind couldn't wrap around what his eyes told him. He stepped back again and stumbled over a large shattered branch, coming down hard on his butt.

The wolf paced out onto the logging road and stood there, amber eyes on him, fur glistening with beads of mist. Its sides moved as it breathed.

It sure as hell *looked* real.

Ramon scrambled to his feet, heart racing.

The wolf turned its head to look over its shoulder.

And there was Alegria, one hand on the gnarled trunk of a yew tree, her eyes as deeply amber as the wolf's. She moved out of the night-shadows, her fingers trailing across the bark of the tree as if reluctant to leave.

"Alegria?" Ramon said, his voice gruff. "Are you my niece?"

She reached fingers up to her face and traced softly down her jaw, as if checking. "Of course."

Her voice was the same, and yet not, rough as if unused, smooth as if aged.

Ramon stepped forward. "Please, tell me what's going on. I don't understand. Where's my little girl?"

A tear pearled up and rolled down her cheek. "I died, Tío. Maybe."

"You're not dead, baby. You're right here." Ramon took another step.

"The Matlose, the thing that came after you, was going to kill me. The boy and his guardian saved me. But to save me I had to die. To become. I'm within the trees now. I'm part of them. And oh, my Tío, it's beautiful." She raised her face, eyes closed, long fingers trailing through the needles of a cedar tree next to her.

Ramon shook his head. He didn't understand, couldn't grasp what she said.

Alegria came forward and stood next to the wolf, one hand on its massive shoulders. "Tío, look at me."

Ramon shook his head again, pressing the heels of his hands into his eyes.

"Look at me!"

He did.

She moved closer to the cedar tree, and closer, until she seemed to meld inside it. She was there, and yet not, surrounded by a deep luminescent red-gold, the heartwood of the tree. She held there a moment and he saw the fissured bark of the tree shimmer as she pulled away. When she stood fully before him, the red-gold held as a halo. And then behind her, light fractured and a darker red glow moved from the yew tree, forming the shape of the boy.

And behind the boy, coming through the trees, was the massive grizzly bear.

Ramon managed to hold his ground but his heart hammered in his chest and terror turned his blood to ice.

"Things older than this world have been released," Alegria said. "You will need to find the man from the hole."

The boy and his grizzly drew even with Alegria. "Keep the dying woman with you," he said. "She must die, but not yet, so watch her."

Ramon shook his head so hard he saw stars. "I'm dreaming. Or I'm unconscious. Or I'm the one dead."

"No!" Alegria said, her voice sharp. "Listen to me. As long as you are near the trees, we may be able to help you. But you need to find the others who are ahead of you. They are coming down from the mountains. You need to trust Marie. Follow her. See what she sees."

The boy held his hand out. Resting in his palm was a small piece of a yew branch. "Give this to my mother. Tell her when she goes home, I will be there."

"Your mother? Who is your mother? I don't understand." Frustration rose through the fear and the flush of it heated his skin. "Tell me what to do. Tell me how to help you both."

"Tío, I love you." Alegria looked over his shoulder. "And I love my sister. Tell her. And remember what we've said."

And then they were gone. Boy and bear, girl and wolf. The drizzle pattered down around him, seeping down the neck of his jacket, dripping from his hair into his eyes. Twilight had deepened and it was almost too dark to see.

"Tío?"

Alegria. Behind him. He whipped around, opening his mouth to call her, but it was Marie who stood in the middle of the logging road. She held a flashlight in one hand, the pale beam pointed at the muddy track. Rain had soaked her long unruly curls and she shivered.

"Come back to the fire," she said softly.

Ramon drew in a deep breath. Marie was there before him, real and solid. No hallucination. Her eyes were steady and clear, more lucid than she had been in days. He drew in another breath as understanding came to him. He was the one who'd had the head injury. Not Marie. He was the one seeing things that weren't there. He joined his niece and let her shine the light forward on the trail back to camp.

They'd only gone a few feet though, when Marie held her hand out and spoke in her soft voice. "This is yours. Don't lose it."

The tip of a yew tree branch rested across her hand. Ramon stared at it then wordlessly pocketed it. She squeezed his arm as if to reassure him.

The man from a hole. A dying woman. His niece part of a tree. Monsters.

The world had gone insane.

Or else he was.

Back at the camp, a large fire burned in a ring of stone. Sharon sat alone in the shadows but the others huddled around the flames.

Ramon followed Marie and she lowered herself next to Artair on a small log someone had rolled up to the fire for a bench. Ramon watched the young man hand her a bowl of something and tug the hood of her coat up over her drenched hair.

He stood, not ready to give up, not ready to admit there was nothing left he could do. The light from the flames played over Marie's face as she spooned up something from the bowl. His throat was thick with pain. Alegria should have been next to her.

June took up most of the space on another small log, sitting under a small fold-up umbrella she'd found somewhere. Ben was crammed in next to her, barely clinging to the last scant inches of seating space, the collar of his wool coat pulled up and a fluorescent green stocking cap pulled down over his ears.

June pointed across the fire and Ramon saw a stump with a bowl on it. Defeated, with no answers, no solutions, and no ideas what to do next, Ramon crossed the rough ground to pick up the warm bowl and sit on the stump. There was canned beef stew and he scooped some up with a spoon, swallowing without tasting. Warmth tracked its way down to his stomach and he shivered.

"We should post guards tonight," Ben said. "Whoever does it should have a gun. And they need to keep the fires going."

"You really think fire will stop more of those things?" Ramon asked. "We were attacked in daylight."

Ben shrugged. "I don't know, son. None of this makes sense. I don't even know if a gun will help. But if not, we have fire and can always try burning them."

"And we need to rest," June said. "The children are exhausted from the shock of today."

"Plus we can't travel at night," Artair said. "The logging road might be wiped out and we'd never see it. But I think we should leave early. Get to Index as fast as we can."

Marie put her bowl on the ground and leaned her head on Artair's shoulder, closing her eyes. Ramon wondered briefly if she was tired, or simply tired of seeing things in the shadows.

"So we push hard tomorrow," he said. Something in his heart twisted in pain. He wished it were a heart attack. Something that could be fixed. Not something irreparably breaking at the thought of leaving Alegria.

Tessa leaned toward the fire and dished more stew into her and Connor's bowls. "Thanks for dinner. We haven't had warm food since the quake."

"Yeah, man. Just cold burgers." Connor grimaced. "When this is over I'm going to deliver pizza or something. No more burger joints."

Ramon managed a smile, but he doubted this world would ever go back to normal. Pizza delivery. They'd need roads first.

"So we have kind of a problem," Connor said, glancing at Tessa as if for confirmation.

She nodded. "Sharon's kind of, like, sick. We thought she was going to pass out earlier. Like, maybe she's running a fever or something."

"Sharon?" Ramon asked, his brain momentarily unable to move past bears and grizzlies and trees.

Connor gestured toward the edges of firelight, to the woman sitting alone in shadows. "We picked her up in Sultan when the dam burst. She's helped us out, but she's got the flu or something."

"So we were wondering if you might have antibiotics?" Tessa looked at June.

June put her bowl down and wiped her hands on her ample thighs. "Help me up, Father. I'll go talk to her."

Ben stood, gripped June's hands, braced himself from old habit, and heaved his wife up. June wheezed as she left their fire and moved to where Sharon sat alone with a blanket around her shoulders, staring into the blackness of forest.

"You kids doing okay otherwise?" Ben asked. "No one else getting sick?"

"We're good," Connor said. "Scared shitless, to be honest. The world's a crazy place right now and it don't make sense. But hey, it's not much crazier than a drive-up window on a Friday night." He managed a chuckle, but it came out forced.

Ramon appreciated the kid's effort to ease their fear and managed a smile that felt just as false. Connor grinned back and Ramon saw the banked fear in the kid's eyes. Ramon wasn't the only one suffering here. He wondered if their families were alive. If not, what would happen to them? What would happen to any of them? He ran a hand over his face and drew in a breath. "Want to share watch during the night? We probably shouldn't do guard duty alone."

"Sure, I can do that," Connor said, glancing at Tessa.

Ramon could almost see the kid's chest puff up. "We'll need to keep the fires going. And do you know how to shoot?"

"No," Connor said. "But if something like that monster shows up I bet I can learn fast."

"I bet you can," Ramon said, and this time his grin felt more natural.

June came back to the fire and lowered herself down with a

grunt. Once settled, she shook her head. "Sharon doesn't have the flu. She's got breast cancer and I don't have anything that can help her with that. Maybe some pain meds, but I don't think Tylenol will be strong enough for what she's facing. And I don't think she'd take them anyway."

Ramon froze in the act of placing a piece of wood on the fire. Across from him, Marie's eyes flew open and she straightened to stare back at him. He heard Alegria's words in his mind.

The dying woman.

9

They stood outside in the early gray morning light. Ethan held his handgun and Anya her rifle. The others clustered close and stared at the outhouse.

A thick spray of blood fanned over the door. Drying clots clung to the rough wood boards. Blood-filled drag marks led into the woods.

Anya studied the tree line but saw no movement. She jacked a shell, rested her finger near the trigger, and called to Bird. When the dog was at her side, she walked the drag marks. No one followed. At the tree line, she glanced back. Ethan nodded to her and she knew he would keep watch.

She had no intention of going far by herself, but she wanted to at least enter the tree line and see if the tracks continued on or not. And if they did, what direction they went.

A soft, cold breeze rustled tree branches. Water from yesterday's rain still dripped under the forest canopy. Salal, ferns, Oregon grape, and bracken were flattened where something had been dragged. Where Zack had been dragged.

Anya swallowed against the ache in her throat. He was just a kid. She thought about all the blood in the tracks and wondered if he could have survived. She walked a few feet further into the woods. Maybe he was out there, injured. Blood always looked like a lot when spread like that, but maybe it wasn't as bad as it seemed.

She came to a downed cedar, the huge trunk split its length by the fall. Shards of wood impaled the ground where they'd landed. Great strips of bark had been peeled as the tree came down against others. Blood pooled and dripped across the destruction.

Movement caught her eye where something blue fluttered from one of the long, shattered ribs of wood. She brought the rifle up. Moved her finger to the trigger. Bird stared fixedly at the same spot, hackles up, but he stayed close to her side instead of investigating. She took a reluctant step forward, and then another. She tripped over roots torn up from the earth and caught her balance on a branch. The flat needles of the cedar brushed her palm and bits of rough bark bit into her skin as she gripped the branch, unable to let go.

It was a long strip of jeans material caught on a spar of raw wood.

And a few feet away, the mangled remains of a leg, the knee joint and long bones, were easily recognizable. There was nothing else above the knee. Skin and muscle were gone from what would have been the calf of the leg, but enough remained to identify it. The foot was still attached, a hiking boot still in place, but canted backwards in a position so alien to anatomy that it was almost unrecognizable as real.

Anya gagged and pressed the back of a hand tight to her mouth. Grief filled her like a heavy weight and she dropped to her knees, hot tears washing over her cold hand. Another child gone. She folded over, sinking to the wet earth, digging her fingers into dirt and roots. The sharp resin scent of the destroyed woods filled her senses but couldn't disguise the smell of blood.

When she her sobs eased, when her shaking slowed, when the deep, deep sorrow pulled back into her heart, she wiped her eyes and nose on her coat sleeve and stood on shaky legs. Bird held guard beside her, watching the woods. He whimpered once, softly.

"Yes," she said, wiping her eyes. "We're going back."

At the clearing, Ethan and Spike were the only ones outside, waiting on the old wooden deck. Smoke curled up out of the chimney and it was almost surreal to see the cabin sitting there cozy and inviting.

They watched her cross the clearing. She shivered, the rifle cold and heavy across her arm. Her fingers, around the rifle stock, were blue-tinged. When she reached the cabin, they didn't ask if she'd found anything. They didn't ask if there was any chance Zack was alive. She knew the answer was written in her face.

"Fuck," Spike said under his breath. He turned and shoved open the cabin door.

Bird followed him.

Ethan waited until Anya had climbed the few steps to the deck beside him then reached out to take the rifle from her. He took her hand in his and the warm touch was so startling, so alien, she almost yanked her hand away.

"We pack up what we can," Ethan said. "We get the hell out of these fucking woods now. I'm not losing any more of my kids. And you're going with us."

Anya simply nodded and walked past him. It was too hard to speak around the painful knot of anger and heartache lodged in her throat. Inside the cabin, she silently pulled her frame backpack from where it hung on a wall. Her emergency gear was already inside. Bird sat by the wood stove, ears up and eyes alert, watching her. She pulled in a ragged breath.

"Go through the shelves," she told the others. "Pack what food you can carry."

"But what happened?" Lucy asked.

Jennifer, face streaked with tears, stood against the wall, arms tightly crossed over her breasts, fingers gripping the shoulders of her shirt. "I had to use the bathroom in the middle of the night. Zack said he'd walk me out. Then he decided to use the outhouse, too. I was too scared to stand out there by myself."

"But not too scared to walk back by yourself," Michael said. "Is that what you're saying?"

Spike grabbed the back of Michael's neck and jerked him backward. "How about we just haul you out into the woods? How about that?"

"Stop it!" Anya yelled. "Pack your gear."

"Zack said it was okay," Jennifer said, gulping back sobs. Her whole body shook. "It was cold so I got back in my bag. I fell asleep!"

Nathaniel crossed the room and pulled her into a hug. She dropped her head to his shoulder, sobbing.

"We all would have done the same thing, sweetie," Nathaniel said, rubbing slow circles between her shoulder blades.

"No," she said, shaking her head against him. "No, you wouldn't."

"It's done," Ethan said, putting the rifle on the table. "Jennifer, take a minute, pull yourself together. Then gather your gear. We're getting out of here."

Anya tied her bedroll to her pack and hefted it up, sliding her arms through the straps. She picked up her rifle and walked back outside. She crossed the clearing to the young yew tree and stood there, her hand on the red bark.

"I'm coming back," she whispered to her child, her little boy, sleeping there in the roots of the tree, within the soft loamy soil. "I'm not leaving you forever."

She didn't know if she spoke to her lost baby or to the lost young boy who roamed the woods with a bear.

Either way, she would come home.

The last thing she did was release her chickens. The others stood in a loose half circle around her as she opened the coop door she'd so recently repaired. She didn't know when she'd be back and she couldn't leave them cooped up indefinitely, even if wild animals might get them out in the open. At least they'd have a chance.

When the chickens simply clustered in the doorway, she gestured. "Bird!"

The dog jumped forward, scattering the chickens, then stood there wagging his tail. Anya turned away. "He loves scattering them. It's how he got his name."

She started across the clearing. Bird and Ethan came up on either side of her.

They walked in silence through the changed landscape in a loose single file with Anya leading and Ethan bringing up the rear. Both of them scanned the forest for movement that didn't belong, for shapes that shouldn't be there, for shadows of antlers. The early morning light was pearly, with low gray clouds trailing in wisps among the trees still standing. A few birds sang, tentatively, in the distance, as if not sure about their new world.

The underbrush was still wet from the rain the day before and it wasn't long before her jeans were damp to the knees. Anya glanced back at Rowan behind her. The girl's hair hung in a thick, damp braid over her shoulder. She kept pace easily, watching the woods. But it wasn't like she was scanning for danger like the others. Her eyes didn't dart from shadow to shadow, her head didn't turn quickly from side to side.

"You don't seem as scared as the others," Anya said, holding back a branch from a fallen cedar so it wouldn't slap back and hit the girl.

Rowan started, as if surprised that Anya was there. She caught the branch and nodded her thanks as Anya turned away to continue forward. The silence stretched long enough that Anya didn't think Rowan was going to respond. But then she heard an indrawn breath.

"I'm good at forgetting where I'm at," Rowan said softly.

Anya picked up her pace in spite of the increasingly steep terrain as they neared the ridgeline. But Rowan kept pace easily and it put distance between them and Michael, who stumbled breathlessly behind them. Jennifer, behind Michael, offered him a water bottle, and Anya was pleased to see the small kindness.

"What do you mean?" she asked, when Michael had fallen a few yards behind them.

There were several more long moments of quiet, but this time Anya knew the words would come.

"I look for things to draw," Rowan said. "When I'm sketching, it's like I'm in another world. I'm not here anymore. Sometimes...sometimes it helps me not hear or see what's happening."

"Have you always drawn?" Anya asked, sensing something more behind the words.

"No," Rowan said. "Only since I was twelve."

Anya wondered what had happened to make Rowan need to escape her world when she was twelve. She wouldn't ask though. One thing her way of life had taught her was to value holding one's peace.

Sometimes keeping your thoughts held tight was the only way to keep your sanity.

"But you know what?" Rowan suddenly asked, her voice stronger as if defensive.

"What?" Anya saw movement up ahead but recognized Bird trotting back to her. His tail was relaxed and wagging, and no hackles were up.

"Everyone else? They all want to get home," Rowan said.

"Well, yeah." Anya patted Bird's head as he joined her. "They want to be home, a place safe without monsters. Seems obvious."

"I get that," Rowan continued. "But sometimes monsters are right next to you. If you have to face monsters no matter where you are, I'd rather be out here on my own. Like you."

"It can be a lonely life, Rowan. And hard." She glanced back but Rowan wasn't looking at her. Her chin was up, watching a raven circling high above them. A week ago trees would have blocked the sky. They would never have seen the raven as he glided on currents of wind.

Behind them, Jennifer walked next to Michael, talking to him. Anya saw him scowl at something she said, and the girl lifted both hands, palm up, as if asking him what his problem was. Behind them, Spike helped Nathaniel over a downed tree and then lifted Lucy over while Ethan waited, scanning back the way they had come.

Rowan watched the raven, clearly done talking. Anya took up the lead again, stumbling over a rock covered in moss. She caught her balance and kept going, hearing muted conversations behind her but not paying attention to their words. She watched the angle of light through the trees brighten as they left the forest fringe for the open ridge. The going was easier now, and they were able to move faster.

Anya's goal was to get them to the power lines and the cell towers above the tiny town of Index. From there Ethan and his students would be on their own. She planned on turning around even though she wouldn't make it back to the cabin before dark. There was safety in numbers, and part of her wanted to stay with them. But her thoughts kept going back to the boy with the bear. To Zack, dying alone in terror. And to her son, buried under the yew tree.

She couldn't leave any of them alone, as crazy as that sounded even to her.

10

Ethan leaned against a still-standing cedar and opened a fruit and nut protein bar. The others were scattered nearby, some sitting on damp ground, some standing, but all staying close. He'd agreed to a brief break but his whole body itched with the need to go. Anya stood the furthest from the group, shifting her weight from boot to boot, one hand on the head of her dog. He watched her study the woods ahead of them, shift to look over her shoulder, shift to briefly meet his eyes, shift again to watch the direction they were headed. Bird, too, was alert, ears pricked forward, silent and still.

Watching Anya, he knew that she felt it, too.

Something shadowed them.

Ethan had felt it about an hour earlier, a sense that something wasn't right. At first he put it off to all that had happened, to worry and fear for the kids. He watched the surroundings as they hiked and saw nothing but quake devastation.

Jennifer took a bite of her granola bar and offered the rest to Michael. He was sweating heavily even in the cool forest air and Ethan wondered if it was more from fear than exertion. Lucy sat on a rock, swinging her feet slowly. She was still favoring her side. Spike handed her a bottle of water, and then went to Nathaniel and checked the other boy's backpack straps. Payton talked without pause to Rowan, but Ethan wasn't sure Rowan knew Payton was even at her side.

All accounted for.

He finished the last bite of fruit and nuts, wadded up the wrapper, and bent to stuff it in a pocket of his pack. When he straightened, Payton came over. "What's up, kid?" he asked.

"Do you, like, know much about being a teenage girl in high school?" Payton fidgeted with the sleeve of her bright pink coat.

"No," Ethan said, lifting his pack and watching the woods.

"To be popular, you have to be pretty and flirty and make sure you show the right amount of cleavage. You know?"

Ethan looked at her in surprise. "Is this really the time to have a conversation on the caste system of school?"

"I'm pretty and flirty and have great cleavage." She looked down at her chest, then up to meet his eyes. "And I work hard to fit in."

"Yeah? So?" Ethan spoke without really paying attention. He watched Anya stop fidgeting and turn north. He watched Bird's hackles come up.

Payton put her hand on his arm and slid it up to his bicep. "I just want to…I guess…apologize. I mean, if we're all going to die out here, I just wanted to put it out there. That I know I'm a pain in your ass not being prepared and all that. I do it on purpose because the guys like rescuing me. But I know you hate it."

"Apology accepted." Ethan started to step away but Payton tightened her grip.

"And…like…I know the boys out here can't keep me safe. Not like you can. So I just, you know, want you to know the real me. To not hate me."

Ethan gently dislodged her fingers, seeing red flags flying in his mind's eye. "What I actually hate are people who lie to themselves about who they are. Or who lie to others to manipulate them."

Payton turned pink but said nothing. She tossed her hair over her shoulder and walked over to Jennifer.

Ethan joined Anya.

"It's pacing us," she said, cradling her rifle. "Or something is."

Ethan looked back at the kids. "Come on," he said, raising his voice. "Pack your shit and get up here."

"What do you want to do?" Anya asked. "Keep going or find some place to hole up?"

"I suppose you can't summon your pet grizzly?"

Anya was startled into a short laugh. "Not hardly."

"Then unless you know some safe place real close, I guess we keep going."

"What's going on?" Jennifer asked from behind them, her voice shaky. "That thing can't be back already?"

"We need to stick close," Ethan said, pulling out his gun. "Anya in front, me in the back, like before. But keep it tight. Keep quiet and watch your surroundings."

"But…what do we do?" Jennifer grabbed Anya's arm. "I thought it wouldn't follow us this far!"

"Calm down," Anya said, shaking her arm free. She paused, something in her memory stirring. Something that didn't fit. But then it was gone. "It may be pacing us but I don't think it's coming closer. Just stay behind me. We're almost to the Wall above Index."

"We need to go back to the cabin," Michael said. "We should never have left."

"That's irrelevant now," Ethan said. "Get moving."

Anya headed out and Ethan let the students pass him. Jennifer stayed close behind Anya, followed by Rowan, and then Lucy and

Nathaniel, with Spike right behind them. Michael took a few steps back the way they had come, but Ethan moved into his path. They locked eyes for a moment then Michael gave an angry shake of his head.

"We die, it's on you, teacher." He turned, stumbled over a tree root, and followed Spike.

"Of course it is," Ethan said, not sure if Michael heard him. And not caring if the kid didn't. After all, he'd known that from day one.

They went maybe half a mile at a fast pace, climbed over a few more downed trees and stumbled into an open swathe of land overgrown with brambles. Ethan realized it was a power line road but the towers were toppled, with heavy cable lines strewn over the warped metal.

"We're going to be electrocuted," Lucy said in a small voice.

"No way," Spike said. "There's no power. If there was, we'd hear those lines humming. We'd see all those blackberries and ferns and shit smoking."

Ethan went past the kids to step out into the clearing and scan the area.

"He's right," Anya said, following him. "So this power access road will lead to the Wall above Index. Plus, you can now see anything coming up on you."

Ethan glanced at the massive downed towers and lines then waited as the kids trailed tentatively into the open to cluster around Anya. Spike had a hand on Lucy and Nathaniel's shoulders, and Jennifer still stuck close to Rowan. Payton stood only a foot or so from him, watching him.

Ethan looked back into the trees. "Hang on," he called to the others. "Where's Michael?"

"He was just here," Rowan said.

Ethan didn't answer. He turned and ran back the way they had come, searching the forest on all sides, terrified he'd find signs of yet another death. But after a couple hundred yards, he stopped. There was no Michael. Not even blood. And the other students were back there, exposed, with just Anya.

"Shit!"

He turned back.

"How could he disappear like that?" Anya asked when Ethan rejoined her. "We were all standing right here. We'd have seen something grab him."

"Unless nothing grabbed him," Rowan said.

"What do you mean?" Jennifer asked, tears filling her eyes again.

"She means, he wanted to go back to the cabin." Ethan wiped sweat from his forehead and pulled in a deep breath, trying to blow out the fury that burned inside. "She means, he may have just taken off."

"I'll look for him," Anya said. "I was going to go back anyway, once you were safe on the power line road."

"No way," Spike said. "You can't go back with something following us. It's too dangerous. That fat ass is on his own. He made his choice and he don't care if it's endangering all of us. Leave him. You go, and it's just Ethan with his gun. It's not enough."

Anya stared at Spike and Ethan saw the anger in her eyes.

"I'm not your savior!" she said, voice rising. "I need to be home with my son! He's unprotected, too. Or didn't you think about that?"

"Your son?" Spike asked. "Man, that kid has a grizzly bear to protect him. What the hell are you talking about?"

Anya's hand came up over her heart and she drew in a ragged breath. They didn't understand. It was her baby that was alone and vulnerable, not the boy. That tiny baby, that tiny heart that had beat like butterfly wings under the palm of her hand for such a short, short moment in time.

"Please," Lucy said softly. "Please don't go. We've lost enough friends already. Don't make us watch you leave and never come back. Don't make us face this alone."

"That's not fair," Anya said, swiping tears off her cheeks. "I didn't ask you all to mess up my life. I was fine by myself."

"We didn't," Rowan said, putting an arm around Lucy. "That was the earthquake. And you weren't fine by yourself. You were hiding in a boarded up cabin."

"Stay with us until we get to town," Nathaniel said. "Until we know what is going on, what all of this is. Until it's safe for us, and for you, to go home. Please."

Ethan moved away, scanning the ground. His kids knew what to say better than he did. And they meant their words. They weren't just thinking of themselves, of their fear, of their vulnerability. There was an odd warmth inside that was suspiciously like pride.

"I can't," Anya said, but her voice was lower, defeated.

"You will," Ethan said, his back to Anya as he stared at the ground. "Because otherwise I'll throw you over my shoulder and haul you out of these damn woods."

"But Michael-"

Ethan turned and held a hand up, stopping Anya's words as relief loosened the knot in his stomach. "He may think he's going back to the cabin, but his tracks go through here. Look. You can see the break in the blackberry vines. The idiot is going the same way we're headed."

Spike laughed. "What a dumb ass."

Ethan came back to Anya. "So we're going to catch up to him before anything grabs him. And you need to stay with us for your own safety. At least until this is all over. Then I'll personally see you safe home. Promise."

"We all will." Payton stepped between Ethan and Anya. "Like, you know, when it's all over. Ethan and I will make sure you get home so you can go back to being alone."

"Oh for fuck's sake," Spike said. "Let's get the hell out of here."

Anya met Ethan's eyes, nodded slightly to him, and turned her back on them, taking point once more. Bird whined once and pushed his nose under her hand. She sank her fingers into the warm ruff of his neck, and walked away from her home.

11

Curtis's stomach growled but he still felt too queasy from his night in the woods and finding the lone eyeball to eat anything he'd packed. Instead, he followed the trail through the damp woods until he came to a spot where a large boulder had come down and taken out part of the trail above him. The boulder was now wedged against an old growth Douglas fir. Curtis stared at it, bemused that the tree held the rock, until he realized he was directly below it.

He scrambled from the trail, plowing through wet Oregon grape until he was several yards away, then stood with a hand pressed against the hitch in his side as his breathing slowed. The boulder had taken out a big chunk of the upper trail as it careened down the steep slope, but he could see where it had come from. And above it, the trail continued. And better yet, the ridgeline was close. He was almost to the top of the Wall.

He climbed through underbrush, staying well away from the precariously balanced boulder and was close to the top when he heard a voice. He froze, his heart tripping into overdrive. He slipped behind a tree, hugging up tight to the bark and straining to hear past the rush of blood pounding in his head.

"You can die out here in the woods if you want, but I'm leaving." There was a pause. "What's that? You think *you* can force me?"

Curtis drew in a soft breath, listening hard. It was a conversation, but he couldn't hear the second person. Where were they?

"You may think you're a tough guy, teacher, but you're not. No…wait…you may think you're a tough guy, teach, but I'm the badass here."

Curtis relaxed his grip on a tree branch. He wasn't sure what was going on, but this didn't sound like a monster that ate eyeballs.

"Yeah. That's better. I'm the badass."

The words stopped but Curtis now heard the heavy breathing of someone ponderously working their way through the forest debris. Branches snapped and rocks tumbled, followed by a high pitched squeal. Someone seemed to have just slipped. Curtis sympathized.

"Listen up Spike, you asshole. No…you fucker. Yeah. Listen up Spike, you fucker. You think you're some kind of hero, but when this is over it's going to be me Jennifer comes to, because you're nothin'. I'll be the one that saves her."

Curtis felt a smile broaden across his face. A scared guy, a kindred spirit, rewriting his history. Practicing the dialog he should have said, wished he'd said, or planned on saying. Maybe convincing himself that he'd actually said those things. There was a time way back in middle school when Curtis had done the same thing. These days he knew he wasn't a badass so instead he gave that dialog to characters in his manuscript. Created the fictional world he would never move through in real life.

Whoever this stranger was, he'd be mortified to find out someone had heard him. Curtis stepped out where he would be visible. He bent over, fingering his bootlaces, and coughed loudly.

All noise up ahead stopped. Except for the heavy breathing. Curtis coughed again.

"Damn bootlaces!" he said loudly.

There was a rustle in the bushes. Enough sound to allow Curtis to act surprised, as if he'd just now heard the noise.

"Who's there?" he said.

"Are you a monster?" There was a distinct quaver in the voice from the bushes. "Because if you are, I'm a badass. Just sayin'."

Curtis covered his mouth to hold back the laugh. Then he straightened. "No monster here. Unless you're one?"

Ferns and salmonberries trembled, then parted, and Curtis saw a very overweight young man come through. His face was flushed and shiny with sweat, even on such a cool day. His trousers and shirt had tears in them and looked like they'd been slept in. His backpack straps were frayed. He looked no more than seventeen, maybe eighteen.

"What are you doing out here alone?" Curtis asked, startled.

The kid pulled his shoulders back. "What are *you* doing out here alone?"

Ah, a defensive, prickly sort. Curtis should have guessed. He tilted his head to one side, studying the young man. Defensive but very scared underneath. Sympathy for the kid settled his own nerves.

"I'm searching for a friend," Curtis said. "And the cell tower repeater. Where did you come from?"

"Silver Creek," the kid responded, stepping closer. "On a field trip with an idiot teacher. We were at a cabin with food and everything. Safe. And he decides we're going to hike out because he thinks that will be safer. Even though some of us kids have already died. We should have stayed at the cabin. Jennifer, one of the girls in my class…one of the popular girls, agrees with me. When we get out of this, he's so fired."

Ah, delusions of girlfriends. Curtis remembered those days. "So where is she, this Jennifer? Did she come with you?"

"Not yet. She's going to follow as soon as she can slip away."

"Okay, then where is everyone?" Curtis looked uphill in the direction the kid had come from but saw no movement.

The young man hesitated a moment. "Well, not really sure. I left them a while ago. Decided to go back to the cabin. But I guess I kind of got…turned around. Not lost. I can find my way through woods anytime. But the earthquake, you know, messed things up." His face drained of color and he glanced over his shoulder. "And then there's this…"

"Monster," Curtis said when it became obvious the kid couldn't complete his sentence. Part of him felt relief, as if he'd just been handed proof that he wasn't going crazy. "It's something that eats people, I think."

"You've seen it?" The kid stepped forward.

"Not seen it, just heard it." Something tickled in Curtis's mind again, a feather touch of a faint memory. But once again he wasn't able to pin it down. "And I think there's a second one back the way I came, but that might have just been some kind of wild dog. Hey, what's your name?"

"Michael. Who are you? And why are your jeans hanging from your pack?"

"I'm Curtis. I'm a professor with the University of Washington. I was here working on gravity experiments when the quake hit." Then he decided on honesty. Something to show Michael that he wasn't alone in the world of being afraid and not being a hero. "And I'm drying out my jeans. I pissed myself last night out here alone in the dark when that thing went by."

"No shit!" Michael laughed, loudly. "I've been scared the last few days, but never that scared! 'Course, I'm a badass, like I said."

All desire to sympathize, offer camaraderie, or be kind, flew away. Curtis decided he could pull his shoulders back and look tough, too. "Good for you. Nice meeting you."

"Wait, where are you going?"

Curtis passed Michael and gestured with a hand. "Uphill, obviously. I told you, I'm looking for a friend."

"But-"

"If you keep going downhill you'll end up in Index. It's been hit hard by the quake like everything else, but there are people. And a few houses left to hole up in when the monsters come out. You should be able to stay there. If you want to find that cabin in case your girlfriend shows up, you're on your own."

Michael looked back the way Curtis had come from, and then looked uphill. "It's dangerous out here alone you know."

"Okay. Thanks for the warning."

"Look, man, maybe I should go with you. For protection, you know."

Curtis grinned, keeping his back to the kid. "I'm not much for protecting kids. But if you keep going like I said, you'll be safe soon enough."

"No, fool," Michael said. "To protect you."

Curtis shrugged, grabbing a tree branch for support as he pulled himself upward. "I don't really need protection. But if you want to come along I don't mind the company. I'm not going to look for your cabin though."

Michael came up the trail so fast rocks and dirt tumbled loudly downhill. "Well, I guess, if you need the company, I can postpone going back to the cabin for a few days. Jennifer will wait for me."

"Not a few days," Curtis said firmly. "Hours. By dark I'm going to be in Index. With people."

"So you don't piss yourself again?" Michael snorted loudly.

Curtis swung around, cheeks flushing. "Look, if you want to be out here tonight, fine, but you're on your own. I survived last night with whatever that thing is. I'm not going to push my luck again. If you see that as cowardice rather than common sense, I don't need company that badly. And I certainly don't need someone tagging along that's going to give me grief the whole time."

Michael raised both hands, patting the air. "Sorry, sorry." He looked around at the forest, the mountains, the destruction, and then stared at the ground. "Sometimes I say things without thinking."

"I suggest you start thinking." Curtis turned back to the trail. "You'll find there's a reason we have brains."

"Asshole," Michael said.

But he spoke so quietly that Curtis pretended he didn't hear. Let the kid have the last word. Though he wasn't so sure the comfort of company was going to be worth this type of company.

Curtis started uphill again, watching the ground and where he stepped. The earth was so disrupted, so broken, that it took his full concentration to keep his balance. But as he walked, he felt the breath of a thought in his mind. Something there he should know. It was like those late nights at the university, working without sleep, his mind so shattered with knowledge that at times it was like everything slipped away and he couldn't grasp a single concept.

The heavy, labored breathing of Michael behind him didn't help. The noise was like raising a huge red flag shouting 'over here!' to monsters.

After several minutes of climbing, Curtis paused, not only to allow Michael to catch his breath and not have a heart attack, but also to get his bearings. The woods were opening up as they reached higher elevation where granite took over, dirt was scarce, and plant life found it harder to sink roots. Off to his left the fault line wavered upward. It was narrower here, probably also because of the granite.

In the deeper parts of Curtis's mind, where reality resided, he knew Henry had to be dead. Not because of the scrap of scalp left on the hood of his car, but because of the thing that had moved past him in the night. Something was out there eating people. It didn't matter where it had come from or what it was. It was there, and Henry was gone.

But Curtis had always been hopeful and optimistic.

And so he looked uphill to judge how close they were to the cell tower and a grin spread across his face.

"Almost there," he called down to Michael. "See? The crest is just there."

Without waiting for a reply, Curtis started uphill again. Almost there. He'd see the reality and that would allow him to walk away from the hope. No Henry and no way to become a hero and fix the tower. And then, finally, he would go back. Downhill would be faster. He'd be with people and warmth and safety before darkness started sending shadows to sift down between the trees.

The sounds Michael made as he worked his way uphill grew fainter as the boy fell farther behind. Curtis didn't care. He craved the end of the trail, the crest of the ridge. To be able to see far, to see there was nothing more he could do.

He pulled himself up over the last downed tree with the help of thick branches, and stepped out onto the somewhat level ridgeline. He straightened his aching back, put his hands on his hips, and lifted his face to the cool air, eyes closed in blissful relief. It was starting to drizzle again, fine misty drops gently settling in his hair and on his skin. He drew in a deep breath and opened his eyes.

A man stood a few feet away, gun pointed at him.

12

Curtis stumbled backward, hands coming up as if they could stop a bullet. "Hey!"

Even as he moved, the man was lowering the gun and raising his own hand. "Wait, wait, it's okay."

Curtis came down hard on his butt, pain shooting up his spine.

"Shit!" the man said. "I'm sorry. We heard something coming through the woods. We thought...well, like I said, sorry. You okay?"

Curtis stared, one hand on his pounding heart, the other on granite, fingers pressed down tight. The man was solid, muscles obvious even under his coat. His black hair hung to his collar, damp in the drizzle.

"You okay?" the man asked again, reaching up to shove his hair back out of dark eyes. "Need a hand?"

"No, no," Curtis said, shoving against the ground and heaving himself up. He twisted from side to side relieved nothing was broken and snugged his pack straps back up. "Wait, did you say 'we'?"

Even as he spoke, he saw people standing several yards back, near the remains of the fallen cell tower. A woman, with a rifle and a large German shepherd by her side and young people, all bedraggled, all with eyes wide with fear, all staring at him. Before they could respond though, there was a loud crashing in the underbrush behind him.

The man immediately raised the gun, slicing the air with an abrupt hand motion, signaling Curtis to get out of the way.

But Curtis recognized the sound of bellows. "Wait," he said. "It's okay. It's just-"

"Michael!" the man said. "You asshole."

There was relief under the words and the man lowered the gun again.

A heavy, hot hand came down on Curtis's shoulder. "Let's go," Michael said, low. "Come on, you wanted to go back. Let's go."

Curtis pushed Michael's hand away and stepped forward, reaching out to the man. "The tough guy teacher, I presume? I'm Curtis Jonason, a scientist working in the area on a gravity experiment for the University of Washington. Or I was. Until the earth quake."

In spite of the confusion in the man's eyes, he also reached out and shook Curtis's hand. "Ethan Reynolds. Environmental Science teacher." He laughed shortly. "On a field trip."

Curtis stepped to one side. "And this, I assume, is one of your students."

Ethan's dark eyes smoldered. "Yes. Yes it is."

"Hey man!" Michael stuttered out. "You were going to get us all killed. I was going back to the cabin where it was safe."

"You little shithead. You put us all in danger, taking off like that, leaving us to look for you. It was irresponsible, juvenile, and incredibly stupid." Ethan drew in a deep breath. "And you stupid kid, the cabin is in the complete opposite direction from where you were headed! What the hell were you thinking?"

"I was thinking I wanted to live," Michael said. His words were brave, but he took a faltering step backward. "And you haven't done a great job so far keeping us alive."

Curtis saw the quick flash of pain in Ethan's eyes.

There was a moment of silent tension before Ethan shook his head.

"Yeah. Well, you still want to go to the cabin, it's back the way we came." He turned to Curtis. "Come meet the others."

Curtis glanced at Michael who stood still, sweat drying on his flushed cheeks. He shrugged and followed Ethan across the rough ridgeline to where the small group waited. He didn't look back, and didn't hear Michael following them.

A girl with blond hair stared fixedly past Curtis at Michael. Her green eyes brimmed with tears, but they didn't fall. Curtis paused, trying to decipher what he saw on her pale face. Fear? Relief? He couldn't tell. Next to her stood a classically pretty girl with long dark hair and a tight tee shirt. Even in the chilly air she left her stylish jacket unzipped just enough to show the tee shirt. And cleavage. Her eyes were focused on Ethan as if Curtis didn't exist. But he was used to that.

He turned to the girl with tears in her eyes, making an educated guess. "Jennifer, right?" he asked.

Her pale cheeks warmed with a quick flush as she turned her eyes to him and nodded.

"Nice to meet you," Curtis said, then thought Michael might need all the help he could get. "I've heard a lot of nice things about you."

Jennifer flushed but the woman with the rifle came forward before she could respond. Ethan introduced her as Anya, and then introduced the other students. Curtis sensed trauma behind all their haunted eyes.

"Where are you going?" Anya asked. "Out here on your own?"

"Here," Curtis said, gesturing widely with his hand. "The quake opened a fault line from Index and I wanted to follow it to find a friend of mine. And I promised some people in Index I'd look at the cell tower to see if it was fixable. To see if there was any way to contact the outside world." He stared at the downed power lines. "To call my mother."

Anya looked over her shoulder at the toppled tower. "I don't think you're going to repair that."

Curtis knew she was right. There was no way to fix total destruction. No way to call out. No way to find out if his mother was okay, or to get help to her if she wasn't. It was hard to swallow past the lump that filled his throat. He pressed the palms of his hands into his eyes as if to push the sudden and overwhelming disappointment back inside.

The young girl introduced as Lucy touched his arm. "Excuse me, but is it safe in Index? I mean, will we be okay there? Can we get there before dark?"

Curtis dropped his hands, sniffled, and shrugged. "Well, I plan on being there before dark."

"Look," the tattooed young man called Spike said, gesturing for Nathaniel and Lucy to join him. "We can talk later. We need to move. Or have you all forgotten what's going on?"

Curtis saw the terror that came into their eyes and the way the kids looked at each other and then outward, into the mountains, as if searching.

Nathaniel put a hand on Lucy's shoulder. "Sorry, but Spike is right. Mr. Jonason, we really need to be someplace safe by dark. Some of us have died. There's something out here hunting us."

"We have my hand gun and Anya's rifle," Ethan said. "But I don't think it's enough. We can't be out here once it's dark."

Curtis shivered. "Oh, I know. I mean, I know there's something out here. I haven't seen it, but I heard it. It passed me last night. And this morning I found..." He looked at the fear in Lucy's eyes. "Well, anyway, I plan on being in town tonight. There aren't a lot of houses left standing, but there's people and fires."

"Can you lead everyone there?" Anya asked.

When Curtis nodded, she touched the dog's head as if to catch its attention.

"Right. Then I'm going home."

"Wait!" Rowan caught Anya's arm. "Even if we're going to be okay, you won't be! You won't make it home before dark."

"I can't..." Anya started, then paused for a deep breath that sounded like a sob. "Please understand. I *need* to be home. I have to go home. If that thing shows up I'll shoot it. But I have to go."

"Ethan shot it." Spike said, his voice rough. "That thing with antlers coming out of its head. He shot it. And it didn't slow the fucker down. Didn't stop it from killing Paul and Zack. Didn't keep it from coming after us. You know it's following us. It's close. You don't stand a chance even with a grizzly."

Curtis felt that feathered whisper in his mind again. But this time it didn't float away. This time it settled and the thought coalesced as if ice flooded his system. "Wait, antlers?"

"Come on, man!" Spike almost shouted. "We need to move!"

"Oh," Curtis said softly, thoughts racing. "Oh, sure. No, you won't kill it with guns."

"How would you know?" Spike asked.

"Because I...right, that reference in...and that story from..." Curtis realized they were all staring at him. "Sorry. It's just, well, I just realized what it is."

"Tell us," Anya said, grabbing his arm.

"No," Spike said, his voice intense. "Tell us how to kill it."

Curtis looked from face to face, uncomfortable with being the center of their focused fear. "Well, a couple references say you can kill it by fire, but who knows? I mean, how can you say definitively what kills a myth?"

"That thing after us is no fucking myth," Spike said.

"Please, what is it?" Lucy asked.

Curtis recognized the basic need to name something, to lessen the terror of the unknown with knowledge. That was something he easily understood. "Well, some Native American legends from the Midwest call it a Windigo. The Native Americans here, the Coast Salish, the Haida, describe it with antlers. You can't see them unless they want to be seen. They..." Curtis paused as his thoughts raced ahead of his voice.

"What?" Ethan asked.

"Well, according to myth, they hibernate for hundreds of years and when they wake up, they gather humans to bring back to their lair and eat. Some tales say they keep their victim alive for years, letting them heal between feasting."

"Who cares?" Spike said. "Let's talk some place else."

Ethan nodded once in agreement then turned to Anya. "You can't go back yet. You can't kill it with the rifle, or your dog. You won't be safe."

"Anya's grizzly, though," Nathaniel said.

Curtis's eyes widened. "You have a grizzly?"

"Talk while we walk!" Spike shouted. He put his hands on Nathaniel and Lucy's backs, nudging them toward the trail Curtis and Michael had come up.

Ethan held a hand up, stopping Spike. "You're right, we need to go. But we're not leaving without Anya."

Rowan caught Anya's arm. "Please. Come with us. Another day or two. We can figure this out. Your cabin will still be there."

There were tears in Anya's eyes. But when Spike headed for the trail, she nodded to Ethan in defeat and followed.

Curtis trailed behind Nathaniel, stumbling over the rough ground. His thoughts raced, remembering textbooks and anecdotes, fairy tales and mythology. It felt like the old days when he'd been working on his thesis, his mind so full of information that he felt separated from the real world around him. His imagination flowed between the facts, racing to illuminate the bare bones of research.

His knee hit a downed cedar and he toppled over the log. He barely noticed when Spike grabbed him by the backpack and hauled him to his feet. He barely felt the pain of the split skin on his knee.

"What is that?" Jennifer asked, pointing through the trees at the huge crack in the earth.

"Fault line," Curtis said, his voice feeling like it was an echo, belonging to someone else. "Opened with the quake. Runs all the way to Index."

The others talked around him, voices low and fearful, but he didn't hear their words, or join in. There was too much to think about.

If the Windigo shadowed these people, hunted them, everyone in Index would have to be warned. No one would be safe. They'd need to stick together. Not just campfires, but maybe one big bonfire. Had the quake disturbed the thing in its lair? Had it always been here, deep in the granite mountains, hibernating, waiting?

"We need to talk," Curtis said abruptly to Ethan. "Compare notes. What we've each seen. Create a working hypothesis."

"Later," Ethan said. "Once we're out of the woods."

Curtis nodded vaguely, attention turned inward to theories and possibilities, causes and effects.

Seeing nightmares.

13

It was definitely faster going back than it had been climbing uphill. They moved in a tight line with Ethan leading this time and Anya bringing up the rear. Curtis noticed Payton stayed on Ethan's heels, frequently gasping out and stumbling, reaching for Ethan's help each time. She slowed them all down with her helplessness, her neediness. He saw the frustration in Ethan's eyes each time he had to catch her. He understood the teacher's frustration, but he also understood what Payton was doing.

When she glanced at him, Curtis smiled in commiseration. She was just doing what they all were, after all, clustering close to the ones most likely to keep them alive.

"Where were you when the quake hit?" Ethan asked over his shoulder.

"In Index." Warmth heated Curtis's cheeks. "I drove into the telephone booth at the general store."

"Kind of hard to drive when the earth is buckling."

Curtis was oddly relieved, as if he'd just been absolved of being a bad driver. "Michael said you were at Silver Creek."

"Yep." Ethan helped Payton around a boulder. "The field trip from hell."

Curtis laughed, but then sobered as Ethan told them what had happened since the quake. As he talked about the students, Curtis looked back over his shoulder at them.

Spike herded Nathaniel and Lucy along, lifting the small girl over obstacles.

Michael wheezed loudly and struggled to keep up. Jennifer, behind him, walked silently, watching their surroundings with banked terror in her eyes. Curtis noticed that Michael didn't hold tree branches to keep them from slapping back on her. The kid wasn't winning any points there.

Rowan followed them, her beautiful face oddly peaceful as if she either didn't realize the danger they were in, or had found some way to remove herself from it. Curtis envied her. He saw how she watched the trees and the wind in the leaves, how she turned to see pale light coming through clouds that hid mountaintops. It was like she was daydreaming or had found a way to completely disassociate from the real world.

Anya, by contrast, also watched the woods around them, but her light blue eyes were intent as she scanned their surroundings for threats. Bird stayed close to her side. It comforted Curtis that she was back there, aware and on guard.

Ethan paused to heave a shattered chunk of fir out of their path. He waited while it rolled a few feet to the side then gestured for Curtis to come closer. But when he spoke, he kept his face turned from Curtis.

"We lost Zack last night." He coughed as if something lodged in his throat and quickly swiped at his eyes.

Curtis didn't know what to say, didn't know how to offer comfort. He certainly couldn't tell Ethan that everything was going to be okay.

Ethan turned back to the trail and Curtis fell in step with him, leaving Payton to follow.

"Can you tell me what happened?" Curtis asked hesitatingly, not sure if Ethan wanted to share details.

"He went to use the outhouse and that…thing took him."

Curtis thought of Michael. "Are you sure he didn't just wander off into the woods and get lost?"

Ethan swung around to grip the sleeve of Curtis's coat in his fist. "Anya found his leg."

Curtis froze, eyes wide with horror.

Anya and the students came up around them and Curtis saw tears and helplessness, anger and fear.

"It might have been any of us," Payton said. "I'd been out to the outhouse earlier, too, but I didn't go alone."

Anya suddenly gasped and bent slightly as if she'd been hit. Ethan reached for her, but she was already straightening, her face bone-white.

"What is it?" Spike asked, looking wildly around them. "What is it?"

Curtis saw the sudden spiked fear in their tension and the way they quickly huddled in tight together, circling to peer into the forest. But he kept his eyes on Anya, not sure he wanted to hear what was coming.

"No, it's not the monster," Anya said. "What you just said, about the outhouse. There's something…something I didn't pay attention to. Something about Zack."

Ethan caught her arm. "What?"

Anya gripped Bird's ruff, sinking her fingers into his fur. "Zack and Jennifer went to the outhouse," she said slowly, as if thinking something through.

"Yeah?" Ethan asked, eyebrows up in confusion.

"We had barred the door."

"Right, to keep the monster out," Spike said. "So what? Let's go, man."

Anya held her hand up. "Wait. Jennifer came back on her own."

"Yeah? So?" Michael stepped up beside Jennifer, chest out and shoulders back. "She was too scared to wait out there by herself. What's wrong with that?"

Jennifer stared at the ground, hands gripping the straps of her backpack so tightly that her knuckles whitened. But then she raised her chin and Curtis saw tears pooling in the girl's eyes. Anya's face suddenly flushed and she shoved through the others to grab Jennifer's arm, shaking her.

"Hey!" Michael reached for Anya but Ethan stopped him.

"Tell us," Ethan said.

"I woke up." Anya pushed Jennifer away from her. The girl stumbled back into Michael. "I heard someone come in from the outhouse. I heard the bar come back down on the door."

"I don't understand," Lucy said.

"I knew whoever had gone outside had come back in and relocked the door," Anya took a step toward Jennifer. "That everyone was safe. It's why I went back to sleep. Everyone was inside and safe."

Ethan's eyes met hers. "Did anyone else use the outhouse that night?" His voice was cold, his words clipped and terse. "Anyone?"

The only answer was the wind in the trees.

Anya grabbed Jennifer again, shook her violently, and then shoved her so hard she slammed into Michael and tumbled backward, coming down hard on the ground. "You fucking bitch."

"What the hell!" Michael shouted, bending to help the girl up.

Jennifer stood and shook off Michael's hand.

"You locked him out," Anya said. "You left him out there. He had no chance. No chance!"

Curtis stared from one to the other, his heart pounding as he realized what Anya was saying. He didn't want it to be true, but realization was dawning on the others, too. Lucy gripped Spike, tears coursing down her cheeks. Nathaniel choked on a sob and dropped to his knees. Rowan, back in reality, staggered away from them. Spike pulled Nathaniel to his feet, put his arm around the boy's shoulders, and drew both him and Lucy close. His face was flushed, his eyes bright with anger. Michael stood, mouth hanging open.

Payton clutched at Ethan but he pushed her off and grabbed Jennifer's arm. "Is that true?"

Jennifer pulled away and crossed her arms tightly over her chest like a self-contained hug. She was pale but her tears were gone. "It was

Paul. His death showed me."

"What the hell are you talking about?" Ethan asked.

"How to keep us safe," Jennifer said. "I realized we needed to keep the thing fed. Curtis said the same thing. Right? It takes food back to its lair and feeds slowly. So if it's feeding, or full, or whatever, then the rest of us have a chance to get someplace safe."

"Are you fucking insane?" Spike pulled Nathaniel and Lucy back from her. "You sacrificed Zack?"

Michael was breathing short and rapid as if hyperventilating. "Is that...is that why you agreed we'd be safer at the cabin? Told me...told me I should go?"

"Of course," Jennifer said. "I thought Zack would be enough. That I'd only have to do it once. But the thing followed us. So I had to feed it again. And you're big. You could feed it for a long time."

"You said you'd join me." Michael's eyes filled.

"I was scared, okay?" Jennifer shouted, eyes going from one face to another. "I don't want to die! I told you all that in the bus when I was stuck! This is the only way to keep us safe, to give us a chance. I did it for all of us."

"But, that wouldn't work," Curtis said, his voice shaky. "Don't you understand? All you did was show it that this group was a regular food source."

"We need to get out of here," Spike said.

Ethan pulled his gun and started down the path. "Come on. All of you. Now."

Curtis immediately followed, glancing back over his shoulder. The students clustered in behind him, Michael wiping a hand across his eyes. Jennifer stepped forward, but Anya caught her arm and pushed her back.

"You don't get our protection," she said. "You can follow or you can stay here, but you aren't with us. You weren't thinking of keeping us safe. You were willing to sacrifice all of us to save yourself. So do it. Save yourself."

Anya passed her and took up position behind the others again. Bird growled low as he followed Anya.

Curtis stared back at Jennifer until he stumbled over a rock and almost knocked Ethan over. She stood in the devastated landscape, face pale but oddly resolved, as if she'd done nothing wrong. He apologized to Ethan and then couldn't help but look back one more time. Jennifer was several yards behind them, but she followed.

Curtis had always believed disasters pulled people together. How could it not? Life was precious and even more so when it was threatened.

They needed to help each other. Not…whatever this was. Kill another in order to survive? What kind of survival was that? Warm tears trickled down his cold cheeks. He wiped them away with equally cold hands. Things would never be okay again.

Behind him, Rowan spoke. Her voice was low, but the words carried clearly.

"See? The monsters are always there no matter where we are."

14

It was late afternoon when Curtis and the others reached Index. Rain was headed their way but still high in the mountaintops, the sheeting curtain slowly hiding the trees as the wind pushed rain down the Wall. He shivered in the chill, damp air, even through his layers of fleece and rain gear. Hopefully the fires were still going.

He saw exhaustion in the eyes of the others around him. The final leg of the journey, crossing all those downed trees blocking the road, had taken it out of the kids. Cold, wet, exhausted, and scared, they barely stumbled along. But the thought of someplace safe, someplace like home, kept them pushing forward.

But all of that was like a thin layer of ice over the deeper betrayal. No one had spoken during the hike. But Curtis saw how all of them watched Jennifer as she followed them. He was the same, continuously glancing back. She stayed within a few yards of them, and several times he caught her with tears on her face.

But he doubted those tears were for Zack.

He wasn't sure if what lodged in his heart was anger at the girl, or betrayal that she had sent that poor boy to his death.

Someone's stomach growled loudly and Curtis suddenly remembered the turkey and Havarti in his backpack. It had been hours since he ate and yet he'd somehow forgotten the food he'd bartered for. When they finally got to a fire, he'd pull that food out and divide it. Even a mouthful would be better than nothing for these kids. Maybe he could get Betty to feed them.

They crossed the railroad tracks in a straggly line, passing a sheriff's truck that looked like it had been driven into a house. Curtis wondered briefly which deputy had been driving and hoped it wasn't the one who'd helped him when he smooshed the phone box. He wondered suddenly if Jennifer had committed an actual crime. If there were some way to lock her up so she no one else would be sacrificed to her fear.

The town seemed almost in control. Small groups of people moved as if with purpose. A backhoe headed toward Alley Oop, with the firefighter, Samuel, walking behind it. Two men carried a body toward the makeshift morgue behind the town hall, and Curtis wondered briefly what they would do with all those who had died. They'd have to find a burial ground, and soon.

In the park someone had built a large fire with debris from

downed trees. It smoked from the wet wood, but still looked wonderful. He saw someone adding a round of wood, and heard the sound of chainsaws in the distance. He veered toward the fire and the others followed.

"Stay here and warm up," Curtis said, when they reached the wonderful heat of flames. "I'll go see if I can find some food."

"We have food," Spike said. "We packed a bunch of crap from Anya's place."

"We just didn't take time to eat," Lucy said. "You know, with that thing after us."

"But we'll eat now," Ethan said, dropping his backpack. "And then we'll figure out what to do next."

"I'll find the deputy then," Curtis said. "I have to tell them about the cell tower anyway. I'll see if there's someplace you can shelter when the rain gets here. Maybe get some rest."

He started to walk away and then realized if they all had food, he didn't have to share his sandwich. He lowered his pack, rummaged around, slapped turkey and cheese between stale bread, and took a huge, ravenous bite as he stood. Slinging the pack over one shoulder, he left the tiny park and crossed 5th Street toward the store.

The little parking lot in front of the store was destroyed. Huge chunks of pavement had been lifted and strewn about like they were pebbles. Water ran slowly from underneath, creating pools in the low spots that he jumped over. It looked like the water main had blown while he was gone.

He turned the knob of the door and then stared at it, startled, when the door wouldn't open. Betty had locked it. He cupped his hands around his eyes and tried to peer through the dimness inside, but saw nothing.

"She's not letting anyone in," a man's voice said behind him.

Turning, Curtis saw the deputy. "No one?"

"Nope. She's locked the inner door so it doesn't matter that the back wall is collapsed. No one goes in. You're Curtis, right?"

He nodded.

"You went up the Wall trail?"

Curtis nodded again. "Max? Your name, right? The cell tower's a mangled mess. No way to fix it. And I didn't find Henry either. But I did find a group of people. They're at the fire in the park. They'll need shelter and we'll need to talk to you about one of the girls. And I think I know-"

Max put his hand on Curtis's shoulder. "Good work. Talk to Louis about a place for them. He's organizing shelters. I'll check in with them as soon as I can."

"Right. Okay." Curtis caught Max's sleeve. "But we should have some sort of town meeting. There was this monster-"

Max patted Curtis's hand. "I know. We chased it into the river. It's gone."

Confusion flustered Curtis for a moment. But then he realized the Windigo must have flanked them, passed them somehow, come into town. Maybe drawn by a larger group of people.

"That is absolutely the best news we've had in days. The kids are going to be so, so relieved." Curtis grinned broadly feeling almost airless with relief.

"Yeah, we were happy to see it go, too."

Curtis raised his bread. "Want a turkey sandwich? I have enough here for a second one."

Max looked as if he was going to say no, but then paused before nodding. "Sure. Thanks. We haven't got a handle yet on what food supplies are like so Louis has been handing out granola bars."

"Turkey is better."

Max laughed. "Sure is."

Curtis watched the deputy cross the street to where a second deputy was coming out of the fire department bay. Max tore his sandwich in half and gave her a hunk. Curtis headed back toward the park almost giddy. The monster was gone. Hopefully drowned in the river.

They were safe. What a fantastic thing.

Well, there was still the whole survival thing to negotiate through, but at least there were no more monsters. And the threat of aftershocks was still there. But he'd sleep tonight. Really sleep. And those kids would be safe finally. He hadn't realized just how terrified he'd been over the past two days until now, when it was all magically lifted away.

~Day 5~

1

Curtis scooped up a spoonful of scrambled egg. Not just a real scrambled egg, but one with chives. He tried not to gulp the food down, tried to savor it, but within seconds he was scraping the little tin plate. The fire burning in a circle of stones in front of him crackled and snapped as pockets of pitch in the cedar caught. The flames warmed his face and hands and knees, a contrast to the chilly breeze going down the back of his finally dry jeans. But…scrambled eggs. He'd never thought such a simple thing would be so wonderful.

A few people in town had chickens. Some continued to lay eggs as if the world hadn't just shaken them all. Early that morning Samuel, the firefighter, had gone around town collecting all the eggs people were willing to share, which turned out, surprisingly, to be a lot. He'd also cut chives growing in a tiny garden patch in front of the town hall, that hadn't been buried in debris. And then he scrounged around for camping equipment and had been cooking eggs for everyone since. It wasn't a lot, but so much better than cardboard-tasting granola bars.

Curtis considered licking his plate.

Seated around the fire, and a second fire nearby, were Ethan, Anya, the high school kids, and Bird, who was finishing his scrambled egg. And licking his plate.

Curtis yawned until his jaw cracked. He'd slept straight through the night, exhaustion quickly pulling him under and the expected nightmares never materializing. The reassurance from the sheriff deputies that the monster was gone had helped, and so had the flickering light of fires around town. They were safe, he wasn't alone, his clothes were finally drying out, and the weight of fear was lifting.

And then when he woke up there was breakfast. It felt like everything was going to be okay and he couldn't help but grin across the fire at Ethan, who looked momentarily startled but then grinned in return.

Curtis ran a finger around his plate to catch a few remaining minuscule bits, and decided he would hunt down the mayor, find out what tasks he could take on. There was so much work to do just to keep going until help came. He licked his finger. Maybe he could help Samuel with the injured, or help the mayor with finding a place to bury their dead.

That thought brought the high school students to mind and his brief moment of contentment died.

Jennifer sat by the second fire but there was space around her. No one spoke to her. Curtis wondered what would be done. What laws had been broken? She'd left a guy out there alone and it had led to his death, but was that illegal? Even if it wasn't, it was morally illegal and it hurt when he thought about it. That poor kid should never have died like that, out in the woods in the dark and alone.

The sound of conversations around him grew quieter and he looked up to see people staring across the ruined street at the crumpled front of the general store. The front door screeched as it was tugged part way open. Betty, cradling her splinted arm, stepped into the doorway, looking around at the groups of people around fires. Her eyes went to the plates people held, with little mounds of scrambled eggs and her mouth opened in surprise. But no one stood to bring her a plate or gestured for her to join them.

Curtis started to stand, to invite her over, sorry now that his plate was empty. Maybe there was still an egg left somewhere. But then Betty's face sagged into something like anger. He wasn't sure, but the lines around her eyes and mouth were deep. It surprised him that she didn't come join them, that no one called her over or offered her something.

He decided he would go talk to her and find out what had happened, but she stepped back into the dark interior of the store. He caught the pale flash of her hands coming up to push the door closed again. Even from where he sat he heard the snick of padlocks.

And then that small sound was washed out by another. A noise at once familiar and yet strangely out of place. People around Curtis stood, food forgotten. He also stood, pulled to his feet by the weirdly out of context noise of an engine laboring down the road.

An old truck with a camper, followed by an even older World War relic of a jeep, lumbered its way up and over the broken railroad tracks at the crossing. As people stared, the two vehicles rounded the corner onto Fifth Street and pulled in to the general store parking lot just like they'd come for groceries or their mail. Granted, the truck was at a weird cant because of the torn up pavement, and the jeep didn't even bother trying to get into the lot, stopping instead behind the truck. The doors of the jeep opened.

Over the past few days Curtis had seen a lot of strange things. Earthquake, devastation, monsters, an eyeball. But none of it prepared him for the sight of McDonald's employees.

He could only stare, and he wasn't the only one.

The two kids stood side by side as if not sure of their welcome. A woman with long blonde hair that might have been stylish at one point but was now just straggly, climbed out of the jeep behind them. Her slacks were torn in places and her silk blouse stained. Curtis thought she looked almost transparent somehow, as if she was fading.

The doors of the truck opened. The driver, an elderly man in bib overalls, climbed out, rounded the front of the truck, and helped a very overweight old lady out. From the back doors came a muscular young man and a teenage boy and girl. They stood by the truck, looking as uncertain as the McDonald's employees.

Curtis glanced at the locals. No one seemed to know what to do. He put his plate down on the round of firewood he'd been sitting on, and waved. "Morning! Are you hungry? I think we've got some scrambled eggs left."

The newcomers looked at each other and then joined him hesitatingly. They reached hands out toward the warmth of the fire and slowly, the expressions on their faces seemed to melt from tension and fear to something almost like hope.

Except for the muscular man, whose dark eyes kept going to the woods, to the trees shattered and those still standing, as if looking for something. There wasn't fear in his eyes though. Instead Curtis thought he saw grief.

The two deputies, Max and Casey, crossed the street.

"Everyone okay?" Max asked.

"We're alive, son," the old man replied. "That's a good thing."

The teenager from the pickup truck pushed forward past the others and grabbed Max's arm. "My brother. Is he okay?"

"I don't know. Who's your brother?" Max asked.

"Samuel Beaumont."

"Head over to the fire department," Casey said, smiling. "I think you might find someone there who answers to Samuel."

Tears bloomed in the teenager's eyes and he sprinted away from them, jumping over cracks in the street as if they didn't exist.

Max looked back at the group and caught the eye of the older woman in the torn silk blouse and too-pale skin. "I know you."

The woman cocked her head to one side, her eyebrows up in momentary confusion. But then she drew in a breath. "Ah yes. You refused to arrest me. Before the quake. You told me there was always hope. You don't have a career in predicting the future."

Casey snorted. "How did you get here?"

"We came from down below. Sultan," the old man said. "The

high bridge is out so we followed old logging roads. Would never have made it without the winch on the old Crusher." He gestured back at the truck.

Ethan stepped closer. "Sultan? Is it okay? Was the quake just local? Can we get cars out the way you came?"

People were crowding in now, desperate hope in their eyes.

The old man paused before answering, looking around at all those craning close to hear his words. He seemed troubled, and Curtis saw how the others in his group glanced at each other. His stomach dropped, knowing what was coming.

"Sultan is gone, son. The quake breached the Culmback dam and the city flooded. Not sure how many people had time to get out. But a lot didn't."

Curtis heard the indrawn breaths, the soft sobs, the quiet moans that came from those around him. It felt like hope blowing away on the cold air. If Sultan was gone, if the highway was impassable, there was no help coming from that direction.

"We moved a lot of trees and rocks with the winch to get the truck through," the muscular young man said. "There are a lot of slides. A car might make it back out along our route but it will be slow and not safe. Plus, there's nothing to go back to."

"Maybe we can go east," Casey said. "Go back the way this truck came, at least to the highway, and then head east over the mountains. Get help from Leavenworth. Or maybe there's radio reception from the top of Steven's Pass."

Max shook his head. "Doubt we could even make it to Skykomish. Think about the tunnel there. Maybe someone could do it walking out, but that would take days."

"Well, there's Rob," Casey persisted. "He's been bringing down people from Skyko One on that raft. Maybe he could take people downriver past the flooding."

"Too dangerous," Max said. "Rafting flood debris."

Curtis barely listened. Maybe someone would try to walk out but it wouldn't be him.

"You don't want to go out there anyway, dude," said the young man who had helped the blonde out of the jeep. "There's things…" His voice faded as he looked at everyone staring at him.

The slightly plump young woman from the jeep moved closer to the kid. He seemed to draw strength from her because he lifted his chin and stood straighter.

"There's monsters out there," he said. "You aren't going to believe us but there are. We saw them."

Max walked over to the kid and put a hand on his shoulder. "We believe you. It was here, too. But it went into the river. It's gone."

"No," the kid said, shaking his head. "We saw it killed. It was torn apart in front of us. Though that fog-"

"No, wait," Ethan said. "It didn't die. It hunted us all the way here."

"The shadows, wisps of fog." The blonde woman rubbed her chest as if she were in pain. "That is what's hunting all of you. You can't kill them."

A deep silence fell over the group. They stared at each other with dawning horror in their eyes. Curtis felt his lovely scrambled egg curdle in his stomach and swallowed against sudden queasiness.

"Okay," Max said, his voice calm and sure and cutting through the heavy silence. "Time to talk this over and figure out what's going on."

The old woman grunted as she moved ponderously toward the back of the camper on the truck. "Build up that fire, boys. Someone get me a big pot of water. This talk is going to need hot chocolate all around."

"Hot chocolate?" Casey asked. "Seriously? You have hot chocolate?"

"And coffee. We have plenty of supplies," the old man said. "And we'll happily share them. Especially the hot chocolate. Like Mother says, mayhap we're going to need it."

"I think we're going to need something a lot stronger," Max said, tossing a piece of firewood onto the flames.

"But in the meantime, honey," the old lady said, "chocolate always helps the bad news."

"And I need books," Curtis said, looking across the street at the still-standing school. "I have an idea. Save me some hot chocolate."

2

Sharon put her hand over the curving slope of her breast, where her skin burned from below. She stood by the fire watching the others as they introduced themselves, found pots, filled them with water from bottles, and acted like it was old home week. She watched, but took no part in their camaraderie. There was something else pulling at her. She lifted her chin and drew in a deep breath.

There was an odd scent in the air that made her edgy. Maybe propane. Which would make sense. Tanks damaged from the quake and venting. The faint stink was a small irritant, like a tiny invisible splinter felt every time a finger brushed it.

She rubbed her skin with cold fingers then cautiously pressed her palm harder against her breast. She smiled in bitterness at the irony of the movement. Her hand pressing, feeling for lumps like a good girl, testing monthly like all the women's health literature insisted she do.

Like it had made any difference.

She still felt no lumps under her palm but there was something there. She'd noticed a faint tingle when they were getting close to town and now that tingle was more like dancing nerves. Like those cancer cells were waking up.

She flashed on the PET scan she'd had last month. Positron Emission Tomography. They'd had her not eat or drink ahead of time. And then fed her glucose. Supposedly if there were cancer cells in her body, starving them and then feeding them sugar made them wake up. In the scan they would then show up as bright red lights. On the screen her body had been pale gray, like a shadow of her life. Like those shadows that had killed the kids.

Everything pearly gray. Except for that breast and armpit, so full of cancer cells that it was a bright red beacon among the shadows, pointing to her death.

That, she realized, was what her breast felt like now. Like the cells had been starved and were now awake and in a frenzy of feeding. Awake and lit up.

She rubbed her skin again, breathing shallow against the burning of her breast.

Soon, she thought. *Soon.*

3

Ethan stared at the high granite cliff behind the town, overwhelmed and heartsick with all he'd seen up there in the woods over the past four days. A big fire snapped, sending sparks and smoke high in the morning air. Other than the sound of the flames, it was quiet. A profound, heavy silence that sat on his shoulders like the heavy clouds sat on the crags.

They had finished their breakfast and their stories and now waited for Curtis to come back from the school, where he'd gone saying something about needing books. The others seemed to feel a tiny bright hope, that maybe Curtis, the timid scientist, would find the answers they needed. But Ethan had no hope.

A breeze, damp and chilly, moved through the town and he shivered. This place of forest and water still tugged at his soul in spite of all that had happened.

It was such a contrast to the years traveling with his parents, being hauled along on their missions through hot and arid countries. Through war zones. Through shattered lives and trauma, carrying the impossible goal of his parents to save the world. How he'd longed for the lush green forests he saw in books and movies. How he'd craved colors other than blood and gun-metal gray.

He'd thought coming to the mountains and the forests would be an oasis. A cool and lush place to be washed clean of all he'd seen growing up. And then when he'd taken the Environmental Science job, he'd been overwhelmed by the desire to show the students the natural world, with no cruelty and no danger.

Instead, here they were.

The survivors in this tiny town clustered around fires, building them up as if roaring flames would keep nightmares at bay. And sitting there clutching cups and mugs and glasses with hot chocolate, or instant coffee, or tea, they'd shared their horrible experiences and the creatures they'd faced.

Ethan glanced at Anya. She sat silent, one hand on her dog's head, watching the flames. The only time she had reacted to the earlier stories was when Ramon talked about his niece and a boy. With a grizzly and a wolf. She had jerked around in shock, and then met Ethan's eyes. He'd recognized Ramon's description as well.

Their grizzly. Their boy.

And now no one knew what to say. Or what to do. And so they waited, watching the school for Curtis's return. Or watching the two sheriff deputies, as if expecting Max and Casey to have answers or explanations.

But they were silent, too.

So Ethan watched the cliff face, scanning for movement. Because there was no help coming and nowhere to go. And the kids were still his responsibility. The fires they sat around, the shelters they found, were nothing more than illusions of safety.

At least the responsibility wasn't on just him and Anya anymore. Max and Casey had guns. Ben said they had rifles and guns in the back of their truck, along with ammunition. He wasn't sure guns would do any good, especially after hearing the description of some of the creatures the others had come in contact with. But he still felt reassured that guns were available.

If only his parents saw him now. With their idealistic dreams and refusal to use weapons even in self-defense. He turned to the fire, pinching the bridge of his nose at the irony. His parents wanted to save the world. He wanted to save these kids. They would have done anything to meet their goal except touch a gun, even if that meant sacrificing their only child.

He would do everything he could, too, including sacrificing his parent's only child. Except he sure as hell was going to touch a gun.

4

Curtis had trotted back from the school with a sheaf of papers and had been madly scribbling on them for the past twenty minutes while people waited, silently. Now he cleared his throat and straightened, unconsciously slipping into his professorial role.

"Okay. Can I have your attention please?"

People shifted their attention to Curtis, some looking hopeful, some just scared, as if they knew what came would just be more bad news. The mayor and EMT, Albert and Samuel, joined their circle around the fire. Betty had come out of the store for something and Curtis saw her watching them from the parking lot. After a moment she tentatively joined them, but she stood at the fringes, cradling her splinted arm.

Jennifer also stood at the fringe, a couple feet from Betty. None of the high school group invited her to come back into their circle. He didn't blame them. He felt bad for the girl but at the same time, was afraid of what she might do next to ensure her own survival. There were so few of them left that they should stick together, value life. And yet she had betrayed them. No one trusted her anymore.

He cleared his throat, looking at his notes as if preparing for a lecture. Which, in a way, he was.

"We know some can be killed." Curtis tapped his pencil on the notebook. "It appears some may not, at least by guns."

"Right," Michael snorted rudely. "Like you know anything about monsters."

"Actually," Curtis said calmly. "We're not talking about monsters."

Casey twisted her empty mug round and round in her hands. "No? What then? Because they sure as hell look like monsters to me."

"You already know the answer to that question." Curtis smiled at her. "You talked about that Sisiutl as a myth of the Coastal tribes in Canada where your family is from. And that's what we're dealing with here. Myths."

"Those are real, son." Ben leaned forward to add a piece of wood to the fire. "As real as you and me. Not myths."

"Oh, I agree," Curtis said. "But real as they are, they're still myths. Are you all up to hearing some theories and some history and some ideas?"

"I'm going to need more coffee, I can tell." Max took up a dented aluminum coffee pot and poured tar-black liquid into his mug.

"Settle in then." Curtis stood and paced a short line back and forth, as if standing at the head of a classroom. "First, I'm going to lay out my working hypothesis. You've all heard about leprechauns?"

"Oh, god," Michael said. "You've got to be shitting me."

"Look." Ramon reached out to grab Michael's arm in a grip tight enough that the young man squeaked. "My niece is out there. Either add something constructive or shut up."

Michael flushed a deep red and jerked his arm free. But he fell silent.

"Um, okay then." Curtis flipped a couple pages. "I'm not talking about what you see depicted everywhere on St. Patrick's Day. The little people have a much more ancient lineage than that. During pre-Christian times, they were real. But according to recorded and documented legends, as Christianity moved in and took over from the old religions, people quit believing in them and quit talking about them.

"And as people quit talking and believing in the old gods, the old deities, the old religions, those creatures grew smaller. They went underground, inside hills, and so forth."

Anya leaned forward. "Underground?"

"Yes. Those old religions and mythical beings did just that. As they lost their power because people no longer believed in them, they disappeared." Curtis turned a page in his notebook. "Like the Tuatha Dé Danann. The lived in Ireland long before the ancestors of the modern Irish. They were skilled in magic and disappeared into the hills when the modern-day Irish ancestors came. They are treated in historical documents as real, actual people, all the way up to the seventeenth century. But the modern world overcame them, too."

"Well, sure," Ethan said. "If you're going to be killed for believing different from what the ruling religion or government dictates, those things you believe in must disappear. We used to see that all the time with missionaries or terrorists coming in to villages. It wasn't so much that the locals gave up their beliefs, they just knew it was safer to quit practicing in public."

"Exactly!" Curtis said with a wide grin, as if a favorite student had just aced a test. "And those old stories did fade. Like leprechauns, they grew smaller and smaller until they were no longer seen. Or rarely seen. And yet we still talk about leprechauns, don't we?"

"And this relates to fucking cannibals with antlers coming out of their head, how?" Spike tossed the dregs of his hot chocolate on the fire, making the flames sputter before flaring back up.

Curtis rolled the pencil between his fingers, staring at his notes for a moment. And then he looked around the group and shrugged, blushing. "This is just an idea, remember. But look. We know that throughout time, old beliefs faded. We know that in several legends similar to leprechauns, the old ones went underground. Or into rivers." He glanced at Ramon. "Or into trees. So ask yourself this. If they went underground, would a devastating earthquake release them?"

Michael laughed out loud.

But he was the only one.

Casey rubbed her palms against her knees. "Two weeks ago I'd have said you were crazy."

"We know what to do then!" Payton sat up straight with a wide smile. "We just have to quit talking about them! Then they'll disappear!"

No one spoke for a long moment and she held her hands out, palms up, as if her point had just been proven by their silence.

"Well…" Curtis glanced from Ethan's pained expression to Ben, whose eyebrows had climbed into his sparse hairline, and tried not to laugh. "Not exactly. It took many generations before previous truths became myths. I don't think we have that much time."

"So what do we do?" Lucy asked from where she sat next to Spike. Her voice was soft with fear.

Curtis flipped a page. "List what we know. The school had some books on myths. Based on what I found, and on descriptions from all of you, I think we can identify what we've seen so far."

"Like the Windigo." Rowan opened her sketchbook and turned it so the others could see a pencil drawing.

"The Pacific Coast version. Then Casey identified the Sisiutl. Or something similar. The legends about Sisiutl being the searcher of truth are as numerous as the legends that tell of it being the monster you saw." Curtis tapped his pencil on the page and spoke thoughtfully. "The Black Dog. Me and Louis saw it. Huge, glowing eyes, a common theme in many cultures. Often associated with ancient pathways, crossroads. They'll turn vicious if attacked but are more commonly seen as guardians."

Marie reached out to clutch Artair's hand as she lifted her chin. "The fog."

Her words startled Curtis. She was such a quiet girl, seated between her uncle and the teenager, with her head down and hands folded in her lap, that it was easy to forget she was there.

Curtis turned to point his pencil at Tessa and Connor. "Not fog. Based on their descriptions I think it's more like shadows, or the Gray Men. And to be honest, those things kind of terrify me."

"And a cannibal doesn't?" Spike asked.

"Well, sure. But the Gray Men. Or Shadow People." Curtis shivered and shifted closer to the flames. "Shadows with no features. Barely there and barely seen. They're common in myths. Some say they are from parallel universes that sometimes overlap with ours."

Michael snorted. "First you're trying to get us to believe in leprechauns and now you want us to believe in aliens?"

Ramon turned toward Michael, who flinched back and fell silent.

Curtis didn't reply, suddenly remembering Henry and his talk about the Hole experiments and parallel universes.

"Curtis?" Ethan asked.

"Oh, right, sorry. Those Shadow People don't necessarily kill you. They can, of course, or they can just eat your soul."

Silence fell again at his words.

"Then we have the grizzly and the wolf." Ramon threw a hunk of wood onto the flames and the sudden flare of sparks made several of them jump.

"Yes." Curtis flipped a page. "And their tree spirits. Another common myth. An external soul. Or trees that hold a soul when someone dies, to keep it safe. Dryads in Greek mythology, Kodama in Japanese folklore...it's pretty much a common theme in any culture. Here, the young boy and the grizzly first appeared to Anya so they have some connection to her, just like the wolf and Ramon's niece connect to Ramon and Marie."

Curtis avoided looking at Ramon, at the pain in his dark eyes.

"They aren't monsters," Nathaniel said. "They helped us."

"Well, sure," Curtis said. "Not all myths are bad."

"Just the fuckers eating us," Spike said.

Curtis shrugged and turned another page. "Have we missed any?"

Marie straightened and stared straight at Sharon.

Curtis saw Sharon shift on the round of wood she sat on. One hand came up to cover her heart. Or maybe her breast. She stared back at Marie for a long moment but didn't speak.

Artair squeezed Marie's hand. "Go ahead."

"The old woman. And the raven."

"Of course!" Ben said, turning to Curtis. "We forgot her. We all saw the old woman, but Marie was the only one who saw the raven on her shoulder."

Curtis's face lit up. "Seriously? You saw the Stone Woman? How cool is that? Is she here now?" He turned in a circle but saw nothing but the grayness of a misty late morning.

"We saw her in Sultan," Ben said. "Right before the flood."

Marie clutched Artair's hand. "Sharon knows the old woman."

Sharon jumped up. "I'm done with this crazy talk." She tossed her mug to the ground, spilling tea into dirt, and stalked away in the direction of Index Avenue and the ruined railroad crossing.

The others watched her leave and Curtis wondered if they should call her back. It wasn't safe to wander around alone but then he couldn't force her to stay with them either. When she disappeared from view, he turned back to the others.

"What's this about a stone woman?" Ethan asked.

"Oh, wow." Curtis sighed. "An old, old myth that crosses all cultures and has been adapted for almost all religions. The Crone in goddess mythology. The Virgin Mary in Christianity. The guardian of the natural world. The heart of the land. The Mother. She's called innumerable things. But as the Stone Woman, she walks among us yet is rarely seen. Sometimes she has a tall staff, sometimes a raven, sometimes both. If you get touched by the staff you die instantly. But she is seriously powerful. I mean, like, power over all life, control your destiny kind of stuff. You treat her with reverence and she'll help you. Look at all the ways people down through the years have prayed to her and worshipped her as the mother of life."

"You sound like you believe in that one," Ethan said.

"Oh, yeah. I mean, can you picture it? An old woman with a raven? It's like the epitome of all mythical stories."

There was a shift of movement at the fringe of the group as Betty took a step forward. "I believe you."

Her voice made Curtis jump. He'd forgotten she was there. She raised her hand to the sky, palm up, as if calling down benediction from a pulpit.

"I believe all of it," she repeated. "All the demons you describe. It's in the Bible. 'They will turn their ears away from the truth and will turn aside to myths.' 2 Timothy 4:4. That's a direct quote from the Word of God. We brought these monsters on ourselves." She turned back to the store and spoke over her shoulder as she walked away. "There's nothing left to do but pray. The end times are here."

The others looked at each other uncomfortably.

"She never used to be like that," Curtis offered, almost in apology.

"Trauma takes people that way sometimes," Samuel said. "They need something to believe in, that makes them feel like someone is in control and able to save them."

Rowan closed her sketchbook and leaned her elbows on her

knees. "No god is going to save us. But we know what these monsters are now."

Anya finally looked up. "So we know what they are. Whether they came from the earthquake or something else, it doesn't matter. We need to kill some of them. How do we do that?"

All eyes turned to Curtis. He poked at the stack of books on the ground with his foot then looked up to meet their hopeful faces.

"Kill them? I have no idea."

5

5

Sharon paused on the other side of the railroad tracks to catch her breath. Walking even that short distance from the fire seemed too far. Which was ironic when she thought of all the hours she'd spent in the gym and the swimming pool, in yoga classes and doing Pilates. Now it was like she was weighed down, being pulled toward the earth that would soon cover her bones.

It couldn't come soon enough.

The faint scent of propane was back. She caught slight whiffs as the chilly breeze eddied around her. Maybe that would be the way to go. Find the tank that was leaking and ignite it. Up in a ball of flame, instantly doused, instantly beyond pain and caring. She lifted her chin and sniffed, turning her head until she caught the smell.

Somewhere down Index Avenue maybe. She started in that direction, going slow because of the torn up street and downed lines. A few cars were canted out into the road, one white SUV tipped on its side. The houses she passed all had damage to them. Several were completely collapsed in on themselves. It made sense that somewhere in all that carnage, gas leaked.

As she made her way down the street, pausing occasionally to catch the scent she followed, she thought about what Curtis had said. Of course the world was now full of monsters. Of course they weren't safe. She'd known that since the day she'd seen the monstrous cells eating her body. She wanted to take Tessa and Connor and shake them, force them to fully see how truly awful the real world was. Maybe then they'd have a chance of surviving.

Index Avenue turned at the end, becoming a short little street that linked to Avenue A and the river that raced deep and wild along the boulders bordering the road. Sharon turned in a circle feeling like some sort of bloodhound. When she picked up the scent again, she headed toward Avenue A. The rushing water drowned out all other sound and its raging power sucked away debris from the quake. Whole fir and cedar trees with root balls still attached scraped the edges of the street as they were swept downstream. Roof rafters were pulled under only to bob back up. Someone's trailer, upside down, went by with tires slowly spinning. The bloated, bobbing carcass of someone was hung up in tree branches. As fast as she saw something, it was gone, downriver.

Sharon flashed on the moment when she'd stood at the remains of High Bridge thinking about jumping into the river. She could still do that. She wondered which method would be less painful, burning or drowning. She laughed to herself at how surreal such thoughts were. If someone had said such things to her a month ago she'd have wanted them committed.

She crossed Avenue A, going closer to the river. But before she reached the rushing whitewater at the edge of the street, an intense knifing pain cut through her breast. It slid, bright and almost incandescent through her racing heart, her stomach, her groin, and down her legs. Her knees gave out and she dropped, coming down hard on broken asphalt. Her breast was a ball of white-hot heat and all she could do was hang her head, dig her fingers into gravel, and struggle to breathe.

The world glowed as if she was seeing an aura and she knew she was going to faint. She rolled onto her hip and shoulder, lying down in the middle of the road. And as she did so, the pain eased in such a tiny increment that she wasn't truly sure it was getting better. Except that she drew in a breath.

Slowly, her vision came back, but she lay there several moments before her heart eased back to normal and the pain faded to a dull, distant throbbing. And then she carefully made it to her knees, and then to her feet. Bits of gravel were embedded in the palms of her hands and blood trickled down her arm from small abrasions on her elbow.

Even though she was determined to die as soon as possible, that didn't mean it didn't hurt when she fell. She sniffled and wiped tears away from her eyes. And when she dropped her hands, the raven stood there at the edge of the river.

The bird was big, even for a raven, with feathers so black they shone blue and glossy. She was sure, looking at it, that it was the same one that had landed on the jeep. Its head was cocked to one side so that an ebony eye stared straight at her.

"Go away." She took a step toward the eerie bird.

Pain tingled brighter in her breast. The raven squawked and stretched out its wings, flapping them.

"Crazy bird."

She wanted to go to the river, to the cool waters that would douse the fire under her skin. But she didn't want to pass the raven. It was just a bird. Except...maybe it wasn't.

Maybe the old woman was near.

The scent rose up on the breeze again. Propane. Or maybe not. Its sweetness tantalized her, pulled her toward the back road out of town. She took a step in that direction, away from the raging river.

The raven folded his wings.

6

Ramon left the others by the fire and walked past the general store and down 5th Street toward the Wall and the woods that made a towering backdrop over the town. He heard footsteps behind him and turned to see Anya and her dog following. He paused for her to catch up.

"Do you think they're up there?" Anya raised her chin in the direction of the granite cliff and the trees.

Ramon shrugged. He knew she wasn't asking about monsters. "Maybe." He ran a hand over the shepherd's head absently. "My niece. She was twelve. When I saw her with the wolf, she was older. A young woman, somehow. But it was still her."

Anya was silent a long moment. And then she started forward, heading for the tree line. Ramon fell in step beside her.

"My son...I gave birth to him in the woods. He was premature and only lived a few moments. I don't know if he would have survived if I had been closer to help. His father was useless."

The last part was spoken in a tone of deep anger. Ramon touched her arm lightly. "Did the father die in the quake?"

"No. Devon left me. Left us. Before the quake."

"Us?" Ramon asked.

"I buried my son under a yew tree. And I couldn't leave him when Devon wanted to go."

A sudden blinding flash of realization hit Ramon. He heard the voice of the boy with Alegria. Yew trees.

"You buried your son under a yew tree?" He put his hand in his pocket.

Anya nodded. "They're incredibly slow growing. The grandfathers of the forest. I thought...I thought it would protect him forever."

Ramon pulled his hand out and opened his fingers where the small tip of a yew branch rested on his palm. He held it out to her. "The boy with the grizzly gave me this. He told me to give it to his mother."

Anya stopped suddenly and gripped Ramon's arm. "Do you think it's my son?"

Ramon shrugged, his fingers tingling from lack of blood flow. "I don't know. But my niece, whatever happened to her, is older. And she's with a wild animal. She said the boy and the trees saved her. So yeah, maybe the boy is your hijo, your son."

Anya let go of his arm and he rubbed circulation back.

"I need to go home," she said, and he heard the quiet desperation in her voice. "I can't leave him out there alone."

Ramon understood. More fully than he'd understood anything else that had been said that day. But he didn't know how to show this woman that he knew the deep need to be with their kids, to keep them safe. Even if they were no longer children. Even if they were no longer fully human. Whatever Alegria was, she was his blood.

"Your nieces," Anya said quietly. "Are they your only family?"

"No. Their parents are somewhere. If they survived the quake. My brother and his wife." Ramon laughed shortly at the irony. "I moved to the States to spy on my brother. My sister-in-law thought he was having an affair. She wanted me to watch him, confront him. She thought it might save the family if I stepped in."

"Was he? Having an affair?"

"Oh, yeah. More than one. Doesn't matter now though, does it? They're dead or missing, and who knows how long it will take for roads to be passable again. It might be months before I can even begin searching for them. So I'm all my nieces have."

"I'm going back as soon as this is resolved." Anya stared up into the mountains. "Whatever this is. I'm going back to my cabin and my child."

"I'm going to have to stay, too," Ramon said. "As long as Alegria is out there in that wilderness, Marie and I need to be close."

He started to turn back, but a low growl from Bird made both of them jerk around in the direction Bird stared. The dog was growling but his hackles weren't up.

Ramon saw movement in the trees. As he watched, heart racing, a man stumbled out onto the street, falling to one knee and then slowly pushing himself back up. He was old with patchy gray hair and a large blood-crusted spot on the crown of his head. His clothes were torn and he was covered in cuts and bruises. He limped heavily as if one ankle was broken or sprained. The man staggered and Ramon ran forward to catch him before he fell again.

"Get Samuel!" he shouted to Anya.

Carefully he half-carried the injured man to the park next to the school and lowered him onto a granite block. He pulled off his jacket and draped it over the man's shoulders as Samuel and Anya came at a run. Ramon saw some of the others following and the old man's eyes filled with tears.

"Curtis."

Ramon glanced over his shoulder to see Curtis part of the crowd.

"Yes, he's here."

Curtis came forward with a broad grin and tears coursing down his cheeks. "Henry! You're alive! I found your scalp. Well, a piece of it anyway. I thought maybe an eagle or something attacked you. I've been searching for you."

"Not an eagle," Henry said, his voice rough.

Samuel cracked a bottle of electrolyte water and helped Henry to take a drink. "Just a little."

"Not an eagle," Henry repeated, reaching out to catch the sleeve of Curtis's raincoat. "A dog. A monster dog. It attacked me. Knocked me into the fault."

"Later," Samuel said. "Right now let's get you to the station."

Max and Casey got Henry to his feet and headed toward the station, trailed by Curtis who was still talking. Or so Ramon assumed by the gesticulating hands.

Ramon started back to the fire as the first drops of returning rain fell. Anya walked beside him and he caught her looking over her shoulder, back at the woods and the mountains, now disappearing under sinking clouds.

"They'll be okay," he said. "My niece. Your son. Probably better than us."

Anya nodded, but he felt her yearning, like a rubber band stretching between her and the woods, pulling her back.

He thought about the things he hadn't said earlier. About the fear he didn't want to voice.

If they found a way to destroy these mythical beings, would his niece, would Anya's son, survive? He wouldn't be able to help kill monsters if it meant the death of Alegria.

And he wasn't sure how to convince people who were terrified that a grizzly and wolf, even if mythical, were safe.

7

Curtis shifted on a hard metal folding chair wishing he could go back outside to the warm fire. Even if it was raining lightly again. But Henry was asleep on a cot and he felt obligated to sit by the old man's side.

Henry's ankle wasn't broken, but badly sprained. He was exhausted, dehydrated, and covered with cuts and abrasions. One large blue-black bruise over Henry's ribs clearly worried Samuel, but in their primitive settings there weren't many options.

"He should be on antibiotics," Samuel said. "But we don't have any."

"You should ask the old man who drove the truck into town." Curtis reached back to rub his aching tailbone. "He said they had a lot of supplies and were willing to share. Maybe he has antibiotics."

"Good idea."

Albert, the mayor and backhoe driver, came inside and gestured to Samuel who walked over to join him. Curtis watched Henry's labored breathing, barely aware of their quiet conversation behind him. They talked about having to find a burial spot for the bodies, how long before the National Guard might show up, which locals knew how to preserve food without electricity. Their conversation grew quieter as they moved further away.

Henry stirred and shifted on the cot but didn't wake. Curtis reached out to tug the army surplus wool blanket up a little higher. He was overwhelmingly grateful that Henry had survived. As much as they argued, he liked to think that Henry was rather like the father he never had. And now, because of the quake, maybe that was all Curtis had left.

His mother lived in Anacortes, a coastal city near the San Juan Islands, and it was unlikely she survived the quake or the tsunamis that would have followed. He'd always been close to her. She understood his fear and knew what it was like to be afraid of everything, to have to learn how to maneuver through life in spite of that fear. She'd never told him to get over it or to be brave, or that monsters didn't exist.

And now she was gone and Henry was the closest thing to family he had left. Curtis brushed away tears.

"There is no sense crying."

Curtis jumped at Henry's scratchy voice. "You're awake."

"Obviously." Henry plucked at the blanket but made no effort to sit up.

"I'm so happy you're okay." Curtis put his hand over Henry's. "I searched for you, all the way up to the top of the Wall. I was so worried you'd died. Or that you were out there, injured, with…in danger."

Henry pulled his hand free and slipped it under the blanket. "You should have listened and heeded my warnings. Although I believe the damage was already done."

"What are you talking about?"

"I told you the Fifth Force experiments were causing earthquakes."

"But-"

"Those tremblers opened the fault and once that pressure was released it was only a matter of time before plate tectonics shifted in response."

Curtis gripped the edges of the cold chair, all thoughts of Henry as a father-figure gone. "You misunderstand what experiments were being conducted. They had nothing to do with causing this. It's just been a matter of time before the Pacific Northwest experienced a major earthquake, and it finally happened."

"If that is what you need for your conscious to rest easy, I understand." Henry tugged on the blanket again. "But I passed the Hole. I smelled radon. I saw the black dog again, the one that attacked me, this time coming out of the Hole. If radiation is leaking out of there, no wonder it has gone insane and has eyes filled with blood."

"Radon gas is odorless." And then Henry's words sank in. Curtis reached out and caught the blanket. "Wait. You mean the Hole isn't blocked? I thought the quake would have destroyed the entrance."

"Boulders came down, of course. Most of the entrance is blocked. But it is not completely closed off. You should never have bored into the granite. Now all the radon is escaping."

Curtis looked down at Henry, at the wispy gray hair, bandaged scalp, and arthritic fingers picking at the blanket and realized it was impossible to change Henry's mind, about radon, about the gravity experiments, about anything. He would have to accept Henry as he was.

"I'm glad you're okay, Henry. As much as you annoy me sometimes, I'm happy you're back."

Henry's fingers stilled and he met Curtis's eyes. "I feared you were inside the Hole. I am, also, relieved you survived. Even though you are the worst type of scientist, unable to see past your narrow view of the world, and even though you are the cause of all this."

The worst type of scientist? The cause of the quake? The words cut deeply. Henry had feared for him, and that meant something. But

Curtis had worried about Henry, too, and searched for him and been alone and terrified because of him. And none of that mattered to Henry.

Curtis stood and walked away with an aching lump in his throat and hot tears in his eyes.

Outside, Ethan sat on a wooden bench, bent over, elbows on knees, and hands dangling loosely. His dark hair hung forward to hide his face, but when the door shut behind Curtis, he straightened and pushed the hair back from his eyes.

Curtis swallowed and wiped the tears away, hoping Ethan didn't notice. He crossed the small stretch of soggy grass and sat down, feeling rainwater soak into his jeans. Ethan gave off an aura of being tough and self-sufficient, of being fearless and all the things Curtis wished he was. And yet at the moment, Ethan's dark eyes seemed vulnerable. They didn't speak, but Curtis felt comforted somehow, as if being with someone else that was hurting allowed him to hurt, too.

Clouds hid the Wall and trailed low into the trees that still stood. Rain fell in a soft drizzle that collected in Curtis's hair and shoulders like silver cobwebs. He felt it trickle down the back of his neck and shivered slightly in the light wind. The afternoon light slanted dull and gray across the town. Curtis thought about those hours of deep panic up on the Wall in the dark.

"I was so scared the night I spent up there." Curtis gestured at the Wall.

"When you were looking for Henry?"

"Yes. I'm in awe of the forest and yet when I'm out there, at work in the Hole, there's always this underlying low-level fear of what's walking in the trees. I just never thought it would be monsters."

Ethan watched the gray streamers sifting through treetops.

"I was worried about bears and cougars." Curtis managed a laugh. "And, okay, spiders."

"Bet you wish that was all you had to be afraid of now."

"Isn't that the truth." Curtis hesitated. "Are you ever afraid? I mean, you know, if that's not too personal."

Ethan snorted. "Are you kidding? I grew up scared, hauled along like luggage. My folks dragged me from one world disaster to another, trying to save everyone. Every single day was nothing but fear. When would the next bomb hit? When would the next old truck filled with rebels and guns come in shooting?"

"Your parents must have been brave, facing all that to help people."

"Sure." Ethan's voice was tight with bitterness. "But their empathy for the world didn't include me. And then my father was killed and I was injured, and afterward I knew I had to take care of myself."

"I'm only confident in front of a classroom," Curtis said. "In the middle of a lecture, with books and words and information. Is that why you became a teacher? To teach kids to be self-reliant, to give them the knowledge they need to move through their world?"

"I wanted to be alone. With no one to be responsible for except myself. But I needed a job."

"And yet you chose a job with people. And not just people, but high school students."

This time, Ethan laughed outright. "Yeah. Go figure. Sometimes what terrifies me is that I'm just like my parents."

Curtis smiled, feeling the hurt from Henry's words ease slightly. "Henry just blamed me for the quake."

"No shit?"

"I know I'm a coward. I try to be brave but I always fail." The words boiled up. "I was so scared looking for Henry. But I was more scared that he was hurt and alone out there."

"And he blames you instead of being grateful?"

"No, it's not that," Curtis said. "I wasn't looking for thanks. It's just, well, I guess I thought we were friends. Sounds stupid to you, I suppose. But I don't remember my father. He died when I was young. I kind of thought…"

"That Henry would take on that role?" Ethan shook his head. "Well, it's his loss."

Curtis glanced at him, but Ethan wasn't laughing at him. And he also wasn't judging him, or blaming him. He sat there talking to Curtis like they were equals. He even seemed to understand about Henry. Curtis straightened. Maybe he wasn't a failure after all. Maybe he was braver than he realized, too.

"Look at those rain clouds." Ethan pointed at the Wall. "See them up there? And how those tendrils come down through the trees?"

"Sure," Curtis said. "It will probably be dumping rain by noon. I see why people describe clouds like that as sheep's wool. Like the mist is caught in tree branches."

"No." Ethan stood. "Look at how they move."

Curtis stood as well, studying the Wall. He wiped drizzle from his face. Those clouds, those tendrils of water vapor condensing into raindrops, sagged downward like long fingers.

But they moved in the same direction, together, as if seeking something.

"What was it you said back at the fire?" Ethan asked quickly. "About those things that steal your soul?"

Curtis's stomach bottomed and he reached with shaky fingers to grip the damp sleeve of Ethan's jacket. "The Shadow People. The Gray Men."

"Yeah, those guys. I think they're headed this way."

8

"What do we do? Oh, god." Curtis turned in a panicked circle. "We need to get everyone together. Find shelter."

The devastated town with collapsed roofs, fallen walls, and shattered homes offered no security.

"The fire department," he said breathlessly, heart racing. "Maybe we can fit everyone inside."

Ethan shook his head. "Walls won't stop those things. They're ghosts, fog, vapor. All that will do is gather a feeding ground. What the fuck do we do?"

"Oh god," Curtis repeated. He grabbed Ethan's arm.

Behind them, a door clicked. Curtis turned as Marie came out of the fire department bay, followed by Artair. She passed them, dark eyes raised and watching the tendrils through the trees. And yet her face was composed and calm. Curtis stared. Did she not realize what was coming for them?

"Marie," Ethan said. "Wait."

She kept going, heading toward the park where Ramon stood with Max and Casey, staring up at the Wall.

"Come on." Ethan went after her, toward Fifth Street and the others, towing Curtis.

Marie went straight to Ramon and he pulled her close to his side. Curtis and Ethan joined them.

"Are those…" Casey didn't seem able to finish the sentence.

"Soul eaters," Curtis said, his voice high and shaky. "What do we do? The river? Will they follow us into the water?"

"It doesn't matter." Max's voice was controlled. "We can't get everyone gathered in time, and no one would survive the river, running like it is."

Casey whirled on Ramon. "Your niece. The wolf. Can you, I don't know, summon them somehow? Fight myth with myth?"

Marie held her hand up. "Wait," she said softly, lifting her hands slightly, palms up, cupping the slight wind. "They aren't coming here."

"Where are they going?" Ramon asked, keeping his arm around her shoulders.

Marie lifted her face, lifted a hand, and pointed. "They are following Sharon. That way."

"That's right," Curtis said. "She went over the tracks to the other

271

side of town. She's alone out there. Someone needs to help her."

"Marie." Max touched her shoulder. "How do we fight these things?"

Marie jumped as if startled and tears filled her eyes. "I don't know. I can see things, like auras. I can...feel some of them. But those shadows, they're just ...emptiness. I'm sorry."

Max patted her shoulder and then his hand went to the butt of his gun in its holster. "It's not your fault. Come on Casey. If bullets won't work maybe the Tasers will. Give them a jolt of electricity. See what happens."

Marie tilted her head to one side and her pupils dilated. She grabbed Casey's hand. "Wait."

The others held still, watching her. Curtis's heart fluttered, like a tiny spot of hope flared.

"Sharon," Marie said. "I think...there's some connection."

"Maybe Sharon has seen them," Curtis said.

"No." Marie frowned. "I think they're drawn to her."

"Okay then." Max ran a hand over his short hair. "Let's go find out why."

He and Casey headed toward the railroad tracks. There was no hesitation. No doubt. No fear. Curtis took a faltering step after them, but then stopped. It was their job to put their lives on the line for strangers. They would know what to do. But still, was he going to be someone who helped, or was he going to be like Jennifer, who put her safety above all else?

"Hang on!" he shouted. "I'm coming, too!"

He ran up to Max and Casey.

"Stay here," Casey said. "It's not safe."

"I know." Curtis's teeth chattered so hard he was sure they heard the sound of his terror. "But I'm coming anyway."

It was the right thing to do. Sharon was part of their group now, family formed by circumstance. Curtis felt tears rise. This was the only family he had left.

Terror was ice cold, making his heart high and light and fluttery. Making his stomach airless and queasy. Making his knees shake until it was hard to walk.

"I'm coming anyway," he repeated.

"Okay," Max said. "You've got guts. Maybe not too smart, but you've got guts."

"Wait up!" Ethan shouted behind them.

Curtis looked over his shoulder. Ethan and Anya, with her dog and rifle, ran to them.

Ethan clapped Curtis on the back, making him stagger. "Can't let you go without us, buddy."

Curtis pulled in a shaky and profoundly grateful breath.

Max and Casey, a few yards ahead of them by now, moved at an easy jog over the tracks. He followed, stumbling. His body shook like the earthquake was now inside him. But at least he wasn't alone.

At Avenue A they paused. Across the street, the river raced fast and full of debris. And in the middle of the street stood a large ebony raven, wide wings spread and head bobbing. When Max turned toward the road out of town, the raven lifted and took flight over their heads. The strong downdraft from its wings blew damp air into Curtis's face as it flew over their heads.

As if leading them.

The rain tapered off as they made their way through the debris of fallen trees and buckled pavement, following what had been the back road out of town. By the time they reached the remains of the little gated community, there were small cracks in the clouds exposing fingernail slices of watery blue sky.

They climbed shattered trunks, crossed downed and dead power lines, and passed collapsed homes without speaking. Occasionally there would come the loud *kwark* of a raven's call, sometimes behind them, sometimes ahead of them. Curtis scanned the forest fringe bordering the road looking for fog, for shadows, for the shape of Sharon somewhere ahead of them. He stumbled frequently, banging knees and elbows on downed trees and torn up pavement, but he couldn't quit searching the woods for what might be there.

In the middle of scrambling over a broken telephone pole, his stomach growled loudly and he flushed. "Sorry."

Anya slipped her backpack down onto one shoulder, unzipped a side pocket, and tossed Curtis a fruit and nut bar. "Here, get some protein inside you. Fear makes you feel hollow sometimes. So you think you're hungry when you're just empty."

Curtis bit into the bar, thinking about the books he'd found in the library. How were monsters killed in the old stories? What might work on fog?

"Silver," he said abruptly. "There's always someone who has a silver bullet."

"No silver bullets," Max said.

"Crosses," Curtis continued. "Salt. I read somewhere that the ringing of loud bells chases evil things away."

"All those stories are about fighting tangible monsters." Anya worked her way around a large boulder that had rolled downhill. "You

273

can't shoot fog, or stab it with a stake, or even sprinkle salt on it. Anything solid will pass right through."

"You don't know that," Curtis said. "You're assuming those old remedies were for tangible things. But salt spread along windowsills and doorways, wasn't to shrivel something up, like a slug. It was to prevent entry. Right? So maybe…maybe we should have told them to find salt for the fire department doors."

"Too late now," Casey said.

"You're smart, Curtis." Anya heaved a big branch out of their way. "Think. You know more about this stuff than we do."

"Okay." Curtis fell silent, thinking.

"Just don't take too long," Max said. "I see movement up ahead."

"I don't know," Curtis admitted. "I'm really sorry. I should know. Or know where to find out at least. Wait, you saw movement? As in monsters?" The protein bar suddenly coalesced into a heavy lump in his stomach.

"No," Max said. "It's Sharon. She's almost to the Hole."

9

Curtis wanted to drop to his knees and give thanks to the Stone Woman that he hadn't been in the Hole when the quake hit. Boulders had calved from the wall, taking trees with them, hitting the ground so hard they'd sunk into craters. They'd fallen to create a tangled mess of rocks and trees piled at the base of the Wall. But the Hole's door wasn't completely blocked and it gapped at the top between debris. And Sharon was carefully picking her way up over the boulders, moving cautiously around giant swords of splintered cedar and fir.

Curtis knew it was up to him to do something. After all, the Hole was his responsibility. He stopped at the edge of the rocks, with one shaking hand resting on the cool granite. "Hey, Sharon. What's up?"

"What are you doing?" Ethan asked him.

"I have no idea."

"Stay put," Max said as he passed Curtis and started up the boulder field. "Hey, Sharon, it's not safe up there. Hang on. Let me help you."

Sharon paused and looked down, her face pale and drawn. "I don't need your help. Not anymore."

Anya came up on the other side of Ethan. "What's in there, Curtis?"

"All my equipment. If any of it survived."

"Tell us what you did in there," Ethan said as they watched Max near Sharon. "What should we know if she gets inside?"

"Basically we were researching the Fifth Force. Newtonian physics. There are four known forces, gravity, electromagnetism, and two nuclear forces. We hoped to find proof of a weaker fifth force operating on the molecular level." He faltered to a stop. "Sorry, I ramble when I'm nervous."

"No, keep going," Ethan said. "What else?"

"What else?" Curtis's mind went blank with confusion.

"Did you find it? The fifth force?"

Curtis shook his head. "Oh, not yet. Henry thought the experiments had to do with searching for parallel universes. Nothing to do with our work at all. He even thought the gravity experiments caused the minor tremors…" He saw their expressions.

"Maybe he wasn't so far off," Anya said. "Where else could these things have come from except some other world?"

"Oh, no, really," Curtis said. "There's no such thing. And even if there were, these monsters are from our cultures, our mythologies. So basically they're from here."

"Maybe from here," Casey said, watching Max climb. "But like you said, they went underground according to old stories. So maybe hundreds of years ago 'underground' was a word they used because they didn't know about alternative realities."

"I haven't seen anything to convince me that there's any such thing as parallel universes," Curtis said.

"And two weeks ago there was no such thing as that, either." Ethan pointed at the mist trailing through the trees on the Wall, drifting closer.

Curtis stared up at the fog. Tendrils separated almost as if flanking them. Did these things reason?

Max paused just below Sharon. "Why don't you tell me what's going on?"

Sharon used a spar of shattered tree to pull herself up onto a large rock in front of the Hole. "Can't you smell that? Something sweet. I need to see where it's coming from. And you need to go away."

Curtis drew in a deep breath. He smelled only the forest, the loamy earth, crushed fir needles, and sweet, damp air.

"Max, let me try," Casey said, starting up the rock pile after Max. "Sharon, can you tell us what it smells like?"

"I told you." Sharon straightened and rested a scraped and bleeding hand over her chest. "Sweet. I smelled it in town but it's stronger here. It cools what's burning in me."

A memory slammed into Curtis with so much force that he staggered. "Come back! Right now! All of you!"

"What is it?" Ethan spun, wild eyes searching their surroundings.

"Max!" Curtis shouted. "Grab Sharon, don't let her go in there. Radon!"

"What?" Casey stopped climbing and stared down at Curtis, her face paling.

"Radon. The Hole. This granite has the highest concentration of radon gas anywhere on this whole planet!"

"But you worked in there." Anya caught Curtis's arm.

"Yes, but it was in granite, not air. Now, with the earthquake?" Curtis pulled his arm free. "Who knows how the quake affected the gas. You could end up with radiation poisoning. You need to come down now! All of you!"

Max and Casey hesitated, looking at each other for a long moment.

"You heard the man. Go back, Casey," Max said. "Come on Sharon. Let's get you out of here."

"Max! Behind you!" Ethan shouted.

A long tendril of mist snaked over a splintered tree and sinuously entwined around Max's torso. He twisted, grabbing at it, but his hands passed right through.

"No!" Casey screamed, scrambling up the rocks.

Without thought, Curtis started up, breath coming fast, legs weak with terror. But Ethan caught his arm and stopped him.

"Stay with Anya. Help her if she needs it." He went up the rocks.

Curtis hesitated, torn between the need to run after Ethan or do what he was told. He drew in a shaky breath and made the safer decision, going back to Anya. But once at her side, he saw the shadow people forming around Max's torso, sliding upward.

"Cover your mouth and nose!" Curtis shouted.

Max dropped to the ground, one hand over his mouth and nose, the other trying to beat off the tendril. The fog took humanoid form and something that was almost a hand, almost fingers, searched Max's face. Probing.

Casey grabbed Max around the waist and tried to pull him away but the fog just floated after him.

And then it entwined around both Casey and Max.

Ethan was almost to them.

"Ethan, wait!" Anya shouted. "You'll just get caught, too."

"Then what the fuck do I do?"

Max shook his head, gesturing for Ethan to go back.

Panicked, Curtis dug shaking fingers into his hair and pulled. He needed to calm down. He needed to think. Knowledge was his strength. He squeezed his eyes shut. What killed shadows? What dissipated fog?

Sunlight.

Wind.

Casey screamed, the sound muffled behind her hand. Tiny bits of fog rose up her neck, seeping into her ears. Max rolled on top of her, putting his hands over her ears. The tendrils paused, shifted, headed back toward him.

Wind.

Curtis scanned the sky. "Yes. Wind."

He heard the coming wind before he saw the huge raven flying through the trees. Its feathers glowed like moonlight on oil as its wide wings swept up and then down. It flew to them, to Max and Casey, and its wings beat strong downdrafts against them. The powerful movement was a hard pressure against Curtis's eardrums. Ethan staggered backward. Max wrapped his arms around Casey and held on. And still the raven beat the air, its wings bringing the storm.

The shadow creatures shifted, disintegrated, melted through gaps in rocks and trees. And Max and Casey were free. The raven lifted up on air currents to soar higher circles around them. But Curtis barely glanced at the raven. The shadow creatures were coalescing, reforming, and softly flowing toward Sharon.

"Sharon! Look out!"

Sharon hoisted herself up over another boulder. She looked back at them and Curtis had a sudden sense that she was no longer there. She looked...luminous.

The raven came down, settling on a tree trunk next to Sharon and cawed once before folding its wings. Sharon glanced at the bird, but then seemed to look off to its side. She cocked her head as if listening.

"It's my time," she said, and paused. "I choose now."

"What's going on?" Anya asked. "What is that?"

The filtered light coming down between tree branches, broken clouds seemed to shift, and an old woman stood next to the raven. She held a tall walking staff and her charcoal gray dress moved in the wind circling her. Hair, gray as the clouds, hung to her waist and blew around her face and shoulders.

"The Stone Woman," Curtis breathed.

The ancient woman nodded to Curtis. "I have not heard that name in many ages. I did not think anyone remembered in this time." Her voice was rough, the voice of age. The voice of the raven.

"Oh, wow," Curtis said, his whole body rippling in gooseflesh.

Bird vaulted onto the boulders and scrambled upward until he was between the old woman and the others. His hackles climbed and his head dropped on level with his shoulders. They clearly heard his growl.

"Bird, here!" Anya started up the rock field after her dog, but Curtis grabbed her around the waist.

The old woman didn't seem aware of the dog at all. She turned her black eyes on Sharon. "My daughter. Will you leave what binds you? Will you take what seeks your fire?"

Max, still breathing hard, glanced at the shifting fog easing toward Sharon. He motioned for Casey to stay where she was, and climbed over the remaining boulders until he could reach out and catch Sharon's wrist. "Come down, now. Come with me."

The Stone Woman raised her staff and the raven launched for Max, wings beating against him. He twisted in silence, struggling against the bird as it stabbed its beak into his shoulder. Down went the bird's head again and again, each time coming up with flesh and blood.

Casey screamed and frantically scrambled toward him.

"Bird!" Anya shoved past Curtis and pointed at the raven. "Bird!"

The dog leaped and slammed the raven, knocking it from Max. The dog and the bird fell, rolling down the rock field, the raven's claws embedded in Bird's stomach. Anya raced toward them, bringing up her rifle one-handed.

"You'll hit Bird!" Curtis yelled.

Anya dropped the rifle and kept going. "I'll kill your raven!" she screamed at the Stone Woman. "You take my dog, you bitch, and I'll kill that raven!"

The dog screamed as they came down on a boulder. The Stone Woman raised her staff and the raven's wide black wings spread. It cawed loudly, once, and lifted upward. It soared the few yards to the Stone Woman, alighting at her feet.

Anya reached Bird and gathered the bloody dog tight to her.

Casey had her arms around Max but he didn't seem able to move. Ethan climbed fast, with almost deadly precision, straight for Max and Casey. He slid over a boulder, granite pulling up his shirt and ripping skin. He hit ground with a thud and then hauled himself up over a tree trunk.

Terror pounded in Curtis's heart, filled his body with airless adrenaline. He could only stand, rooted, useless to help.

Ethan, breathing hard, pulled Max's arm up over his shoulder. Casey slipped under Max's other arm and between the two of them they lifted him to his feet. Blood flowed heavy from deep puncture wounds across his shoulders, arms, and neck.

"Come on, big guy," Casey said.

Max slipped and sagged but Casey caught him, taking his weight. She couldn't keep them from falling though, and both were pulled free from Ethan, coming down hard on rocks.

Casey got to her knees, and then to her feet, tugging on Max. "Ethan! Get Sharon! Don't let her go in the Hole."

Max sagged out of Casey's grip. Ethan started toward her, then twisted around and ran for Sharon.

Curtis took a stumbling step forward, and then another, and then another. He pulled himself up onto a boulder, jumped to the next one, and climbed to Casey. Breathless, heart racing with panic, he reached for Max.

Ethan was almost to Sharon.

The raven spread its wings next to the Stone Woman, and cawed loudly. Curtis flinched away, but then gripped Max who groaned in pain.

Casey got hold of him on the other side, and she and Curtis pulled him to his feet.

The raven, head cocked, beak bloody, watched them. Dread shook Curtis but he held tight to Max, knowing what he needed to do. That he needed to speak old words from books.

"I fear you not!" His voice was high and tremulous. "I claim this man! I claim these people!"

The Stone Woman cocked her head, eerily mirroring the raven. "I hear you, my son. I bind you to your claim. But the daughter is mine."

The raven lifted airborne again. This time though, it simply landed between Sharon and Ethan, holding place with its wings spread wide. Ethan, breathing hard, froze.

"We just want to save our friend," Curtis said. He gestured to Casey and they moved Max downward a few feet. "We don't want anything to happen to Sharon."

Sharon didn't appear to have heard him. She moved away, nearing the collapsed entrance to the Hole. The heavy metal door tilted where it had been pulled free. She tugged on it briefly but when it didn't budge she bent and twisted around, working to squeeze through the opening.

"Ethan!" Anya pointed into the trees.

Ethan looked up. The Shadow People seeped closer to Sharon. But one tendril separated, sifting in his direction. He scrambled backward, falling over rocks, picked himself up, and vaulted downhill. The fog slowed and then coiled back toward Sharon.

She paused in the opening of rock. Her hands came up to cup her left breast. Her eyes closed and she swayed.

The ghostly wisps thinned and then coalesced into vague human forms that slid with a purpose straight for Sharon.

"How do we stop them?" Curtis shouted at the Stone Woman.

The wind around the Stone Woman grew. She lifted her staff but didn't speak.

Horrified, Curtis gripped Max and Casey. He stood transfixed and helpless to stop something that had no substance, no being. Something that Sharon now passed her hands through.

"No!" Anya yelled. "Sharon, no!"

Sharon lifted her face to the sky and opened her mouth. The vapor swirled around her body as if caressing her. Tendrils curled around her left breast and clung there like a suckling baby. Others slid over her shoulders and around her waist and arms and legs.

And flowed like water into her mouth.

Sharon drew in deep shuddering breaths, her body convulsing.

But she sucked down the mist, swallowed the shadows.

And then turned and forced her way through the narrow granite opening, disappearing into the darkness of the Hole.

10

The shadow people were ice in Sharon's veins. For the first time in weeks her breast cooled, the fire of dying cells extinguished. To be pain free, fully pain free, was an exquisite joy. She slid into the narrow opening to the Hole, rocks tearing her clothes and skin.

The damp air was filled with the sweet scent that pulled her forward. It smelled like life and she couldn't draw in enough.

With each breath she pulled in though, they shivered under her skin. They flooded her body, making her very cells tingle. She felt their deep hunger, their unending need to seek, to find, to devour life. And yet at the same time, as she breathed, they pulled back.

What she found to be life, they feared.

And she understood how trap them.

She sucked them inside, baited them with the food they craved; her body, her immune system so gloriously alive and fighting. And then fully inside her, fully feasting, she continued to draw in breaths of radon gas.

She felt her way deeper under the mountain, deeper into the blackness, deeper into that sweet and calling air. With each breath they fluttered inside. The shadows, cringing.

She drew in a breath for Tessa. For Connor. For the old married couple. For the students. She'd kill the shadows. Catch the intangible and hold it and save the others. And then she drew in a deep, deep breath, pulled it all the way in to that deeper panic she'd been trying to kill for days.

Because finally, *finally*, death was here.

And by god, she was going to take these bastards with her when she went.

The mist twisted deep inside, wrapped around her lungs and squeezed. They wanted to stop her breath, to allow them to escape. But the air she found sweet was a weight inside chaining the shadows to her soul.

Pain arced through her heart, a bright searing heat that doubled her over. The shadow people cut into her, working to make her stop breathing. The blackness of the Hole pressed against her eyes but pain was there in tiny starlight sparks at the edges of her vision. She fell, hit the rocks, heard her bones splinter, and breath escaped on soul-breaking screams.

Vapor seeped from her mouth and nose, cold like ice. For the briefest of moments she thought she had failed, that they would escape. And then she sensed their terror, their twisting from the radon. Sensed their disintegration. Even those still inside her. Pain came back as a bright fire, white light, shining, all encompassing, until thought was no more.

Tiny sparks of cancer cells flared and died. Grayness filled her body, trapped and twisting and struggling.

Seeking to consume life.

But there was none.

11

Curtis hauled himself over the rocks until he stood at the cracked door. Cold air pulsed out as if the mountains breathed. He put his hand on the rough granite and leaned forward, listening. He heard the faint sound of water and knew it was the underground stream that used to flow beneath his workstation.

All the work he'd done, gone. It would be a long time before anyone returned to research and studies. Time would be taken instead with simple survival. And even when people did return to things other than survival, no one would come back here. He'd make sure of that. This place would become the grave of a woman who had sought death, and in that seeking, saved them.

Some day he would talk to Henry about the Shadows. About the Stone Woman's words that they were not of this place. He didn't believe in parallel universes. But they had to have come from somewhere. The quake had released old monsters. Maybe that fault line, the radon, the Hole, had somehow opened something else as well.

Whatever it was, this was now a place to stay away from.

He leaned in a little further. "Sharon! Are you there?"

He heard nothing so he yelled again, feeling her name tear his throat. Silence. He shouted again, and once more, until he felt tears on his cold cheeks. Until a warm hand came down on his shoulder and Ethan spoke next to him.

"Come on. She's gone. We have to get back to town and it's going to take a while with Bird and Max injured. We don't want to be out here after dark."

Reluctantly, Curtis followed Ethan back down the slope. Max stood next to Casey, heavily bandaged and using her for support, but upright. A type of sling had been fashioned with cedar branches and Ethan's jacket, and Bird, also bandaged from Anya's first aid supplies, rested on it, panting lightly.

The wind had dropped to a strong breeze, and Curtis caught movement in the trees where the Stone Woman stood. "Look," he called to the others.

The wind around her slowed. The raven stretched his wings and landed on her shoulder. She moved into the trees that still stood, moved through them until she was barely visible. But then movement stilled and they heard her ancient voice from the forest.

"She sought death and so she summoned me. She is now gone from this realm." She pointed her staff toward Curtis. "You claimed these people. They are yours to save."

There was a brief flurry of rising wind and then she was gone.

"If I'm supposed to save everyone, you're all screwed." Curtis felt sick to his stomach at the thought. What had he done, claiming his friends before the Stone Woman?

"Bigger guns," Max muttered under his breath. He groaned as Casey helped him over a log. "We just need bigger guns."

Ethan reached for the poles in front of Bird and Anya took the ones at the back. Together they lifted the dog and carefully made their way toward the ruined road, trudging slowly towards the remains of the town. Rain came back down the mountains and shadows lengthened. Real shadows this time, reaching out as the daylight disappeared behind ridges and high crags.

"Wish I'd known her," Ethan said. "Sharon."

Max chuckled. "I got dispatched to a road rage call. Before the quake. It was Sharon, taking on this kid who'd almost rear-ended her. She was something."

"This will be hard for the McDonald's kids," Casey said. "I think she was kind of a mom figure to them."

"They won't be alone." Anya shifted her hands on the poles to get a better grip. "People will watch over them. Sharon would have wanted that."

Curtis was quiet as they walked, searching the road and the forest fringe. But he wasn't sure what he hoped to see. Sharon, or the Stone Woman, or the raven. The Stone Woman had relinquished his friends to him. Queasiness churned again and he pressed a hand to his stomach. He wasn't capable of saving people.

But for Sharon, to honor her, he'd at least try to be braver.

~Day 6~

1

Anya ran a hand over the bandages around Bird's stomach. She felt only the normal warmth of the dog and no heat of infection. At least not yet. She lifted her hand, but when the dog wriggled suggestively on his back and whimpered, she scratched the uninjured part of his belly.

"You're not going to milk this for attention, mister."

Bird's tongue hung out. He was a sucker for belly rubs.

They were on her sleeping bag under a tarp hung from rope tied between a bent light pole and the frame of a mangled car. A makeshift tent to keep the drizzle off while they slept, fitfully, near a fire someone had built the night before and others had kept burning during the dark hours. They were only one of several shelters along Avenue A. Safety in numbers, she supposed.

The sleeping bag was still warm from her body, and it felt good to sit there for a moment, with nothing to do except check her dog and rub his belly, sinking her fingers into his fur. The spring sun was just coming up, and the rain had eased off during the night. The light wasn't bright enough to make the world look clean and new and safe. It only illuminated the destruction of the place and the trauma etched in deep hollows on people's faces. It wasn't even enough to warm the air. But at least it wasn't raining.

Anya shivered in her damp jacket and thought about just shedding it and crawling back into the somewhat dryer sleeping bag. But then Bird snorted, rolled over, and stood stiffly, ears up and tail wagging. She followed his gaze and saw the two young McDonald's workers coming toward her, bowls in hand.

"Morning," the girl said. Her eyes and nose were red as if she'd been crying.

"Morning. Sorry, I don't remember your name."

"No worries. I'm Tessa, this is Connor."

The young man lifted a bowl in greeting. His eyes were also red. "June, the old lady who came with us? She saw you were awake and sent us over with oatmeal for you and your dog. She said if you come to the fire she'll have hot chocolate soon."

Anya's stomach growled. "Oatmeal? She made oatmeal?"

"Real oatmeal," Tessa said. "She made it with water since there's no milk, but it even has brown sugar in it."

"Oh god, that sounds wonderful."

Tessa handed her a bowl with a mound of oatmeal still steaming, and a spoon.

Connor put a similar bowl down in front of Bird. "June says they never grabbed pet food when they were stocking up. Sure hope this doesn't give him the shits."

Anya laughed, and the sound startled her for a second. How could she laugh? "Even if it does, he'll think it's worth it."

She gestured with the spoon to her sleeping bag, and scooted to one end. Connor and Tessa hesitated, and then sat cross-legged next to her. Connor rested a hand on Bird's back as Anya scooped up still-warm oatmeal. It tasted wonderful, but was tempered by raw sadness that was a weight on her heart. She put the spoon down after a second bite.

"Sharon should be here eating breakfast with us," Tessa said, tears rising in her eyes.

"I'm so sorry." Anya lifted the collar of her damp coat and pressed the cold material against the tears in her eyes. "She saved us. From those shadows."

"I think she was dying." Tessa sniffled. "Just from things she said. And June said something about breast cancer. But Sharon helped us get here, kind of took care of us like a mom. I don't think she wanted to, but she did anyway."

Connor bent, burying his face in Bird's thick fur as his shoulders shook with silent sobs. Tessa's breath caught on a gasp of pain as she folded over him, crying and clutching his coat with both hands.

Bird turned his head but didn't move. Tears ran down Anya's cheeks as she put a hand on each of the kids. She understood loss. She knew they didn't need her words. They needed what she had never received from Devon. Comfort in touch, in shared grief. And so she cried with them and let their pain be hers.

Connor finally straightened, wiping his eyes with his hands. "Sorry. It's just...everything. Sharon, this hell, being scared all the time." His voice broke as more tears pooled. "Our families. We don't even know if they're alive or not. We're alone now."

Tessa broke into fresh sobs and Connor put his arm around her shoulders, crying against her hair.

"I'm so sorry," Anya said again. "I know this doesn't help right now, but you're not alone. We can't take the place of your family, but we're here. And we won't forget Sharon or what she did for all of us."

Tessa abruptly pushed up to stand. "It doesn't help. I know it will, later, but right now-" Her voice broke as she cried. Raising a hand as if to stop any more words, she walked away.

Connor hesitated, then stood and went after her. At the edge of the park, Tessa stopped, shoulders bowed and hands over her face. Connor came up behind her and put his arms around her. She turned and buried her face against his shoulder.

For the briefest moment Anya deeply wanted someone to hold her like that, to take on her grief. She pushed down the hurt, the vulnerability.

"We don't need anyone," she told Bird.

The dog thumped his tail once, and burped oatmeal fumes.

He'd finished her oatmeal when she wasn't looking. Anya picked up the two bowls and stood. She could handle grief and fear and loneliness. She was strong. "We don't need anyone."

Maybe if she repeated it often enough, she'd convince Bird it was true.

She left the dog on the sleeping bag and headed toward the fire built in a ring of stones next to the burned out shell of the museum. It was big and burning bright, and she felt the heat of it on her face when she was still a few feet away. And June was there, overflowing a canvas camping chair. She had a long stick and she was using that to turn a pot of water that was steaming on a rock close to the fire. On a round of firewood next to her sat a circle of tin mugs with powdered cocoa mix in each one.

Ben stood next to her, adding more wood to the fire. He nodded to Anya when she came up to them.

"You look not much bigger than Marie," he said.

"What?"

"Want a dry coat?" He gestured toward their old truck and homemade camper. "We got us some extra clothes when we were stocking up. And mayhap you could use something warmer."

"That would be wonderful. At least until I can get my jacket dry." She shivered, wiped her eyes, and held her hands out to the heat of the fire.

"Let me get somethin' for you then." Ben tossed a piece of wood on the fire and left them.

June bent, wheezing, for the pot and tipped hot water into a mug. She stirred it briskly and then held the mug out. "Warm up your insides, too. We were sure sorry to hear about Sharon."

"The kids are hurting," Anya said, feeling the ache in her own heart.

"Give me a hand up."

Anya put her mug down then braced herself and heaved June upwards.

"It's been a long time since my children were that young," the old woman said, gesturing toward the park where Tessa and Connor stood. "But I'm still a mom. And a grannie. You leave those kids to me and I'll take care of them."

Anya started to speak, but then closed her mouth, not even sure what she wanted to say. But June paused and then folded Anya into a tight hug.

"You're not alone, neither, no more than them two kids are."

Anya couldn't speak past the lump in her throat, but June didn't seem to need any words.

"Drink that hot chocolate before it gets cold," she said, walking away.

Ben came back and handed Anya a quilted jacket in virulent purple. His eyes followed June's slow progress to Connor and Tessa, and he nodded to himself. "Mother will take care of those two. They're our kids, now."

Anya shed her damp coat and tugged on the new one, not caring about the color. It was dry and warm and she zipped it to her chin before picking her hot chocolate back up. "She's a good woman."

"That she is," Ben said. He took Anya's old coat, shook it out, and spread it across a round of firewood.

"What do we do now?" Anya asked, watching the high flames. "What happens to us now?"

Ben lifted his chin to toward his old truck. She saw Max and Ethan at the back of the camper, pulling shotguns out.

"Now we take care of each other," he said. "And then, mayhap, we kill us some monsters."

2

Ethan stood by another fire, over on Index Avenue, that had been built in the yard of the collapsed church. His students were around him, some sitting, some standing. They'd had oatmeal for breakfast, thanks to June, and had eaten in shifts, washing bowls as they finished and then serving others. He broke open a shotgun he'd taken from Ben's camper, and slid a shell in.

Rowan sat cross-legged on the ground, oblivious to the damp. She had her journal open and her hands rested across a sketch easily recognizable as Sharon. She watched the flames, her green eyes far away, and Ethan wondered what she saw.

Jennifer stood at the fringe of their group, arms over her chest in her familiar self-contained hug. Her eyes went from one to another, but no one acknowledged she was there. Not even Michael, on his second bowl of oatmeal. She'd refused her serving when June handed it to her, and Michael had quickly taken it.

Spike had left a few minutes before, but now came back to the fire, carefully holding three steaming mugs. He handed one to Nathaniel and one to Lucy, and then stood next to them holding the third mug. Ethan saw how he asked Lucy something, how she put a hand to her side and twisted back and forth, and assumed Spike had asked about her ribs. He watched Spike put a hand on Nathaniel's shoulder and squeeze, how Nathaniel managed a smile. Somehow, in the midst of all their fear, in the midst of losing their former world, Spike had created a tiny family. He'd taken these two as if they were the most vulnerable, and made them his own.

Payton, of course, stood too close to Ethan, shivering. He shook his head. "Why don't you go talk to Ben. See if he has something warmer you can put on."

Payton stepped closer and slipped her fingers into his. "I'm fine when I'm with you."

Ethan tugged his hand free and scowled. "Lay off, Payton."

Jennifer laughed suddenly. "She's only following nature, just like I did."

The low conversations stilled as everyone turned to her.

"What are you talking about?" Michael asked.

"All this." Jennifer threw out a hand, waving at the destruction around them. "The world goes to shit and we all go back to caveman days. Survival of the fittest. I found ways to survive. And all Payton is doing is surviving the only way she knows how. By finding the alpha male to protect her."

"At least I didn't kill anyone!" Payton said.

"I didn't either," Jennifer said. "Not directly. I did what I needed to, just like you're doing. Or trying to do." She laughed again. "You had guys surrounding you in school all the time. Show a little tit, sway those hips, and they all came running. I saw it all the time. Miss Popularity. Doesn't work so well out here, does it?"

"Just shut the fuck up," Spike said.

Jennifer glared at him, her eyes defiant. "What we were, who we were, before the quake, doesn't matter any more. That's all dead. Our families are probably dead. Our lives are over. This is who we are now. Who the quake forced us to become. We're not a bunch of high school seniors worried about graduating."

"That's true." Rowan closed her journal and stood. "Who we were before, how we faced our demons at home, doesn't matter any more. This is who we are now, like you said. Which means you are someone who betrays others, who tricks them, who lets them die. That's way worse than Payton acting the helpless female."

"Knock it off," Ethan said in his old, firm, teacher-voice.

"Time for a 'we got to stick together since we're all we have left' speech?" Michael asked. "Time for some brave wise words that will inspire us all to live happily ever after?"

"No." Ethan flipped the shotgun's safety on and slung it over his shoulder. "Time for you to fucking grow up. You and Jennifer and Payton. Just…grow the fuck up. A woman just died to save you, and the way you're acting, it wasn't worth it."

He left them and was almost back to Avenue A, regretting his burst of anger, when he heard the sound of running footsteps behind him. He glanced over his shoulder and sighed heavily when he saw Payton. She reached his side, used one hand to push her long hair coyly back, and linked her other hand through his arm.

"She's wrong, you know. This, between us, isn't some survival game. It's not some cave-man thing." She giggled. "Though I don't mind cave-man."

"Payton-" He tried to swallow down the anger and then gave up, pushing her hand from him. "Do you even care about what happened yesterday? Do you even care that one of us died? Or that Sharon died for us?"

She sobered. "Look. Of course I care. I'm not some cold bitch like that Anya. But I also know Sharon's gone and we're still here. That's what's important now. You think anyone in this little shitty town is going to care if tonight, our sleeping bags are zipped together? The only thing that freak, Jennifer, has right is that we have to look out for ourselves now."

Ethan took a step closer. "I've watched you for a long time now."

She smiled and flipped her hair again. "I know you have."

"And what I've seen is a manipulative little girl. You play the helpless role on any guy who happens to be handy. I've seen you doing this for months. Even John, on the bus."

"John? Who?"

Ethan stopped, fury washing through him. "John. The guy who tried to help you with your cell phone when we left on this field trip from hell. The kid who didn't survive the bus crash. The kid who died out here in the woods and you don't even remember him."

Payton looked genuinely confused. "But he's dead, like Sharon, and lots of others, so what does that matter now?"

The anger, so quickly kindled, just as quickly shifted to sadness. "It matters way more than you're obviously capable of feeling. I'm not going to play your game, Payton. I'm not some naïve kid with raging hormones. You're going to have to find someone else."

He walked away and left her standing in the middle of the road. When he reached Avenue A, he looked back. She still stood there watching him. He couldn't tell if it was confusion on her face or resignation. Or hell, maybe fear, what did he know? He felt a twinge of guilt, but squashed it. Sharon and John and Amy and Paul and Zack deserved to be remembered and mourned. Payton on the other hand, didn't deserve his guilt.

He headed toward the general store but then saw Anya by a fire in an ugly purple coat, talking to Ben. He changed direction, crossing the street to her, leaving Payton to fend for herself.

There were more important things to do than pander to a manipulative, selfish teenager.

3

Casey saw Max at the back of Ben's truck and went to them, giving in to the overwhelming need to reassure herself Max was okay. She caught a whiff of herself in the light breeze. Her clothes were smelly and damp after six days in the same uniform, in rain and mud. She glanced at her shirt and saw brown stains across the front. Max's blood. Her stomach gave a funny little flip, almost like fear. She knew, of course, that he was human like anyone else. Yet she'd still, somehow, imagined him invincible.

But now, he'd been hurt. Sharon was dead. Monsters were still out there in the woods.

Kind of put what remained of life into perspective. Things she would never have been able to give words to a week ago now needed to be said. The loss of Sharon made it clear that death was on all sides.

She saw Ben hand Max a rifle and say something that made Max laugh. Then he winced and put a hand to his neck, before shaking his head and reaching in to the truck to pull out a box of shells.

She stumbled to a stop in the street.

That laugh. She'd always loved that laugh.

Max looked up, saw her, and limped to her, concern in his eyes. "You okay?"

"Fine," she said. "Just thinking about Shep."

"Oh." Max ran a hand over his face. "Yeah. Shep. Your boyfriend. Hope he's okay."

"Same here." Casey took a deep breath. "Because if he is, I'm going to need to break up with him."

"Is that so?"

"That's so."

4

Curtis watched the sun come up as he paced Fifth Street. Down past the school, turn, back past the park, turn again. He'd refused the offer of oatmeal, barely aware of one of the McDonald's kids offering it to him. His mind whirled, thoughts chasing themselves around and around and then swinging back to Sharon.

It hurt so deeply to think about her, this woman he'd barely known. He couldn't remember if he'd even talked to her in the short time they'd been in town together. Yet at the end, right before she'd gone into the Hole, she'd looked at him. And in her eyes he'd seen pain, and a deep panic.

And resolution. And strength.

In spite of her fear, she'd been strong. How had she found that willpower? What had made her decide to go, when she had to have known what the decision meant?

She'd protected them by killing the shadow people. At least the ones that threatened them here. Curtis assumed there were more, in other cities and feeding off other groups of people. But for now, this area was an oasis, free of soul-vampires, and all because of Sharon.

He wished he'd known her better. He wished he'd taken time to talk to her, share her company, find out what the source of her pain was, and maybe the source of her courage.

Because now the Stone Woman had made him responsible for the others and he had no courage, no strength, no tools to save them from all the monsters that still surrounded them.

Curtis paused in his pacing and dropped down to sit on a block of granite at the edge of the park, barely aware of the cold rock chilling his jeans and butt.

He didn't have the tools of bravery and strength like Ethan and Sharon and the others. But he did have his own gifts, the things he was good at. Intelligence and the ability to problem-solve. He knew how to research and find resources and piece information together into a working thesis. It might not be the same as fearlessness, but it might be enough to allow him to honor Sharon's sacrifice. If he came up with a plan of defense then maybe he could help that way.

His fingers itched for a keyboard, or even a book. He needed some sort of resource. And then he remembered a resource he did have and hadn't yet used. He stood, wiped granite grit off his jeans, and headed to the fire department.

In the converted bay, Samuel was checking the splint on Betty's arm. There were several cots with people on them, including one with Henry, who raised a hand and beckoned Curtis over. But Curtis continued past him and went toward Samuel. Because sitting on chairs near him were Marie and the teenage boy. He didn't remember the boy's name but knew Samuel was his brother.

He'd figured the boy would be with his brother, and where the boy was, Marie would probably be, too. And he was right. As he got closer, he saw that Marie and the boy were holding hands.

"Can I talk to you?" Curtis asked Marie.

When she nodded, he looked around, found a folding chair, and set it up next to her.

Curtis drummed his fingers on his knee. "We know the Windigo is still out there. Plus the black dog. The Shadows are gone. The Stone Woman and her raven are still around, maybe, but I don't think they're a threat. We know that your group killed another monster. The one your sister called a Matlose. We know one creature went into the river. We know about the bear and the wolf, and their companions, but they are most definitely not a threat-"

Marie interrupted, her voice quiet as always. "But what you don't know is if there are more."

"Exactly." Curtis sat forward. "So I'm wondering if you can, I don't know, sense them somehow. We need to know what we're up against, how many more there might be, where the ones are that we know about, so we can plan a defense. Something long term, I'm thinking."

Marie stood. "I'll be right back," she told the boy and Samuel, and then turned her dark eyes to Curtis. "Will you go outside with me?"

Once out in front of the fire department, they sat on the stone bench where Curtis had been with Ethan the day before. The rainclouds hadn't completely gone, but they'd broken up enough that weak sunlight was coming through, angling down the Wall as the sun rose. The bottom of the small river valley where the town sat was still in early morning twilight though.

Marie closed her eyes and sat still, with her hands in her lap and palms turned up. Curtis waited silently for several minutes before she sighed, opened her eyes, and turned to him.

"There are many more. I don't understand how I sense them so I don't know exactly what it is I feel. Before my head injury I always saw things others didn't. Like auras. I didn't tell anyone, not even my parents. I didn't want to be thought of as a freak."

"Understandable," Curtis said.

"After I got hit on the head, it was like everything amplified. For a while I thought I was dead. But it was just because everything looked so weird. Like the world was here, but not here. Everything was surrounded by auras, even the shadow people. And I don't just see them. I can feel when they are near. It's like the tingle right before you get shocked."

"That's a good analogy," Curtis said. "And might be exactly what you are sensing. Their energy."

Marie nodded again, but he sensed she wasn't really listening. She looked up at the granite wall towering over the town. "So yes, I can sense them. And there are many out there in the mountains. And spreading down below to the cities. Everywhere that people are, all those myths you've talked about are going. They've all returned."

"Thank you," Curtis said. "That's what I was afraid of. That Sharon died only to give us a small reprieve. Can you help me gather everyone? I need to talk to them."

Marie stood. "Of course."

She went back into the fire department. Curtis stood as well, and started across the street toward June and the McDonald's kids standing by the park. He wasn't sure what exactly he would say, and his hands shook with nervousness. But the seeds of the plan were there in his mind, taking root and growing.

5

Curtis pulled out the folded and stained papers he'd used to scribble notes on mythical creatures, and found enough blank pages to start drafting out his thesis on defense. He sat on a stump of firewood, head down and writing, barely aware of the others gathering around the fire.

Marie did a good job convincing people to come listen to him. Some, like the mayor, declined to join them, instead heading out in the backhoe. He and a few others were going to try and clear the road all the way to the Hole, where they intended to block it off completely as a memorial to Sharon.

But most had come to the fire. When Marie touched his shoulder and he put down his pen, they watched him. It was like being back in the classroom.

"Think back to your American History classes," he began. "Remember what life was like in the 1700s and 1800s. Men hunted and fished and trapped. Women foraged for native plants, for food and medicine. Clothes were made from skins and furs. Shelters were built from logs and mud chinking. Light came from animal fat and beeswax. Food was foraged and preserved by drying and salting and fermenting."

"I doubt anyone remembers how to do that," Tessa said doubtfully.

"I do." Anya shrugged when everyone turned to look at her. "It's how I live."

"We do," Ben said. "That's the advantage of being old farts. We're mayhap not as old as what you're talkin' about, but we remember the Depression and how our folks survived."

"What did people do back then?" Curtis asked. "They built forts. Lived within walls. What were those forts built out of? Logs, like their homes."

"I think I see where you're going with this," Max said.

"It's obvious." Curtis pointed in the general direction of the Wall. "All these downed trees. We build an enclosure with gates we can guard. We make sure we're all inside at night and we stay close during the day. We let nothing in once it's dark. In the daylight, we hunt and fish, but in groups. No one goes out alone, or without weapons."

"You're thinking we're going to be on our own for a long time," Ethan said. "But really, how long will it be? It's spring. I bet in a few weeks we'll have contact somehow with the outside world. Even if it's just National Guard."

"True," Curtis said. "But think about it. Even after contact, what will happen? They might be able to fly in supplies. Maybe airlift out our ill or wounded. But where will they take us? If the quake was devastating to the whole Pacific Northwest, they'll probably have to take people to camps, like in eastern Washington, or out of state. Resources will be maxed here. Remember Hurricane Katrina? So many people moved out of state because there were no resources?"

"I'd rather stay here and take my chances by the river than go to Yakima or some desert place like that," Samuel said.

Curtis shrugged. "Whether we go or stay will depend on how long it takes contact to come, and what they tell us about the outside world. Once we have information we'll know more what to expect and can make decisions. But in the meantime, we have the monsters. And we need shelter that's more secure than tarps."

Silence fell around the crackling fire.

"And so we build a fort," Max said finally. "And arm some guards."

Curtis pointed at Anya. "And maybe set traps. Marie says there are more myths out there than just the ones we know about. I'm willing to bet Anya knows how to build traps."

"No." Max massaged his bandaged shoulder. "Traps won't work. We don't have any, and anything we could make won't be big enough or strong enough. You've all seen these monsters. They won't be killed by a snare."

Curtis sagged, deflated. "I didn't think about that."

Spike tossed a piece of wood on the fire. "What the fuck else are we going to do? Might as well try it. It's not like we have a whole lot of options here. We might be able to come up with something that holds the motherfuckers long enough for us to shoot them."

Curtis nodded to him, relieved. "That could work. But, honestly, I don't know anything about killing monsters."

Max laughed. "That's okay. We'll figure something out."

"One thing," Ramon said. "My niece is out there. We aren't trapping or killing any bears or wolves."

Anya had been standing silently slightly behind Ethan, but now she moved closer. "I'm going back home. I need to be with my son and I need to make sure he stays safe. Whatever it is that he's become, he'll be in danger from anyone hunting the monsters. I think if I go home, he will follow me." She looked at Ramon. "And maybe your niece, too."

"But we need you to teach us how to live," Curtis said. "And aren't we your family now?"

Anya blew out air in frustration. "Every time I say I need to be home, you people find a way to guilt me in to staying. Not this time. I'm going."

"When are you leaving?" Ethan asked, scowling.

"As soon as Bird is well enough to travel," Anya said. "So if anyone wants to pick my brain about skinning and preserving, there's a couple days to do it. Then I'm gone."

6

Curtis walked up the berm of land where Ethan stood in the middle of the railroad tracks, hands in the pockets of his dirt-stained jeans, studying the looming granite wall intently. Curtis had a sudden urge to tell him to get off the tracks but then remembered there were no trains.

Rain clouds were thinning, pulled into long gray tendrils that slowly trailed through the trees, pulled upward by a wind he couldn't feel. But these gray tendrils brought no fear because, thanks to Sharon, they were nothing more than thinning mist. Weak sunlight broke through clouds in a few spots, dappling the granite and creating deep shadows in cracks.

"Some of my kids died," Ethan said, tension obvious in his jaw, in his bunched shoulders. "From the quake, from Jennifer, from that thing. It's still out there and I want to kill it. Not wait for it to find its way down here to hurt someone else."

Curtis's heart stuttered in sudden consternation. "You'd have to go back to the woods. And besides, how would you kill it?"

Ethan shrugged. "No idea. But I'm going to kill it. And not just for my kids. If Anya leaves like she says she's going to, she'll be alone to face that thing."

"She has a pet grizzly," Curtis said, and then shook his head. "What a strange world we're in now."

"And what if the grizzly doesn't show up when she needs it?" Ethan asked. "She'll be on her own."

Curtis was silent a few moments. He thought he understood why Ethan was worrying about Anya, but he wasn't sure how to point that out without embarrassing both of them.

"Anya's pretty tough," he finally said.

"But she'll be alone."

Curtis thought a moment. "Well, traps don't sound like they're going to work. Guns didn't do much good. The Hole is blocked now, so no radiation."

"What about fire?" Ethan asked. "That's one thing we've got."

"If that worked, it would have to be a big fire," Curtis said. "And long-burning. To make sure, you know? Plus, you'd have to pack in an accelerant, a way to get a big fire going fast. I mean, the Windigo won't just stand there and watch while you add moss to sparks."

Ethan laughed. "No, I suppose you're right. A two-gallon gas can might be enough. That won't be heavy to pack. If I can find some gas."

"Hey!" Curtis caught Ethan's arm. "My Bug, my car, is sitting down at the edge of town. There's still some gas in it. Unless someone has siphoned it."

Ethan nodded once. "So. You want to come along?"

Curtis's insides turned to water and his knees suddenly felt as if they'd been sucked into one of Henry's parallel universes. No he most certainly did not want to go along. But...he didn't want a friend going alone, either.

"Sure. Why not?"

~Day 7~

1

It was so early the sun wasn't up yet. The air was chilly and damp, but the rain continued to hold off. Curtis stood next to his car, facing it so the headlamp he'd borrowed from Samuel would light up the gas cap. Ethan twisted the cap off and inserted a piece of garden hose.

They both wore backpacks loaded with enough food and gear for a few days. It hadn't taken much to find what they'd needed. Old Ben had let them raid his camper.

The others wanted to go with them. Casey and Max had been the most insistent. And Anya, of course. But Bird couldn't travel yet and she wouldn't leave him behind. And besides, Ethan seemed stuck on the idea it had to be just Curtis and him. Brains and Brawn, he called them. Curtis had been flattered. And so they'd sneaked away in the early dawn.

Curtis wasn't feeling so flattered now.

"There's a lot of mountains out there," he said, rubbing his hands together for warmth. "How are we going to find it?"

"Maybe it will find us at night when we set up camp. Then we'll be able to come back sooner." Ethan sucked on the end of the hose, got gas flowing, and spit off to the side. "But I have a general idea where it might be. Didn't you say these things took victims to their lairs?"

Curtis nodded, then realized that made the headlamp light bounce. "Oh, sorry. Yes, they have lairs. Typically caves. Well, according to the old stories anyway."

"One of my kids, Paul, was killed when we were crossing a slide." Ethan pulled the hose out of the full can. "He got trapped by a falling boulder and then that thing got him. It took...it took Paul's head."

"I'm sorry," Curtis said, his stomach doing a little roll of nausea.

"It went uphill from the slide. Later, Anya saw it at her cabin, and it left Paul's head there. Our bus driver, Val, also disappeared in the same area, where our bus went off the road. So I'm thinking this thing's lair is somewhere in the area of Silver Creek."

"It's going to take a couple days to get there."

"We made it here from Anya's cabin in one day of pushing hard," Ethan said. "Maybe another day from her cabin to where our bus is. And then we still have a lot of area to search."

302

Curtis was quiet while Ethan capped the little gas can and straightened. His thoughts whirled around fear and monsters, myths that came up from the same earth that had swallowed them when people quit believing in them.

"We might be able to narrow the search area some," he finally said. "But it means letting me run back to town for a couple minutes."

"Can you do it without bringing a horde back with you?"

"Sure," Curtis said absently, his thoughts flying. He dropped his pack. "Don't leave without me."

Back on Avenue A, he jogged through the gray light, passing people sleeping under tarps and in tents. He went straight to the fire department, and inside, walked swiftly between cots until he reached Henry. He gently touched the old man's shoulder, waking him. When Henry's eyes opened, Curtis touched his lips with a finger and knelt beside the cot.

"You're familiar with Silver Creek, right?" Curtis whispered.

"Of course." Henry propped himself up on one elbow. "There is a rare lichen up there, *Niebla cephalota*, that I've been monitoring. Why haven't you been to see me?"

Curtis flashed on their last conversation when Henry said the earthquake was his fault. He wanted to tell Henry how much those words had hurt but then he remembered his mother and her admonitions to be polite to elders.

"Sorry. I've been busy."

"Well, since you're here now, I will explain to you what makes that lichen so rare-"

"Maybe another time," Curtis said quickly. "What I need to know now is, are there any fault lines in that area? Any caves?"

"Fault lines?" Henry's eyes sharpened. "So you finally admit to the parallel universes. Well, of course there are fault lines all over these mountains. Some caves, lots of old mining tunnels."

"Mining tunnels." Curtis sagged back to sit on the concrete floor, weighed down by sudden discouragement. "I didn't think about all the mining that used to go on here."

"Copper, silver, garnets," Henry said. "There are old mines all over. There was a famous mining town up in that area back in the 1800s. It is all reclaimed by the forest now, of course."

"But fault lines that maybe the quake opened?"

Henry closed his eyes as he thought, then opened them and nodded as if agreeing with himself. "No. Well, yes, technically. But they are small and you would need to know what you are looking for to find them. They would be like fine filaments, or hairline cracks in an eggshell.

If you are hoping to find an opening to a parallel universe, I would suggest the mines. Look for one that has been widened by the quake. Opened."

Curtis thought about myths. About stories that stayed with the land, that became tales told around campfires.

"Henry, are there any…I don't know…ghost stories about that area?"

"Ghosts do not exist." Henry waved a hand dismissively.

This, from a guy who believed in parallel universes. Curtis grinned. "Well, old stories then. People disappearing, that kind of stuff."

"Well, there are stories about Bigfoot sightings in that area, and it's where I would expect to find the creature. But I do not see what folklore has to do with the reality that we are threatened by the very science you studied."

"But?"

"But nothing. No ghosts. No local folklore."

Curtis balled his fists in frustration. And then jumped at a low voice behind him.

"No ghosts," Samuel said, bending down to speak quietly and not wake others. "But we get more calls up there than anywhere else. It's always been weird how many hikers get lost there."

"A lot?" Curtis stood, his legs tingling as circulation came back.

"No." Samuel straightened. He glanced around the room, but people still slept. "But steady, you know? Over many years. I've heard the stories. And do you know Bert and Ernie?"

"The town drunks? The two homeless guys?"

Samuel nodded. "Ever wonder why homeless guys would choose to come to a tiny town in the mountains instead of someplace with fast food and dumpsters?"

Curtis shook his head.

"Because Bert's from here. His family was here for generations, so he says."

"Bert is mentally unstable," Henry said. "He believes he is one of the last remaining descendants of the Skykomish tribe. When he got tangled up in Fred's electric fences running from the police, and fell in the goat's water tank, he thought those electric shocks were Martians zapping him with ray guns. His brain is pickled."

Samuel gestured for Curtis to follow him and led the way back to the door. Outside, he spoke in a normal tone of voice.

"Bert says the Skykomish avoided Silver Creek. They had stories, going back generations."

"Of a monster." Curtis shivered.

"Of a being that came out of the earth."

Curtis caught Samuel's arm. "I'm willing to bet that if we found elders who knew the old oral stories we'd find correlations with that thing showing up only after the earth moved. And I'm willing to bet we'd find tales that said the thing terrorized the area over a span of time and then eventually left."

"I don't follow," Samuel said.

"That's okay." Curtis waved his hand, thoughts flying. "Ethan doesn't want anyone following anyway."

He left Samuel standing there looking confused, and ran down the street. It all made sense. The creature would break free after an earthquake. Obviously not one as devastating as this one. Maybe even just tremors that shifted old faults. But it would come to light, it would feed, probably over weeks or months, or maybe even years, and then it would go into hibernation, or something similar. People would stop disappearing, fear would ease, and loss would become just another story.

Back at his car, Curtis found Ethan sitting on a downed Cedar, finishing a granola bar. He told Ethan quickly what he'd learned and then held out his hands.

"But that doesn't narrow the search at all," Ethan said. "If anything, it adds to it as we now have to look for mines. Now we're going to be out there longer."

Curtis deflated. He looked around at the woods, at the dawn light lifting the darkness. The old familiar fear settled across his shoulders, as heavy as the weight of the pack he picked up.

"Guess we better start walking."

~*Day 9*~

1

It took them two days just to reach the totaled bus. They stood at the edge of the slide looking down at it in bright spring sunlight. A cool breeze moved through what remained of the forest, bringing scents of rich loamy earth, waking after the winter. Stellar's Jays and Varied Thrush sang in the woods. Near Curtis's boot, a small trillium, or Wake-Robin, was beginning to open. One of the earliest native flowers, it bloomed here as if nothing had happened. It came back just like it always did, in spite of the destroyed landscape.

"Amy's still in there." Ethan wiped the back of his hand across his eyes. "She died when the bus crashed. I thought I'd get the kids out, be back in a day or two with search and rescue. To recover her body. But she's still there. So is John. He died from injuries the day after the quake."

Unless they've been eaten, Curtis thought, but knew better than to say. Instead he shook his head. "I can't believe any of you survived that crash."

Ethan just shrugged. Or maybe he was shaking off the thought of his students. Curtis didn't know.

"Where to now?" Ethan asked.

"I have no idea," Curtis answered. It seemed hopeless now that they were here, surrounded by nothing but wilderness.

Ethan studied the terrain. "This whole Silver Creek area was mined for copper, silver, garnets. Silver would have been the most common because of these mountains. Granite, veins of quartz."

"You have an idea?"

"I'm an Environmental Science teacher, for fuck's sake!" Ethan spun in a circle. "I should be able to figure this out."

Curtis waited silently, recognizing the signs of a brain also spinning, racing into familiar ground, pulling out premise, possibility, known facts, breadcrumbs.

"Henry said there weren't any major faults around here. So it's got to be an old mine and it's got to be close because that thing showed up almost immediately. Plus, the lair can't be too high up the mountainsides. Old time miners wouldn't have gone rock climbing. Well,

306

they would have if the possibility was strong enough. But they had to have a way to get the ore out. So there'd be old donkey trails or horse and cart paths, overgrown now but still visible if you know what to look for."

Curtis didn't interrupt, knowing the flow of words was Ethan thinking, processing, out loud. He'd done this himself, many times, and he knew an interruption could derail thoughts with as much finality as a quake derailed trains.

"One thing," Ethan said, gesturing. "The quake has actually helped. Yeah, it caused this whole shit-storm, but it's also helping. Because of the slides, the downed trees, we can see the bones of the land. You see, there, and there?"

Curtis looked where Ethan pointed, simply nodding and not speaking.

"If it wasn't for the quake, this would all still be deep forest. We'd have to take educated guesses about what was underneath the forest canopy. But see those knobs of granite? And those small ravines?"

His hand dropped to his side and Curtis heard discouragement creep into his voice.

"The lair could be any of those. If it's even in this spot."

"Where did you first see the thing?" Curtis kept his voice low, a nudge to get back on track rather than an interruption.

"That first night. We were all still in the bus...we were looking for a way out, looking for Val, the driver. Zack..." Ethan's words faltered to a stop.

"Zack?"

Ethan shook his head. "Zack. The boy Jennifer led to his death. He was headed out through the hole where the front windshield had been. I went to him to see if it was a safe evacuation spot. I saw our lights reflecting off eyes. I thought it was Val, ejected from the bus."

Ethan paused again and Curtis knew it was time for another soft nudge. "But it wasn't."

"But it wasn't. So...the first time we saw it was there, near the front of the bus. The quake had just happened. It didn't have time to travel far."

"So if it came from that direction, what looks promising out there?"

"There's a creek." Ethan pointed. "The old miners used water for sluicing or panning. If we follow the creek upstream, if it goes roughly southwest there, where it starts to climb? Maybe there."

Curtis felt airless suddenly, feather-light, shivery with a wash of fear-fueled adrenaline. He swallowed against the coppery taste and tugged up the straps to his pack. "What does it mean when terror becomes so familiar you just kind of shrug and go, 'okay'?"

"That's courage," Ethan said. "Being terrified but at the same time thinking, 'let's get this shit over with'."

Curtis's voice shook as much as his hands. "Then let's get this shit over with."

2

The spot was easier to find than they expected; a short hike upstream following the small creek that tumbled green and white over rocks, Ethan spotting a small, overgrown trail, and then Curtis seeing the sign.

An actual sign, with an arrow pointing the direction to go. The board was half rotted, with moss trailing from it. But when Curtis pushed the damp moss away the words some hopeful miner had burned into the wood were still legible. Copper Chief Mine.

"We've guessed right so far," Curtis said, following Ethan. "But there's still nothing to prove the thing is here."

It was strange, he thought, how time affected fear. After a while it faded, even though the circumstances were still the same. Was it just adrenaline wearing off? Was he, maybe, becoming braver?

Ethan pushed through salmonberries just beginning to leaf out, took a couple steps, and then stopped. "I think we found your proof."

Curtis looked over Ethan's shoulder. A hole in the rocky side of the hill, thick timbers visible just inside, dripped with moisture. Maybe at some point in the past it had been a natural crack in the granite, but it had clearly been blasted into an opening large enough for men to pass through.

And in front of the opening, lying bedded softly on moss and fir needles as if put to rest, were bones. Some white and new, some stained and old. Fragments and whole pieces. Not enough to make a pile as if it were a dumping ground, but enough to create an image in Curtis's mind of the thing going in and out over many generations, dropping bits as it went.

A few of the bones still had pieces of tendon or muscle attached. One of the longer bones had deep gouges. Claws or teeth, Curtis didn't know and didn't want to. He stood, frozen, as Ethan put the gas can down and bent to pick something up. He fingered it and Curtis saw orange material before Ethan carefully put it back, almost reverently, on the moss-covered stone.

"Time to build a fire?" Curtis asked, hating the hopeful tone in his voice. He wanted very much to go home.

"Focus, evaluate, act," Ethan said, almost as if talking to himself. "We need to make sure it's in there."

"Oh, no, we don't." Curtis moved closer. "They always do that in horror movies. Go in when everyone in the audience is screaming 'don't go!' or 'it's behind the door!'"

"There's no door."

"You know what I mean."

"Yes, but think, Curtis. We set the fire and it's not in there. Maybe it comes back while we're still here. Maybe it tracks us back to town. Finds us one night out there alone in the woods. Sure, we have materials to build campfires, but we won't have gas for an inferno to kill that thing. We'll have used it all up here, building a fire for nothing. We'll have wasted the gas, and it's not like we can just trot down below to the nearest town with a gas station."

Curtis swallowed. "You convinced me at 'finds us one night' but all your points are valid."

"Sorry, buddy." Ethan put a hand on his shoulder. "You stay out here. I'll go in."

Curtis straightened. "Look, yes, I'm scared. But that doesn't mean I can't go."

Ethan shook his head. "Listen. I'm not going in any further than I have to, and then getting the hell out of there. But you need to be here as back up. I grew up always having to plan for worst-case scenarios, and this is it. If that thing isn't in there and shows up here, you have to warn me. If that thing is in there and I can't get out, you have to burn us. You understand?"

"Oh, I understand perfectly," Curtis said.

He saw it all clearly. Ethan would go in, there would be horrible screams, he'd be forced to make a dramatic decision, which of course would be to not set the fire and be a hero instead. He'd rush in to that black opening and fight the thing, rescue Ethan, drag his bleeding body out, and set the fire. In a big dramatic burst of flame, the thing would come out writhing and screaming and would die before them.

He saw it all. And none of it would happen outside of his imagination.

Because he wasn't a hero.

"We might as well pull the first aid supplies out now," he said morosely.

Ethan looked confused, but he simply patted Curtis on the shoulder and turned for the mine. Curtis watched him go in, watched the light of his headlamp illuminating dripping rock walls briefly before being swallowed by the darkness. He picked up the gas can and moved near the entrance. He slipped off his pack, dug out a tin of matches, and began gathering sticks to mound before the opening. He was sure they'd want the fire, fast.

Behind him the mine opening breathed ice-cold air on him. He knew it was the changes in air pressure, the barometric differences between warmer surface air and colder underground air. He knew first hand from all his time working in the Hole, how it could be upwards of ten degrees colder in that blackness than out here. But still, it was eerie to feel the movement of earth-breath.

His shaking hands moved fast, piling up fuel for the fire. He kept waiting for the screams to start, but only silence and his own pounding pulse filled his ears.

When the gunshots came from inside the mine, it was so sudden, so unexpected, that Curtis yelped and pressed a hand to his racing heart. He ran to the mine opening, listened for a brief moment, and then ran back to the fire. The thing was obviously in there with Ethan. If the gun didn't kill it, then it would be coming out any second.

Curtis frantically pulled larger branches onto the pile of tinder, and then grabbed the gas can. He fumbled with the locking cap but couldn't get it to come free. Breath coming fast and rapid, he twisted off the whole nozzle instead.

From inside the cave he heard scuffling. Something coming out. He upended the can and wildly splashed gas over the wood, then fumbled out a match and struck it.

Nothing.

He grabbed several more and got one to light. He used the small, fragile flame to light a handful of the matches and tossed the whole thing onto the soaked wood. The fire went up in a loud whoosh of air and blue flame.

Curtis jumped back from the heat.

Ethan staggered out of the mine opening, threw up his hands to protect his face from the bonfire, and stumbled a few feet to the side. He fell to his knees, shuddering.

"Did you kill it?" Curtis went to his side. "Is it dead?"

Ethan shook his head and rubbed a trembling hand over his face. After a moment he put a fist to the ground and pushed up. "Val is in there. Our bus driver. She...she was still alive."

"Oh god."

"She's been in there all this time. It's been feeding on her. Strips of skin flayed off. Muscle peeled-"

Curtis held his hand up. "No more," he said helplessly.

He suddenly remembered the screaming he'd heard that night when he'd been alone in the woods. The eyeball in the morning. It had to have been the Windigo bringing Val here, to this hell. The horror that poor woman went through. He gritted his teeth against the sorrow that welled up.

"She was still alive," Ethan repeated. "I don't know how. But I know death. I've seen it so many times…she was too far gone."

Hot tears washed over Curtis's cheeks. He knew what was coming.

"I…I shot her."

"You had to," Curtis said. "You couldn't leave her like that."

Ethan suddenly kicked viciously at Curtis's backpack on the ground. "God, the pain she must have been in. For days."

"But she's free of that now." Curtis stepped back from the rage in Ethan's eyes. "I know those are just words. I know they don't mean anything right now. But it's true."

Ethan ran a hand over his face. "Maybe, but it doesn't help. She wasn't alone, Curtis. There are…pieces. My kids. Oh, god, my kids."

He bent, retching and shaking. Curtis could do nothing more put his hand on Ethan's shoulders, a small circle of warmth, of human contact. When Ethan wiped his mouth with the sleeve of his jacket and straightened, pulling in a shaky breath, Curtis handed him a water bottle from the pack.

Ethan took a mouthful of cold water, spit, and then swallowed more. He capped the bottle, pressed a thumb and forefinger against his eyes a moment, and then looked at the blazing fire. "There goes the gas."

"And I didn't get it close enough to the opening." Nausea was a solid weight in Curtis's stomach. "I'm sorry. I thought it was in there with you. I thought you were shooting it. I thought it was coming out-"

Ethan stopped him by raising a hand. "Curtis. Knock it off. I get it."

"But what do we do now?"

"We close that mine for starters," Ethan said, anger flaring again, bringing color back to his face. "No way is that fucking thing getting back in there."

"Okay…but…" Curtis hesitated and then drew in a breath. "But how? I mean, if the quake wasn't enough to close it off, how will we? Obviously the granite is pretty solid here."

"What do you want me to do?" Ethan turned on Curtis. "You want to just walk away? Let that thing come back here and keep feeding? Let my kids, let Val, end like that? Never buried, left to rot?"

Curtis stepped back from the fury. "Of course not. I just don't see how we're going to close it."

Ethan drew in a ragged breath and pushed hair out of his eyes. "I don't know."

"Maybe-" Movement in the trees caught Curtis's eye. He fell

silent, words gone, thoughts gone.

Ethan glanced at him then turned in the direction Curtis stared.

It was there. Tall and thin, man-shape and yet not, its head too large, and the antlers reaching up sharp and branching. The eyes were black holes reflecting nothing. Its long fingers, ending in claws, twitched and moved as if already peeling them.

Curtis's heart raced, fleet and fast. Every primordial cell in his body screamed to run. But he couldn't move.

"What do we do?" he whispered.

The woods stretched out on all sides, infinite and wild. There was no safe place. Not even an old Volkswagen Bug to race to.

Ethan pulled his gun, aimed, and fired at the thing's chest. It recoiled and put a clawed hand to the small hole in its chest where black blood flowed. And then it moved fast and silent and straight for Ethan.

Ethan fired again, and again, as the thing rushed him. Black blood flowed freely from several holes but the wounds didn't slow the thing down. Curtis froze as it grabbed Ethan, ripping claws down one side of his face.

Ethan screamed.

Curtis couldn't breathe. His muscles were water. He couldn't move. Terror was ice, stopping his heart.

The thing lifted Ethan off the ground and without a glance at Curtis, took long, loping steps toward the mine opening.

Its lair.

Where it would feed for years on Ethan. On his friend.

Heat like fire raced through Curtis. It felt like rage. It felt like power. He grabbed the free end of a burning branch from the fire, holding it up like a flaming sword.

"Leave my friend alone!"

Curtis charged forward without thought, pulled by the animal screams of Ethan. He shoved the branch at the creature's back and shoulders. Blood poured from deep slices in Ethan's cheek. The thing lowered his head toward Ethan's chest, as if to bite out his heart.

Tears poured down Curtis's face. Flames caught and grew in the material around the thing's waist. Curtis shoved the fully engulfed branch upward into the Windigo's antlers, even as flames scorched his hands. The branch caught in the antlers and Curtis twisted it back and forth, spreading the growing flames.

The Windigo screamed and dropped Ethan, long claws madly scrabbling at the branch, at the flames that grew and spread fast, fed by orange cloth and old antlers.

Ethan fell to the ground, not moving.

The Windigo spun, screeching. The dark pools of its eyes found Curtis. He jumped back, away from its burning, reaching hands.

But claws caught at him, sank deep into his chest and neck. He felt deep, deep pain, and the hot flood of arterial blood spurting from his neck. He struggled but the thing pulled him close in a parody of a hug. He heard the sizzle of his hair catching fire, felt the agony of his skin burning. Something deep inside screamed.

Mother.

And she was there, in the trees, in the rising wind, the earth's mother, the Stone Woman, arms out to take him.

And he was gone.

3

Ethan groaned and slowly rolled over onto his back. One eye wouldn't open and when he managed to raise a trembling hand, he felt caked and coagulated blood over the whole side of his face. His cheek burned and with that pain came the memory of the thing slicing at him with its claws.

Curtis.

He struggled to sit, managed to get to one knee, and then slowly, to his feet. Deep tremors shook him and it felt like ice moving from the wounds down his neck and into his chest.

Smoke and the sweetish stench of burning flesh filled the air. Ethan had smelled that before, that distinctive scent of death.

Curtis had done it then. Burned that fucking monster alive. Avenged his kids. Saved him. Ethan managed a twisted smile. Curtis would be the hero of the day when they got back to town.

He took a shuffling step toward the smoking mound that was all that was left of the Windigo. Flames licked at the scorched antlers.

There was something wrong though, and it took a moment for Ethan's pain-filled brain to realize that a charred hiking boot rested in the burned remains. That there were too many bones. That the flames hadn't been hot enough or big enough to completely burn the two blackened bodies.

He couldn't take it in. Couldn't grasp what was there before him. Hot tears poured down his face, burning in the cuts. He sank to his knees, collapsed to the ground, and dug his fingers into the soft and loamy forest floor.

Not Curtis.

The best of them all. The kind and gentle light that was always in his eyes. His awkward confessions of fear. His willingness to face that fear for his friends.

Not Curtis.

Rage and helplessness came out in a wordless shout that split wide the drying blood. Fresh blood flowed and he didn't care.

Movement at the periphery of his vision made him come up on his knees.

The wolf and the grizzly.

The boy and the girl.

They came forward out of the trees but Ethan didn't move.

Didn't care. The wolf came up to him and sniffed his face. And then licked the sliced wounds. Licked away blood and tears. Ethan tried to push the wolf away but the girl knelt and caught his hands. He looked into her amber eyes but felt nothing.

Because nothing mattered any more. He should have been the one to die, not Curtis. The loss of his friend would be on his soul forever.

"You're too late." He shoved the wolf away, sobs welling up, gut-wrenching and heart-breaking.

Too late.

4

Ethan walked through the forest gingerly, pain a warm burn across his face. He wore his backpack and had Curtis's slung over one shoulder. He had to pause occasionally to pull the strap back up. Each time he did, it felt like loss.

He didn't recognize this new world. This wrong place where he walked, with a grizzly and a wolf pacing ahead of him, with the boy on one side and the girl on the other.

It was all wrong.

It should have been Curtis next to him. Curtis, clutching his backpack straps and watching the woods around him nervously. Curtis, hands shaking and fear-filled eyes, stepping forward to go with him anyway.

Curtis's death was his fault. If he hadn't been so focused on wanting to kill that thing, Curtis would still be in Index. That knowledge, that sorrow, was a heavy weight on his shoulders as he walked between the boy and the girl.

Ethan was surrounded but he was alone.

Grief was a deep, deep cut that would never heal. Grief for Curtis. Grief for his students. It widened within him until he was nothing but seeping tears and empty shell.

He walked through the night. He knew he wouldn't sleep, and the thought of making camp…building a fire…sickened him. And so he kept going, walking through another day until suddenly he realized he was alone.

He had no idea when his companions had faded away into the forest. The sun was sinking behind the mountains when his boots, somehow, found the remains of pavement.

He stood there staring with dark eyes full of confusion and pain. Somewhere in the fog of his mind he knew he should continue, that he was close to town. But he couldn't take another step. He couldn't go back there and face bringing up words that would need to be said.

Ahead of him something shifted in the gathering twilight. He took a stumbling step back in sudden panic.

But it was Anya, rising from where she'd been seated on a log. She came forward with her rifle over her shoulder and Bird limping at her side. When she reached him, she looked deeply into his eyes and then put her hand to his injured face. The wolf had cleaned the deep gouges

317

but the wounds were raw and seeping.

The sudden warmth of her hand made the deeper wound of grief bleed again and his hot tears spilled over her fingers.

"I've been waiting for you," she said with tears in her eyes.

She pulled his head down to her shoulder, enfolding him tightly.

Holding him for as long as he needed to be held.

High overhead, high above the trees, high above the land, a raven circled on the wind.

5

Ethan sat on the tailgate of Ben's truck with a wool blanket around his shoulders. June pressed a cup of hot chocolate into his hands but he simply held its warmth, not sure what to do with it. Samuel stood next to him, disinfecting his wounds and pulling the ragged edges of flesh together with butterfly bandages.

"These are going to leave nasty scars," Samuel said. "You should really have stitches."

Ethan didn't respond, didn't care.

The others stood in a semi-circle around him that grew as more people joined them. Even Bert and Ernie, the town drunks, were there. They all stood, tears in their eyes. Touching each other. Why was it, that when there were no words, the only thing left was the soft touch to share the pain?

A faint sound came from downriver and grew slowly into the steady thump of helicopter rotors. Slowly, as if drugged by their grief, people turned to watch the chopper come in, an oddly incongruous sight after so many days alone in the woods. In the openings on both sides of the chopper men watched the ground, aiming guns downward.

The helicopter was able to land in the little park by the school and once the rotors slowed enough, two men and one woman got out. The men in the side openings remained with their guns, silently scanning the town and the woods. The pilot and co-pilot were armed and wore National Guard uniforms. Their passenger was an older man in a suit, complete with tie. They crossed Fifth Street and approached the group around the old truck. There was an odd quiet, as if these people from the helicopter were aliens from another world.

But then the stories came, spilling over one another, telling the strangers in shaky voices what had happened. Albert, as mayor, took the lead, sharing loss, explaining about the Hole, and radon, about the monsters killed and the ones still out there. About those who had died.

When he was done, the man in the suit introduced himself as being with FEMA's disaster recovery team. He took up the story. Massive earthquake. Seattle toppled. Freeways collapsed. Infrastructure gone. Everett, Edmonds, up to Canada, all along the coast flooded and gone. Landslides. Millions of decomposing corpses, human and animal. Devastation.

And monsters.

Everywhere.

There were as many theories about where they came from, as there were monsters.

There were even some, the man said skeptically, who believed not all the beings were monsters. That some helped.

Ethan looked at Anya and Ramon, but no one spoke.

"Right now," the man continued, "We are simply in the triage phase. Finding the worst hit areas, finding the critically injured. With the freeways and arterials destroyed, we can only go by air. The military is sending every resource they have, and other countries have started sending aid. My job is going up the Skykomish valley here, assessing each and every town."

"If we take back roads, is there any place we can go?" Max asked. "Gold Bar? Sultan? Any of those towns stable enough to take us?"

"Sir," said the man, not able to meet Max's eyes. "There is no place, anywhere, stable enough for refugees. There are no resources. It's bare-bones survival."

"What the fuck?" Spike shoved forward. "You saying there's no place for us to go? Did you not hear the part about fucking man-eating monsters?"

The co-pilot stepped forward, one hand going to the butt of her gun in its holster.

Max caught Spike's arm. "Calm down."

Ethan wasn't sure if he spoke to Spike or to the co-pilot.

"We are absolutely clear on the danger everyone is facing," the man said. "But the fact is, there isn't anywhere to go at this point that isn't facing the same things. We are working, like I said, on assessment. In the next week we hope to be able to start dropping supplies to people."

"Supplies?" Casey asked. "And those will include big guns, right? Monster-killing guns?"

"Food and medical supplies," the man said. "If we can get ways to help you defend yourself, then yes, those will be included. But our focus right now is on getting the injured to aid and setting up camps where we can evacuate people. The Red Cross is working to establish refugee camps in eastern Washington, Idaho, and Montana."

"So the reality, son, is we're on our own." Ben gestured at the helicopter. "And that's just for show."

"It's for reassurance," the man said, frustration leaking into his voice. "We're doing all we can."

"Then I guess that means you'll leave us one of those big guns you got there." Ramon gestured at the chopper.

"Look," the man said. "I understand. Believe me. But right now-

"

"Right now, you're fucking useless." Spike turned to Lucy and Nathaniel. "We're on our own, just like before these assholes showed up."

"You're right." Anger flickered in Ethan. "They're useless and not going to help. And they're too late. If they'd come sooner, maybe some of us would still be alive."

Max cupped the man's elbow in his hand and turned him toward the helicopter. The co-pilot started forward, but Max waved a hand at her. "Back off, hero. I'm just escorting your boss back where he came from."

"But don't you want to know-" the man began.

"No," Max interrupted. "What we want is for someone competent to come back for our injured. What we want are those food and medical supplies you mentioned. Plus dry and clean clothes. Temporary shelters. And big guns. We've already killed some of these monsters."

"You've killed some?" the pilot asked in surprise. "How?"

"Well, not with the help of the military," Max said. "So until you can bring us what we need, you're no use to us. Go back where you came from. In the meantime we'll take care of things on our own."

"Well...okay then." The man gave Max a small salute. "You've managed better than most. You're going to make it. Everything is going to be fine. The government is involved now and resources will soon be coming in."

"And we'll be here," Max said.

The man gave Max a hearty slap on the back, making Max wince, and then followed the two in uniform back to the helicopter.

"Useless piece of shit," Spike said when they were out of earshot.

"But the ones that come next won't be," Max said. "The next wave will be people who can actually put boots on the ground and help."

"We just have to hang on until they get here." Casey watched the rotors of the helicopter pick up speed. "Guess we better start building Fort Curtis."

~*Day 13*~

1

Ethan zipped the last pocket on Curtis's backpack and shouldered it. The pack was heavy with supplies from Ben's truck. It wasn't as sturdy as his old pack, but it had belonged to Curtis and Ethan couldn't leave it behind. In the bottom of the pack was a coffee can with ashes.

"You sure you're okay with this?" he asked Spike. "Taking on the responsibility of this crowd? Michael can be an asshole. And Max says he thinks they can try Jennifer for manslaughter once the military comes back. Which means you have to keep an eye on her, make sure she doesn't take off. And-"

"For fuck's sake," Spike said, laughing. "We've been over this already. Get the fuck out of here. They've already left and you're going to have to catch up."

Ethan walked to the top of the railroad tracks before turning back to where Spike stood a few feet away. It tore something inside him to leave his kids. But overlaying that responsibility was the deep, deep chasm of grief. He wasn't sleeping at night. He wasn't eating.

Anya told him he needed solitude.

Anya told him he needed to bury Curtis's ashes under a yew tree.

Anya wouldn't let him sink into the black hole in his soul.

So he talked to Spike. Asked him to make his little family of Nathaniel and Lucy bigger. To include all the students.

"Hey, Spike," Ethan said. "Couldn't have done all this without you."

Spike lifted a hand. "And we wouldn't be alive if you hadn't been with us. You're okay. For a fucking teacher."

Ethan managed to smile.

Then headed for the solitude of the forest.

2

Anya and Ramon climbed the trail to the top of the Wall. They went slowly, at Bird's pace. When they reached the top they paused under the ruined power lines and gave the healing dog a long drink from a water bottle.

"You sure you won't stay?" Ramon asked.

"I'm sure," Anya said. "I need to be home."

Ramon looked out into the forest, where a few birds tentatively sang. "I want to find Alegria. But Marie is here and I can't leave her, either."

"I'll watch for your niece. I'll make sure they know to stay out of sight for those who will come to kill monsters."

"And I'll keep them safe if they come this way," Ramon said. "But I don't like you going out there alone."

Anya pointed back down the path where Ethan climbed steadily in their direction wearing a loaded backpack. The wounds on his face were healing but still raw. And the sorrow in his dark eyes was just as raw.

"Don't worry," Anya said. "I won't be alone."

~*Acknowledgements and Monsters*~

As always, fiction allows you to get away with things. While the locations mentioned in this story actually exist, those familiar with the mountains will know that it takes longer than a couple days to bushwhack Jumpoff Ridge to Index. And finding old logging roads to solve the problem of downed bridges over the North Fork Skykomish River is also a bit harder than it sounds here.

The town of Index is a wonderful, unique place full of friends. They may think they recognize themselves here, but they will be wrong. As any writer knows, bits and pieces of many people come together to create characters. So hey, friends, you're just seeing bits of yourselves. With the exception of Rob, kayaker extraordinaire. And with the exception of Mark and Sandy and the Espresso Chalet where Bigfoot lives. Stop by sometime and try a Lift Ticket. I dare you.

The Hole in the Wall is closed up now, and I'd like to thank Keith Curtis for allowing me to interview him about his Fifth Force experiments. I have taken his words and tossed in some artistic license because, unfortunately, he never mentioned parallel universes…the gravity experiments and radon gas though, are real.

And heartfelt thanks to the friends who offered honest advice. Susan for your editing and keeping me on task, Jenni, for always loving everything I write, no matter how rough. And Art and Sabrina. Silver Creek and Jumpoff Ridge owe their presence to you. I will always remember the two of you sitting side by side, laughing as you both made sure I knew how impossible it was to bushwhack to Index from Barclay Lake. The story was worth spending three years writing to see Sabrina laugh. Your river spirit will always be with you and we love you.

Art of course, gets to be mentioned again, because there would be no stories without him.

For the purposes of this story, I tried to stay close to mythical creatures of the Pacific Northwest and the cultural heritage of the characters. With that in mind, the following creatures made appearances.

Amarok

A giant wolf in the folkore of the Inuit people. Also similar to the Black Dog or Fairy Dogs of Celtic mythology. And also similar to the giant wolf Fenris of Norse mythology. All are giant dog-like animals that are either the guardians of the places they haunt, are killers of those they stalk, or herald the end of the world.

The Grizzly Bear

Common in legends of the Pacific Northwest, these bears renew the world. They are both ancestors and way-showers. They are teachers, guardians, and healers.

Sisiutl

A myth from the Coastal tribes of British Columbia. A two-headed monster with forked tongues that seeks truth. But if it finds fear it will send you spiraling and the corkscrew spinning will cause you to leave earth and wander as a lost soul forever.

Cailleac Bhuer or Stone Woman

An old woman with a walking stick and carrion crow on her left shoulder. She can be either dangerous or, if treated with respect, a guide. In some myths she dwells in a land of winter. In some, her staff is buried under a tree and retrieved after Samhain to bring forth the spring. In Scotland she is known as the Blue Hag, who walks the highlands at night. Some see her as the crone goddess. Variations of the Stone Woman can be found in many cultures. Because she walks the Pacific Northwest in these pages, I have chosen to give her a raven.

Shadow people

More of a ghost story than a myth, these are humanoid forms made completely of featureless shadow. Some say these are other-dimensional beings with their realms occasionally intersecting with ours. Some see them as travelers, scouts, or invaders. They commonly are seen as a sign that evil comes.

Wendigo or Windigo

A creature of North America, most commonly seen as a man-like cannibal that keeps its victims alive while it slowly eats them. Sometimes described as looking similar to Bigfoot. Sometimes described as a tall, thin, man-like shape with talons and antlers.

Wood nymphs, dryads, and naiads

Spirits that live within trees. Combined in this story with spirits of yew trees, which, in pagan beliefs symbolize psychic awareness, spirits, and the death passage. I keep hoping these will show up when I walk in the woods.

Matlose

Matlose is a famous hob-goblin of the Nootkas. He is covered with black bristles and has teeth and claws like a bear.

A wonderful resource for every mythical creature imaginable is *The Element Encyclopedia of Magical Creatures* by John and Caitlin Matthews.

~Play List~

Writing comes easiest with music to help drown out the outside world. Each story seems to end up with its own individual play list. So if you're interested, here are some of the songs that helped create the mood of this story.

If you like the partial list, the complete playlist can be found on Spotify, under 'This Deep Panic Playlist'.

A Deep Slow Panic – AFI
On the Nature of Daylight – Max Richter
Fehu – Wardruna
Wolf Totem – The Hu
Rún – SKÁLD
Winterwolf – BrunuhVille
Cantus – Connie Dover
Light From Darkness – City Of The Fallen
Across the Snow – Tartalo Music
The Willow Maid – Erutan
Trøllabundin – Eivør
I Don't Believe – Chrom
Throw Off the Bowlines – James Paget
The King of the Highlands – Antti Martikainen

Made in the USA
Coppell, TX
07 June 2022

78556559R00194